CW01494551

Pen Friends

Pen Friends

Michael Thorn

MACMILLAN
LONDON

First published in 1988 by
MACMILLAN LONDON LIMITED
4 Little Essex Street London WC2R 3LF
and Basingstoke

Associated companies in Auckland, Delhi, Dublin, Gaborone,
Hamburg, Harare, Hong Kong, Johannesburg, Kuala Lumpur, Lagos,
Manzini, Melbourne, Mexico City, Nairobi, New York, Singapore and
Tokyo

British Library Cataloguing in Publication Data

Thorn, Michael
    Pen friends.
    I. Title
    823'.914 [F]   PR6070.H68/
    ISBN 0–333–45568–1

Typeset in Linotron Baskerville by
Wyvern Typesetting Limited, Bristol, England

Printed in Hong Kong

for Pip

Part One

"Do we have to, Papa?"

"Yes, we do."

"But Mr. Tappan is such a horrid man. I don't think he deserves to get his letters."

It had been a good dry summer, by West Massachusetts standards. Father and son picked up dust at their heels as they walked to the Stockbridge Post Office.

"Mr. Tappan is a fine gentleman, who lets us live at the Red House for very meagre rent. And, Little Man . . ." As the father's tone changed to that of a mock threat the boy, taking the cue, began to run and to scream at the same time. "Little Men . . ." Mr. Hawthorne gave his son a friendly flick on the bottom. Julian hiccupped with laughter and shrieking. "Little Men, I say . . ." and the boy received another flick, "should not abuse their elders. Does the Little Man understand?"

Mr. Hawthorne gathered his son up in his arms and snarled with bared teeth at the boy's knees.

"But . . ."

"But, but, but."

"But . . ."

"*No* buts."

"He wouldn't let you pick his apples. Mama said. She told Una and me that we can't pick the apples, even when they're ripe, because of nasty Mr. Tappan."

"Stop it. I'll have to put you down now. Look what a sweat your father's in. Oh, for a sea-breeze. The air can be devilish still in these bowl-shaped valleys."

"Anyway, you don't even like the Red House."

"It's the climate, not the house. You never know whether it's going to be too cool or too warm but it's always one or the other. Yes, Julian, I detest it. *I hate Berkshire with my whole soul.*"

3

The boy put his hands to his ears but his father took one away, saying, "Here, grab on, we must reach the Post Office before it shuts."

*   *   *

Julian was running up and down a grassy bank, trying to distract his father from reading the papers. They were returning from the Post Office and Mr. Hawthorne, feeling thoroughly overcome with the heat, had decided to take a rest beneath a primaeval pine.

"What sort of tree is it, Papa?

"How can you tell?

"But *why* doesn't it have *proper* leaves?

"Why is the grass another colour in the shade?

"Would any of these weeds be good for Bunny?

"I do wish Una was here. I could tumble with her over the thistles."

The paper was temporarily closed with a flourish. "Julian. Your father is taking a rest. Ever since your mother went away I've had day after day, minute after minute of cross-examination. Just for a few moments let my mind dwell upon things of its own choosing. Please. Why not run and gather a posy for Mrs. Peters?"

Mr. Hawthorne went back to his paper, shortly to be greeted by a salutation in Spanish from the other side of the fence. He turned round and, seeing a dark-jacketed, behatted figure on horseback, acknowledged the man as he would any polite and sociable stranger, then turned back to his paper. But the Spanish salutation was repeated and Mr. Hawthorne was prompted into recognition of the rider by Julian scampering up the bank, shouting, "Mr. Omoo, Mr. Omoo, Omoo, Omoo!" The boy ran past his father and was already climbing over the gate by the time Mr. Hawthorne had stood himself up.

"Why, Herman Melville!"

Mr. Hawthorne followed Julian over the gate, Melville got down from his horse and, putting the child up into the saddle, they all set off in the direction of the Red House, which lay two miles distant.

"Mrs. Peters told you where we were to be found, then?"

"No."

"You have not been to the house?"

"No."

4

"So – you were not riding expressly to meet us. What brings you so far from Arrowhead, then?"

"Sit a little straighter in that saddle, Julian. That's the way." Melville walked beside the horse, holding in one hand the reins, and with the other supporting the boy's back, his fingers splayed from shoulder to shoulder. "No, I was just out riding. As you know, I was lately in New York trying to push my *Whale* through the press. Well, I'm still shaking the city out of my hair. But you were right to be expecting a visit. Did I not promise, by last pen, to roll down to you at the earliest good chance? Well, here I am, ridden not rolled, and what a good chance that we fell upon one another on this road. And so then, Julian – out foraging with your father are you? On a manly rampage, eh? No little Una with you today?"

"Sophia went two days ago to West Newton," the boy's father explained. "She took Una with her. They won't be back till beyond the middle of the month."

Melville slapped his thigh and let out an excited holler. The horse frisked a little and shook its neck, so that Julian cried to be put down. As Melville lifted him to the ground, he said, "We must hit upon some little vagabondism. Most of the haying's done, I'm as disengaged as I'm likely to be this summer, and the Duyckincks are expected next week. Graylock. We must go and do our vagabonding there." He put his hand on Mr. Hawthorne's shoulder and grinned at him. "And look, you have a wondrous book completed and, no offence to your good wife, you are alone, alone in these valleys to repair yourself of all the hard work done. High times we'll have, with brandy and cigars. It'll be Paradise. And fit weather for it. Let us hope the sun, ruling so grandly this first August day, prospers in its supremacy. Like the Elizabethan in me, eh? Enough, we must hatch American conceits together. You and I."

Melville tightened the grip on his friend's shoulder. It was then that he noticed that his companion was uncommonly red, and blowing hard through his nose. The difference in their ages spanned some fifteen years. Indeed, Mr. Hawthorne at this time, August 1st 1851, was only three years short of his fiftieth birthday.

*   *   *

When they came to the house Julian took Melville to view the

5

Bunny, while Mr. Hawthorne went inside to arrange tea and cakes with Mrs. Peters. He had not been pleased with the terseness displayed towards his son earlier on and when his housemaid had bustled away to do her duty he stood at the small-framed window studying his companion's manner towards the boy. He saw Melville crouch to the child's height, his jaw opening and closing rapidly, no doubt exercised in the telling of some South Sea narrative. He remembered when Sophia had actually screamed out loud, and almost torn the covering off one of their armchairs, just as Melville had lifted up a poker at the climax of one such tale. In comparison there seemed something lame in his own story-telling – his children were complimentary enough and all of the retold myths which he had completed that summer had firstly been read aloud to Una and Julian. But he lacked the magic touch of fabricating long, oral stories at will. His was a more distilled, reflective talent and even though his wife had wept openly at the end of *The Scarlet Letter* when he had recited to her the final installment, Mr. Hawthorne felt keenly in this respect a sense of inferiority, of inadequacy almost, in Melville's presence.

Melville *was* telling Julian a story, but not about the South Seas. It was a most alarming account of the destitution he had seen on the streets of Liverpool. From Bunny they had passed on to rats, and from the rats they had passed on to beggars and waifs.

Mr. Hawthorne opened the window and called them in for tea. When he saw the strength of Mrs. Peters' brew, Melville said he would have just half a cup, as tea tended to keep him from sleeping.

"Did you know it was my birthday?"

"Today?"

"Of course today. I am thirty-two."

"This calls for a cigar."

When the two men lit up, Julian said, "Mama doesn't permit smoking in the living room."

Melville smiled at the boy through the smoke. "Ah, but it's a man's domain now. This is a splendid cigar, Nathaniel. A pity we haven't the brandy to go with it."

The conversation before supper was about publishers and books. Julian became so bored that Mr. Hawthorne decided they should take an early supper together, so that he could get the boy to bed. No sooner had Mrs. Peters cleared away the cakes and washed up the teacups than she was being asked to bring out the cold meats. But Julian would have none of them, insisting he was not hungry. Neither was he tired and Melville had to assist the boy's father in getting him up the stairs by improvising a scene in which a shipwrecked whaler was pursued ·by a pair of native cannibals.

"Having trouble with the boy?" Melville asked when Mr. Hawthorne eventually reappeared.

"Oh, it's his mother's conversation the Little Man misses. Veritable inquisitors are our children, as you know, and Sophia encourages it."

"Yes, it's a strange thing, this maternal emphasis on the vocal faculty. Elizabeth would be having Malcolm deliver stumping speeches and she worries when he can only manage a Gimme Dat. The boy's only two and a half, I tell her. I was backward in speech till I was pubescent."

Mr. Hawthorne chuckled. "And made up for it since."

"Not everyone would say so. They wouldn't say so at all. I have enough of the unfathomable silence about me to make acquaintances stand back. Silence is too near to truth for people's tastes. Truth, when it is sounded, is ridiculous to men. I fear my new book may plumb too great a depth and make me a laughing stock."

"Must mean you're pleased with it."

"It's a wicked book."

"There is wickedness in all good writing."

"But only to be trodden down." Melville began to pace about the room. "The dice are loaded every time. Ach, I was possessed by dark powers while I wrote this book, Nathaniel, and something of the darkness I caught from you. There is blackness in your work. A mossy, damp, peaty blackness, which in me has turned cavernous and bottomless. I've written about a white whale, but the whiteness mirrors the blackness. Both are mires."

"Have another cigar. You'll feel better about it once it's through the press."

Melville turned, and became voluminously theatrical. "So be it. Let me stay late and fill your lady's parlour with the billowing clouds of pagan incense."

Having no fear of the six-mile horse-ride home in the pitch of night, Melville settled, cigar aflame, into delightful "ontological heroics" with the friend whom he had met for the first time just twelve months previous. Their acquaintanceship in all that time had been intense but desultory. They had had not even half a

7

dozen opportunities for exchanging their innermost visions, so that invariably those few occasions which had offered themselves were, on Melville's part at least, sucked dry of possibility.

"Is it belief or resignation? There is some such foregone stead-fastness behind every word you write. You *know* the way it lies in Paradise, and yet you let loose but a smattering of your knowledge. While I search and seek and stalk, every book an expedition of discovery. Yes, and as the oceans turn upon themselves, so I come back to the same beginning – a family homecoming, with no treasures won, no new wisdom gained."

"You under-estimate yourself. I'm sure you are not the same man who went to sea at the age of nineteen."

"And that I'm not, but I wonder if all the learning and new-gained sophistry have been merely pasted on to the same youthful heart. There is something of my Ahab in me, made manic by spectral images of the Truth. It was blessed work, just recently, building shanties from sun to sun, working myself as if I were a hired man."

"That is something Sophia berates me for. I have not the ability to be my own taskmaster for anything other than writing. If we ever owned a property it would have to remain as found at time of purchase, or we would need the capital to spare to have improve-ments made professionally. She is the industrious one. Did you know she has started painting again? Now the children are older she claims to have more time, managing to sketch away in the midst of the dual inquisition, and little Rosebud more often than not asleep."

Mr. Hawthorne did lean his head towards a small canvas on the most distant wall but Melville could not distinguish its subject, and did not get up to make closer inspection.

"This is just my point. You seem compelled by a calmer genius, drawn along by a more soporific star. If barometers of our brain could be read, yours would be balmy, mine tumultuous. You smile?"

"Was I not meant to?"

Melville never did quite learn to read that smile. It grew to madden him, thinking that it denoted an amused detachment – the ironical detachment with which the initiated view the stum-blings of an apprentice.

The night grew black. Mr. Hawthorne lit the lamps and then, when moths began to flutter round, closed the casement.

"It strikes me," Melville continued, while his companion was engaged in these activities, "that you have resigned yourself philosophically to God's Providence. And feel that others should do likewise."

"Don't all my important characters fight against their allotted fate?"

"There is more calm endurance there than resistance. Anyway, what is it that Boethius says about Fate? That it's just God's way of bringing about through circumstance his Providence. So, whatever your characters do is determined, or self-determined, it doesn't matter, and in the end leads to pre-ordained conclusions. I know you profess never to go to church and yet you seem to have a firmer faith than me. I think there is something pagan in you, Nathaniel, some love of the natural world which I can't muster."

"Oh, you should have heard me tell Julian today how much I loathe these Berkshire hills."

"But that is it. The fields, the clouds, impel you to fervent reaction. While I just use them as a solace. Sitting on my piazza with a pipe in my mouth, or climbing the slopes of Saddleback with my nephew Sam. It's only the sea that can break through my stand-offishness. And wind. The way it gusts across the tall grasses."

Mr. Hawthorne chuckled. "You twist us about so. I, the fervent one? You, taciturn? A while ago it was somewhat different. And let me tell you it's the sea *I* miss here."

Melville humphed, without a smile. "Analogies, analogies; do they have to be mathematical equations, each side holding true in different circumstance? Truth doesn't always hold the centre ground. Doesn't demand exact equivalence. As the readers of my *Whale* will have to grant. Or be led a right dance trying to balance one comparison with another."

Unable to think of any apt reply, Mr. Hawthorne stretched and said, "You must forgive me. I don't seem able to hold the thread. Parenthood saps the metaphysical energies."

Melville stood and picked up his dark and heavy jacket from the back of a chair. "Yes, I'd better be mounting my horse. Now look, we must marshal a party next weekend. With the Duyckincks. You must bring Julian and spend a few nights with us. I shall send a wagon."

"Yes, I should think we could manage just one."

"Just one! There's no one here to miss you, man! And there's

9

Lizzie and Augusta who can take the child off your hands for a bit. Malcolm mightn't be much of a conversationalist but he'd be something of a playmate, for all the difference in age. Agreed?"

The two men were at the door. Mr. Hawthorne nodded his head in assent.

"Good. Adios. Don't come to the barn. It's a clear night, and if you don't blow out your lamps too sharpish I'll see my way all right."

*　　*　　*

The next day the boy awoke insistent that Bunny should be given away. He had promised it to Ellen Tappan, or some such tale. Mr. Hawthorne happily acquiesced in the arrangements, glad that they had such a practical transaction to accomplish and relieved that, for a while at least, he might be spared Julian's incessant cross-examination.

He had had a short night's sleep, having lain awake for some time after Melville's departure. He felt numb, and somewhat compromised in the face of the younger man's speculations. He ought not to listen so passively and yet he was sensible that his own reticence in matters philosophical was bound up inextricably with his creative impulse. Were he more eloquent he should not feel the same need to write – to fashion his weird brand of emblematic romances in sentences so classically chiselled.

Julian, let it be known, had enjoyed no better a night's sleep than his father. Visions of a rodent, equal in size to Bunny and with oddly similar ears, though with no fluffy stump for a tail but rather a long, worm-like piece of flesh – visions of this rat kept looming before him, despite his turnings on the pillow, despite the clenching of his eyelids.

They had risen at half-past six, gone to the barn for milk, and were discussing plans for the day over breakfast.

"I have to go to Ellen's."

"I thought you didn't like the Tappans."

"I have to give her something. I've promised it."

"And what splendid gift would a Little Man like you be taking the fair creature."

"Bunny. I'm taking Bunny."

His father had known something was amiss, from the moment the day had begun, with toilet and frizzing of hair. There had been

10

no questions, no quizzing. In their place an ominous sense of impending disclosure. And here it was.

"But, Julian, you can't give Bunny away without Onion here. Whatever would she say when she gets back."

"Ooona doesn't like Bunny. She's nasty to him. She puts him up in the apple trees. Right up high so he can't get down."

"Then what about your mother? It's your mother has to nurse Bunny when he catches chill."

"It was Mama's idea. I heard her say to Cara that he was messing our carpet and that at Highwood they had more room."

"Your mother said nothing about it to me, and you've left it very late to mention it."

"Today's Saturday, isn't it? We agreed to keep it one more week."

"You're quite certain of this?"

"Yes."

It was right that Sophia had made it known on occasion that Bunny's habits did not exactly fit him to be a constant occupant of the sitting room, but he had very pleasant little ways, and a character well worth observing. Mr. Hawthorne did not know any other beast, and few human beings, who, always present, and thrusting a little paw into all the business of the day, could at the same time be so perfectly unobtrusive.

Eventually he did allow, at ten o'clock, Mrs. Peters to accompany Julian over to Highwood, with Bunny wrapped in some of the outer bedding from Rosebud's crib.

*   *   *

Melville stabled his horse after arriving home from the night's talk with Mr. Hawthorne and then, so that he could take off his boots before going into the house, sat on his north-facing piazza – an extension he had had built the previous month. His step across its boards toward the only chair (the rest of the household found the aspect there, even in midsummer, too cold and cheerless) gave out the hard hollow echo of new wood. Being the type of man who could be rather careless in his thoughtfulness, Melville now let the spurred heels of his boots jangle harshly against the floor. The noise set off a scurry beneath him, as some small startled animal bolted in fright.

The next morning at 7.30, while Melville was still asleep, his

11

sister, Augusta, brought him and his wife breakfast in their room. Lizzie carefully sat up and raised the pillow as a backrest.

"Oh, Augusta, how sweet of you. I'm sorry we're not up yet. I didn't want to disturb Herman. He was very late in, you know."

"You're not to be getting up early from now on, anyway. This month brings you to the last stage of your confinement." She stood looking about the room for a place to put the tray.

"What have you done with Malcolm? I heard you go to him earlier on."

"He's with his grandma."

"Oh, dear, she'll be testing his improvement and making remarks all through the day."

Augusta, having chosen to put the tray down on the washstand surface, handed Lizzie her coffee and roll. "She was just the same with us. I expect Herman told you how worried she was about *him*."

Lizzie smiled. "Some things never change."

"And where did our adventurer get to till so late last night?"

"Did he wake you too, then? I must scold him when he stirs. To Nathaniel Hawthorne's, I think."

"I dare say he needs the rest then. I gather they talk rather deeply about things. Aren't men funny? They think our conversation so full of prittle-prattle and yet worship us as the profounder sex."

Lizzie, putting down her coffee cup, said, "And I don't like these women who try to play it man's way. These new bloomer-stockings or whatever, and talking-shops. Mrs. Hawthorne's sister is very involved in one, I believe."

"I know Lizzie, you're doing the woman's part, swelling up with new life."

Lizzie blushed, not through the direct reference to her condition, but the unintended affront made upon Augusta's spinsterdom.

"Oh, Augusta, I . . ."

"Don't be silly, and keep Herman there as long as you can. Now I'll go and see to the two young Samsons."

Melville was no longer asleep. He had been awoken by Augusta's entry into the room and, lying still in a disguised state of continued slumber, had overheard the entire conversation. Eavesdropping had been a vice of his ever since, as a child, he had discovered that by feigning interest in something else, a toy or a

12

book, the adults around him would talk as if he were not present. Many a family summit on the subject of dollars and debt had he been party to as a boy, and although, now that he was much older, the subterfuge had to be more oblique, more offstage – standing beside a door drawn ajar, hesitating on the stairs, waiting by an open window – and therefore more meditated and, by the same token, more sinful, the taste for overheard exchanges, particularly those that related to himself, was too firmly established to be forgone. And there was something delicious in this morning's evidence that he could occasionally regress to the more childlike, the more angelic, mode of witness.

Having feigned sleep, he next had to feign stirring himself out of it. He began by making nuzzling noises, then by stretching his legs, and finally rolling onto his back. Lizzie was sitting up and looking down her nose at him. On her mouth was a smile of sweet affection, but such was her husband's angle of vision, and such the screwed-eyed manner of his first look at the day, that he perceived her expression as one of derision. The misapprehension (though it lingered more than such, and was by no means the first time Melville had misconstrued the attitude of his betrothed) was dispelled by the touch of her hand upon his forehead, her fingers gently stroking hair off his brow, only to be displaced by another from which he immediately recoiled. Whether it was that he felt suddenly like a child being petted by his mother, or like a white man being pampered by a South Seas paramour, and that either one of these impressions did not fit comfortably into the accepted dramatisations of the marital bond, you will be better able to judge once you have been introduced to the other Mrs. Melville.

As a result of a single, violent convulsion Melville was sitting up beside his wife, a little further down in the bed, and looking back at her startled face. Elizabeth was full of the timidities of a wife whose normal and comely domestic aspirations were forever being thrown awry by the seismic startlings of a man who, whatever philosophical statements he would make in his work, could not live his life within a closed frame.

"Sorry, Lizzie. I only half awoke, and did not know where I was."

He insisted on going to the cow. She forbade it. "Sam will go, or one of them will." He explained his late night, telling her of Mr. Hawthorne's difficulties alone with Julian.

"So I've invited him over next week, when the Duyckincks are

13

here." She scolded him gently for the dropping of the boots. It did not matter, the two Sams had kept the house up with midnight chatter. He said he would take the boys out for a hike later in the morning. She said he wasn't to feel he had to, if there was work he should be doing. "Not for a bit. A spell of drifting between strong breezes." She told him that Malcolm was with his mother, and could not then retain him: "Come on then, the child needs rescuing."

Later in the day, having made explanation for his late rising to his mother, and ensuring that Malcolm was transferred to safer parts of the household, Melville set off in the direction of Monument Mountain with the two step-cousins Samuel. Both under twenty years old, they were quiet and simple boys who put Melville in mind of, by virtue of their names and companionship, David and Jonathan. They asked, naturally, of his sea-faring days and he was still glad to oblige with a colourful yarn. And yet it was he more than they who was put in the envious position, walking behind them during lulls in the conversation. Such open brotherhood seemed more than ever a vestige of lost innocence, incompatible with the restraints of a property-owning maturity.

*　　*　　*

Julian was away just forty-five minutes. At quarter-to-eleven he was back, empty-handed and obviously upset by the transaction.

"They took him, then?"

The child did not answer, but looked at Mr. Hawthorne's shoes.

"Have you done something wrong, Julian?"

"No, Papa. Not naughty. But I don't think it's right for Ellen to have Bunny. When she realised she could keep him she lifted him up by the hind legs and dangled him in the air *and* tickled his tummy with sticks. I don't think Mrs. Tappan can make her behave, and Mr. Tappan's horrid and Ellen is . . ."

Mr. Hawthorne knelt down and put two arms round his son in a timely effort to prevent the onset of hysterics. "Remember, Julian, it was mother's wish." He thought privately it might have been a greater kindness to have drowned the beast. "Let us cheer ourselves up with a walk to the lake. We've time before dinner. Come on, it's warm enough to go as we are."

It was another cloudless day, but at 11 a.m. still not too warm. Monument Mountain was almost entirely covered in mist except

14

where its peak pushed through on the western side. Somewhere in that distance went the three hikers from Arrowhead, and Mr. Hawthorne, walking along with his subdued infant companion, thought again of Melville's visit and the impression it had given (confirming the same one gained from a recent exchange of letters) of a mind torn from all natural moorings. He looked at the trees, the mountain peak and the head of his boy, and he blessed the solace of his own contentment. They could call it smug complacency if they wished; but be damned for doing so. He loved his wife and children and had a talent which, after long years of monastic execution, was at last being rewarded and applauded. Strange world; yesterday he was ranting at this landscape, today it seemed the perfect setting for his mental poise.

They found a boat drawn up on the shore of the lake and fastened to the root of a tree. The boy was allowed to climb into the boat and play around in it. There were some fish in the bottom, evidently dead for some days past, and when he saw them Julian pleaded with his father to take him fishing.

"The boat is locked."

"But it's only tied." Julian clambered up to the boat's prow and pulled on the rope, lifting the tree root some inches out of the ground.

"It's someone else's."

"Look – they've already been fishing today. They won't come back."

Mr. Hawthorne turned towards the old fish being held up by Julian, its body so decomposed it was about to part company with the fin.

"If you really want to go fishing, we'll have to call on old Mr. Farley after dinner. He's got a boat."

Enough said. They spent the afternoon drifting in the middle of the lake, with Mr. Hawthorne very content to give Julian over to the arcane wisdoms of the Waltonian. There was, briefly, something hurtful in the way the boy made himself so easily receptive to the other man's instruction, listening intently with an expression of avowed respect which he rarely, if ever, showed his father or mother. He was more aggressive with them, never quietly soaking up their words but forever quizzing and prompting them, wringing them dry. Never mind; Mr. Hawthorne comforted himself, slouching back with his neck resting against the edge of the boat and using Julian's bundle of warmer clothing as a soft bolster, with

15

the thought that this was how it was between fathers and sons. He had no grounds for satisfying himself with such an assumption, his own father having died during his infancy, but it was characteristic of the man that he should brush perturbation back with the unbending fibre of a vague but confidently intuitive philosophy. "My business is merely to live and to enjoy," he had once said, and although a good portion of this sensualist statement can be attributed to its timing – soon after his marriage to Miss Sophia Peabody – it still points to a sharp difference between himself and Melville. Indeed, it will be instructive to leave Mr. Hawthorne to his bobbing daydreams on the ripplets of the Stockbridge Bowl, while Julian, pulling in a small bream, enjoys the ecstasies of huntsman's first success, and to move landward a few miles to the north, where Melville and the two Sams have just picnicked on spartan provisions.

* * *

The two young men, made sleepy by a glass or two of well-fermented cider, were stretched supine on the mountainside. They had stopped for lunch as soon as there was a perceptible gradient in the land, a proper ascent requiring an initial train journey to North Adams or Williamstown. Melville sat up straight, striking two pieces of flint together, as a boy would, in hope of producing a spark. He was thinking hard and aloud about arrangements for the weekend. "It is the drink mainly. Given the number in the party – a dozen at the very least – how much in the way of brandy and champagne can we get up there? Mm? Now I know you won't be with us. Though you're welcome to stay on, and if the weather holds we can set up two hammocks across the piazza. The crossbeam should be strong enough, I remember mentioning the possibility to the carpenter. Of course, it's Mrs. Morewood I should be asking. A professional organiser of a party, that lady is. There does seem to be some mathematical conundrum I can't yet fathom. The larger the party the more can be carried. But also the more stomachs to fill, the more gullets to swill. Can you work that one out, Samuel?"

Melville lobbed one of his pieces of flint at the nearest youth, who simply rolled over, saying, "Oh, Uncle Herman, I don't know." The older man rather resented the example of indolence set by this younger generation and came close to throwing the second piece of flint, much harder, in the same direction. Instead, he stood and hurled it high and wide into the open air.

As it happened he might have joined the boys in their languorous wasting of the afternoon. Next weekend's picnic with the Duyckinck brothers and Mr. Hawthorne would venture into less grand geography, in a different compass direction, and with fare more humble than that enjoyed by these three today. It would, after all, be left to Mrs. Morewood, that doyen of picnic adventures already referred to, to marshal an expedition upon Graylock, and as that will become an episode from which Mr. Hawthorne was excluded, let us give him the rest of the week to himself.

*   *   *

At the end of the afternoon's fishing, with Julian safely and unquerulously in bed, Mr. Hawthorne found himself in conversation, for only the second or third time inside a year, with "that nasty man" Mr. Tappan. Spotting his landlord passing by the edge of the orchard garden, Mr. Hawthorne had gone outside braced for a further tussle concerning the rights to the fruit – a controversy which, as the reader knows already, had permanently prejudiced young Julian's opinion of the entire Tappan household, and one which had intriguing undercurrents to be developed later.

"Ah, good evening, Nathaniel, I wanted to catch you without the boy. Is he in bed? You see, we find the animal quite troublesome. Ellen mistreats it; the dog is always trying to get at it; in short, not a very desirable acquisition. A pity to have to snub the boy's generosity but we shan't be able to keep it. This has nothing, nothing to do with the other business."

It was obvious now that Sophia must have had nothing to do with the proposal. Mr. Hawthorne was sure Mrs. Tappan would have allowed Bunny a longer trial if she had – unless, despite her husband's embarrassed assurances, she was just being awkward in the manner of their other dispute – but he didn't try and corroborate this. It seemed immaterial now whether Julian had been telling the truth or not.

"We were finding the same ourselves. I wondered if it were best to put the creature out of existence but the boy was insistent Ellen should take it."

"No. You can't do that. We'll turn him out into the woods if you won't take him back."

17

And so it was agreed that Bunny would return to the Red House next morning. Mr. Hawthorne went inside, crushed some currants in a bowl and ate them. Then he read *Pendennis* until bedtime.

In the middle of the night Julian had another nightmare. He was playing with Ellen in the Tappan house when her face seemed to lengthen and her cheeks become fluffy. She held her hands in a peculiar way in front of her chest and protruded her upper teeth at him. He went to find Mrs. Tappan and tell her that Ellen was scaring him but instead he came upon the rear haunches of a giant rat. The creature turned in time for Julian to see Bunny's tail disappearing into its masticating jaws.

Mr. Hawthorne was woken by the boy's screaming and found him thrashing about in a perfectly soppy state, having wet the bed. He went downstairs and fetched a clean nightgown, attributing the unprecedented accident to the maternal absence.

At breakfast Julian was told that he could go and fetch Bunny back, which he did promptly, at nine o'clock. Later, the three of them had dinner together – bread and custard pie – and then Julian was back to his speculative self, smashing every attempt that his father made at reflection into a thousand fragments so that Mr. Hawthorne could not say that he preferred the boy merry or morose.

The week was a continuum of similar exasperation, allayed now and again by little incidents which, in their uneventful life together, became elevated into adventures. There was the discovery of a remarkable echo in the middle of the woods. Julian called "Mama", "Una" and many other words. When he shouted his own name and the sound came back, he said that it was Mama calling him. On Monday the weather had grown temporarily chilly, though still dry. The water had dropped five or six feet in the lake and the trees' foliage had so shrunken that the shade seemed less dense – or such was Mr. Hawthorne's impression. He was of a delicately balanced constitution and the inconsistent temperature made him catch cold, which he dosed with Nux Vomica. On the Tuesday Julian was stung by a wasp while getting over a fence by Mr. Tappan's oatfield, an event which did nothing to improve that family's reputation. Once home, Mr. Hawthorne bathed his leg in Arnica, Mrs. Peters already having left, and the following morning administered two globules of Aconite to ease the swelling. Later on the sting improved, but the day was spoiled

18

by another "accident" suffered by the Little Man while walking home from the village. The father hoped that he might be able to keep these two episodes from his wife who would be likely to interpret them sombrely and to have guilty thoughts for having left the boy behind. On Thursday a Mr. Waldo called, together with his little girl, and Julian was asked to show them Bunny, Mr. Hawthorne secretly hoping the other father might be persuaded to take it off their hands since its character seemed to have been wholly spoiled by its half day at the hands of Ellen and the Tappan dog. But no such offer was made. When they had gone Julian had a tantrum over a piece of bread, bellowing and beating his father terribly and putting up rampageous resistance until bedtime.

*   *   *

Evert and George Duyckinck had duly arrived at Pittsfield in the middle of the week just as the weather was beginning to deteriorate and, having had a rather interrupted excursion to the Ashley Pond on Thursday, the Melville wagon drew up at the Red House between eleven and twelve o'clock on Friday morning with no precise plans for the rest of the day and, thinking it likely that dinner would be provided by Hawthorne, with just teatime victuals aboard, and those amounting only to mustard sandwiches and gingerbread. But Mr. Hawthorne had nothing to give them, it being Mrs. Peters' day off, and so, a ride and picnic being proposed, he fetched his last bottle of champagne and they set out.

They took the road towards Hancock, Melville having scotched his plans for a mountain ascent, a scheme which had been bequeathed to Mrs. Morewood and was timed for later the following week. Evert Duyckinck made room for Julian on the front seat, while George and Mr. Hawthorne held conversation in the back. In appearance the two New Yorkers were typical city gents of their day – they seemed not to have made much sartorial accommodation for the rustic way of life. They and Melville had been acquainted ever since 1844 when the sailorboy returned from the South Seas to begin his apprenticeship as a writer, and it had been the Duyckinck library which had been responsible for the transition from *Omoo* to *Mardi*, from straight if fanciful recollection of maritime experiences towards an idiosyncratic form of figurative fiction.

19

While Evert enquired politely of Julian after his mother and sister, Melville drove the wagon with a dogged taciturnity, holding the reins in his lap, and looking askance at the landscape, away from his companions in the barouche. The truth is he had been in a black temper ever since we left him berating the laziness of his nephews. With the *Whale* book some way off the final stages of printing he had found himself already contemplating a new work, so that just when Elizabeth might have expected to find him a more communicative companion she had once again detected the vague and wayward look in his eye which she knew by now to be the sign of imminent composition. Her attempts to combat this perception by trying to root Herman in the practicalities of farm-life and fatherhood – she had tried to talk to him about further improvements to the interior of the home, about efforts they might be making to help prepare Malcolm for school – had either been ignored or answered in eruptive volleys such as, "Good God, I've just spent two months putting up new out-houses, I'm a writer not a frontiersman," or, "I thought my mother was making efforts enough in that direction". To which she could have replied that for almost the entire month of June he had been away in New York and that his labouring work had been much more sporadic than he cared to claim. As for his mother, it was all very well for him to bemoan the fuss which she made of her grandson but he did very little personally to liberate him from her clutches. Added to this there was the sexual restraint which Elizabeth's pregnancy now dictated. There was nothing remotely prodigious about the frequency of their love-making at normal times, but Melville was sufficiently a man to share in the symptoms described by Burton which afflict those who are required to abstain from Venery.

"I have *two* sisters," Julian corrected Evert Duyckinck. "But Mama has taken them both away."

"What is the new sister's name?"

"Rosebud. She will be cross when she comes back because we've lost her crib blanket."

"Oh?"

"Yes, you see we gave Bunny away to nasty Mr. Tappan and we've got him back now but they've kept the blanket. We wrapped him up in a blanket when we took him there but they just brought Bunny back."

"Well, I expect your mother will sort that out when she returns. When is she coming back?"

"Never." Julian gave his fib away by laughing immediately and then turning towards Melville. "Mr. Omoo. Yoo-hoo." Julian, frightened by the stern aspect which he saw turned toward him, said the first thing that came to mind. "I like your beard. I wish Papa would grow a beard." Melville made no answering remark and the boy turned round for a comforting glance at his clean-shaven Papa who was listening to George Duyckinck speaking about a new business venture the two brothers were engaged in. It had something to do with literature but Mr. Hawthorne was bemused by the financial details and rather bored by the whole explanation.

So that the mood of the party was rather cool when Melville drew the carriage up into a pleasant grove and indicated that it was time to alight and arrange things for a picnic.

What little repast they had with them was contained in one basket which, having been placed on the ground, they all sat round. Melville opened the napkinned bundles and handed sand-wiches to each person, including Julian, who was the first to bite into one, immediately exclaiming and hopping about with an open mouth. Mr. Hawthorne took a peep between the layers of bread. There was a little cold meat to be sure, but wholly camouflaged by oodles of dark yellow mustard.

"Better open the champagne and let him cool himself with a sip," said one of the Duyckincks, which prompted the other to quote from Keats' Ode. Melville took the jolly black bottle and without more ado levered out the cork with his thumbs and let a half-tumblerful brim over into a glass quickly held out by Evert. Mr. Hawthorne looked on uncomfortably while his boy supped the forbidden beverage and reflected that the number of secrets he intended keeping from Sophia on her return was multiplying. Julian downed the drink quickly, without realising what he was taking, and to stall any offer of a further glass Mr. Hawthorne enquired what else there was for the boy to eat.

"There's only gingerbread," Melville replied. "All hot stuff, though he'll probably find it cool enough after the mustard." He investigated more napkinned bundles until he found one which contained the gingerbread. The food might not be various but there was plenty of it, suggesting to Mr. Hawthorne that the three men's plans for the day had been wholly different and had been adapted in response to his own empty larder – a reading of the situation which seemed to explain Melville's downcast mood.

21

Julian filled himself up on the cake and then gambolled about amongst the low branches of the grove, allowing the adults time for a smoke under the trees and a chat about literature.

"I can see where you get Pearl from," Evert remarked, as he was handing around the cigars.

Mr. Hawthorne smiled in a half-timid way, and answered hesitatingly, "Una's the girl. Julian was only a squib when the *Letter* was written."

"Mm – I didn't mean the boy was the model, merely that it is clear that, against the popular belief, you do write from life."

Again the Hawthorne smile. "I like to disguise the fact as far as possible. Much as I may use real experiences, and I've kept notebooks for that purpose over the years, I'm far happier for the readers to consider my books Romances, as I've made plain in preface after preface."

"I don't see *you* as a notebook man, am I right, Herman?" George was the first to ignite his cigar and he passed it around for the others to use as a light.

"No. Only on trips. And then the barest of Logs."

"What was it you said to me in a letter a while back . . .?" Evert sucked on his cigar and let the smoke drift upwards in breath-free rumination. Then, jerking to life and tapping a small amount of ash onto the ground, continued, "Yes, it was an image of the creative act. Something about scraping a book off the brain, like taking an old painting off a panel. An uncomfortable, but evocative metaphor I thought."

"It may not be true but it's damned close to the feeling one gets at the end. It's a ticklish and dangerous business writing a book, a good book that is, but there's more devastation to the brain than is in my poetic analogising. I think really it gets scraped away more as someone eats a ripe melon or avocado, scouring down to the skin. It's a better conceit for explaining the crazed or grazed headache which is quite peculiar to too much work at the writing desk. These dandies don't know what we go through, eh?" Melville slapped Mr. Hawthorne's knee.

"Well, I confess I don't have the capacity for such onslaught. As can be seen well enough. Your output already far exceeds mine."

"Ah but money spinners mostly, and not very efficient ones at that. I was speaking just now of *real* writing."

"And which of your works would you include in that category?" George asked.

"The present one definitely. But this conversation is turning too personal. Haven't you two any gossip for us backwoodsmen?"

"Not really, have we, George? We've been working very hard ourselves."

"I suppose it is a bit rich, your coming from the hectic city to find the both of us free to take buggy rides in the woods." Melville lay back on the grass. "Still, this is turning into a pleasant little frolic. Wish I'd brought the brandy flask." And, propping himself up on the elbows, said to Mr. Hawthorne, "Sorry about that. I haven't had much excitement in me the past few days."

Evert and George exchanged a glance, telling one another they were relieved to find their host thawing out at last. Melville had said hardly a word to them until now.

Julian, realising at last that his acrobatics were being ignored, sped up to Melville and jumped onto his stomach.

"Oh-ho, and who are you running away from in such a hurry? There are cannibals in these woods. They'll put you in a pot and eat you for dinner."

"There aren't. Will they?" Julian looked to his father for peace of mind.

"Mr Melville is an expert on these matters. He ought to know."

"I tell you what, Julian."

"Yes?"

Evert stood up and held up his hand for the boy to hold. "You see that tree at the edge of a rise over there. If I were to lift you up onto the first branch you could keep look-out for us. Cannibals aren't choosy. Much as they like young flesh they won't turn their noses up at ropey old stuff like us. So they might jump on us all at any time. They'll be coming from over there, won't they, Herman?" Melville gave a single, serious nod. "So, you know your job? Just holler the minute you see anything suspicious."

As Evert lifted a bemused Julian off the ground and carried him about fifty yards to the look-out tree. Mr. Hawthorne remarked to the others, "It sounds harsh, but it's such a relief to be rid of his attentions, even for this quarter-hour or so. Sophia has been gone ten days and it seems I haven't had a moment to read or think."

"What did I hear the boy saying about Bunny?" Melville asked.

"We gave him away. He says it was his mother's plan, but I'm fairly sure that was an invention."

"He seemed very fond of the creature the other day."

"Yes, but it's not an animal that returns affection. I have been

23

tempted often enough by the Evil One to murder it."

These words did not, on the face of it, strike any discord in the company. With Evert returned, the two Duyckincks asked after Mrs. Hawthorne and tried to discover what plans the family had for the future. If Melville had listened closely he might have been alarmed to find how temporary the Hawthornes' future residency in the Berkshires was due to be, but although he watched with the air of one who was intently listening, he remained perplexed and tantalised by the remark about wanting to kill the pet rabbit. There would always be something elusive, something secret in Nathaniel's character and Melville wondered if, in this offhand confession, he had stumbled upon an important pointer. Could there be, running through this quiet, outwardly gentle man, a hidden seam of latent violence, one that remained perhaps continually closed, but which nevertheless was always threatening to split asunder. He would have to get out the *Tales* when he was home and see if there was any evidence in the work. Further contemplation of this matter was cut short by an outbreak of whimpering from the look-out tree. It was not a cry of alarm, but one of displeasure. All four of them stood up and walked over to see what was the matter. It was Melville who reached up and took Julian down from his perch. The boy had obviously been crying for some while and was now worked up into an infant delirium.

"Ellen – does that – with – Bunny. So – he can't – get – down." The boy's words were interspersed with deep inhalations which racked his body and made his head vibrate. The Duyckincks said they'd pack the picnic away and Melville went to see if the horses were still thirsty.

Mr. Hawthorne knelt down at his boy's feet, and dabbed at his cheeks with a handkerchief. "Naughty Papa. Leaving you up a tree. I thought you were excited by Mr. Duyckinck's little game." Julian took the handkerchief in his own hands and, giving two peremptory pats to his either cheek, quickly returned it to his father, and ran off towards the carriage, shouting, "Can I sit in the front again?"

The party, having set off down an unfamiliar track, in a direction which they took to be west by the position and trajectory of the sun, stopped a half-mile on beside a girl who was playing outside a fine old house.

"What road is this?" Melville called over to her.

"To the Shakers."

"How far?"

24

"Two or three mile."

Melville turned to George and Mr. Hawthorne in the back. "Shall we go?"

"Are they the cannibals?" Julian asked of Melville. And "Are they monsters? Do they have four legs? What do they shake? Will they be shaking today?"

In the back Nathaniel smiled. He smiled when Melville became impatient on the fifth question, he smiled because Julian was obviously over the upset in the tree, he smiled because the weather was clement, not too warm but dry, and he was in interesting company and on his way to an experience which would re-satisfy an old curiosity, he smiled because he felt pleasantly void of creative incubation – these ten days alone with Julian had severed his mind completely from all thought of writing – and lastly he smiled because he felt an absolute confidence, imbued perhaps by his two glasses of lunchtime champagne, that Phoebe (his affectionate name for Sophia) would in due course return safely with his two daughters, and once again life could attune itself to the feminine balance which, all through his youth and manhood, he had found the most commodious.

A very different train of thought tracked out the lines of expression on Melville's face. Already the enjoyment of this masculine rendezvous, which over lunch had effectively counteracted his attack of tristimania, was beginning to pall at the prospect of the evening's return to Arrowhead. He had read secretly, in the past month, *Reveries Of A Bachelor* by Ilk Marvell, a pseudonymous bestseller. It was no work of literature but it had rung a deep and grievous chord in this particular reader, mirroring as it did so unambiguously, right down to the psychological motivation for solitary cigar-smoking, his own mode of meditation. The fact that he, a husband and a father, could identify so strongly with this misogynous work was a source of pain and trouble to him.

Mr. Hawthorne, spotting an old man up ahead dressed in a gown, and grey, broad-brimmed hat, tapped Julian on the shoulder and informed him that this was a Shaker. Evert Duyckinck, it turned out, knew the old fellow from a previous year's visit and, jumping down from the carriage and getting a short greeting over with, introduced the gentleman as Father Hilliard and invited him up onto the back seat alongside George and Nathaniel.

"If we drive him up to the house, he says he'll see it's all right for us to go in. He's one of the Elders of the village, so there should be no problem."

They were indeed allowed into the principal dwelling-place, a large brick edifice with interior walls of polished wood and plaster as smooth as marble. Spittoons were provided but gave no evidence of ever being used. On one side of the entrance to the two dormitories hung the hats of the men, on the other the ladies' bonnets. There were no washing conveniences in any of the sleeping chambers but a single sink and wash-stand was provided for the whole group, and Mr. Hawthorne could not help remarking, fastidious soul that he was in matters of toiletry, that of the four Shaker pillars – Virgin Purity, Christian Communism, Confession and Separation from the World – it was apparent that cleanliness was not considered a part of the first. And he was quietly amused when Julian let it be known that he wished to relieve himself, thus conferring on the establishment the only mark of consideration of which the foolish place was worthy.

On their departure they saw women sewing or otherwise at work in the doorways of auxiliary dwellings. They looked pale and careworn, nothing emanating from them of the ecstatic raptures supposed to be part and parcel of their religious services.

"A hateful and disgusting place," Mr. Hawthorne announced, when they were away from the domestic settlement and the few field workers still about were either too distant or too elderly to hear. "The sooner the sect is extinct the better."

Evert turned around, knocking Julian into Melville's lap, who growled good-humouredly at the boy. "I think, to be fair to the movement, one must experience one of their religious services. Shall we come over again on Sunday, Herman, and Mr. Hawthorne could join us?"

"Well, I wouldn't bring Julian to that, and I've no one to leave the boy with."

"You're still invited to Arrowhead. These two are already sharing a bedstead but there are hammocks we can put up on the piazza this mild weather. Then Julian can stay behind with the women."

"Yes, there are any number of those at the Melville home," George put in.

Melville said to Evert, not as an underhand remark, but for Mr. Hawthorne to hear, "He's an awkward cuss. Invitation after invitation I give him. Never taken up. I think he's put off by my masculine reveries and thoughts on the infinite. A pagan, feline soul is our Nathaniel." Melville turned round and beamed, to disguise a real sense of frustration. Such jesting words were not, anyway, the kind to persuade Mr. Hawthorne to alter his plans, since he was of that class of shyness which, when its foibles are mocked, hardens them for something more solid to duck behind.

In discussing their impressions of the Shaker settlement they mistook the direct road back to Lenox and ended up having to ride some fifteen miles through unknown regions. It was the most picturesque ride Mr. Hawthorne had ever been on, travelling up heights and into glens, and he determined to find the way again so that he could return to the scene on foot with Sophia.

It having been already five when they had set off from Hancock, they were still driving along well after sunset, but by then they had made out Monument Mountain and Rattlesnake Hill and other familiar features so that there was no real fear amongst the adults of being lost. For Julian though it must have been the wildest and most unprecedented adventure, and he kept looking round at his father with such a peculiar expression as might a child use on a particularly breathtaking fair-ride.

Although troubled with doubts as to the result, Mr. Hawthorne felt under an obligation to invite the party to take supper and rest the horses before going on to Pittsfield. Mrs. Peters would be back on duty – her day off being taken from 3 p.m. one day to the next – but there was no telling whether she would absolutely refuse to co-operate at such an hour.

However, she bestirred herself, like the black angel she was, and despatched Mr. Hawthorne to Highwood for some loaf sugar and whatever else Mrs. Tappan might bestow, so that in no time an adequate meal of poached eggs, scones, jam and tea was at hand. Julian had fallen asleep on the couch without so much as taking off his hat, and when he had to be stirred in order to be undressed for bed and was asked whether or not he had had a good time, the naughty Little Man answered with a grumpy "No".

"Hm, it's good to see him being as headstrong as Malcolm. I wonder sometimes whether we ever entirely grow out of such contrariness; that there is ever a diabolic impulse in us which seeks to cast a negative hue over all our pleasure." Melville said this as he slowly crumbled some loaf sugar into his tea, Mr. Hawthorne first having reached the foot of the stairs after depositing Julian into his bed.

27

"Calvinism." George Duyckinck spoke the word as if it were an apt summary of what Melville had been driving at.

"No, I used the word 'impulse'. I might just as well have said instinct. By which I mean that it goes deeper than any particular religious orthodoxy. Right back, I suppose, to the Eden story."

"Original Sin *is* a particularly Calvinistic doctrine," persisted George.

"I'm not arguing that. But they are interpreting a truth of the heart which remains a truth for all our race."

"I thought you found the South Seas relatively free of this – er – guilt thing," said Evert.

"Guilt doesn't play a part in this, which is totally irrational. In seeking to rationalise it most Christian sects have only succeeded in making their adherents more prone to its influence. Religious explanations should seek to heal, to alleviate heaviness of the heart, not pile on weight after weight. They have the right method in the East, though the wrong answers. The object of a Buddhist treatise, say, is always to lighten the load, to explain tribulations so that they can be avoided rather than gloated over."

"I didn't know you were so interested in the East," said George.

"Your brother's library holds many wonders. I read ravenously while writing *Mardi*. But perhaps Mr. Hawthorne will be more inclined to support your notion of persistent Calvinism."

They looked towards the other writer. "All I've got to say on that matter is in the *Tales*."

Melville smiled. Evert Duyckinck explained unnecessarily that it had been a fair reply – writers ought not to be expected to elaborate on their fiction.

"What! Not even for the benefit of their own personal search? Don't talk rubbish, Duyck."

They had finished eating and the Duyckincks lit a round of cigars before departing, Mrs. Peters bustling in to tidy away the debris of the meal.

"Tuh-tuh. Whatever would Mrs. Hawthorne think," she said, upon picking up a plate in which cigar ash had been disposed.

"I am not normally permitted to smoke in this room," Mr. Hawthorne explained. The Duyckincks laughed and George, being one himself, referred to *Reveries Of A Bachelor* – a dangerous moment for Melville, who did not want his own familiarity with the book exposed.

"A nasty piece of woman-hating, but it's selling wonderfully

28

well. Looks like it might out-run Curtis. I suppose it must make you fellows despair – the public taste for frippery."

"I've made a private decision never again to pander to it, which doesn't bode well for my purse. We'll have to see what happens to this *Whale* of mine."

Conversation continued until the last butt had been pressed out. Melville repeated his invitation to Mr. Hawthorne but it was once again parried. "Well, try and make it over for the mountain climb. It'll be on Monday now, organised by the Morewood machine. We'll be going by rail up to North Adams so you could meet with us there. What about Sunday? Shall we pick you up if we go back to Hancock?"

"No, I think not." Mr. Hawthorne shook the Duyckincks' hands and wished them continuing enjoyment on their vacation.

The carriage set off for Pittsfield in full moonlight at 10 p.m., the occupants able to read the time readily by the huge Lenox clock face.

"An impressive man – Mr. Hawthorne," George remarked to his brother.

"Yes, a fascinating mixture of authority and vulnerability. Fancy admitting that your wife won't let you smoke in your own drawing room. Would you put up with that, Herman?"

"Oh, I come under sufficient feminine sway in other respects." He flicked the reins to hurry them homeward.

*   *   *

George and Evert Duyckinck disturbed one another awake before 6 a.m. The rest of the house was utterly quiet, and so they whispered their accusations.

"You woke me."

"No, *you* woke *me!*"

"You scratched my leg with your toe."

"You kicked me first."

It was good-natured banter. They were rather amused at having to share a bed and, in due course, propping up their pillows, both engaged themselves in the writing of letters: Evert to his wife, and George to a lady friend. They scratched away at some length and in time began to hear sounds in the house which indicated that its other occupants were on the move. There were peripheral noises at first – doors being opened, steps in the hall,

29

the murmuring of voices. But all of a sudden the low burble was exploded by a thundered "No!". Unmistakably Melville's – his was the only other masculine voice under the roof, the two Sams having left for a weekend hiking expedition – the noise shook George so that he spattered ink on the sheet. He gave his brother a Darn It look, while they both ceased writing to see what would ensue. Nothing of any note developed except that doors seemed to be closed with more of a bang and steps in the hall became less tentative – but then this is the natural way with noises in a house as the morning hour progresses.

Had their hearing been more acute they would have caught the sound of sobbing emanating from the Melville bedroom. Elizabeth, although dressed, had fallen gently back onto the bed, minding her condition, and was weeping into her pillow. The tiff with Herman had been of no real consequence, but she did abhor being shouted at, especially when there were guests in the house. She had only asked him if he might take his mother to Mrs. Morewood's Musical Party proposed for later in the day, and when he had refused she had stupidly pressed her request. Stupidly, that is, because, as already remarked, she had perceived that he was newly preoccupied and it would have been wisest in the circumstances to protect herself from his attendant ill temper. She had probably felt that her pregnancy invested her with a degree of natural protection, as by rights it should have done, and had as a result handled her husband with less perspicacity than usual.

Melville himself had run out through a heavy storm to milk the cow, taking a smoke with him. He wondered which of his sisters would go in to comfort Lizzie – Helen or Augusta – and wished that he could be there to hear what was said. What he found most disagreeable about married life was the aspect of negotiation, of reaching a mediation between two separate wills. Over matters such as the choice of curtain material he simply could not muster the strength to haggle, and let Elizabeth have her way – though he knew that even this displeased her, since it suggested he was disinterested. When larger issues were involved, he tended to behave as he had done this morning, bluntly stating his position and then withdrawing himself from further opportunity for dissension. He did not think that Elizabeth would be able to read his *Whale* book with any real understanding, which was a pity, for he had put into it many warm statements of support for the family and home life which would reassure her. His next book must be set upon the land and contain more domestic scenes than heretofore; perhaps it could even be a book that Elizabeth might delight in, or would the Devil take his pen again? Having milked the cow, he sat down to smoke and to augment these vague plans for future work while the rain kept up its hullabaloo on the barn roof.

It was Helen, the older sister, who went into Elizabeth's room. "Lizzie, whatever is it?" She sat on the edge of the bed and put a hand on Elizabeth's shoulder. Elizabeth, without raising her head, wiped her eyes and forced a smile.

"I'm sorry, Helen. I'm a little fragile at present."

"It didn't sound as if my brother was handling you with much care. We all heard him shouting."

"I'm sorry. It's just – Herman uses himself up so when he's writing and then when the book's over he's got Mr. Hawthorne and now the two Duyckincks – I know they're no trouble, they're both charming men, but I can't help but feel a little left out."

"When the new baby's here we shall have to get you out and about a bit more."

Elizabeth tiredly sat herself up. "It'll be winter then. Herman will be writing another book – he's already mulling it over – and the nursing will keep me tied till after Christmas."

"Do you want me to have a word with Herman for you?"

"Could you, Helen? He gets so touchy with me and he's much more suspicious of Augusta. I think he'll listen to you because he knows you're on his side as far as the writing goes."

"Aren't *you*?"

"Oh, I am proud of him, Helen, yes. And I know he's never worked so hard on anything as with this new book. And yet he doesn't seem to have much faith in its success. Is it very strange?"

Helen had been acting as Herman's copyist. "It *is* different from anything he's done before, but it has the same elements which have made his other books popular – the sea, and masculine adventure."

"Do you think he misses it very much? All his books seem to harp back to his sailing days."

"No, no, Lizzie! He's quite expansive in this one, about the joys of the fireside and so on."

"I do wish he'd make more show of enjoying his home, then."

"Anyway, we'd better see about breakfast for the Mr. Duyckincks. Tell me, though, just so I know for when I speak to Herman, what was it about this morning?"

31

"The quarrel? Oh, it was stupid. I asked him to do something that I didn't really want anyway – to take your mother with him to the Morewoods' Musical Party."

"Silly Lizzie. Scared to ask for anything herself. And not quite the thing to ask of Herman now, is it? Well, I'll take advantage of the next occasion that presents itself. I won't go out of my way, so it shan't be obvious. You stay here and get yourself properly freshened up. Let's all enjoy the weekend."

Helen left the room, closing the door behind her, and Elizabeth went to the wash-stand to sluice her face, pushing the cold water hard against her eyes, and holding it there while it trickled through her palms.

The weather was too unpredictable to allow for any excursion. The showers were extraordinarily heavy and there was thunder in the sky. Word came from Mrs. Morewood during the afternoon that the Musical Soirée would go ahead, but must needs be held indoors. It was debated whether or not to risk the carriage ride through the storms, one of the Melville horses being of nervous disposition, and for a time at least Elizabeth was hopeful that Herman and the guests would remain at home, which had been her real wish all along, and she did suggest that an evening of card playing might make up for the loss of musical entertainment. It can be imagined then how displeased she was to learn of the gentlemen's eventual decision: George would spend the evening at Arrowhead while Evert and Herman would attend the Morewood party. If the guests themselves were split over whether or not to go it would have taken no great persuasion on Herman's part to dissuade the keener party. The inference was obvious, and hurtful. It was Herman who wanted the trip to go ahead and Evert had volunteered to accompany him. Perhaps the two brothers had even tossed for it.

*   *   *

Across at Lenox the weather was even worse, the thunder reverberating off Monument Mountain, and allowing Julian to venture out into the garden for only short intervals, with the result that once again Mr. Hawthorne felt driven to distraction by his interminable babble.

Between four and five o'clock, in the midst of one of the heaviest showers of the day, came a salvo of knocking on the door. Julian and his father ran as quickly as possible to see who it might be, Julian chanting hopefully on the way, "Mr. Omoo, Mr. Omoo."

On waking in the morning he had announced, apropos of the previous day's adventure, that he loved Mr. Melville as much as Papa, as much as Mama, and as much as Una. When Mr. Hawthorne had enquired why Rosebud was excluded from the family litany Julian had answered, "She's not ready yet. When she's bigger."

Mr. Omoo was not on the doorstep, but a young man with jacket drawn over his head for shelter. There was a carriage at the gate which Mr. Hawthorne recognised as belonging to the Englishman, Mr. James, whom he had met a short time ago while returning from the Post Office.

"Could my mother and father call on you? We're having a hard time of it driving through the rain."

"Yes, yes, of course." Mr. Hawthorne watched the invasion from the coach with less relish than the words implied. Here he was, acting as host for the second day running. If only Phoebe had been there to see!

The carriage contained seven in all: Mr. and Mrs. James, their eldest son, their daughter, their little son Charles, their maidservant and their coachman. The coachman did not come in and the maid, at Mrs. James' suggestion, stayed in the hall. Charles was a month or two younger than Julian, a fact which furnished sufficient conversation matter to start upon, although Mrs. James proved so greatly afraid of the thunder that safety within four solid walls was all the hospitality and entertainment she required of this particular social call. The elder son and the daughter took the part of saying nothing, which Mr. Hawthorne presumed to be the English fashion. Little Charlie went to play on Julian's rocking horse and Mr. James proved the only one to whom it was necessary to talk.

He was renting a furnished house at Stockbridge, the land of which contained a portion of the Negro swamp at the foot of Monument Mountain. He was a prolific writer whose eventual output would total a staggering hundred novels and twenty-six volumes of history.

"My birthday today. Typical, ain't it. The weather, what?" He was a portly man with moustaches stained by tobacco. Mr. Hawthorne offered him a cigar, but it was refused, thus avoiding a third transgression of Sophia's edict.

33

Julian brought Bunny in and let him loose on the floor.

"Ah, the animals I had when I was a boy. Twelve owls at a time, I remember, and we had a raven who stole the silver spoons. For a short while we had a squirrel who could build towers with my mother's cotton spindles." Mr. James mentioned various other pets and their attributes, the authenticity of which Mr. Hawthorne began to doubt as the list extended, but they were described with the type of seriousness which succeeds in convincing children of anything, and induced such raucous laughter in Julian as his father had never heard before.

The mythical menagerie may have become increasingly bizarre had not little Charlie come forward tearfully holding out a long tuft of hair in his hand.

"What on earth is it?" Mrs. James broke her silence and for a moment Mr. Hawthorne was himself a trifle startled.

"Looks like a little girl's pony tail. Have you got a sister?" Mr. James asked Julian.

"Yes."

"Oh, please God, no." Mrs. James put her hand to her throat plainly believing that her child had scalped an erstwhile unnoticed occupant of the house. But at last Julian turned and saw what to him was immediately, "Horsey's Tail. He's pulled off Horsey's tail."

Julian attacked Charles savagely with his fists and the two Little Men had to be hastily separated by their Papas.

"I think, if the rain's over, we'll be heading along at this point. I'll just pop Neddy's rear appendage back on. There, Julian, good as ever. See, he can swish it about as well as before. Well, sir, it's good to have made this call at last. Sorry it had to be a forced stop, but much obliged for the shelter. Come and see us any time you're down in Stockbridge; you know the place. I have some English periodicals you'd be interested in."

*   *   *

George Duyckinck had declined the musical evening through simple weariness, not out of any particular relish for a card game. He did not seem able to stand the travelling and the late nights as well as his brother and was feeling the effects of the morning's early waking. As for Evert, there had been no toss of a coin, and no persuasion had been necessary to seduce him into going – he

34

enjoyed Herman's company too much and was a natural socialiser. The two evening entertainments on offer simply did not strike an even balance on his scale of prospective enjoyment.

The household had sat down to a sizeable meal at midday so there was little eating to be done later on. Helen brought tea and cake to George's room at seven and let him know that the card-players would be collecting in the smoking parlour in half an hour's time.

George put aside the book he had been reading – a volume of sailor's yarns from Herman's library – and took up pen and paper to bring his letter to Joanna up to date. "Evert woke me early this morning with a paroxysm of his lower limbs (I have not told you yet that we share a bed!), and I am feeling so utterly weary that I have stayed behind this evening while brother and Mr. Melville attend a musical evening at the big house, Broadhall. I cannot imagine any of the local ladies' talents come up to your own – either musical or otherwise – and anyway the weather is appalling. Not just 'grand showers' as they say but electrifying upheavals in the heavens, the noise of which has been amplified so much by the hills I really have quite a sore head and will probably play whist like a dolt. Cards, you see, are on the itinerary for us stop-at-homes. It is Mrs. Melville, Herman's wife, who seems the most keen. She actually tried to tempt Evert into staying behind for a game. It put us both in the devilish difficult position of having to choose between husband and wife and I'm sure that the outcome appears to her the most blatant of compromises. She is well advanced into her second pregnancy and I think the heavy languishing is beginning to play upon her nerves. The elder Mrs. Melville made her appearance at luncheon. She had been out of sorts for a day or two and had been staying in her room. I shall be the only male participant at the gaming table tonight and in view of what I have seen of the two Mrs. Melvilles I trust you will forgive me for hoping that I have one of Herman's maiden sisters for a partner."

Adding his customary valediction, George joined this page to the account of yesterday's picnic with Mr. Hawthorne and put all inside an envelope ready for posting, then, brushing his hair and sprucing himself up as well as he could without the aid of a mirror, he made his way to the smoking parlour.

"Mr. Duyckinck, how nice to see a man with no hair on his chin. Do come and sit down. You have either myself or Frances for a

35

partner. We shall play a dummy hand on this table." Mrs. Melville Senior and Frances, the youngest of Herman's sisters, sat at two adjacent sides of a table which was otherwise empty. It was a wooden-topped table with engraving around its perimeter. Herman's wife and the three other sisters formed a complete group at the second table, which had an orthodox card-playing surface of green felt. George was brave and took a chair opposite Frances, who blushed slightly at the ripple that came from the other group.

"They seem to find it amusing that you should choose youth over wisdom. When they are my age, they will learn it is the way of the world. Now then, if you could deal, Mr. Duyckinck, but do be careful of this shiny surface. We have only the one card-table, as you see. Hearts are trumps. Dummy hand to lead. You stay with your partner for three games before changing. I hope you don't mind the fire, Mr. Duyckinck. I insisted Herman light it before he went out, and that's why we're in here instead of the drawing room. It has been such a dark day I thought we could all do with a little fireside cosiness. I certainly could. Have had a little chill you see, that's why you haven't seen too much of me."

George had managed to deal the cards so that each hand fell in a compact-enough pile. He straightened the dummy hand and then began to study his own.

"Yes, I do like to see a man's chin," Mrs. Melville Senior continued as she adroitly rearranged the cards in her fan. "Both Herman and Allan are so old-fashioned I think, the way they keep their beards, and a dirty straggly old thing our Herman's is becoming. I love to notice the fashion and see the alterations in style; for a while, you know, we lived on Broadway, in the twenties, before the financial collapse. Are people actually wearing those bloomer-stockings? Preposterous, but very amusing. Could you turn the dummy hand over for me? Thank you."

George began to question whether or not his wisdom might after all have been better served by going along with Evert and Herman, but it soon became apparent that Mrs. Melville Senior was a competitive lady and once the game had commenced she gave it every concentration. Frances, on the other hand, kept looking across at her sisters and broke all the cardinal rules for the second player with the result that several times George was forced to over-ride a card of hers which was already winning a trick. Added to this, Mrs. Melville had extraordinary luck with the

36

dummy hand, and George moved on at the end of three suits with very little to show on his scorecard. These scorecards had been drawn up by hand, with all the disproportionate precision that bored young rural women could bring to the task. Movement about and between the tables was stage-managed in such a way that Mrs. Melville Junior could remain where she was.

George's fortunes improved to such an extent that at the end of twelve hands he stood in second place, behind Mrs. Melville Senior, and for the first time became aware that they were playing for a prize. In the meantime he was sent away with Helen to arrange sherry glasses for those who wanted them. He was to help himself to as much gin as he wished.

"I'm very glad, Mr. Duyckinck, of a chance to speak to you on my own." Helen spoke as she was filling a decanter with sherry from a small barrel. "It is about Herman. Nothing serious. This year he has been so wholly engrossed with the *Whale* book – I expect you've heard about it – it's due out in the autumn – that Lizzie hasn't seen a lot of him and now she's a bit down in the dumps, telling herself that Herman isn't being much of a father to Malcolm and such like. I had promised to talk to him myself, but it would be much better coming from a man. And now that Allan's in New York we haven't got his influence to call on any more."

"I thought he was here for the climb."

"Yes, he and Sophia will be staying at Broadhall. I expect Herman and your brother will meet them tonight. I don't know when they were arriving. But they'll be going straight back to New York. You wouldn't need to say you'd spoken to me or anyone else. Just draw attention to what you've probably already noticed before I'd mentioned it. You see, he's *such* a dreamer he probably genuinely doesn't notice Lizzie's doldrums. And we're all a little concerned for the arrival of the baby. She really must be in better sorts in time for the confinement. The gin by the way is in the darkest barrel."

George filled a glass straight from the tap.

"Take a little flagon of it up with you."

"No, the glass will be adequate. It's really Evert you ought to talk to. He's much closer to Herman than I am."

"Perhaps you could mention it to him, then?"

"I'll try."

"Thank you. Now we had better get back or we'll be the subject of card-room tittle-tattle. Could you carry the tray?"

Evert had not come back by the time George returned to their room with his prize – a box of playing cards, containing two decks and a booklet explaining different forms of one-handed Patience. He straightway undressed and got quickly into his nightshirt without washing, intending to make maximum use of the empty bed. To begin with, he left a lamp burning for Evert to see by on his eventual return, but finding himself unable to drop off to sleep directly, he later extinguished it. Even in the dark, and in the cool expanse of the crisp double sheets, deep repose eluded him. He kept thinking over his short interview with Helen and each time he drifted off into a light slumber he was shaken back to consciousness by dreamlike substitutions of Mrs. Melville Senior's face for the sister's, a supplanting which occurred with such insistence he really did begin to doubt his own recollective trustworthiness.

He made a special effort to think about Joanna, but by ghoulish adjustments to the facial features, beginning sometimes with the nose, sometimes with the mouth, the older Mrs. Melville would reassert herself. It turned into a battle of wills within his own mind, until he was so powerless to alter the course of his thinking that, had his eyes not been wide open, he might have been said to have been in the throes of a nightmare.

He did not hear the horse and cart ride up to the house, and only became aware of Evert's presence in the room when the curtain was drawn back.

"Mmm? Eh?" He hunched himself forward in perplexity. As he blinked his eyes, beads of sweat fell down from his brow. "Oh, Evert." He slumped back into the pillow.

"It sounds like you've had a night of it. What did you and the ladies get up to?"

"I won the prize. Why did you open the curtain?"

Evert was momentarily silhouetted naked, before slipping into his nightclothes. He then began putting his jacket and trousers on a hanger. "The moonlight. You didn't leave me a lamp."

"I'm nervous of sleeping in a room with a flame."

"Oh, we had a lovely moonlit ride home. The skies have quite cleared and the air is much lighter. Not quite soon enough. There were fewer guests than expected. Weather scared them off. What was your prize?"

"A set of Patience cards. So it was disappointing, was it?"

"No, no, we had a grand old time. The piano playing wasn't up to much but because of the depleted numbers there was an excess of punch to help dull the musical ear. Herman overdid it a bit. Became quite garrulous just now in the buggy. A pretty thing or two I heard about his mother."

George sat up, instantly interested.

"No, George. I'm not going to divulge another man's drunken confidences. I wouldn't want him to do so mine."

"That is very Christian of you, Evert."

"Thank you, George."

"Only I have been fighting the most nightmarish visions of Mrs. Melville."

"She didn't strike me as being that venomous at luncheon."

"No, but she's weirdly possessive."

"Ooh, ve have a vitch in ze houze."

"Quieten up, Evert."

They fell silent and George found that Evert's presence in the bed, just as it restricted his bodily movements also seemed to put at an end the restiveness of his brain. The two of them were asleep within minutes.

*   *   *

It was the Sunday before the mountain climb. Mr. Hawthorne spent it once again wrapped up in the company of Julian and, despite the child's continuing babble, they had an enjoyable day together. Here, in Mr. Hawthorne's own words, without trimming, without invention, is his end-of-day thanksgiving:

> Thank God! God bless Julian! God bless Phoebe for giving him to me! God bless her as the best wife and mother in the world! God bless Una! whom I long to see again! God bless little Rosebud! God bless me for Phoebe's and all their sakes! No other man has so good a wife; nobody has better children.

He did well not to go to Pittsfield to join the Shaker excursion. The mood of the day there was not good, though who can tell how it might have improved had Mr. Hawthorne turned up. Certainly Melville wished that he might appear, and in fact held up the departure for Hancock in hope of his showing at the last minute. The plans for his new rural romance needed mulling over, and Hawthorne was the man to speak to.

39

Only the three men set off for the religious service and they had quite a ride, the Duyckinck brothers having been thrown into reserve by the burden of their individual confidences. It was a reticence that contrasted in a ghastly way with the frenzy of the transported Shakers. Prior to the dance the glass-eyed preacher had put Evert in mind of an escaped maniac, whilst Herman could not help but see him as the incarnation of Ahab, leading his flock just as deluded and implacable a dance as the crew of the *Pequod*.

They returned to the farm by the most direct route, overtaking those fashionable visitors who travelled at a more sedate pace.

"Your mother wants to speak with you."

Herman was changing out of his Sunday dress and stood trouserless at the end of the bed, long shirt-tails covering his thighs. There was something incommensurate in his wide-shouldered and broad-beamed torso being held up by these small knees and narrow shins. Although he was of average height, much of it was made up from waist to head, and his legs, which had performed well enough in his maritime days, now that he led a more sedentary life seemed to be suffering an accumulation and stagnation of the blood.

"Look, Lizzie. Do you still not see that vein stand out? On the left leg." He bent to point it out to her, at the same time turning his foot so that the inside of the leg, down which the swollen vein ran, was visible to his wife.

"We can always call a doctor in if you're worried. I've been saying you need to see one for a little time now."

"Yes, yes. What's this about my mother?"

"She's sitting on the piazza."

"I don't believe it. What does she want?"

"Only a talk, I think, and says she hasn't seen a lot of you. She was a little disappointed you didn't go and read to her while she was poorly."

"She hates my reading. Says Augusta's ten times the reader I am."

"Yes, but a mother likes being read to by her son, however poor the cadence."

"Mmm. Well, I'll go and sit with her, I suppose. She hasn't Malcolm there, has she?"

"No, I've just come from the kitchen where he's helping Frances and me make some scones. She's wonderfully good with him and I do hope she can be a mother one day. Actually I think he'd like his Papa to put him up on a horse later."

"I *am* in demand, aren't I." Herman hitched tight the belt on his trousers and smiled at his wife, who moved forward into his arms, and, laying her cheek against his shirt, said, "Thank you."

"Why, Lizzie?" He bent away from her, gripping her arms lightly at the elbows.

"For that smile."

Herman pulled her back into an embrace. "Oh, am I such an old grizzly beard as that?"

* * *

"Hello, there. Are you coming round to it at last?" His mother had taken the only chair on the piazza, and covered herself in two rugs, one being used as a shawl, the other as a knee-blanket. "It's a very warm day, Mother, do you need to be wrapped up like that?"

"Herman, I shall *never* come 'round to it' as you say. I still maintain it was a selfish, stubborn and anti-social act of yours to have this porch placed here, and not on the south side of the house, when we would have been much better anyway knocking down the old chimney indoors."

"It's a piazza."

"What?"

"A piazza, not a porch. And you know why I chose this side of the house." Herman gestured towards the view.

"It only makes me feel more chilly, looking out on that bald-headed monster."

"You shouldn't be chilly now, Mother. It's a wonderful warm August we're having."

"Shade is *always* chilly."

"If you were sitting on the other side of the house you'd be scorched to crackling."

"It's no use trying to win me over now. No lady in this house is going to take their life in their hands and sit in a north wind whatever the time of the year. You knew that when you had it built and you are secretly pleased that you have it to yourself. You are becoming strange, Herman. A strange, secret, solitary son."

Herman turned his back on his mother and, leaning on the piazza rail, cast his eyes upon Graylock.

"It's no use turning away from me. I want to have something out with you. For almost a year now you've been looking quite distracted. And you appear to have forgotten completely that you are a husband and a father. Oh, I've seen it all before, don't forget.

41

The same distracted look in your father's eye when he became demented by financial troubles. But he never for a moment lost sight of his family. He cared for us diligently until . . ."

There was a quiver in his mother's voice which made Herman rage and, still looking at the mountain, a reservoir of suppressed and unspoken resentment welled over in his mind: You false-hearted shrew. It was your social snobbery and your hypochondria which drove my father to his grave; not the loss of his money, only what you made it signify. I saw the fortnight's derangement. I heard the crazy twist-tongued ramblings of his pell-mell brain. A twelve-year-old boy is not stupid. I understood the jealous ravings against Uncle Peter. You dare to lecture me now about regard for my wife and child. Look at the example *you* set. How many times did you desert Father and drag us all off to the Gansevoort home, you evil bitch?

Melville was momentarily numbed, and deafened, by the recognition of his own hatred, which he immediately recoiled from, as if the malevolence stemmed from a devilish possession of his faculties.

His mother was continuing. "We only have your interests at heart. We want you to be happy. And if writing your books no longer makes you happy, there must be other occupations you are fit for. You are an intelligent man."

"Mother, writing does make me happy. The only thing that pains me is that what I feel most moved to write – that is banned, it will not pay. Yet, altogether write the other way I cannot. So the product is a final hash, and all my books are botches. As for Lizzy and Malcolm, I shall try to give them more of my time. I do mean that."

"Well, I'm glad to hear it." Her mission apparently partially completed, Maria Melville arose from the chair, gathering the rugs together under her arm. She moved across to the railing and gave Herman a maternal kiss on his bearded cheek. "I do wish you would take that thing off. Mr. Duyckinck looked so dapper and modern last night."

Melville chuckled; not in any effort to keep hidden the venom of his recent thoughts, but in a natural show of familiar spirit. "I don't think I shall be obliging you on that score."

Opening the door into the house for his mother to pass through, Herman stayed on the piazza and sat on the vacated chair. Despite the brutality of his unasserted opinions regarding his mother, he felt, at the end of the confrontation, peculiarly indifferent. He remembered his brother Gansevoort's last letter, written from London a month before his death, in which he had spoken of the insensibility which was stealing over him, and Melville felt concurring premonitions of mortality creep over him now. He was put in mind of the seeds taken from an Egyptian pyramid, where they had been buried a thousand years or more, then shipped to England and planted in English soil, where, even after so long a hibernation, they developed themselves, grew to greenness – and then fell to mould. He had been just such an undeveloped seed until his twenty-fifth year, since when three weeks had scarcely passed that he had not unfolded within himself. And now he felt arrived at the inmost leaf of the bulb, he wondered if shortly the flower must fall to mould.

He looked down at his palms. There were four blisters there made by hoes and hammers. Dollars damn me, he thought. And then, despite their soreness, he rubbed his two hands together in response to a sudden chill breeze which fanned through the piazza.

*　　*　　*

Although they had not been expected until eleven, the Morewood troupe, consisting of Mrs. Morewood, her sisters Mrs. Pollock and Miss Henderson, Allan and Sophia Melville, and a clergyman by the name of Mr. Entler, all arrived at Arrowhead soon after ten o'clock.

Melville and the Duyckincks not being quite ready, the party was invited to stop off for coffee, and it was while rummaging in his large stairway cubbyhole that Herman chanced to overhear another conversation about himself. This one was brief and spoken in hushed voices. He was crouched with his feet placed precariously between various boxes and was having to use his hand on the sloping ceiling of the cupboard for support. The door had fortunately swung to of its own accord; while searching for the old hacking stick which he thought might come in handy on the climb, he had been forced to keep elbowing it back open to give sufficient illumination for his search.

There was first the sound of heavy footsteps on the stair, followed by a lighter set.

"Allan."

43

The heavier step came to a halt. "Helen!"

"Allan, could you keep an eye on Herman during this jaunt?"

"Why are you whispering?"

"I don't know who else is about. Just to see what kind of spirits he's in. He has seemed so languid since getting back from New York."

"Exhausted, I shouldn't wonder. He worked frantically there, or such was the impression. I don't remember us seeing him more than the once."

"And you did write us that he drank rather much on that occasion. If you could anyway."

"Is anything amiss?"

"No. No."

"Well, I was on my way to see Mother. Just languid, you say."

"Yes. And Sophia? I must catch your wife before she goes." The two of them began to walk away, Helen's voice simultaneously rising by several degrees.

Melville stayed in the cupboard a little longer, but did not continue the search. When he surfaced he made a special effort to appear energetic, in the first instance racing between the house and the barn to get the carriage ready. They would be using both the Morewood carriage and his own to take them to the Pittsfield station and then hire just one carriage at North Adams for the ladies.

With the complete party finally assembled, the Melville sisters came out to wave everyone away. Lizzie knelt down, holding Malcolm's hand, and Herman jumped from the carriage to give his boy a goodbye kiss.

"Daddy's climbing the big high mountain," Lizzie explained.

"Gray Rock," Malcolm mouthed.

"That's the one," said Herman. "Though it's Gray-*lock*."

"He can't say 'l' yet."

"Can't he now? Never mind."

"Doesn't Mama get a kiss?"

"Of course." Melville kissed his wife, leapt back into the cart and flicked the reins in one smooth movement so that the Morewood contingent was taken by surprise and had to set off some yards behind. Languid, eh?

There was a subdued atmosphere on the train as it took them north-, north-west alongside the River Hoosic. Baskets and other picnic appliances were stacked in the centre aisle of the carriage so

44

that when the train pulled in to North Adams the ladies, who had been allowed onto the train first, had to climb over them and leave the men to do the shifting.

There was a hotel a few yards off from the station and the two Melville brothers went inside to arrange with the crippled landlord the hire of four horses and a four-seater wagon. The wagon was to be driven by him to the start of the mountain passage and would be ridden back the following morning in order to pick them up. The four horses could be taken with them as nearly up to the summit as they cared to make them go. Did they have enough provisions with them? Only he just happened to have a pair of fine fowls going spare in his larder, a party of vacationers having that morning cut short their allotted stay. The Melvilles decided to take the birds and came out from the hotel holding one each, gripped about the neck as if wrung by their own hands.

They walked back to the station where the others were waiting for the baggage to be picked up. The vicar and Mrs. Morewood's sisters had travelled to Williamstown (where there was neither hotel nor vehicle contractor) to ease the transportation situation, and from there would be rejoining the group on the arranged path of ascent.

The climb proper consisted of three miles of the toughest bog and stumbling ground that the forces of mountain torrents and the rotting of mists and snows could put together. Once they had said farewell to the cripple from North Adams, and arranged a pick-up time for the morrow, they sat down to await the trio from Williamstown and to muster strength for the bog. Presently they heard shouting, both male and female, and Melville, forgetting the bad blood in his legs, ascended the trunk of a tall tree, from which look-out post he managed to guide the Rev. Entler and the two ladies towards them.

Two of the horses were used for baggage, the ladies taking turns on the other two. Melville led one of the pack-horses by the rein, as did his brother Allan the other, and the pair of them started the climb side by side.

"You're looking well, Herman." Melville imagined he heard a slight emphasis on the word "looking" which, if he'd been correct would have had the effect of turning his brother's compliment into a tentative query.

"I'm feeling good." There seemed to be nothing to be gained yet from divulging to Allan the domestic antagonism to his chosen career. If it were to blow up into anything more than it was now, then he might wish to enlist Allan's support. But there was a fair chance that it would die down after Lizzie had given birth and, anyway, he had every intention of becoming this winter a more attentive husband and father. He enquired after Allan's own two little ones, Maria and Florence, which led on to reminiscence about their Fourth Avenue days together, so that the two of them passed the early stages of the climb familiarly enough; but there was something so circumscribed about this conversation that Melville began to hanker after wider themes.

He called Mr. Entler across and invited him to hold the rein. The pastor was keen to show willing, but could not conceal his nervousness.

"The horse'll plod along regardless, and Allan here'll see you're all right. It's just a question of leading her around anything too suspect." Melville left them to it, and went to join George and Evert, who were walking a little way back with Mrs. Morewood's sisters. These ladies moved away as Melville approached.

"What a magnetic effect to have upon women," he said drolly.

"Wish you'd demonstrated it sooner," said George. "They seem to think Evert is a talent scout from the New York concert halls."

"Yes," Evert picked up, "they kept wanting to know what I thought of their piano pieces the other night."

"Handled like a gentleman, no doubt."

"Like a liar."

"Is it or is it not gentlemanly to conceal the truth? Ah, much lies behind that question, does it not?"

The Duyckincks were not in philosophising mood and could not be drawn. They were, when all was said and done, as their work avowed, an encyclopaedic pair – that is, of summarising and not of meditative bent. Melville walked beside them for a little while, but restlessness returned, and he excused himself with the claim that he must rescue Mr. Entler, who seemed indeed to be having his arm pulled hither and thither by the horse.

The pastor, however, was disinclined to admit defeat so readily, and Melville ended up taking over from Allan, who was glad of the chance to see how Sophia was coping with the ascent.

Having told the vicar to adjust his grip on the rein, Melville remarked, "A dank and smelly domain, is it not?"

"But there is charm in God's wilder haunts, don't you think? Something which the aspiring soul finds freedom in?"

"So – is God's stamp on this bald-headed hump?"

Mr. Entler looked at Melville in surprise. "Why, of course. Upon all his creation. Yes. Moses received the Law from base rock and Christ himself went out into the Wilderness."

"He was tempted there."

"The Devil haunts the mind, he has no physical domain."

"You must forgive me, being an old sailor, for thinking at times he might."

"We all have our treacherous capes where we get tossed about. Life teaches us to have eternal hope that the storm will pass, just as Life itself will pass to leave a deeper calm than anything we have yet known."

"The becalmed sailor prays for the return of breeze."

Mr. Entler was not the man to pick up such delicately poised statements. He proceeded, "But I have read your *Typee*. There seemed to be Paradise enough in that book."

"I am glad to hear you say so. Not all Christians have found the book agreeable. I fear you will find more of the infernal regions in my latest work."

Melville was glad to have found someone willing to partake of expansive conversation, but he still regretted that Mr. Hawthorne was not there to join in such diverting ruminations. He remembered the parallel jaunt last summer (in fact the occasion of his and Hawthorne's first meeting) when it had been Monument Mountain that was climbed. The whole feel of that trip had been different, more masculine, with imposing figures like Holmes, Sedgewick and Fields in the party. This retinue, put together by a lady, was wholly more feminine. But champagne might give them a pulse yet.

"Won't that champagne taste sweet when we get to the top?"

The pastor gently shook his head. "It'll be the water for me. I don't take alcoholic drinks."

Melville pursed his lips and, putting a strain on the rein, strode out ahead of Mr. Entler.

The last of the three miles was tough going and all conversation ceased while each member of the party put their entire strength into reaching the summit, where twenty years or so previously the students of Williams College had constructed an Observatory, the ruins of which were to be their camp.

They were all blown horses when they reached this refuge, gasping and dripping with perspiration. Mrs. Morewood, who had gained something of a victory for her sex by being first to complete the climb, handed out half tumblers of porter to the exhausted arrivals and, inbetweentimes, spread a dinnercloth on the damp boards of their ramshackle hotel. Out came the layers of ham, and out came the silver gilt mugs for the Heidsieck champagne. Open went the mouths, hungry and thirsty, till the cloth was all but cleared, and several bottles drained.

While the rest of the party handed round the cherry jar, Melville took an axe and wielded it against the fallen trees lying about. The clergyman helped him gather the broken logs. "Thank you, Mr. Antler." Mr. Entler took the misnomer to be a joke, induced no doubt by the champagne, and did not seek to correct it. "What does the divine wilderness make of our intrusion I wonder?"

"You talk as if there were no such thing as verdure in nature. The earth is not all empty ocean and windswept crag."

"Grass can grow into a jungle. Much of our country was primaeval forest until the settlers came at it with these." Melville raised his axe. "It might seem that God needs Man, as much as Man needs God."

"God *needs* none of this at all. We are all here by his grace alone. But, yes, we have our part to play, we have certain obligations as custodians . . ."

"But wait, I don't feel *obliged* to cut this wood, unless it be out of a certain sense of chivalry towards the ladies. The fact is our night ahead would be grim without a fire."

"Oh, yes, we embellish our circumstances . . ."

"With the simple human craving for warmth and comfort? Where does God come into this? What is it Lear says? 'Allow not nature more than nature needs, Man's life is cheap as beast's.' Yet the New Testament seems to exhort us to do just that. To think as little for the morrow as the birds of the air. I confess that I resist this, as Lear does."

"Yet in all the saints there has been exhibited a disdain for worldly comforts."

"Saints don't marry; don't become fathers." The two were walking back now, their arms piled with logs. "Good, my brother's set some kindling wood alight."

The ladies were already lying down, wrapped in some buffalo robes left behind by a winter sleighing party. The Duyckinck brothers had started on the brandy. Inside the Observatory an empty champagne bottle had been used to hold a sperm candle.

48

When the fire had been properly lighted a division of the sexes unfolded, the women remaining inside the cabin, the men gathering outside beside the flames.

Evert passed Herman the brandy. "Are you sure we can't tempt you, Antler?" The Reverend shook his head. Melville went on, "I like to think there'll be brandy and champagne in Paradise and that the angels are half-tipsy the whole time. Maybe the Devil's just suffering from a chronic hangover."

"The Devil uses the bottle as an instrument, I don't doubt."

"Mm. Well then, George, are you going to consort with the Evil One?" Melville handed the bottle to George, who took it without comment.

"It sometimes seems to me that the promise of Heaven has been one of the least helpful of Christian bequests," Evert remarked. "The old Jews contented themselves with life's discontent. They let the natural law prevail and didn't put instinct at variance with Fate. But now the world has been renounced and faith, good works, good heart, must aim straight at Heaven."

The Reverend sat crosslegged, his fingertips touching and retouching. "But we daily pray for God's will to be done on earth as well as in Heaven."

"Perhaps it is already being done." Melville turned some logs with a long stick. "Eighteen long centuries and more have passed since Christ's coming. Has there been any measurable improvement in man's heart?"

"The spreading of the Gospel is a slow business. But the work is being done."

George spoke up. "Too often they spread not the word of Christ, but codes of behaviour from a different culture, as Herman showed in *Typee*."

"George, Mr. Entler has already been good enough to say kind things about my first book, don't turn him against it now. But, anyway, dreams of Paradise have eternally held sway in man's yearnings. Eden and the land of milk and honey are but two examples. The difficulty with surrendering to the natural law is first deciding whether it is wholly good or part good and bad and, if the latter, which instincts are to be cultivated and which shunned."

"Well stated." Mr. Entler seemed set to add some commentary, but their campfire gravity was broken by a burst of ringing laughter from inside the Observatory.

49

"The ladies seemingly," Evert observed, "have picked on jollier topics."

At this the men too tried to inject some merriment into their discourse. Allan, who had been exceedingly quiet thus far (and hanging upon each one of his brother's words in deference to Helen's whispered entreaty), now told a joke that had no relevance to the occasion except that it involved two mountaineers. It was probably in questionable taste for soon afterwards Mr. Entler announced that he was going to lie down and when he had left George wondered out loud whether he would find the female conversation more or less jarring to his spiritual fastidiousness.

"You know, you married men don't know what an act you constrain your wives to perform for you. I mean, not personally, but as part of accepted family values."

Evert smiled at Melville. "It's Joanna, George's lady friend, gives him all this. She's part of the growing women's movement."

"I do think their cause is valid, yes. We have made unreal demands upon them and one only has to look at the general state of health amongst womankind in these States to see the toll it's taking."

"Come along, George, there will always be a few pasty types, of either sex. Lizzie hardly seems to be languishing, does she, Herman, and Margaret can outstay me at anything."

Herman could not suppress a ribald thought concerning Margaret, who was Evert's wife. He wished he could share in the admiration for his own wife's fortitude but he tended to agree more with George's picture of a sickly sex, though he did not see a straightforward connection with a masculine conspiracy. The whole subject of relationships between men and women and one another held a growing fascination for him and one which he knew would be a considerable force in his next book. But the hour was late, and they would need to be up at dawn.

Inside the Observatory, Mrs. Morewood was still sitting bolt upright, wide awake. She said that in the morning she would report on the number of rats that had passed over everyone's buffalo robes.

*   *   *

They were up at four, aroused, inevitably, by Mrs. Morewood. She was already dressed and spreading out the cloth which

50

showed the stain of past devourings. It was to be the two fowl for breakfast and Melville and the clergyman set up in partnership again to rekindle the embers of the fire. When it was beginning to smoke profusely, they put in some large stones, and then held the birds into the reeking fumes by means of an elementary spit fashioned out of a mysterious piece of metal found in the Observatory. It was shaped like a shepherd's crook, but with the double curvature at either end and had, perhaps, like the robes, been left behind by the winter sleighing party.

The early hour was not conducive to conversation and Melville, anyway, was in one of his silent moods. The mountaintop was ensnared by the inevitable morning mist and the two of them, while crouching and resting the elbows of their working arms upon their knees, looked neither upon one another nor at the singeing meat, but out upon the milky blankness. Some vague connections Melville was making with the mists at sea and with the spectral whiteness he had made much of in his *Whale* book. Of the shiftings in Mr. Entler's mind, assuming there were any at all, there is no telling.

As soon as the birds were supple enough each to be torn into four or five separate portions, they were taken inside the Observatory, where the rest of the party had been passing dawn-weary pleasantries. The chicken was washed down with water made flavoursome from rinsings in and out of the brandied-cherries jar, and it was evident that without the chance transaction at North Adams they would have been making a stomach-groaning descent. Either they had all eaten more than anticipated the night before or, for once, Mrs. Morewood's preparations left room for criticism.

Their descent of the mountain was retarded by the enthusiasm of the ladies for picking mosses and wild flowers, strawberries and yellow raspberries, with the result that they were a little late for their rendezvous with the crippled carriage driver, a fact which might go some way towards explaining the ensuing fracas.

The said vehicle contractor had been directed to take them straight to the railway station. Instead, it suited his plans better, or, out of sheer contrariness, to deposit them outside the hotel and leave them to shift their baggage the rest of the way by hand.

"What's the man doing?" Mrs. Morewood shouted, when he proceeded to unload their baskets and cases.

"It appears," said Allan, "that he's taking us no further."

51

"Driver!" Mrs. Morewood was by no means a fatalist. "There's some mistake. We're not staying at your hotel. We're leaving on the eleven-thirty train. Please take us on to the railway station."

"No mistake. Don't go to the station. Always stop here. End of run. I'll thank you to settle the bill now."

"Let him sing for his money," said Evert. "Ladies, out of the carriage. We'll settle this matter."

The gentlemen waited until the females had collected themselves and were making their way to the railway station.

"Right," said Allan. "This cheating bastard can just jolly well follow us for his money; come on, Herman."

The two Melville brothers went to lift the largest hamper, but the cripple put his club foot on top of it.

"The bill," he demanded.

"Get off our property!" Allan stood up close to the swindler and bellowed the words down into his face. The contractor cowered perceptibly and threatened to get the sheriff onto them and to hold up the train and to Use His Influence. Having stated his intentions he walked off as importantly as his limp would allow, in the opposite direction to the station, leaving the way clear for the removal of their baggage.

They were all assembled on the platform, congratulating themselves on the forthright way in which they had dealt with the charlatan, and wondering what course of action they should take regarding payment of the bill, if the train were to arrive immediately.

In anticipation of further friction, the ladies had been positioned at the far end of the platform, in charge of the luggage.

"Perhaps I should pop the money down now," Herman said.

"You will not!" Allan was in belligerent mood. "You'll not let that rascal win the day."

"I do think we have a duty to future customers of his not to accede to his demands but to stick by the terms of our arrangement," Mr. Entler pronounced.

"The baskets *were* all empty. There was very little heavy baggage." Herman was still feeling conciliatory. He did not like these situations and he was conscious of the growing number of village vagabonds collecting outside the station fence, obviously having heard reports of an affray.

"It's not so much the relative justice of the case" – George stated his position – "as the downright surliness of the man."

"The fellow's an ape. The whole thing's preposterous. If the train comes we should get on and he can follow us to Pittsfield if he's so inclined. The blockfooted cheat!"

"Is it Christian of us, Entler, to take this attitude?"

The clergyman flushed at Mr. Melville's direct appeal to the moral precepts of his faith. "We all have our afflictions to bear," he bristled. "Some more obvious than others. The art is in not making them excuses for brutish behaviour."

Melville sighed and turned, as if to retire from the predicament, but just as he did so the crowd of local onlookers began to stir and buzz, and out of their midst came forward the innkeeper, in company with an officious personage – presumably the sheriff. They strode up to Melville and the crippled one said, "This is the man. He it is who struck the bargain."

"Then sir" – the presumed sheriff handed Melville a rather blank-looking roll of paper – "you, sir, are under arrest and must accompany us . . ."

"Go with you? Where?"

"To the hotel."

"You have no business to take me there. The man wants paying, he can be paid here, where he should have dropped us anyway."

"The bill is made out at the hotel, sir."

"Then where is the demand? I haven't been presented with one. Your arrest is worth nothing." Melville pushed the roll of paper between the cripple's legs, where it stuck, and Allan and the Duyckincks could not help but snigger at the obscene spectacle thus made.

"How much are you owed?" The sheriff turned to the publican.

"It's all down on the bill. He must pay me at the inn."

"The journey's terminus was here, sheriff. The man's a malefactor, a fraudulent worm, he tarnishes your township and it behooves you ill to spring to his defence."

Herman moved between his brother and the sheriff. He felt in control of the situation now and did not want the tension exacerbated. Taking from his pocket a folded quantity of dollar bills, he counted off a certain number, handed them to the sheriff and said, "This was the fare we agreed on. I could pay less for failure to complete the contract. But there – you are paid in full. Take it now. I'm not moving from this platform."

The innkeeper snatched the money from the sheriff's hand and turned to go back to the hotel. As he did so, the roll of paper fell from between his legs. The sheriff bent to pick it up and then he too walked off without a word.

"Snakes!" Allan shouted at them. "You were too generous, Herman. They stung us there."

"No," Mr. Entler said. "We behaved correctly. We stood by what was right and just on our side of the bargain. One must never . . ."

Further commentary on the moral lessons to be taken from the incident was curtailed by the noisy approach of the Pittsfield train.

Settling themselves into the carriage, Mrs. Morewood clapped her hands together into her lap and said, "Well, we shall have the afternoon free. I propose a fishing party."

*   *   *

On this Tuesday morning Mr. Hawthorne received a letter from his wife, fixing her return for Thursday. The news was received joyfully by Julian, who was beginning to miss his mother very much. That night he had had another of his nightmares about Bunny (although he told his father it concerned dogs, for fear of Bunny being given away again) which his father put down to too many currants, so noisome had been the boy's stomach in the middle of the night. In this dream Bunny had remained a rabbit in shape, but had grown fourfold in size, brayed like a donkey and gone about snapping its teeth together.

After dinner Mr. Hawthorne sat upstairs in the bedroom, reading a *Harper's Monthly* borrowed from Mrs. Tappan before their squabble, and letting Julian play outside unattended. It was the first time, since his mother had gone away, that the boy had been allowed to venture into parts unseen. The notice of Sophia's imminent return had put Mr. Hawthorne at ease, almost as if she were already downstairs fulfilling her function as watchful wife and mother. At length he began to think it time to look the boy up. He went to the barn and the currant bushes, shouted around the house without response and sat down on the grass to wait for him to appear.

By and by Julian ran from one side of the house, holding up a little fist and shouting, "Papa, Papa, I have something good for you!" And, stopping in front of his father, opened his palm to reveal a squeezed-up pulp of blackcurrants, gooseberries, and other assorted fruit. Mr. Hawthorne took two gooseberries which happened to be not entirely crushed, and told Julian that he could keep the rest for himself.

"But Papa, the currants give me bad dreams, you said."

"A little handful in the middle of the day won't harm."

Julian sauntered off, looking perplexedly at his open hand. When he was at the other side of the house he went quickly to Bunny's hutch, opened the door, and fingered off the purée into the rabbit's food platter. There *was* some thought of vengeance even in so young a mind. For all he knew, Bunny would find the crushed fruit delectable, but secretly he hoped it would induce such disturbance of the Bunny-brain as it had done of his own.

He repeated the procedure the next day, and the day following that, a little disappointed that there had been no visibly unsettling effects. He added to ensuing concoctions some of those berries which he had been expressly forbidden so much as to touch.

During this time he complained to his father of a multiplicity of minor ailments, chief among which were stomachache and headache, which Mr. Hawthorne treated with Aconite and Belladonna.

They waited all day on Thursday for Sophia's return, Julian crying out at intervals, "Oh, I wish Mother would come *soon*! I want to see her, to see her. Rose will be grown-up by the time they arrive."

After the boy was in bed and under the watchful eye of Mrs. Peters, Mr. Hawthorne went to the Post Office, fully expecting a letter from his wife explaining her non-arrival. There was nothing, and the absence of any word was bitterly worrying, even though there were countless possible explanations for the sudden delay, caused he was sure by last-minute considerations, possibly bad weather in the Boston area; otherwise there would undoubtedly have been a letter for him.

On the Friday Bunny was out of order. It was Mrs. Peters who first noticed him having shivering fits and these became more frequent and more severe as the day wore on. Julian announced that it was scarlet fever, the only disease with which he was conversant, and seemed to hold out little hope for the animal's survival. Mr. Hawthorne did not share this pessimism, thinking it possible that Bunny was merely suffering from the sudden onset of autumn. It was certainly a chilly day and when, during their morning walk, Mr. Hawthorne had discovered a patch of sheltered sunlight next to Shadow Brook, he had stretched out on

55

the bank, lit a cigar and basked there, while Julian fished with a stick, threw stones into the water, and stepped in "cow-mud".

They had spent the afternoon at home, still awaiting Mama's return, and keeping a concerned eye on Bunny. Julian did not administer any more doses of his berry brew, a forbearance which managed to wipe his childish conscience clean of any thought of guilt or responsibility.

After the boy was in bed, Mr. Hawthorne went on another jaunt to the Post Office, which again had no letter for him, only a great box directed to Sophia herself, and probably containing all her purchases. The mystery deepened, and he felt most disconsolate as he climbed once again into an empty bed, a little after ten o'clock.

During the night he had a series of bad dreams which centred around his phobia of being caught in a tract of bushes. He found himself in that part of the woods where he and Julian had discovered the echo, and now he could hear Sophia's voice calling him – "Nathan – ye – el, Nathan – ye – el". As he made to move towards it, the undergrowth crossed and intertwined itself about his legs, it brushed his face and seized hold of his clothes with a multitudinous grip, until he felt as if it were almost as well to lie down and die in rage and despair. Then his wife would call again, and he would thrash his legs and split the branches with a simple, powerful flexing of his two fists. Suddenly, during one such foray, the dream changed, and he felt not hard bark beneath his grip but a soft furry fleshiness. The sensation came too late to stop the frantic twisting of his fists, and Bunny's neck was split in two. Dropping at Mr. Hawthorne's feet, the rabbit twitched once or twice before releasing an emission of blood through its nose. The woods were silent. Sophia called no more for Nathaniel who, turning, ran back through the track he had pioneered with his own bare hands.

On waking in the morning, he went straight to the kitchen where Bunny's hutch had been placed overnight to keep him warm, with a foreboding of what had happened. Sure enough, there lay the little beast, stark and stiff.

Julian took the news with more of interest and excitement than affliction, and attributed the mishap to the agency of Giant Despair.

"It's the wickedest thing He's ever done, wickeder than when he made me step in cow-mud or stung me with a pickle."

After breakfast a hole was dug and Bunny placed inside. Julian expressed his hopes that by the next day a flower would have sprung over him, and later on, obviously continuing to give the matter thought, but in no sombre light, he remarked, "Perhaps tomorrow there will be a tree of Bunnies, and they will hang all over it by their ears."

At the end of an afternoon spent sailing a toy sloop on the Stockbridge Bowl, Mr. Hawthorne wrote in his Journal: "It is nearly six o'clock, and they do not come! Surely they must, must, must be here tonight!"

Part Two

Mrs. Sophia Hawthorne, née Peabody, had been born in Salem on September 21st 1809, the third of what were to be six children, three boys and three girls – a fourth girl dying at the age of seven weeks and causing Mrs. Peabody, who was an early believer in prenatal influences, more than the average degree of remorse for an event of this kind. The father had attended medical lectures at Harvard, but had chosen dentistry for his profession. He was, nevertheless, known as Doctor Peabody, and later developed an interest in homeopathic medicine.

While Sophia was still something of a child, the family moved out to Lancaster, a small township in central Massachusetts, north of Clinton and the Wachusett Reservoir. Elizabeth, the eldest child, was well into her teens at the time of this move and, in 1820, when she was sixteen, she took over the school which her mother had been running. While "Miss Peabody" was busy teaching class, the two younger sisters, aged fourteen and eleven respectively, joined in kissing games with a family of boys called the Clevelands. It is reported by some biographers that Sophia was chosen more often than Mary in these games, but this rings of malicious and unsupported bias.

In 1822 Elizabeth moved to Boston, thus establishing her independence and detachment from her two younger sisters, to whom she wrote admonitory and chiding letters as if she were their maiden aunt.

Eventually, the age difference between Mary and Sophia also began to tell and, when the family moved back to Salem, Mary went to join Elizabeth who was by this time teaching in Maine. In 1825 the two sisters returned to Massachusetts and opened a school in Boston, at Brookline.

It was at this time, separated off from her two older sisters, that Sophia's headaches began – a "cannonading of her temples" as she termed it, which was to be a chronic affliction of her young womanhood. Other descriptions of the pain and of flashing colours in her dreams might suggest the diagnosis of sinus trouble or migraine, but there were extenuating circumstances affecting the hypochondria of nineteenth-century women, and particular ones surrounding nineteenth-century American women, which determined that their symptoms be treated with a reverence per se, and that little effort be made to explain or cure the affliction. Illness was at the same time a confirmation of female frailty and a brazen cry for attention and sympathy. Most families were large enough to bear the burden of at least one invalid, and so the sickly person was told to lie down, to stay in, and generally coddled and pandered to so that they became the focus of activity for the more hale and hearty members of the household. It was a dangerous syndrome, as testified by the record of those poor creatures who literally languished to their deaths.

In 1828 Elizabeth, finding that her Brookline school was flourishing, decided that she could afford to bring the clan to Boston, but it was a short-lived prosperity and the family soon found itself back in Salem. Sophia's headaches intensified as a result of the enforced withdrawal and her mother put her on a diet of white bread and rice. The lonely girl occupied her time with efforts at becoming an artist and with reading Elizabeth's letters describing her forays into the masculine world of thought and speculation. She had, in her spare time, been the copyist of William Ellery Channing; she had already met Bronson Alcott and was seeing much of the widower, Horace Mann.

And so the year is 1833, when such entanglements that bind Herman Melville and Nathaniel Hawthorne together are but beams in the eye of God's Providence. General Jackson rides on horseback through the streets of Salem, and Mr. Hawthorne is there to watch him pass, but another fifty moons will have to wax and wane before he makes his first visit to the Peabody home. Sweating horses pull a stage the last furlongs of its journey into the centre of Boston, and out steps the gangling figure of Orestes Brownson, thirty come September. He has travelled one hundred miles from Walpole, New Hampshire, to drink and talk with his friend George Ripley. In Salem, the future Mrs. Hawthorne suffers her fierce and palsying headaches. She dreams that her sister Elizabeth lies dead in a coffin which has been set on the front parlour table. She wakes screaming, and crying out that she loved

Elizabeth, she loved her. This same Elizabeth, in Boston, tries tirelessly to renew the shattered faith of Horace Mann, whose hair is pure white, singed to the roots and beyond by the crazed and tubercular death of his teenage wife. A broken man at thirty-seven, he is energyless to rebut the Channing-style sermons which slip so effortlessly from this formidable woman's tongue. Formidable, at twenty-nine. She had, after all, been a working teacher, a "Miss Peabody", since sixteen years of age. The quieter middle sister, Mary, walks out on these exchanges in jealous hostility. Her time will come but not for another decade, and had she known, as her other sister Sophia knew, through epistolary confidences, of the transformations occasioned by her exiting, she would have been more inclined to suffer her jealousy and remain an awkward presence in the room. Study this interlude and judge the matter for yourself.

"You are a gloomy Calvinist, Horace. A wallower in your own misery. Your stubborn refusal to turn away from this blackness is a grave error. Oh, I see what you've come to. You think to immerse yourself in your suffering is exactly what God craves. That there can have been no other reason for your cruel bereavement. But you are approaching forty, Horace, a dangerous time for a man of your abilities, and for one whose equilibrium has been shot through with grief. Don't you see that the perilous time for the most highly gifted is not youth; no, the perilous season is middle age, when a false wisdom tempts them to doubt the divine origin of the dreams of their youth. Think back to your youth, Mr. Mann, I plead with you. Acknowledge that your heart was clearer, more buoyant then. You did not court your wife with such downcast looks, I'm sure. Do not concentrate on the dark hand of Fate, but gaze into the waters of your own soul. Though the surfaces are rippled, even tossed about a bit, by the trials of this world, you will find deep layers of calm just below." And so she rattled on. Not for nothing had she taken lessons in Greek with a shy nineteen-year-old Emerson. Not to be wasted were the nine years she had spent as secretary for the eminent Unitarian preacher Dr. William Ellery Channing – those Saturday morning walks together, talking theology and the next day's sermon.

To watch this wizened man, who had so mysteriously won her heart, soak up these interminable spiritual indictments, with no more resistance than the continuing desolation writ upon his face, was utter purgatory for Mary. On this occasion she left the room

63

as soon as Elizabeth made reference to Horace's dead wife. The nerve of her sister was sickening.

As it happened, Elizabeth had been fully aware that she was taking a monumental liberty (one of her abiding virtues was to be her disregard for the conventional rules of good taste), and this was calculated as her final shot, the one which could not fail to ruffle Mr. Mann's intractability. The silence which followed was disappointing. Elizabeth was an impatient woman; once she'd delivered her set-piece she was not inclined to return to the attack and certainly not to shift mood with idle conversation. She sighed – there was even a faint tut-tut on her tongue – and got up to leave. But at the door she hesitated. To leave him thus seemed too unfeeling. And so she turned, and did what she had never done before. She went and took his hand. He looked so mutely and so sadly grateful that it went to her very heart and she gripped his hand still tighter. He broke down at last, drawing Elizabeth nearer and throwing his arms around her, letting the tears flow. She held in her other hand a book of Socrates which was in line with his sight. He grew a little calmer, drew away and said, "He conversed with wisdom and so he suffered death. How mysterious, mysterious world!" And, losing his calmness again, he clung fast to her and sobbed out the single word, "Homeless", to which she had no reply.

In such a way did it come about that, when a journey to Cuba was proposed in the hope that it would prove a restorative pilgrimage for the ailing Sophia, Mary volunteered to be her companion, not in any genuine eagerness for the voyage, let alone the eighteen months of exile, but in a desperate bid to convince Mr. Mann of his true feelings, so that he might declare his love for *her*, and object to her departure.

It was a cold winter day, late in this year of 1833. A new financial panic was as yet affecting only those in the merchandising business, or those who lived off invested capital. The Peabody family, as it arrived at the Boston wharfside ready for Mary's and Sophia's boarding of the *Newcastle* seemed a picture of middle-class well-being, wrapped as they were in great-coats and scarves. There was a commotion concerning a lost luggage-boy and Sophia had to take off her gloves to press cool fingertips against her temples. While Mary kept a watchful eye for Mr. Mann, Elizabeth acted as go-between for her brother Nathaniel, informing her father of his plans to marry and go West. Mr. Peabody expostulated angrily that it was out of the question. Nathaniel was to stay in Salem and train to be a doctor. Mrs. Peabody was lecturing her youngest boys – George and Wellington – on the realities of a seaman's life, lest the imminent view of the departing vessel planted seeds of wanderlust. With Sophia away from home for so long, she did not want to lose her three boys as well.

At last it was time to embark. There was still no sign of Mr. Mann, but the luggage-boy had reappeared and he now led the way up the ramp, the two girls having kissed farewell to their mother, brothers and sister. Mr. Peabody accompanied them on to the ship to ensure that their cabin was in order and that the Captain was cognisant of the fact that he had two unchaperoned young ladies aboard.

They spent a short while arranging their things, then when their father had returned from his talk with the Captain, had kissed them each firmly, and had told Sophia to get herself better, they accompanied him back on to deck and kissed him once more before he descended to the quayside.

There was an awkward ten-minute span while nothing particular happened beside George and Wellington shouting out, "Bring us back some cigars," and suchlike. Mary and Sophia merely waved; Mr. and Mrs. Peabody stood strangely motionless side by side; then there were shouts from the crew, the ramp was removed and the ship began to slip away from the wharf's edge.

Almost simultaneously Mary spotted him – the ice-capped flagpole of a man moving alongside the Peabody family. He stood next to Elizabeth and waved. Mary's own waving, which had become frantic as soon as the ship lurched, now turned limp and mesmeric, as she strained to read the expression on Horace's face. Why had he come late? It must have been intentional. He must have been lurking somewhere waiting for the ship to move. He could not bear the pain of parting. Too unsure of her feelings he did not dare declare his own. And yet she did not like that familiar proximity between Elizabeth and himself. Had it been mutually arranged between them, to avoid embarrassing the rest of the family and to prevent a scene that might have jeopardised the visit? Now that she was out of the way would they announce their engagement and be man and wife at her return, perhaps with a first child already born?

But as the distance between them increased Mary seemed to read the image of his gaze with greater clarity, so that it was as if

65

they were staring at one another across the space of a small drawing room. And his look was one of ardour, of fervent, desperate longing. He *did* love her! Oh what pain, to be sailing away from her soul companion!

And, in the full despondency of her pain, normal laws of perspective were re-established so that Mr. Mann became so small as to be indistinguishable from the rest of the family group.

And thus it was that, of the two young women who went on waving, only one partook of that sense of excitement and expedition which was more normally reserved for the masculine race.

Sophia turned her head to the ocean and let the sea wind blow back her hair. Mary slumped her chin into her chest and sniffed away a tear. And the ship sailed due East, right out into the Atlantic, ready to take the sweep of Cape Cod.

Back on the quay the Peabody family remounted their carriage, Mr. Mann being invited to dine out with them in a hotel. Mary's reading of his expression had not been far wrong, but her suspicions regarding his late arrival, although understandable, were mistaken. As someone who had been a regular family guest during the previous months, Mr. and Mrs. Peabody had expressly invited him to attend the farewell, thus proving their ignorance of Mary's feelings. He had engineered his tardy arrival out of deference to family privacy, not wishing to inhibit any display of emotion with an outsider's presence, and his subsequent discovery of dormant feelings of affection for the departing Mary (he had experienced the same telescopic clarity of sight) had put him into a deeply contemplative state of mind. He had been blind! The creature had been silently adoring him all the while. And he had dismissed her as an ineffectual leech hanging upon the imperial assertiveness of her older sister. What a fool! And how hurtful to the memory of his dead wife, who had been so like Mary in her tight-lipped reticence. Their courtship had been one long gaze – not a scrap of conversation had defiled it. And here, this stockier strain of womanhood who, according to one observer of her ways, "had too much of the man in her familiarity and freedom", and whose firm shoulder was being pressed against his own as they journeyed along in the carriage . . . this well-meaning but domineering harridan had beguiled him out of reading properly the signals from the silent one. Oh, they came back to him now, the episodes of Mary's patient waiting in the wings, ended always with an undemonstrative departure from his sight.

66

"Don't you think so, Horace?"

Mr. Mann turned to Elizabeth with such distracted expression on his face that she was compelled to re-elaborate her question. "Nathaniel. He wants to marry and move out West. Papa insists he stay in Salem and become a doctor. Mother is frightened she won't see him again. But there are prospects in the West for any young men willing to take them. A great work of pioneering and settling to be done. And within ten years the railway network will link every state to one another. Don't you think he should be allowed to go?"

Mr. Mann looked at the twenty-two-year-old Nathaniel and at Mr. and Mrs. Mann, all allowing Elizabeth to summarise the argument. My God, he thought, does she throw everyone into silence? He began to give an opinion, "I . . .", but could only shake his head.

"I apologise, Mr. Mann," Mrs. Peabody said. "Elizabeth shouldn't make you side in a family dispute."

Mr. Peabody agreed that they should have it out another time. Just now they should celebrate Mary's and Sophia's voyage and toast to its success.

"How long are they gone for?" Horace asked.

"A year at least," said Wellington.

He looked to Elizabeth for confirmation and she nodded, without reading the panic in his eyes.

*　　*　　*

On to 1837, and the economy which has tottered for four years finally tumbles, leaving 100,000 workers idle in New England, and causing the failure of 618 banks, a state of affairs which results in the bankruptcy of Gansevoort Melville. It is a sad year also for Mr. George Bancroft, historian and would-be Ambassador – his wife dies while giving birth to their second son. Horace Mann is made the First Secretary of Education in Massachusetts and delivers an inaugural talk at the Lenox courthouse. During a long hot summer there is a street riot in Boston, blamed upon the Irish population of Broad Street. In the coolness of approaching winter, on November 11th to give the precise date, Nathaniel Hawthorne makes his first vaunted visit to the Peabody home.

At thirty three years of age, the narrow way of Mr. Hawthorne's life was just about to open out. Its pattern for the past decade, since his graduation from college, has been, for the greater part of each year, an unerringly cloistered one. For ten months he stayed in his Salem home, waited upon by a mother and two sisters who were as monastic as he. His habits were regular. After his evening walks, varied only by the report of some spectacle, such as a fire, of which he was notably fond, he would partake of a bowl of thick hot chocolate. During the day he wrote the tales which lately had been appearing, pseudonymously, in the *Token* and the *New England Magazine*. Not until the previous year had his identity been publicly disclosed, so that a collection called *Twice-told Tales* was now in print with his own name on the jacket.

But his young manhood was by no means as unhealthy as this routine might imply and, judging from the character of the mature Hawthorne, probably a good deal less rigorous than some biographers like to suggest. Much of his writing time was taken up with leisurely entries in his Journal – sometimes an account of observations remembered from his peregrinations about the town (he had a particularly sharp eye for the habits of dogs); sometimes a brief statement of an idea or proposition for a story (inspiration came more readily than the ability to give it expression).

It was the summertime which constituted his major break from the confines of his cloister. For two months of the year he would set out on youthful expedition, sometimes alone, sometimes in company. He went just far enough to win a proper sense of liberty. In 1833, that year in which Sophia and Mary had left for Cuba, he had spent the summer at Swampscott and had fallen in love with a fisherman's daughter who kept a little shop at the seaside settlement. Her name was Susan and Mr. Hawthorne called her his mermaid. It was not the only love affair he harvested in these ripe months of the year, but none found a permanent place in the storehouse of his heart. He was drawn, during these annual spells of freedom and forsworn penmanship, to earthy girls of the serving order, and who can tell what initiations he could thank them for, and whether they were elementary or advanced.

Before we join Mr. Hawthorne on the threshold of the house in Charter Street, let us see how he spent the summer just past in the companionship of his collegiate friend Horatio Bridge, at the latter's paternal residence, where he had independent quarters. Also lodging with Mr. Bridge was a queer little Frenchman, a Monsieur Schaeffer.

*   *   *

Mr. Hawthorne arrived at Bridge's residence on July 3rd 1837, a day before his thirty-third birthday. The house was pleasantly placed on a mound of land half a mile from the outskirts of the town. A gravelly track led down to the road, beyond which rolled the Kennebec, a river of no small reckoning, being over a quarter of a mile in width. A large flat sand island interrupted the river's current opposite the house, before it was further thwarted by the workings of the Mill Dam, a project into which Bridge was pouring the entirety of his fortune. His aim was to control the lease on ten waterwheels to be placed on the opposite bank, beyond the dam.

The guest retired early on the first evening – to a bare room at the top of the cavernous house, half of which was lived in by a Captain Harriman and his family, an occupancy which was so unobtrusive as not to be noticed. Having dined on nothing more than cold crackers and cheese, with a glass or two of claret wine, Mr. Hawthorne felt not entirely replenished at the end of his travels and consequently a weary light-headedness induced him to leave the unpacking of his things until the morning.

Kneeing himself up on to the tall hard bed, and letting his head drop back into the deep pillow, his eyes surveyed the contours of the high-ceilinged room, lit by the expanse of the clear starry sky. There were no curtains and the bare window frame added to the bleakness of the bedchamber so that, despite it being midsummer, Mr. Hawthorne, in turning over on to his side, pulled the coverlet tight about his neck.

The activity of Irish labourers working on the dam woke him earlier than he had intended. Before dressing, he stood at the window and admired the Maine countryside. That which lay beyond the far river bank was suffused by a rising mist, part of which still rested on the earth, while the remainder ascended so high as to be part of the clouds. His gaze was drawn away from this hazy distance by a sudden movement closer to the base of the building, and he inclined his neck in time to see a serving girl turning a corner of the house. Ths vision was brief, but the profile was sufficient to give him a favourable impression of her bosom.

In the kitchen an unexpected figure, dressed ungainlily in blue coat and cotton pantaloons, was busying himself at breakfast. He turned his crooked eyes on Mr. Hawthorne.

"*Bonjour*, Monsieur Pont. And you must be the Monsieur de l'Aubépine. Monsieur Pont has spoken me about you."

Mr. Hawthorne was a little slow at picking up the Frenchifica-tion of his and Bridge's names and there was an awkward moment or two while he decided which of the stranger's eyes to look into.

"Yes, I am Mr. Hawthorne."

"Then make yourself seated and join me at my breakfast."

Mr. Hawthorne did as he was told and sat at a rude, unpolished wooden table, at which there were no place settings, although some cutlery had been put down on a dishcloth.

"Do you like the kipper?" Mr. Hawthorne nodded a reply. "Good, I shall cook the kipper."

He was a tiny fellow, not much older than twenty, and with a general monkey-like aspect.

"Are you enjoying it in America?"

Mr. Hawthorne's polite enquiry was interrupted when the outer door of the kitchen opened and in came the same serving girl he had seen earlier. She smiled shyly at them both, then walked across the kitchen to a metal pail which stood on the stone floor. Into the pail she poured milk from her bucket. She seemed to pour the milk with excessive care, tipping the bucket only gradually. Her hair was black and fell in a tapering swirl between her shoulder blades, against the clean ruffled whiteness of her blouse. Mr. Hawthorne imagined what sweet combinations of smell and touch would come to pass for one who laid his cheek upon her shoulder.

After she had left the kitchen by the same outer door, and not without a second coy acknowledgement of them both, Mr. Hawthorne spoke to the Frenchman: "I didn't know Bridge had a servant."

"Ah, she is the worker of the family. She brings us the milk in the mornings. But as you see. And now, *par excellence* . . ." He rushed to the table with a plate balanced on the palm of one hand. "Schaeffer is my name. Monsieur le Berger."

"Thank you, Schaeffer." Mr. Hawthorne reached for a knife and fork and then began to pick at the yellow ochre fish, while Mr. Schaeffer sprawled across the table on one elbow, carefully studying the guest's enjoyment of his birthday breakfast.

As Mr. Hawthorne was chewing the last mouthful of rather tough fish Schaeffer stood up and declared, "*Je hais – je hais les Yankees!*" and with that snatched the scarcely finished plate away, leaving the American with a redundant knife and fork in his hand and a bemused smirk on his face. The Frenchman continued, "I am a philosopher. A seeker after Truth. And I must spend my day with the petty minds of your earthbound citizens. Teaching

70

them the beautiful cadences of a Latin tongue. I must be c-razy, no?"

As this rhetorical enquiry was accompanied by the divestment of his shirt, Mr. Hawthorne was inclined to answer in the affirmative, but it transpired that Schaeffer was merely preparing to shave, soon working up a great lather on his face and continuing, "But we must not let the Yankees make us dull. *Vive la gaieté.*" He turned and, with a flourish of the razor and a fiendish grimace on his snow-celled face, broke out into a French chanson, while hopping round and round the table. "Fun; it makes the heart good, and helps us to love the world," he observed seriously, once back at the glass and beginning to remove the mask from a face grown graver in concentration. "Look, I have removed my white veil," he said, turning towards Mr. Hawthorne. It was a pallid enough visage even so. "And I should just as gladly expose my whole heart."

Mr. Hawthorne was surprised at this pointed reference to one of his own stories, *The Minister's Black Veil*. He hardly considered himself a cosmopolitan author.

"You know some of my stories, then?"

"Only the one. A student of mine is very much admiring your work. She translates into French for me. It is too sad. *Vive la gaieté.*" And, gathering up a little bag such as a musician might use for sheet music, the effervescent little man took his leave of the kitchen.

Mr. Hawthorne returned to his room to begin putting his belongings in order. Once his clothes had been properly folded and hung, he sat down next to the window on a hard upright chair. There was no desk or table at hand and the wash-stand surface was too high and in too gloomy a corner of the room to be of use, so he opened his Journal on to his lap and contemplated making an entry. He wished to record something about Schaeffer but pedestrian sentences of character study were continually gusted away by thoughts of the serving girl.

Nathaniel Hawthorne was an extremely handsome man. Too many people have seen only photographs of him in portly middle age – whiskered, and rather gruff-looking. In his thirties he had all the looks associated with Byronic romanticism – high forehead, large eyes, full slightly slanted lips. So there was nothing ridiculous in the erotic daydreaming to which he surrendered himself, until stirred by an explosion from the nearby quarry.

71

Simultaneously Bridge knocked on his door and Mr. Hawthorne closed his Journal without having made any mark therein.

"Good morning. Have you organized breakfast for yourself? Sorry I didn't show, but had to be down at the dam."

"Yes, Schaeffer cooked me a kipper."

"Cooked you a kipper, eh?" Bridge came well into the room and, pressing both his hands astride the window frame, leaned forward at a forty-five degree angle to the floor. "Forgot to fill you in on him last night. He's a sort of lodger really. French tutor. Bit of a wandering scholar. Wonderful company for a solitary old rogue like me."

Mr. Hawthorne put the Journal down on the floor, between one of the bed-legs and his slippers.

"Startle you, did it? The bang from the dam-works. They do that three or four times a day. Damn nuisance, eh?" Bridge began to do press-ups, bowing his head close in towards the glass, giving Mr. Hawthorne a horrid mental flash of the ghastly scene to be produced should one of those hands slip and propel Bridge face first through the window pane.

The two of them went into town for lunch, and dined at the hotel. There they witnessed a drunken scuffle between the tavern keeper and a guest, the tavern keeper raving like a madman. Mr. Hawthorne noted the pathetic tone mingled with his rage.

Walking home they passed a carpenter who was cutting out large poster-sized letters for the purpose of printing out "MARTIN VAN BUREN FOREVER" on a flag. He asked Bridge, as a fellow supporter, for assistance, but Bridge replied, "Let every man skin his own skunks," thus giving Mr. Hawthorne a pithy summation of a mental attitude which he would feel to be his own at many periods of later life.

The aftermath was uneventful and Mr. Hawthorne was pleased to find that his presence made no notable alteration to his host's way of life which, in its independence and freedom from the forms and restrictions of society, was so different from his own existence at Salem.

The evening was spent in literary and philosophical discussion over a leg of cold mutton, which was devoured rapaciously by Schaeffer, all the while declaring that the Yankees, in contrast to his own race, ate too fast and too much. Mr. Hawthorne did not once remind his friend that it was his birthday and despite the fact that he went to bed without setting eyes again on Nancy – such, he had learned, was the milkmaid's name – he retired with a marvellous feeling of well-being.

It was a day or two before he was shown the workings of the mill dam at close quarters. Before that, Bridge took him strolling along one of the Kennebec's sidestreams which ran its course through dense pinewood. They came to where an old dam had been built across the brook many years ago. The pine logs had a red rottenness about them which arrested the eye and the soul, striking them both with the beauty of decay. There were, too, giant toadstools under the trees and, beside the path, smaller yellow ones, about the size of hard-boiled eggs. The brook foamed and struggled easily enough through the near side of the crumbling rampart, but towards the far shore the dam was still sufficiently sound to bank up, with the aid of a natural wall of rock, a broad and deep pool. At the top of the crag stood a white pine, completely stripped of its bark and seeming to crown the spot with a ghastly but graceful emblem of ruin.

Bridge went off to fish for trout and Mr. Hawthorne bathed in the pool, attracted by the wild and peaceful traces of previous times. Treading water in the midst of the pond, he looked up at the naked mast-head. It was easy enough to fancy a tribe of Canadian Indians come down from the brook in search of lead and assembling beneath its white silhouette for the purposes of pagan ritual.

The next day was a Sunday and work on the new dam was at rest. Bridge took him first of all to see the shanties of Irish and Canadian labourers. It was a dark afternoon and already flickers of candlelight could be seen through the windows and open doors.

"Continually quarrelling over these turf huts, they are. Sometimes twenty people in just one of them, a square foot between them. No wonder they have some mighty rows. I have to be their umpire and have picked up enough French from Schaeffer for the purpose, although, to be fair, it's the Irish that cause most fracas." All the while Bridge was raising a hand to various occupants standing in doorways, and Mr. Hawthorne was struck by this image of his friend as arbiter and adviser, Time having transformed him from a free and wild young man into an adult purveyor of integrity and wisdom. He himself felt not so entirely exorcised of his youth. The quiet days of his twenties, his use of the family house as sanctuary, had immolated him in habits of independence in such a way that he could not now envisage himself becoming a man of the world after Bridge's fashion. And yet the next few years would see him making the effort to transform himself into just such a thing.

By the time they reached the dam itself the light had degenerated into premature dusk. A chaise, which had drawn up on the road to examine the work, drew away from them, the riders appearing to give one another ominous shakes of the head. Mr. Hawthorne could understand their alarm. The dam, which was half-finished, looked like the ruins of one destroyed by spring freshets; none of the slow decomposition of the old dam beneath the white pine – here the impression was one of violent and rapid destruction. In the gloom of the evening, stray logs from the saw mill at Waterville could just be seen rolling along the eddies and then crashing against the dam's fortifications, before carefully navigating themselves through the space still to be bridged. Mr. Hawthorne stood at the edge of the bank looking down at the steep precipice carved away by the current. A few feet down, the earth turned yellow. Bridge, noting his friend's observations, began to give the technical justification for his own enterprise.

*   *   *

Another week passed by. One of those weeks where the vacation life seems more real than the one left behind. This feeling was intensified for Mr. Hawthorne by the fact that, on many evenings, Bridge would go to bed early, in order to oversee the dawn parade of labourers from their mud shanties, leaving Schaeffer and himself to pursue their conversations alone. Sometimes they would sit outside in the late summer twilight, Mr. Hawthorne occasionally letting his concentration lapse, and trying to catch a glance of Nancy, whom he imagined dressing herself in silks and acting ladylike behind green blinds. Then, when they retired indoors, it was as if he were the host of the establishment; that this big house was his own, his own capital was risked on the river outside, to him did the French Canadians appeal for protection from the Irish, and he it was who gave orders to the milkmaid.

"I am *très* interested in mesmerism," declared the Frenchman one night, after they had ensconced themselves in Bridge's drawing room and Mr. Hawthorne was puffing on his nightly cigar. "Would you care to be my subject?"

"No, sir."

"That is very adamant. I assure you that I have experience. For

74

some of my customers it is the only hope, no?"

"But you are not my teacher. For what purpose . . ."

"Oh, but you *should* learn French. I have helped Monsieur Pont with his. It is the second language of the world." Schaeffer stepped up from his chair, and began to make weird animated pacings on the hearth rug, all for effect. "But let me hypnotise you to prove the viability of the . . . No, you say viability, to wound?"

"Vulnerability."

"The vulnerability of the mind. Come." He drew some kind of a trinket from his jacket pocket and leaned towards Mr. Hawthorne.

"No!" In the violence of this riposte Mr. Hawthorne spilled cigar ash into his lap and he slapped it clear with wide-ranging flicks of both hands, also designed to keep the Frenchman, and his diabolic emblem, at bay.

"Ah. I see. Man with the veil."

"The mind has many secret chambers, Mr. Schaeffer, into which even friends and loved ones never set foot. Why should I invite an intruder?"

"Am I not your friend?"

"Friend, not mesmeriser."

"Oh, *je hais les Yankees* and their fear of dark corners. You believe in the shadows. Why not cast some light on them?"

"You would not mind a torchlight pointed at your own?"

"Not at all. I have never yet sinned with woman."

Mr. Hawthorne coughed out a lungful of cigar smoke.

"It is true. I vow it. I swear it by the law of reason and morality, the only absolutes to which I bow my head."

"And yet you may be capable of murder."

"What! What you accuse me of? What evidence do you possess? Have I ever lifted a hand in violence? Have you seen me swat a fly even? This is gross . . ."

Schaeffer was pirouetting in scandalised scorn of the accusation. Mr. Hawthorne got up and put a hand on his shoulder. "I only meant your abstinence from one excess does not rule out another. I implied nothing personal. We are all murderers in degree."

"Agh, you talk such prepostery."

"In a few years you may not find it so. Our potentialities grow murkier and more menacing with age."

"That is because you shrink away in the shadows, you shun the clear light of reason. I have seen the picnic parties here. The old sit in the shade of elm trees and it is only the young who play out on the sunny green. Not so in France. We all love the sun in France. We let it press its warmth deep into our organs."

Mr. Hawthorne sat back down, and smiled. He re-lit the stub of his cigar, had three more puffs, and went to bed.

In dropping off to sleep he catalogued the accumulated sightings of Nancy – how many times seen with empty bucket; how many times returning with bucket filled; standing outside washing, her bare arms in the tub, and the handkerchief across her bosom pushed low; coming into the breakfast room to deliver her freshly collected milk. It was this last which Mr. Hawthorne relished most; the sight of her bending down, hair unruffled by any breeze, and the sure conviction he now had that she took more than necessary care not to spill any milk in order to prolong her proximity to him. Her smiled acknowledgements had become much bolder and warmer. Indeed once or twice she had neglected to nod farewell to Schaeffer, who had not noticed the slip in etiquette.

Heavy rain beat against the window. Mr. Hawthorne had grown to like this room, with its bleak, half-furnished feel, and yet it was part of a general air of impermanence about the house which he found unsettling. Bridge seemed obsessed by his project and to give little attention to the domestic side of his existence. There had been no hot meals since Mr. Hawthorne arrived, aside from the odd kipper or sausage rustled up by the Frenchman at breakfast. His host possessed claret wine in abundance but the bottles were touched only frugally, often as a sudden afterthought. The ambience of calm and liberated independence, which Mr. Hawthorne had so admired on arrival, he now saw to be simply a characteristic of the crazed engrossment which ruled his friend's life.

A gust of wind threw the rain with increased force against the window. Mr. Hawthorne had a premonition, strengthened by the violence of the night's weather, that his friend's project was doomed. The house itself, standing on its mound so close to the rushing and impeded Kennebec, seemed insecure, as if the angry waters, when they finally broke, might aim with conscious accuracy at the architect of their barricade.

The storm woke him intermittently during the night with the result that he slept later than usual into the morning. Schaeffer had already left by the time he entered the kitchen. A note placed conspicuously on the table read, "You are lucky Yankee I did not murder you while you sleep. *Vive la Gaieté!*" It made Mr. Hawthorne chuckle, albeit uneasily, not being totally sure of the jest intended. He would have liked it better, and laughed more freely, if the Frenchman had not used a carving knife as paper-weight. A loathing of sharp blades affected both his practical and subconscious life and he quickly took steps to hide this particular knife away; but just as he picked it up the outer door swung open and Nancy, also later than usual, came into the room with her bucket, bumping the door closed behind her with an accomplished swing of her shoulder.

Mr. Hawthorne blushed and quickly hid the knife behind his back. He blushed initially because he was always nervous of being left alone in a room with a solitary female. He was more alert than others to the sexual chemistry implicit in such situations. He blushed secondarily because he realised how stupid had been his reflex action of concealing the knife.

Nancy smiled and then knelt to pour the milk. Mr. Hawthorne noticed that although her skirt was fastened at the back, several buttons beneath the topmost one had come loose, revealing an inch or two of petticoat.

He put the knife down on the table top. Nancy poured the last drop from her pail and then left it tilted steeply, as if the flow were still continuing. But Mr. Hawthorne had a keen ear and was well attuned to the noise of the milk's pouring. He knew that her bucket was empty. She was trying to give him opportunity to speak. That was all. How long might she kneel there? He tried desperately to fashion a suitable sentence. One that would invite arrangements for a meeting without presuming too much. In the end she rose before he could put it together and they merely passed one another the customary farewell smile. Her own lips were pulled a little tighter than usual. The smile was just as pronounced, still held the essential message of affection, but disappointment spread it wider across her face. The door closed. Mr. Hawthorne lifted the knife and stuck its point hard into the table top.

On leaving the kitchen, without having had any breakfast, he became aware of an obstreperous chattering coming from one of the front rooms. Locating the source of the noise, he discovered that the cat had left feathers and two badly mauled carcasses all over the carpet, although there was still some crazed twittering coming from behind the fireboard. Mr. Hawthorne took the board away and found three young birds clinging with their feet against one of the jambs. The heavy rain had evidently washed a nest of chimney swallows down into the fireplace and the adult birds had escaped from one danger into the claws of a more fatal one, while the young ones had been forced to keep to the original predicament. They had a few slate-coloured feathers but a combination of fright and infancy rendered them immobile.

When Mr. Hawthorne saw Nancy on her way back round the house, passing the front window, he did not hesitate to engage her assistance. He rushed over and pushed up the casement.

"Nancy, there are three young birds in the fireplace."

She disappeared with such headlong urgency, not answering a word, that he returned to the fireplace wondering whether she intended helping or not, and uncertain as to whether he should start some form of rescue operation by himself. He felt like the schoolchild who has only pretended to understand the teacher's instructions and sits in front of his task in perplexed agitation.

But within a minute or two he heard movement in the hall and Nancy came into the room carrying a basket filled with cotton wool.

"Are they very little?" she said, coming to the fireplace.

Mr. Hawthorne stepped aside and quietly showed them to her. She knelt down and with gentle confidence placed each one into the softly cushioned basket. "Get a little bread and water." He sprang to obedience like a surgeon's assistant and returned from the kitchen with a cup of water and a hunk torn from the loaf. Picking bait-sized pieces from inside the crust and dipping them into the water she offered these to each of the crying mouths.

"You must hang the basket from a window so that they can escape when ready." Her voice had a wonderful understated authority. "And continue feeding them the soaked bread." She stood up to indicate that her part in the rescue was completed. Turning to go, she said, "You can keep the basket."

Mr. Hawthorne felt his shoulders tighten and a rush of warmth spread up his spine. "Nancy!" he blurted. "I am going to the Old Dam this afternoon."

She smiled. And then left the room, again not answering a word, so that he was thrown a second time into the same state of childish uncertainty. He was heartened, though, by the sight of her running, in skirt-flirling vivacity, back past the front room window. It was true that she was late for her duties, but she did not normally hasten to them.

Mr. Hawthorne took the basket up to his room and, fastening to its handle one of the leather straps from his suitcase, suspended it outside the window so that it hung just a foot below the outer sill. He went back downstairs and returned with more sodden bread. He tried to push some into their mouths but they seemed satisfied by Nancy's efforts and there was much less of a squalking now that they were in the open air.

It was a long, long morning. Bridge was out for the day, executing some financial transactions at the bank. Mr. Hawthorne found himself unable to settle to anything. He went downstairs to browse in Bridge's minimal library. He came back upstairs to check on the baby birds. He went down to dispose of the bones and feathers in the front room. He went up to see if the fledglings were thirsty again. He went down to boil a handkerchief. He came back up to find two of the birds already escaped. Their wings had not seemed developed enough for flight and it was significant that, for Mr. Hawthorne, "escape" was the only interpretation of their disappearance.

He did not think it entirely proper to leave the solitary mite to fend for itself the entire afternoon, and yet the restlessness of the morning had been due to his impending rendezvous and to renege on it now was an impossible consideration. He tried one last time to push crumbs down the little one's throat. He touched the tiny cranium with a fingertip previously kissed, and then pulled the window down firmly across the leather strap.

*   *   *

The day was blessed with cloudless sunshine. No wind rustled the forest leaves as he walked to the Old Dam. There was no noise but the brawling and bubbling of the brook. It would have taken a sharp and obtrusive sound to catch his attention, so absorbed was he in mental prognoses of the afternoon's outcome.

He decided to bathe before Nancy was likely to arrive and stripped off his clothes at the foot of the edifice of rock. He noticed now that it was not such a natural face of stone as he had first thought but had been roughly hewn out by the irregular strokes of workmen. And yet the roots of trees which must have been many decades old had no soil between themselves and the rockface.

He bathed quickly, swimming in a tight spiral, first in towards the centre of the pool, and then back to the edge. To dry himself he sat up tight against the wall of rock, in a sunspot, at a point where he could be fairly certain of not being seen. He put on his clothes while there were still one or two water droplets glistening on his body, particularly in the hairs of his chest, and then, keeping to the lower ground, walked a small way into the underbrush, to find a shady waiting nook. But remembering Schaeffer's disparaging remarks about "Old Yankees", he chose in the end to move back closer to the path and to lie down in the full beam of the sun.

There seemed to be a sexual power in the sun's heat which beat down into his organs so that, as he drifted into an afternoon drowse, contemplating the milkmaid's arrival, he fell prey to a grossness of thought which consisted in seeing Nancy in a variety of attitudes corresponding to some black and white drawings that had been passed round at college. Gradually, these static, mono-chromic visions took on a fleshier hue, and as the state of his slumber deepened, so did he participate more fully in their manipulation.

He would find Nancy standing amongst the trees. She could hear him creeping up towards her but would feign obliviousness. She would be standing in front of a double-trunked tree, its dual stem forming an inverted arch at thigh height. As he came up behind her he placed his hands on her hips. She fell back against his chest and he nuzzled his face into her hair and neck, so that she squirmed with pleasure. He kissed her ear and her cheek and, opening his eyes, looked into the dark tunnel between her bosom which, as she leaned forward to press her rear into his waist, was almost wholly revealed. He slid a hand across her stomach and pulled the ruffled kerchief away. She stretched then like a cat, raising her arms and placing a hand high on either trunk. Then, looking over her shoulder, she took one arm away and with a deft flick of her hand unfastened the clasp at the top of her skirt so that both it and her petticoats fell together . . .

Snatching imaginary bedclothes away, he jumped to his feet, and there, where he had lain, he fancied the earth looked black, as if scorched by the incandescence of his lust. He stumbled away, to a place from which he could see most of the surrounding terrain – the bathing-pool, the high white pine and the path leading up to it. There was no sign of her, and he took the path himself, deciding to take up a look-out post beside the ghostly landmark.

When he had climbed above the wall of rock he stood beside the pine and scoured the visible length of brook. Still no sign. He had been subject to an arrogant delusion. She smiled no more on him than on Schaeffer, and only out of politeness. Her assistance with the endangered birds had been an act of pure charity, and her departing beam had been a gentle way of rebuffing his clumsy utterance. He kicked a little loose earth over the edge of the rockface and watched its untidy splash in the water below. Then he sat among the roots of the plain white tree and, with a conscious act of the will, resisted the return of a satyric sensuality.

He must have sat for an hour or more, his hopes raised just once by a small group of children, two boys and a girl, passing through the solitary valley. The girl had suffered some wrong from her male companions and walked a goodly distance behind them, calling out at spaces with an indistinct indignation. They soon passed out of hearing and out of view and Mr. Hawthorne was left to return to his mindless meditation. For most of this space he sat with eyes open, contemplating the patterns of roots as they spread out towards the rock edge, and intermittently observing an insect traversing their mountain ranges. Eventually the still heat and the bubbling brook lulled him once again into a shut-eye slumber.

He sensed his territory being encroached upon, a shade passing across the blinkered glow beneath his eyelids. Opening them, he started, and, clutching his chest, let forth three or four cries of uncontrolled panic. The fourth cry transmuted itself into pained laughter and, on his knees, he said, "Oh . . . Oh," and chuckled.

Mr. Hawthorne was, on the surface, relaxed and assured. But the air of quiet was a cultivated, habitual exterior beneath which lay a closely coiled centre. It was partly because he had so great a potentiality for relaxation that he was so prone to these sudden frights which, in the average person, would have produced a mere "jump" or "start".

"Oh . . . Oh, forgive me."

On this occasion, added to the strain of being wrenched from the subliminal seabed was the initial shock, on opening his eyes, of believing that his swinish counsellor had called him forth for further sensual speculation.

Nancy put a basket on the ground and sat beside Mr. Hawthorne. "I'm sorry I frightened you."

He reddened at once, embarrassed by his ridiculous behaviour and uneasy at finding himself at last alone in the woods with his milkmaid.

"What is in the basket?" It was a similar basket to that which held the surviving bird. A red cloth covered its contents.

"A little tea. Some bread and currants."

"Are the currants mashed? I love mashed currants."

Nancy shook her head.

"No matter."

"Is the other baby bird still safe?"

"The other one?"

"Yes, I found two beneath your window. The third one must have pushed them out."

"But the nest was big enough for all."

"Shall we start on the currants?"

There was something unreal about the way the untutored girl conducted herself. She drew back the red cloth and handed him some bread and blackcurrants.

"Have you a knife?" She had, and he used it to smash and smear the currants into an instant jam. "Tell me about your family."

Her hand stopped midway from the basket to her mouth.

"It's just that your hands do not seem the hands of a serving girl."

She dropped her currant and made a show of inspecting them, first palm-up, and then their backs. They were small, white and neatly tapered, the middle finger extending a sophisticated distance beyond the rest. She shrugged, and picked up another currant. "I like to be secretive. I like this. This meeting."

They were silent then, while finishing their short tea. Afterwards, Mr. Hawthorne getting up first, they both stood at the rock's edge and looked down at the broken dam.

"Mr. Harriman says the new dam'll end like that, and much sooner. I don't like your friend Mr. Bridge, he doesn't speak to me. And the mistress whispers awful things about him and the Frenchman."

She was speaking more in character now, and Mr. Hawthorne felt nettled by the cheap insinuation of her remarks. Suddenly he found her no longer mysterious but coquettish, and he made use of his temporary sense of superiority by suggesting a walk into the wood.

While bending to tidy up her basket she turned and smiled. It was the smile, Mr. Hawthorne thought, of a girl of loose morals, vulgar and collusive.

Entering among the trees, they found the soil strewn with the leaves of preceding seasons. There was a path, but scarcely worn, and it led the way through an enlacement of boughs and twigs beneath which they had to duck and dart. At one point Nancy trod on a rotten log of pine and lurched forward as her foot sank into the mouldering substance. She reached out for support and they continued hand in hand.

The last time Mr. Hawthorne had walked regularly hand in hand with a girl had been with Susan, on the beach at Swampscott. Hand-holding then had been a simple seal of pleasure which they had broken fitfully, as Susan sprinted a little way to chase the tide, or as she bent to pick up a shell. Nancy was a different girl – Mr. Hawthorne became, as he had not with Susan, acutely conscious of the fact that she was probably only half his age, and their hands were clasped in a different spirit. Those three or four summers ago he had pursued his love in the open, under the watchful eye of Susan's fisherman father, so that the flirtation developed with a precious and adolescent self-consciousness. Now he was in the primaeval forest with a girl who lived apart from her family.

Such recollections and uncomfortable comparisons were suddenly expelled from Mr. Hawthorne's mind when, against expectations, Nancy broke away from his hand, and began to run, as best she was able, across the soft loam, towards a tree of horrid familiarity.

"A seat!" she cried. And on reaching the double trunked tree she sat down upon the inverted arch which it formed at thigh height.

Mr. Hawthorne had a real inclination to turn away and leave her there, to walk briskly back to the house; but the solicitations she beckoned his way were not to be resisted.

As he approached she gathered some of her skirt into her lap to make way for him. There was space enough, although no real length of horizontal bark and the sloping of either trunk pressed their bodies in towards one another. As their shoulders pushed together Mr. Hawthorne lost much of his apprehensiveness and indeed might have submitted himself with some willingness to the realisation of those prurient imaginings.

*   *   *

When Mr. Hawthorne reached his room he did not straightway check the well-being of the baby birds. Instead he wrote some retrospective passages in his Journal. He described Nancy in a

83

detached, observational way, without hinting at any involvement. But he wrote about the Old Dam with an expansive intensity which hinted at an emotional engagement with the setting.

He closed the Journal, and then washed, changing his shirt. Only then did he pull up the window and look outside at the basket. It was still safely secured, hanging steady in the breezeless air. The bird had turned grey and there was a dry mattness about the new colour which immediately betokened Mr. Hawthorne's mistake. He had hung the basket in the full glare of the afternoon sun and the little mite was baked to a turn, although still breathing with an irrevocable rapidity.

He rushed to the basin and wet his hand in dirtied water, and then let droplets fall from his fingers on to the baby bird's beak. Its eyes, which were open, didn't even blink. In order to aim the liquid more directly down the bird's throat he made a tiny paper chute out of a piece of paper torn from the back of his Journal. The contraption worked satisfactorily, but no observable quantity of water was swallowed and Mr. Hawthorne succeeded only in flooding the nest's bedding. The bird, he told himself, would at any rate feel cooler, and expire more comfortably.

He saw Nancy walking across for the early evening milk but resisted the impulse to call again for her aid, since in part he blamed her for the ill conclusion of his ministry, neglecting, as she had, the whole question of sun and shade. Again he was reminded of the black and white college drawings – initially coveted, but later cast aside as sad and worthless curiosities.

Lying down on the bed he attempted a late siesta, trying to expunge the memory of the afternoon and to blank out all thought of the festering form beneath the window. He managed to rest mindlessly for about an hour and then became aware of the Frenchman singing his French melodies in a distant part of the house. He checked the bird. Its condition was unchanged, so he shook the creases out of his trousers and jacket before going downstairs.

Bridge had returned from an afternoon's fishing with two fair-sized trout – sufficient for supper since he himself had to talk over the next day's work with the Canadian leader of the work force. While Schaeffer was preparing the fish, Mr. Hawthorne spoke about the cat's marauding and his concern for the survivor.

"Ah!" the Frenchman turned, licking sauce off his fingers. "Let me see it. I will mesmerise it back to mirthful song." He led the

84

way to Mr. Hawthorne's bedroom, chanting Latin songs for the dead and giggling all the while.

The sun had set but the sky, which was still clear with only a wisp of developing mist in the horizon, maintained an eerie brightness. Mr. Hawthorne carefully lifted the basket into the room and held it in both hands towards Schaeffer.

"*Mon Dieu!* The little thing is wrecked, wrecked." Without any warning he then lifted the minuscule frame up by the neck, laid it carefully out on the windowsill, put his hands together in further Latin prayer, after which he placed his right thumb on to the little bird's skull and pressed it flat, as if he were crushing a pea or bean.

"The heart – it is sometimes too strong." He left the room, continuing the intonations of a Catholic priest as he descended the stairs. Mr. Hawthorne stood pale and shaken, with tears welling in his eyes. They were tears of anger, pity and shame. He felt shame because, shocking though the Frenchman's action had been, performed as it was in a fit of theatrical bravado, he saw that it had been the only sensible remedy and that he should have delivered the stroke himself, many hours previously. He felt shame because the whole episode seemed inextricably linked to his dalliance with Nancy and he could not help but reflect upon the irrational notion that three innocent creatures had had to suffer the consequences of his own corrupt thoughts.

He shook himself busy, forcing himself to lift the baby bird's body away from the windowsill and dropped it to the ground below. He drew his case from beneath the bed and began to fold his clothes inside. Lastly, he untied the leather strap from the basket and laid it across the lid of the case. In the morning he would bind it round the fully-packed load and inside the empty basket (he had already removed the sopping cotton wool) he would place a short, businesslike note for Nancy, thanking her for the loan. And then he would stride away from the mouldering dam and the scary pine and the boiled-egg fungi, from the busy Kennebec and the Irish shanty towns and the unfinished construction work; from Bridge, from Schaeffer, from Nancy . . .

He cheered himself up in just such jauntily conjoined determinations, and then went down to eat the Frenchman's marinaded trout and to smoke a final cigar in his company.

* * *

Three months have passed. Mr. Hawthorne stands across from the weatherboarded house on Charter Street. It is a large square block of a house, with a low almost flat roof, and two broad brick chimneys at front and back. There are three storeys, four windows on each floor at the front, and three on the side which looks out upon the graveyard. A plain iron railing, founded on a high-foot stone base, fences off the gravestones from the road, but there is no similar boundary at the side of the house, so that the burial ground seems to be its very garden. Two steps lead up from the pavement to a cramped pseudo-classical portico, the slanted roof of which rests on two rounded pilasters. Patients of Dr. Peabody, in fact any visitor or returning occupant, must stand on the second step to knock at the door. A third step, which can only be crossed after the door has been opened, forms the actual threshold to the house.

Miss Sophia, at this moment, was upstairs in her room recovering from another of those headaches which, since her return from Cuba two and a half years ago, had once again begun to plague her with a chronic recurrence. Outwardly she was unaltered by the trip to southern climes. Submissively enough she had returned to being the sickly hostage of her nineteenth-century family and the only observable difference in her condition was that she was beginning to paint with a growing industry and confidence. Copies mainly, but they were selling, and for fair sums.

However, behind the sickly façade, her inner life had been changed forever by those languorous days in the sun, and in some part her willingness to resume the invalid's role was due to the fact that it allowed her to indulge in nostalgia. Just so had she been engaged upon this dull New England afternoon.

All that riding! Forty-five miles in one day. The horse Guajanon not going fast enough for her, until Fernando lent her one of his spurs and fastened it to her heel. At first she had stopped each time her hair fell loose but in the end she rode with her ringlets flying free.

The Morells' country house, La Recompensa, where they stayed, was a sprawling one-storey dwelling with long verandahs. There were guests, mostly young men from neighbouring estates, every day. She remembered the feminine shyness these young men displayed whenever she started to sketch them in her notebook, covering their faces with pocket handkerchiefs and then protesting when she pretended to lose interest. And the dizzying waltzes on the open verandah while Dr. Morell played the grand piano on nights which were like "velvet" with wave after wave of orange-tree perfume filling the humid air and, between dances, from somewhere in the distance, a Negro voice singing in Spanish.

Her curtain had been half-drawn to relieve the headache, and dusk was falling as she opened her eyes on to the quiet, dimly lit room, and looked with melancholy vacancy upon its contents. On a bedside table lay a copy of Schiller's poems, beside an untouched glass of water. In an armchair near the window slumped a sewing bag which she had embroidered in her childhood. There were two pictures on the wall, one of her own originals and a copy of a mediaeval painting of the Ascension. A third painting, also by herself, and not hung, was leaning against her wardrobe. The wardrobe door was open and she looked with distaste at her dull winter apparel. In the same piece of furniture, inside one of the compartments for small articles of clothing, she kept her drawing materials – sketchpads, pencils and pastels. If it were not for the way an empty sheet of cartridge paper enticed her, and her ability to fill it with meaningful lines, she felt she would have gone mad, or expired in a far more desperate act of submission than charac-terised her present existence. The thought did not disturb her. She let her gaze drift upwards to the high cold ceiling and then back down to settle on the tasselled curtain pelmet.

Further reveries of the long Cuban summer were interrupted by a heavy, urgent climbing of the stairs. The tread was unmistak-ably that of her sister Elizabeth. The door was knocked upon and opened in one continuous movement.

"Oh, Sophia, Mr. Hawthorne has come and you never saw anything so splendid. He is handsomer than Lord Byron. You must get up and come down."

Sophia turned on her side.

"Sophia, you will come down and introduce yourself?"

"I think it would be rather ridiculous to get up. If he has come once, he will come again."

The Peabody family had originally moved into Salem when Mr. Hawthorne had been a ten-year old boy. The doctor had attended Nathaniel, trying to cure a mysterious limping ailment that had blighted the central years of his childhood. Such treatment as was administered did not meet with significant success and the failure proved prophetic of the medical practice in general so that Dr. Peabody now prescribed his homeopathic cures purely as a hobby and concentrated his remunerative efforts on dentistry.

It was during Elizabeth's absence upstairs that Mrs. Peabody gaily reminded Mr. Hawthorne of this historic connection between the two families. He huffed a response, not wishing to delve further into the embarrassing mysteries of his early years. Mrs. Peabody's sense of embarrassment was more immediate. A newly-discovered writer had appeared in their midst and there was nobody here to laud him. Elizabeth, when she had first begged the visit had been under the misapprehension that Mr. Hawthorne's sister was the author of the *Tales* appearing in the regional journals, and no doubt made claims that the "whole family" was anxious to meet the local genius. And here he was in an empty drawing room!

Elizabeth came in alone and Mrs. Peabody decided to leave her in her own predicament, manufacturing some business to attend to in the kitchen. Mr. Hawthorne stood and bade her goodbye. "'No. I shall be back in a moment. Elizabeth, won't Sophia come down? She *is* on her way?"

"No, Mother."

"The girl has such awful heads."

Mr. Hawthorne smiled a polite sympathy in reply to this information.

"So good of your sister to badger you into coming," Elizabeth said, when her mother had left the room. "You know, we were all quite convinced it was she who wrote the *Tales*. Why have you remained hidden so long? No, don't tell me. I know the answer . . ."

And from that moment on Elizabeth made it plain that she did know the answers, not only to Mr. Hawthorne's past, but to his future as well. He had been quite right to nurse his talent in solitude through the impressionable years of youth, but now, in the primacy of life, he must work in the full stream of public affairs, at an occupation sufficiently lucrative to relieve him from financial anxieties, and yet not so arduous as to deprive him of creative time and energy. She would use all her influence to procure him such a position. A government post was what she had in mind.

They sat together on the same settee, Mr. Hawthorne well back on the seat, Miss Peabody perched at an angle on the edge of the cushion, half of her extensive buttocks supported. Nathaniel's life at this point had been utterly free of the organising influence (with the exception of the "wicked uncle" who had masterminded his early education). Neither his mother, nor his sisters had ever made the slightest attempt to steer him into a career, for the simple reason that they liked too much to have him at home. Mr. Hawthorne had been his own man too long to take Elizabeth's presumptuousness at all seriously. Had he known how utterly incapable she was of resisting such machinations, he would have experienced, on that strange uncomfortable settee, a significant sense of foreboding. As it was, he sat with an amused smirk on his face, taking the onslaught partly as jest – a hostess's way of making conversation.

"Tell me," he said at last, "is your sister often confined to bed?"

Miss Peabody was rather startled by the abrupt neglect of her subject matter, but as that subject was himself, she forgave what otherwise would have been a rude evasion.

"Oh – Sophia. She is often in her room, yes, and otherwise spends almost her entire existence housebound. It is very sad. A year or two ago the family sent her to Cuba, with my other sister Mary – I'm afraid Mary is working away in the country at present, she'll be most cross to have missed you – and for a time it seemed to have made her more robust but the improvement didn't last. Poor thing, I sometimes think she's too ethereal for this world, especially a stormy coastal spot like Salem. The wind absolutely finishes her."

"To Cuba? That must have been a shock. For a delicate New England girl, I mean."

"Well, she didn't stay with the natives. The family has friends there. But yes, it was quite an experience for them both. They were away for more than a year."

"That long?" These moments on the settee, these first snippets of information about his future wife, would remain with Mr. Hawthorne for ever. It was as if he were sitting down to write a story and scribbling notes about a possible leading character: "youngest of three sisters, too frail for this world, time spent in Cuba". No wonder his writer's heart was captivated. In later years husband and wife would claim to have fallen in love at first sight, but in the husband's case it was really on first hearing.

"And how does she fill her time? She doesn't socialise with visitors, I see."

"Her headaches are very debilitating you know. I'm sure she would be down to meet you if she felt at all fit . . ."

"I didn't mean . . ."

"No. Well – she draws. And paints. And reads."

"An active solitude then?"

"There *are* periods of depression but personally I put these down to her chronic ingestion of opiates. They are medically prescribed of course and Sophia is quite proper in her use of them but our father – he practises homeopathy as you know – thinks the dosages far too high."

Mr. Hawthorne had heard enough. He didn't want too full a picture and, pointing at a low coffee table on which lay a volume of the classical poets, he said, "And for yourself, you read too?"

Oh, yes! she did, but it was essentially an active life she led. And for the rest of his sojourn on the Peabody settee Mr. Hawthorne was entertained to a verbal impression of her bustling path through the world.

But as he left the house it wasn't this litany of hectic activity which rang in his ear, nor was it the considerable frame of Miss Elizabeth Peabody which remained in his mind; no, as he stepped down through the portico and on to the road, as he walked across to the other side of the street and looked up to see just one lighted window in the upper storey of the house, the words that held his inner voice in an expectant trance were "Cuba", "painting", "Sophia" and "headache".

*   *   *

Before Mr. Melville is brought before *his* bride-to-be, it is necessary that we should hover above a New York landing stage on a stormy October night in 1830. A middle-aged man and his eleven-year-old son wait at the Cortlandt Street dock for a boat delayed by the ill weather. Allan Melville is forty-eight years old, his importing business is in liquidation, his wife (who has journeyed ahead with the other children) severely depressed, their spacious home at 675 Broadway empty, and all their furniture packed off on the Ontario towboat. They wait for the passenger ferry to take them up the Hudson River as far as Albany, home of Peter Gansevoort, Herman's uncle and source of considerable ill-feeling between the Melville parents. Maria stands accused of loving Peter more than she loves Allan, so it is with a sense of moral as well as financial defeat that Allan now contemplates the move. The plan is that he shall work as a clerk in a fur store. Living quarters have been found for them on Steuben Street. And he must thank Peter for making these arrangements.

During a break in the rain Herman began to kick a stone up and down the dock platform, while Allan sat on a bench at the back of a covered porch, deep in a despairing reverie. The winding-up of his business and the packing-up of the household (much of which went under the hammer) had drained him entirely, so that for a while he was incapable of feeling the paternal instinct and Herman, had he been a senseless child, might have fallen into the Hudson River.

It was typical of Maria that she should abandon ship before the final day of the move. Herman had been left with his father for "company", an excuse much used for posting her children out to various aunts and grandparents. Frequently, during the summer months, the family would be completely fragmented, split between three or four different households. Allan would be left to sweat his way through the business and the New York heatwaves alone, or be given charge of the most unruly children for fear that they might give other relatives too hard a time. And, during the rest of the year, it was only rarely that the family was together for a continuous period of any reckoning and although this was to some extent characteristic of the nineteenth-century middle-class household (it was one of the ways of coping with large numbers of children) there is no doubt that the Melvilles practised such shiftlessness to excess, and altogether understandable that Herman, for all his merry stone-kicking on the boards of the port, would later view this night as emblematic of his mother's treachery.

"Herman, it's coming on to rain again. We must get ourselves into the waiting office."

Allan, a simple man with a conventional belief in God and Heaven, had always been self-pitying. One summer, putting "Bachelor Hall" at the top of the notepaper, he had written in desperation to Peter Gansevoort: "I hope you will take my utter loneliness into generous consideration and not detain Maria and the children an unreasonable period to gratify personal wishes. Their absence is already prolonged beyond my hopes and intentions." And all this summer past Maria had exaggerated the mental agitation that their financial troubles caused her in an attempt to persuade him that it would be wise to remove to Albany before the moment of final collapse.

"Come on now, before you're blown away into the river." He didn't realise the boy had been playing his solitary game for nearly thirty minutes, such time being filled not entirely with acerbic estimations of his wife. No, there had been enough of the better times together to give his nostalgic desperation an agonising edge. He remembered particularly a party given two or three years previously by the entire clan of Melville children. It was something they had been hankering after for the whole of that winter and Maria had finally consented with an uncommon degree of good cheer. She even went out to purchase confectionery and mottoes as these had become a regular feature of parties in the neighbourhood.

The appointed day, a Thursday in February, arrived, and so did the snow, but Allan came home specially at four o'clock so that he could organise the transportation of guests. Forty invitations had been sent out and twenty-five accepted, so there was quite some mêlée. It lasted from seven until midnight. Herman was not yet eight. The two older children, Gansevoort and Helen, were twelve and ten. All the children partook of lemonade port wine, and for eats there were plum cakes, blancmange, oranges and dried fruits, large portions of which many of the boys emptied into their breeches pockets. Despite the late finish there was school as usual the next day and Allan could remember to this damp dreary minute the sense of well-being he had felt that Friday morning, leaving the house still bearing signs of the invasion and bidding his children a good day at school, urging them to keep their eyelids open. Because it had been a children's party even Maria seemed to have enjoyed it and not to have been troubled by her usual doubts as to whether all the social nuances had been observed.

His memory was not able to serve him up many similar family festivities and as he ushered Herman into the waiting room he failed to acknowledge the greeting proffered by two elderly ladies sitting with suitcases at their feet. In response to this rebuff they looked at one another and hunched their shoulders. Plainly their wait for the boat was not to be enlivened by social intercourse with this fellow.

Herman stood up on the seating to look at a print of the Hudson Falls. Pictures of such fuming torrents fascinated him. His father had taken to bringing home maritime scenes on his return from transatlantic business trips and there were many suchlike in his grandfather's home at Boston, although the most compelling family antiquity was a bottle filled with tea leaves that the Major claimed to have found at the bottom of his boots after playing his part as one of the invading Mohawks at the Boston Tea Party. Herman was something of a favourite with his Boston grand-parents and the Major had picked him out, rather than Gansevoort or Allan, to be the recipient of his old man's memories, a selection which had an effect akin to the Biblical handing on of a birthright. This night, alone with his father on a storm-shaken dock, at the moment of family ruin, enhanced the boy's belief in himself as chosen son, so that despite the element of maternal betrayal there was a compensating warmth in the experience.

It was none too warm a night, though, in the draught-ridden waiting-room and the boiler had not yet been given its winter flame. Mr. Melville decided to go to the office to see if he could discover how much longer the boat would be delayed.

"You won't get anything out of them," said one of the ladies when he had told them of his intentions and asked them to keep watch over Herman.

"No, the office clerk was most brusque with Dorothea."

"Yes, a frightful man. Disgustingly uncouth. I expect he's gone home by now, or is stewing himself in a tavern."

"He reeked of drink as it was. If all the company workers are like him I think it better we travel up-river by horse and carriage."

"You see what you can find out anyway."

"Yes, they might talk better to a man. Now, my dear, what is your name?"

It was 7 a.m. before the boat left the dock. Allan and Herman had spent part of the night in a nearby hotel, the proprietor of which had kindly said, in reply to a request made by Allan on behalf of the two old ladies, that coffee could be taken in the lounge. In the event they refused to believe that the boat would be subject to so serious a delay and, scared of missing it, refused to budge from the waiting room. When father and son returned from their hour or so of warmth and comfort the ladies were stonily silent. Allan made Herman lie down on the varnished seat and covered him in his own overcoat.

Towards morning more passengers arrived, either turning up for a later boat, or having received correct information regarding the delay. The boat docked at Albany at eleven o'clock and by midday the Melville family was fully assembled at their new residence.

Despite the winding-up of the business many urgent debts had been left unpaid in New York, including the last quarter's rent for the house on Broadway and Allan felt himself pursued for the rest of the year and was consequently forced to borrow both from Peter and his own father, although Peter would later claim to have been the sole benefactor of his sister's family.

The children went to school – Herman and Gansevoort to the prestigious Albany Academy. Maria busied herself with social engagements, and Allan tried foolishly to recoup his former standing by devoting a pointless amount of energy to the fur business. Pointless, because all his early industry had been fired by Maria's social ambitions and these, now that she was amongst her own family and associates and in a lesser metropolis, were nowhere near so keen.

There was a short let-up in Allan's endeavours that summer, when he and Maria drove by stage with Herman and Augusta to Uncle Thomas' at Pittsfield. Thomas was a "bit of a character". His first wife, a French girl named Françoise, had died very young, but he had nine children by a second marriage. He frequently went to jail for petty debts.

The road to his farm lined with elms, and the larch-shaded porch looking across the meadows to South Mountain, became elemental images of Herman's boyhood and he was to remember this particular trip as one of the few manifestations, and definitely the last, of relaxed masculine zest in his father. The two brothers embraced at the end of the summer day's travel by stage, with the kind of boyish warmth to be found in a Van Dyck painting.

Despite the vacation, by the end of the year Allan was in the depths of a profound exhaustion, of the kind that would not allow him to sleep, nor to halt his fevered rationalizations. On January 5th of the New Year he marked in his Bible verses 4 and 5 of Psalm 55: "The terrors of death are fallen upon me." On January 9th occurred the first indication that his mind was going.

He was confined to the house, and the following day presented the melancholy spectacle of a deranged man. Brother Thomas rushed to Albany on the eleventh to find him "maniacal". He stayed at his side for the full protraction of the illness, without hope, and with no desire for it. He wrote to one of his brother's closest friends, the lawyer Lemuel Shaw, that he ought not to hope for Allan's recovery "for in all human probability he would live a MANIAC!"

During the most severe spells of derangement family attendants would find subtle ways of restraining Maria from being at her

94

husband's side. But not so the boys, whose withdrawal would make Allan writhe and rage and send bedside trayfuls onto the floor. Not that he was truly bedridden until the last few days of the illness. The most fearsome times were when he sat motionless in a chair, eyes wide open and focused upon a distant horror of the unknown life. The boys then, together with Uncle Thomas, took up successive stations of vigil. Gansevoort at this time was sixteen, Herman was twelve; a difference in years which dictated differing degrees of emotional response – Gansevoort's more immediate, Herman's more deepset.

Allan Melville died at 11.30 p.m. on Saturday January 28th 1832, and was buried the next Tuesday in the common burying ground of the local Dutch church. Before two months were past Gansevoort had left school and was, on Maria's account, carrying on the fur and cap business and feeling duly important because of it. Herman, who also had to leave the Albany Academy, was more able to indulge in a mood of mourning and less able to find a compensating air of importance in the position of junior clerk that was found for him before his thirteenth birthday at the Albany branch of the New York State Bank. He also felt some discomfort at the way in which the mantle of firstborn son had been bypassed, a discomfort compounded by the experience of the summer.

In the middle of July the Melville family fled a cholera outbreak in Albany and went to stay with Uncle Thomas in Pittsfield, where the accumulated number of children rose, at a stroke, to seventeen. They arrived on July 14th. Two days later Peter Gansevoort wrote to his sister regarding Herman's position at the bank. It appears that his absence from duty endangered his future employment, for, despite the continuing threat of contagious disease, the lad was packed off forthwith on a return stage to Albany. It was July 18th. He had been in Pittsfield less than four days.

Forced to stay with an uncle he disliked (to put in blandly); banished from an uncle he loved; spending his thirteenth birthday in isolation from his brothers and sisters; performing tedious paperwork amongst colleagues much older than himself; receiving nothing but admonitory letters from his mother regarding the care he must take to avoid the cholera; and simply stuck in boring Albany when he could be under the Pittsfield elms; these would have been unendurable but for the newly discovered pleasures of solitude and an immersion in the books of James Fenimore Cooper. It was not, then, a happy summer, but an important one.

In the first part of September a fire broke out opposite his grandfather's residence in Boston. The Major took it upon himself to pass out flasks of hot coffee to the firemen and in so doing caught a chill which terminated in acute and uncontrollable diarrhoea. He died on the sixteenth of the month.

For Herman the event was significant beyond the sadness which it brought. He had felt great affection for his grandfather, but boys are always ready to accept the demise of old men.

One of the three executors of the Major's will was Lemuel Shaw, and a messy, acrimonious job it turned out to be, since the considerable sums of money that Allan had borrowed from his father had been conducted as strict business transactions and one in particular had been paid direct to, and endorsed by, Maria. The legal upshot of this was that complainants against the Major's estate claimed "authority to sell the share or proportion of the said Allan Melville's estate of his father the testator for the purpose of securing and realising the amount due from him by notes and other securities".

All through the spring and summer of 1833, while Mr. Hawthorne dallied with his fisherman's daughter and the first signs of a new financial panic became evident, the wrangling went on. The air had been cleared somewhat by the death in April of the Major's wife, Priscilla, but Maria continued to take the affair personally, grumbling about the utter desertion of her children by the grandparents.

*   *   *

Eighteen thirty-four began. Sophia and Mary Peabody were in Cuba. Helen Melville prepared to undergo an operation on her lame leg, a disability with a precise physical cause, unlike the strange affliction suffered by Mr. Hawthorne. Gansevoort wrote avidly in a New Year Journal. And still there had been no resolution of the financial situation.

It was a better year, however, for Herman. Although not yet fifteen, his abrupt initiation into the world of wage-earning had matured him beyond his years. Gansevoort was disconcerted one Friday night in March when, on a trip to Schenactady (the next town northward up the Hudson River) he had stumbled upon Herman in company with a Mr. Leake. The two of them had been sent there on bank's business and were whiling away time in Davis's bar-room.

Herman had already been treated to two small tankards of beer and perhaps because of this it was the older brother who found himself most embarrassed by the chance encounter.

Mr. Leake spotted the ill-at-ease young man. "Herman, your brother's tracked you down."

Herman turned, and seeing Gansevoort, didn't hesitate to call him over.

"Hello, Herman."

"This is Mr. Leake. The bank sent us up here on a little business."

"And we're having to wait for a car. Can I buy you a drink?"

Gansevoort, glancing at Herman's glass, now almost empty, declined, and after a moment or more's polite conversation concerning the state of the fur business he explained that he had an appointment to meet a friend and departed.

Mr. Leake immediately bought Herman a third glass of beer, while outside, in the cold evening air, Gansevoort made sluggish progress towards the house of Hiram Haight. He makes an interesting, almost a tragic study, does Gansevoort, and we shall be hearing more of him yet. The interlude in the bar-room sets the two brothers in very typical relief.

Yes, it was a better year for Herman; in the main because he spent much of it in Pittsfield helping his Uncle Thomas through a period of physical incapacity, raking in the hayfield and smoking his first cigars with cousin Robert in the hayloft, and although the following Spring found him working at Gansevoort's store, Maria made it perfectly clear that his assistance was a temporary measure and that he was not being groomed for a business partnership; so that even when the crash of 1837 left Gansevoort bankrupt and the family was once more thrown into financial crisis, Herman's adolescent development took its own course and again he spent a good portion of the year in Pittsfield, strengthening his comradeship with Robert and, in the Fall of that year, taking up a teaching appointment at the Sikes District School.

Herman was absent in May of 1838 when Maria and her children were driven to move out of Albany, to a lesser abode in the tiny township of Lansingburgh. Uncle Peter seems at last to have become exasperated by Maria's constant requests for loans and by her irrepressible desire to keep up appearances, so that when she wrote from the new house requesting a hundred dollars for the purchase of blinds, he replied that she would better have done without the blinds than give her landlord the unfounded notion that she had means to pay the rent in advance. But he sent the money.

Herman, when he visited the new home during the July break, felt an unequivocal separation from the domestic circumstances he found himself among. He was approaching nineteen years of age and his current employment had placed him securely on the threshold of an independent life, but schoolteaching was not a lucrative occupation and he had no thoughts of remaining in it for any length of time. He had already begun to speak of going to sea and now requested Gansevoort to use what influence he had with the shipping traders of New York to secure for him a position on board a sailing vessel bound for England.

In the meantime he returned to Pittsfield sooner than he had need. He no longer stayed with his uncle and cousins but, so that he was within walking distance of the school, had taken up lodgings in a remote house located on the summit of a "savage mountain", or so he liked his mother to believe.

* * *

He had a poky attic room with a marvellous view of the valley cut out from the roof. The window was shuttered, not glazed, but when the shutter was closed beams of light slid through cracks at its ill-fitting edges. In the winter, as a new guest, he had been too embarrassed to keep asking for oil for his lamp and had spent much time reading his school books downstairs, and making the acquaintance of Mr. Tyson, the residing landlord.

Tyson was a lean Yankee who, since the death of his wife, had raised a family of twelve with the help of the older girls, one or two of whom performed menial tasks at neighbouring homesteads. None of the boys was yet of an age to earn a living, and five of the middle children were Herman's own pupils, but there was a strict understanding that school was school and it wasn't to be brought into the home.

It was ridiculous really that they should agree to take a lodger (an approach had been made through Uncle Thomas on Herman's behalf) and overcrowd their dwelling still further. Three children had had to be squeezed elsewhere in order to free the attic room and certainly there couldn't have been much profit left from the rent he paid, for their hospitality was prolific. Mr. Tyson may have been lean but he had the appetite of a gannet and had educated his children in like manner. The bounteous bulk that passed through their fourteen bodies each digestive round was testimony to God's fecundity.

"You've lost weight, boy. What's that mother bin doing with you? Ah, if there was a mother in this house we'd all be more solid-boned. Kath, you'd best fetch Mr. Melville a bowlful of something. Now, how's things? That brother of yours any better?"

Gansevoort had been living and working alone in New York for some months and had been in Lansingburgh to rest off a bout of nervous excitement, which had given rise to talk amongst the relatives that he might be suffering from an inherited proclivity towards brain fever.

"He will be. Just been working too hard, trying to get the whole family back on its feet."

"Huh! I could tell him a thing or two about that. Anyway, he'd better have more flesh on him than you. A tough old business it is, being father to a family. I know your mother's still alive, but she can't be expected to provide."

"Our uncle's been very good."

"Generous, I suppose. With loans of money and all that. I'll tell you something for free. I don't let anyone give *me* hospitality. It'll backfire one day. Never lend, never borrow. That's our creed, up on this mountaintop."

"But if people like to help out, especially if it's their own family . . ."

"We're all one family, ain't we? But I bet your mother wouldn't accept so much as a parcel of morsels from the likes of me. Nope, you just need faith in the Good Lord. He'll provide for those that's got the guts and stamina to make it on theirs own. We don't do so badly here. Well, do we?"

"No. Proudly."

"Not a crumb that we swallow ain't been reared, sowed or paid for by us-selves. Look how he handles the critters. Any that don't pass muster, well, you know as well as I do, it's tough out there, tense and scary. This country started to grow up tough. Seems to me there's too much paper money. People are soft with paper money. Here she comes. This lass'll make someone a fine mother. But I don't want to lose her yet, so you'd better not have aims in that direction."

Herman blushed and busied himself with eating the thick vegetable broth. Kath was roughly his own age and not unpretty but he had not once looked at her in a romantic light.

"Did you hear about the explosion at the gunpowder plant?" Herman pursed his lips and raised his brow in query. "It went up a week or so ago. Thought for a while old Graylock had turned volcano. There are some 'at says it was on purpose too. And that there are one or more government spies arrived amongst us to wheedle out the perpetrators. It'd be easy enough for them to slip in amongst the summer travellers. He's finished, Kath. Better bring him some more bread, the feller's been on starvation diet judging by the rate he downed the soup."

Kath fetched the plate off Herman's lap.

"That was splendid."

"He's only trying to woo you, girl. You can do better than a bankrupt clerk turned schoolmaster."

*   *   *

Mr. Hawthorne was likewise being waited upon by a local Berkshire beauty – a flighty young country hoyden by the name of Eliza Cheeseboro. He had been in Pittsfield itself up until a week ago (indeed there are some who, citing evidence that he travelled under a pseudonym, believe he may have been acting as one of the government agents referred to by Mr. Tyson) but he had now removed himself a short distance to the village of North Adams, and stayed at the inn run by the same cantankerous cripple who was to provoke such a stir amongst Mrs. Morewood's retinue of mountaineers.

Eliza, giving her usual substantial attentions to various favourites, reminded one guest of his promise to carry her home with him over the mountain.

"I'd make you fat old so-and-so puff a bit."

"Give me a big enough piece of the pie my dear and I'll puff my heart out for you."

His friends roared, but Eliza shouted them down. "I suppose you'll be wanting the whole pie for yourself."

"And why not, I can manage it."

"Come on, Liza, pass it around a bit."

"That's the girl – a fair helping for us all."

"Behave yourselves. Whatever is the new guest to think?"

"He looks ready for a piece as well."

There were more roars; Mr. Hawthorne blushed and tidied the cutlery on the plate left empty from his first course.

"Take no notice of the coarse old country codgers. Will you have a piece of pie?"

"Yes, please."

One of the others, behind Eliza's back, rose from his place and, wimpishly going up to another, mocked: "Will you have another piece of pie?"

"Oh, yes. And a helping of arse to go with it."

Eliza put the whole pie dish down on Mr. Hawthorne's table, with a crash that made it bounce, and turning to the rest like an angry school ma'am said, "Behave yourselves now. We'll have no more of *that*."

The men bowed their heads like sulky dogs and ate their pie, looking up over their spoons in big-eyed, burlesque contrition.

Mr. Hawthorne returned to his room as soon as the meal was over, and proceeded to write in his Journal, describing both local characters such as still made merry below and geographical features such as Hudson's Cave and the Notch, both of which he visited more than once. There is something strange about these long, lifeless studies. They paint a picture of a lonely vacationer obsessed with anonymous observations, many of them isolated jottings stored away for future use – "The shadows of water-insects as they swim in pools of a stream". It was characteristic of Mr. Hawthorne all his life to use his Journals as a storyteller's depository but it was normal during his summer jaunts for a narrative momentum to carry him over from day to day, so that observations became more context-bound. It was also usual for him to be more sociable, to enter into conversations and extract little biographies from those he met. There *is* the odd story here, but overheard rather than drawn forth by his own promptings.

Why this studied inwardness? It is not yet the "year of years" which sees the full burgeoning of the love between Mr. Hawthorne and Sophia Peabody, but they have met socially once or twice and he already knows that, if he so wishes, he can make her his. More probable, therefore, than intimations that he was operating as an undercover agent, is the proposition that his observational obstinacy was a form of bracing himself for a change in life. The earlier months of the year had been more sociable than any he had previously experienced in Salem. He had been out walking with

101

the two Elizabeths (his own sister and Sophia's sister) on numerous occasions. Miss Peabody made it known, as we have seen before, that she considered herself the custodian of his talent; indeed, following the death of his friend Cilley, the two of them had had a fierce row concerning his political friends, Elizabeth making it clear that in her mind such associations were detrimental to his work and character, and she continued to press him into taking up some form of government employment. There was a natural tension between the two young women, and on some afternoons Miss Hawthorne would refuse to come out for a walk, blaming her reluctance on the wind, the sun, or clouds in the south.

For some considerable time Mr. Hawthorne continued to hear more about Sophia than see much of her, though by now the two of them *had* set eyes upon one another, and during one of Elizabeth's spells out of town had walked abroad together. An impression of the emotional conflict thus caused can be gained from a letter which Sophia wrote to Elizabeth at some point in the earlier half of the year.

> After dinner Mary went out to take the fresh, intending to finish the afternoon by a walk with Miss Hawthorne, and I commissioned her to bring home both her and her brother, if he should go, that I might give him my fragrant violets. Just after seven, Mr. Hawthorne came. He looked very brilliant. His coming here is one sure way of keeping you in mind, and it must be excessively tame for him after his experience in your society and conversation, so that I think you will shine the more by contrast.

The letter oozes sisterly betrayal and it is easy to imagine how smartly Elizabeth would have pooh-poohed such twaddle as "his coming here is one sure way of keeping you in mind". It also explains the ponderous manner of Mr. Hawthorne this summer. Elizabeth had expressly told him that Sophia's "condition" condemned her to a life of sisterly spinsterdom, so that if he were to set his sights on the younger sister it would not only be a romantic rebuff to Elizabeth, it would represent also a total and churlish disregard of family advice.

And so it was that although his eye and pen were aimed at the Berkshire surroundings, in the pretence of creating some neutral space within which to make a decision, his heart, which had no doubt as to what it resolved, kept up a suitor's vigil outside the house on Charter Street.

*   *   *

Back on the mountainside Melville sat up late with Tyson, listening to more homespun philosophies. It was Wednesday night. He had until after the weekend to prepare for work and intended reading for a second time John O'Taylor's *District School*, which had been a Christmas present from Uncle Peter, and in its graphic portrayal of the evils alleged to exist in Common schools made consoling reading for any young teacher who had found schoolmastering a less straightforward business than anticipated. He hiked about during the rest of his free time, alternate days of which he spent going into Pittsfield or striding out on his own into the hills. Cousin Robert was betrothed to be married a month hence and was making strenuous work of the final days of courting, so that Melville was deprived of masculine companionship. More often than not, on his hiking days, he would set off in the direction of Graylock, and might sometimes have taken the Adams stage to speed him closer to its ranges.

On August 15th he attended the Commencement at Williamstown College, an annual event marking the start of a new college year, which had become an occasion of great social merriment for the local population, with academic involvement peripheral. The rival societies at the college would wear pink or blue buttonholes and there was a form of ritual reception for new students, but otherwise it was a day for street dancing, peddling, and tavern-drinking.

Melville's own school year had begun at the start of the week, but he had been given leave to close for the day and to accompany any pupils who wished to go to Williamstown. Several of them had already made plans to attend with their families whilst others, including the Tyson children, were positively hostile to the invitation.

"I don't want any children of mine – and nor do other right-minded folk round here – getting notions from dandies with pink daisies in their jackets. If I was you I'd keep the school open and let those that want to stay do some good honest learning." That was all Mr. Tyson had to say on the matter.

The weather had turned wet and windy at the weekend and the

schoolhouse was already redolent of the previous winter. When Melville woke on this Wednesday morning, and opened his attic shutter, which had rattled through the night and allowed him only a fitful sleep, it was as if he were looking at the world through several layers of poor quality tracing paper. Fog was a permanent aspect of the region's weather; although in the summer months it was often the harbinger of a fine day, particularly in the depths of the valleys, there was something too oozy, too dripping about this one to allow much hope of a blue sky.

After breakfast Tyson made a show of giving each child a list of chores for the day, as if to stress the frivolity of his guest's plans, so that once Melville had ensured that he was adequately clothed, he set off down towards the road along which the North Adams stage travelled. He assumed there would be extra public carriage this day, and many private barouches prepared to offer wayfarers a lift, but it was still early, and he would be happy enough to walk much of the way.

Mr. Hawthorne, being the closer, arrived at the Commencement proceedings first. Despite the grim weather, there was a considerable gathering of people and, possibly because of the weather, a number of the men were already the worse for liquor. One in particular was very riotous in the crowd, elbowing people aside until at last a ring was formed and another that he had unwisely antagonised challenged him to a wrestle. The match was ended at the first throw, which came sooner than most in the crowd had had time to procure a decent view.

The weather, although still overcast, had turned warm, and those that did not quench their thirst on cider or beer were burying their muzzles deep in the flesh of juicy water melons. This was particularly true of the blacks, who were there in surprisingly large number. (Massachusetts had never been a slave state, but the neighbouring New York had.) Mr. Hawthorne amused himself for some good half hour by studying this contingent in his adopted manner. Most striking was the degree to which the younger amongst them – well dressed and aspiring to decency – cast looks of scorn, shame or sorrow at those few of their elders who, in drunken or merely joyous liberation, gave vent to the sort of grimaces and ridiculous antics assumed by many to be characteristic of their race.

Not before feeling overwhelmed by the increasing humidity, and beginning to despair of ever completing the walk, Mr.

Melville had been picked up by a Pittsfield family, one of the daughters of which he was vaguely acquainted with, through Robert's wife-to-be. There were three young ladies in all, and room was made for him in the rear of the barouche next to the one he knew best. The other two whispered and giggled together and turned round occasionally with looks which tried to impose romantic significance to the seating arrangement. They were a farming family, and the yeoman status of the girls was given away by their sunburnt necks in contiguity with the delicate fabric of their dress; which was fortunate, for if his companion had been a lady of any refinement Melville would have been deeply embarrassed by the antics of her sisters. As it was he knew her as a cowhand and petty blasphemer.

On arriving at Williamstown the family extended an invitation to "Herman" to join them for the duration of the Commencement but he excused himself by claiming that he had arranged to meet up with some of his older school pupils.

As he was making his first tentative steps through the crowd, a bat, flying blindly about in the sultry half-light, settled on his arm and proceeded to creep up towards the shoulder. He allowed interested people in the crowd a moment's look at it before shrugging the creature clear. The bat had left a scattering of dust on his sleeve, which he banged off with his hand. A puff of uncleanness rose and fell in the damp air.

"Roll over – stroll over – bowl over – get yourselves over. Don't shake off your bat-grime entirely, sir. Devil's snow can be mighty fortunate in little doses. Come on everyone. Roll over – stroll over . . ."

A peddler was setting out his wares and Melville was among the first to join the bystanders.

"We're selling everything in mixed lots today – at rates knocked down beyond reason – you couldn't afford to steal them at the price – the remorse of conscience would cost ye more. Here we are then" (reaching into his boxes) "to get us started – a paper of pins, a lead pencil and a shaving box. The three items for ninepence. No paper money please."

In succeeding lots appeared cakes of shaving soap, bracelets, wooden combs, boxes of loco-focos and suspenders. A noticeable tactic was to mix up masculine and feminine items in one batch so that the purchaser was forced to buy at least one article he or she would not normally use. The majority of transactions were made by men, though they were often goaded into it by female companions, and the peddler made good mileage out of such market forces by drawing private debate out into the open.

"Won't he shift yet, my dear – I'm sure you can promise him a little favour in return. Quiet now, while she whispers it in his ear." Or, using a different tack, "I can see by your face sir, you are a miserly customer. Observe the narrowness of his nostrils. See how he pinches the very air he breathes." Occasionally such a target would walk away in angry outrage, but more often than not they responded in the desired manner. And the peddler would say, "There's the lucky man," and slap the purchaser on the back in friendly glee, to make up for the rudeness of his bargaining.

After a while he began to titillate the crowd by pretending that his boxes of jewellery and suspenders were empty. He would hold up a small lot of pencils and steel pens and, losing his humour temporarily, would baldly state a price and threaten that the auction would not continue before that lot was sold. Women wasted themselves in wailing beseechments.

Mr. Hawthorne, who had joined the rear of the crowd, made a bid for one such collection of writing implements. He passed his money forward, and the pens and pencils came back the other way. Melville played a part in this conveyancing procedure, handling both the money and the pens, without setting sight upon the bidder. Probably each of us, by examining the friendships of our maturity, can cast back and find them strangely premonitioned in close but unapprehended encounters in the past. What part these play in the mysterious merging process which brings certain of us together in "fated" friendships is interesting to ponder.

By the time the peddler had stopped his trading and had taken himself off to the tavern, Mr. Hawthorne and Melville were already there. The bar-room was crowded and each was standing at some distance from the other. The landlord, thinking that the mist and dullness betokened November weather, had lit a huge fire, obviously intended to last the entire day. Many, whose garments had become wet or damp, were standing right over it and smoking in the fireside heat.

Mr. Hawthorne was thinking of Eliza Cheeseboro. He was too intimidated by her saucy boldness to be much interested in her romantically, but he could not help but wonder what kind of a wife she would make for a man and what kind of a character would be best suited to match up with hers. Elizabeth Peabody had made much of the theory that successful marriages depended upon a complementary adjustment of personalities – one partner's forcefulness to be balanced by the other's tractability. It did not escape him that this doctrine bolstered objections to Sophia as a partner, on the grounds that the two of them were too similar, particularly in their reclusiveness.

Eliza had been involved in a strange affair of stealing early in the morning, before his departure for the Commencement. A justice of the peace had entered the breakfast room and, together with a witness, had gone up to a lady of forty or upwards, who had come to take passage by stage and was siting there by virtue of its being the warmest haven from dispiriting weather. The commotion had been orderly up until the arrival of the hunchbacked proprietor, whereupon there was a noisy rising from chairs. Eliza was told to fetch Laura the chambermaid and the two of them ordered to search the suspect from head to foot, inside and out.

Apart from the inevitable table gossip, Mr. Hawthorne might have discovered nothing more of certainty about the incident had he not, half an hour later, while dressing himself for his day out at Williamstown, overhead Eliza and Laura in conversation beneath his window. The woman had been accused of stealing a needlecase and other trifles from a factory girl at a boarding house. Apparently, her undergarments belied the ladylike image of her outer aspect and manners, and a quantity of hard liquor had been found in her handbox.

Laura – I feel sick; her body will haunt me the rest of my life.

Eliza – My, didn't it reek.

Laura – All yellow and withered, like a dead bird.

Eliza – You know what I heard someone say about you? That it was enough to make anyone's eyes start square out of their head to look up at such red cheeks as yours.

Laura – And I used to wish so that the ruddiness would fade and leave me pale and ladylike. Not any more. Do you think she was innocent?

Eliza – We didn't find anything, did we?

Laura – No, but the justice hardly told us what we were looking for. There were some queer bits there, in the handbox.

Eliza – And she'd have given it all up bar the spirit flask. Poor thing. Let us find husbands quick before we end up like her. It's easy to be harsh, but what kind of a life does a woman on her own

107

lead, when it comes to it, and her cheeks no longer burn?

And thus did Mr. Hawthorne consider her prospects, somewhat pessimistically deciding that within the small society of North Adams she would probably succumb in desperation to a portly-paunched, brandy-burnt bodach considerably older than herself. It would take an exceptional young man, possessing sufficient confidence of bearing, to give her a proper sense of wifely servitude.

Melville, in another part of the bar-room, considered marital matters too – in particular, the consequences of his cousin's betrothal which had more or less spelt the end of their friendship. The conflict between romantic love and masculine camaraderie was to cast an abiding shadow on his temperament but there would be a long period, beyond this midday, before he would again feel the pangs of juxtaposition.

"Remember them! Remember! Remember your dreams . . ."

The peddler, in conversation with a group of seated men, had suddenly raised his voice, so that all in the tavern could hear. Evidently the conversation had been proceeding at crossed purposes for the men made sundry replies which provoked from the peddler a pained bellow.

– "Ay, we'd have prettier wives if dreams weren't lies."

– "And tumble as many young milkmaids as bent their buttocks awards us."

– "Work up a flush on a virgin's collarbone."

– "Doing things to a lady in a covered barouche while her husband drives for home."

"The dreams of your youth, you fools! Remember your hopes and aspirations!"

– "No different, feller."

– "The same old pulp."

"You dreamed of this? Did you dream of nothing more?"

And, while ever-increasing permutations of this question poured from his mouth, the peddler, pronounced insane by an instant majority opinion, was lifted upright into the air and taken outside, his bags of wares thrown at his feet.

The incident did not immediately affect either Melville or Mr. Hawthorne. The world was fuller then of noisy eccentrics, but the peddler's admonition was to reverberate more strongly in the younger man's heart, though we must leave him now until the latter half of the next decade.

In June 1839, his brother's contacts having borne fruit, the nineteen year old set sail for Liverpool. The next five years were his sea-going ones and interested readers had best turn to Mr. Melville's own books, for we are not going to don lifejackets and join him in the tossings and turbulences of the liquid element.

*   *   *

In January of 1839 Mr. Hawthorne was appointed to the Boston Custom House as measurer of coal and salt at a salary of fifteen hundred dollars. The appointment was directly attributable to the machinations of Elizabeth and she must have felt that the successful culmination of her efforts subjected Mr. Hawthorne to a significant emotional claim. She had been able to bring her plan to fruition by virtue of a fortuitous marriage struck the previous summer by one of her Boston friends – a widow, Mrs Bliss, who had married the historian George Bancroft, recently appointed leader of the Democratic party in Massachusetts and Collector for the port of Boston.

The marriage took place in that summer and the newly combined family of four children (two plus two) set up house in Winthrop Place. By this time Bancroft was a wealthy man, the paper value of his riches amounting to seventy five thousand dollars.

The precise debt that Mr. Hawthorne owed Miss Peabody is complicated by the fact that a year previously Horatio Bridge had written to Bancroft requesting a job for Hawthorne. It is, at the least, unlikely that a man newly appointed to a position of influence would have made appointments at the suggestion of his wife without there being additional advocacy of the candidate.

In any event, here is Mr. Hawthorne, already five weeks into the job, making his first Journal entry on the theme of employment:

> Yesterday and the day before, measuring a load of coal from the schooner Thomas Lowder of St. John's, New Brunswick. A little black, dirty vessel. The coal stowed in the hold so as to fill the schooner full, and make her a solid mass of black mineral.

He does not bother repeating the details of his daily round and entries soon turn to talk at the Custom House – talk about ghosts and temperance. But even entries such as these dwindle to undated observations of "objects on a wharf" or the names of schooners as opposed to other vessels. The truth of the matter is that he and Sophia were now exchanging letters in which their love for one another is openly and ardently disclosed. Mr. Hawthorne made several weekend visits to Salem, away from his dreary Boston room. The courtship began in earnest and the Journal, his occupation and any plans for story writing all give up pride of place to the object of his endearments.

In addition, Mr. Hawthorne found himself pretty much exhausted at the end of the day. He had been won over by Elizabeth's enthusiasm for the position, and had taken it up believing that he would be able to carry on writing every evening after work, drawing, as she had put it, upon the rich material that life along the docks was bound to throw up. Not the least wearing aspect of the job was the continual need to wash and bathe away the coal dust. He was not unhappy, though. It is comfortable for a man newly in love to pursue menial and regular labour during the early period of romance. Such demands upon his time enhance the moments spent together and the sense of being gainfully and respectably employed greatly diminishes certain mental agitations.

Early in May he had a weekday off work. He had known of it some time in advance and, planning a pleasant surprise for Sophia, had murmured nothing of it to her. The weather, which in April had turned dry and warm – a mixed blessing, since it made the dust more pervasive – was now in the midst of a seasonal backlash. Mr. Hawthorne had an aversion for flannel vests and so wore two shirts, one on top of the other. Thus clad, he set off for Salem early, hoping to spend the whole day with his beloved. But when he arrived at Charter Street it was only to be told that Sophia was in Boston, spending a night or two at the home of Caroline Sturgis. He could not help being somewhat amused that his secret scheming had met with such a cruel irony. It had not been easy playing the part of the trickster and he had felt real fear when ringing the Peabody bell. What if Sophia were to be badly shaken by the visit? Or she might simply have made her own plans for the day – a painting, a sculpture – and be irritated by their disturbance. She might be in the midst of a headache and be unable to throw it off without due warning. Yes, the more Mr. Hawthorne pondered, the more it appeared to him that Fate had managed things kindly. Nevertheless he made every effort to get back to

110

Boston at the earliest possible moment. Even so, he arrived at the Sturgis house too late in the evening to contemplate taking Sophia out, so he merely left a card at the door making an appointment for eight o'clock the next morning outside the Atheneum gallery. He went back to his room, took off his two shirts, marvelled at his clean body and, weary from the to and fro travelling, went early to bed.

The next day was horribly gusty. He put on two shirts again, and went out in his winter coat. Sophia was waiting ahead of him, standing a step or two up at the front of the gallery. She waved eagerly and ran to meet him. They did not embrace but joined hands in a bundle of fingers and knuckles.

"How did you know I was in Boston? Are you an archangel spying on my every move?"

"I wish I were. It would have saved all my journeying yesterday. No, I went to Salem."

"To see me! But your work!"

"I had a day off. They give us so many a year."

Sophia let out a pained squeak.

"What is it?"

"I have been wicked. And God has punished my furtiveness. I knew I was coming to Boston but said nothing in my letters. I hoped we might walk by the wharves and catch sight of you while you worked."

"I was secretive too."

"You knew about your holiday?"

"Yes."

They looked at one another with a mock sternness. "We each have every right to be rather cross," she said, and laughed. The wind, gusting with an extra force, threw them off balance. Mr. Hawthorne immediately insisted that he escort her straight back to the Sturgis house. She should not be out in such weather, especially so early in the day.

Sophia found a new lease of physical strength this spring and early summer and chafed against just this kind of protectiveness. One day, a month later, writing a letter from Salem, she said, "When some other callers had departed, came Mr. Hawthorne. It was a powerful east wind and he would not let me go out." And yet, with Elizabeth's warnings still ringing in his ear, we can quite understand Mr. Hawthorne's caution. Besides, such gentlemanly concern was a part of the courting pattern. Still, their relationship

could no longer be described as tentative. Moving ahead one more
month we find Mr. Hawthorne writing:

> *Mine own*, we *are* married! I felt it long ago; and sometimes
> when I am seeking the fondest word, it has been on my
> lips to call you 'wife'. Are we not married? God knows we
> are.

In the same letter, however, he declared that they should seal their
lips to the world, lest the world misjudge them.

*   *   *

Mr. Hawthorne resigned his post in January 1841. It is by no
means certain, with the change in political ascendancy resulting
from the success of Harrison's *Hard Cider/Log Cabin* campaign,
that he would have held on to it anyway. He gave it up in order to
join Brook Farm, a communal settlement situated at West Rox-
bury and founded by George Ripley. Mr. Hawthorne had
attended the Ripley debates held at the new bookshop opened by
Elizabeth Peabody at number thirteen, West Street, Boston and
there can be no doubt that he joined the collective in full anticipation of setting up home with Sophia there. He had worked and
saved hard for two years, and now sunk all his capital into the
project. Why should a man, deeply in love, and considering
marriage, join a commune? It is not difficult to hazard an answer.
Love makes men idealistic. At one and the same time they like to
steal away with their beloved and then, having enjoyed physical
and spiritual intimacies, to mix again with the multitude. In Mr.
Hawthorne's case there may also have been some lingering
unease, springing from Elizabeth's warnings, that his young wife
would prove more of the invalid than expected, coupled with a
straightforward craving for conviviality and brotherhood after so
many friendless years.

By early 1842 the "engagement" had reached the crisis point
common to long courtships. Mr. Hawthorne, who by now realised
there would be no place for the two of them at Brook Farm, was
forced to confess in one of his letters to Sophia – a confessional tone
pervades many of his letters during this period – that he had not
yet informed his mother of the engagement "because of the strange
reserve in matters of feeling that has always existed among us". It

is a mark of Sophia's spirit and impatience that she immediately took it upon herself to write to Nathaniel's mother with the news.

Mr. Hawthorne left the Farm and married Sophia on July 9th 1842 – the same day that Herman Melville, and his friend Toby, deserted ship in Nukehuia.

*　　*　　*

After Brook Farm Mr. Hawthorne had arrived back at his mother's house financially ruined, without any hope of setting up, from his own resources, a marital establishment. And yet, by their wedding day, a large old parsonage in Concord had been made available to them, with even a pre-planted vegetable patch waiting to be harvested.

Mr. Hawthorne had visited the house in early June, to look it over. The clergyman had lived there for sixty uninterrupted years and the rooms showed all the dust and disarray that might be supposed to have gathered round him in the course of that time. It had required some energy of imagination to conceive the idea of transforming such a musty edifice, where the good old minister had been writing sleepy sermons for more than half a century, into a comfortable modern residence. He had returned to Sophia in trepidation and sought not to exaggerate the solemnity of their prospective dwelling.

He need not have worried. The challenge of refurbishing such a place fired her artistic enthusiasm. Hers was the organising influence and Nathaniel was happy enough to take orders, although not so happy with her insistence, three weeks after taking possession of the house, that he venture at last into the study. The combination of manual labour and sexual union promoted an empty and ungoading lethargy and there was little impulse to write. "What is there to write about at all? Happiness has no succession of events; because it is no part of eternity." He did write; but only in his Journal.

As older furnishings gave way to such modernisms as astral lamps, gilded Cologne bottles, silver taper-stands and alabaster card-vases, one relic of the previous occupancy remained upon the mantelpiece. It was a stuffed owl, its feathers sized in undisturbed dust.

"Nathaniel, the thing is hideous. It cannot stay."

"But look at the expression, the way it pulls its beak into its chest, fearing the very banishment you suggest."

"Then take it to your study, and be two wise birds together."

"I fear its sulky eyes would fret me still, and even more so if behind my back. I do not like to see the haughty thing so sullen."

"Then let us despatch it to the wild again."

Mr. Hawthorne went up to the bird and addressed Sophia's proposition directly to the creature. "No," he turned, "there is no apparent hunger for escape. Rather, it has kept too long to this imprisoned perch; it fears its freedom, fears its life."

" 'Thaniel! Silly." Sophia came up close. "The thing is dead. Its eyes are glass!"

"Then you must be its bailiff."

Surprising her husband, Sophia lifted the bird off the mantelpiece and ran with it at arms' length out of the room. Mr. Hawthorne pursued her, out of the house and round to the vegetable garden, which had been planted for them in advance of their arrival by Mr. Thoreau. Sophia stood on the edge of the lawn's kerb, breathless and flushed. The owl had fallen, beak-first, into the sloping gutter which drained away into the hedgerow.

"There – it can perhaps persuade its lesser feathered brethren to pillage other pastures."

"We are to have forbidden fruit in our paradise then?"

She took both his hands and pulled him into an embrace. Both of them, fired by the burlesque argument over the owl, and by the genuine ardency of freshly consummated desire, wished to go inside, but neither could make so bold as to risk interruption by visitors, of whom there had been a small but persistent number. There was George Prescott who brought the morning milk – three pints – but also turned up some afternoons, with an offering of flowers. Mr. Emerson came, often bringing Ellery Channing in tow. The afternoon was a prime time for that pair. Then there was Mr. Thoreau, who would look in to see how the vegetables were coming on, but not normally until the evening. The butcher came two or three times a week, at no regular hour of the day. And then there was Miss Hoar, a spiritual lady who flitted in and out as if she were in truth a visitor from the ethereal world.

Mr. Thoreau did call later, and fitted the owl on a frame where it might be better seen by smaller scavengers. After he had gone, Mr. and Mrs. Hawthorne at last went to their bedroom. Sophia laid her head down beneath a cadmium moon, painted as part of an unfinished allegorical figure on the headboard of the bed.

114

There was, in the garden of the parsonage, a considerable orchard, planted at the time of the Revolutionary War, and in its prime during the occupancy of Dr. Ripley, who one year earned a hundred dollars for his barrels of apples alone. There were peach trees, pear trees and cherry trees too. And although all had grown beyond optimum size their fruit was still abundant.

Mr. Hawthorne spent his days in heavenly idleness. In the mornings he picked ripe vegetables and berries. After lunch he retired to his study to sleep or to write in his Journal. In the afternoons he walked with his wife. Passing a farm on one of these rambles, he remarked, "Our domain wants only for a creature to mediate between the human and the vegetable."

Sophia suggested they acquire two horses and Mr. Hawthorne, who had read her Cuban diaries, responded, "I'm not sure I can resurrect those dashing hidalgo days. No, I was thinking more of a – a pig." In naming the animal he skipped up onto the tufted grass beside the path, as if he feared some physical retribution for so ridiculous an idea.

"A pig!"

"Yes, a pig. I grew very fond of the porker at Brook Farm and took much amusement in studying its character. I seriously think it is our duty as custodians of our paradise to support one of the lower creatures and I declare it ought to be a pig, though I have no design to feast upon its flesh."

Mr. Hawthorne and his wife spoke often in this bantering way about their plans for the household and the garden, but the summer went by and few of their dreams were realised, except for minor adjustments to the function of rooms in the house.

Visitors came to stay for a weekend in the middle of August and, though their arrival confirmed Mr. Hawthorne in his image of himself as a man who had finally grasped a tangible existence and locality in the world, he was as pleased as his wife to wave them on their way back to Boston.

Another of the passing visitors not so far mentioned was Margaret Fuller, a personage with whom Sophia had been associated since 1839, when Miss Fuller began her series of "Conversations" (a type of informal seminar then in vogue) at the Peabody home, and later at Elizabeth's bookshop in Boston. Sophia can hardly be said to have been drawn to Miss Fuller and many times averred that she had not the slightest interest in "this movement", by which she meant the nineteenth-century version of feminism.

115

Margaret Fuller had been brought up to lead a life of intellectual vigour. The infant learning régime imposed by her father had induced nightmares and somnambulism. Her greatest desire was to be recognised as a thinker, a philosopher. Too many women of her day sought heroism in acts of charity and deeds of social service, Elizabeth Peabody being the quintessential type, whereas she had the gall to interrogate God and to scrutinise the soul.

Her categorisation of sexual humours may be nothing more than an encapsulation of sexual stereotypes – it was exactly that – but its design was to increase appreciation of woman's secret influence and to dispel the image of woman as purveyor only of sexual favours and charitable works. To this end she made the following type of pronouncement: "The especial genius of woman I believe to be electrical in movement, intuitive in function, spiritual in tendency," or, "Male and female represent the two sides of the great radical dualism," and it is easy to project ourselves into Mr. Hawthorne's head, and to recoil with him from such idle pontificating.

Sophia stated her own mind plainly enough, in a letter to her mother. "Queen Margaret Fuller has been here pronouncing from the throne. Even before I was married I could never feel the slightest interest in this woman's movement. Home, I think, is the great arena for women."

Regal pronouncements were not sufficient for Miss Fuller. Without fail she left behind a "little volume" for Nathaniel and Sophia to read. Mrs. Hawthorne, unlike Mrs. Melville, would remain throughout her life a keen reader, but we have heard her view on the Fuller canon. Mr. Hawthorne was never so voracious a reader as Mr. Melville, and that which he did read he did not like programmed.

So one Sunday afternoon finds him walking back from Mr. Emerson's place having returned one such unread volume which had been left by Miss Fuller the evening before. He came, by mistake, into that part of the woods known as Sleepy Hollow, and perceived a lady reclining near the path which bent along its verge. It was Margaret herself. She had been there the whole afternoon, meditating and reading. Grateful that he no longer had the book in his hand, he responded to her call of welcome.

"So someone else does know of this retreat. Not another soul has broken my solitude the whole afternoon."

"I came this way by mistake."

116

Mr. Hawthorne sat down and Miss Fuller, who had raised herself on one elbow in greeting, now lay back flat in the grass and held her hand as sun-shield over her eyes.

"It is wonderful to lose oneself in the woods. Especially for a woman. For once one can feel what it is like to be a pioneer, walking into pristine territory."

"Such open sanctuaries as this are a pleasure to stumble on but I confess that I am tormented to death when my way is unexpectedly barred by a tract of undergrowth."

"There are many such bushy tanglements in these woods," Miss Fuller warned him. "As in living from day to day, you must brace yourself for the snarled and ravelled trail."

The day was warm. And he was ill at ease in finding himself in such close society with a single woman. Mr. Hawthorne let her condescending philosophy pass. A breeze fluttered the pages of the book that she held out in the grass, her thumb in its spine, holding place.

"I feel the influence of autumn in that breath of wind," he said.

"Oh, no! The day is beautiful. Don't let us quit summer so soon."

"I am not familiar with country signs, but there is surely something ponderous in the gathering of the crows." A company of which were apparently holding a sabbath festival in the tops of surrounding trees.

"They are heavy-gaited and black, but not automatic harbingers of woe. Appearance, Mr. Hawthorne. You must not judge on appearances. We women know too well your crass scale of judgement. I speak of your sex in general, of course." She raised a hand in a gesture supposed to allay any offence. For a second the pages fluttered freely and her place was lost. She closed the book and then held it just above the waist of her skirt.

Conversation continued to pass, with an ease which did not allow Mr. Hawthorne occasion for embarrassment. But he was not to be saved from the sensation altogether. In the midst of their talk they heard footsteps above them, on the high bank, and then a voice calling to Margaret from among the trees. It was Mr. Emerson, who scampered down to join them.

"Hello, Margaret. Delaying our friend on his return? He seemed in a hurry to get away from me. Returned a book of yours by the by."

Mr. Hawthorne blushed burningly and asked Emerson if he

knew the time. It was nearly six, so that he had ample reason to hurry on his way.

* * *

At the beginning of September the Hawthornes acquired a little paddle boat. They bought it off the impecunious Henry Thoreau for seven dollars and promptly rechristened it so that the *Musketaquid* (Indian name for the Concord River, river of meadows) became the *Pond Lily*. Mr. Hawthorne spent the greater part of the month trying to acquaint himself with the skills of boatmanship, making small voyages up the North Branch but never with a view to equalling the previous owner's paddle power. Mr. Thoreau had once followed the river down to the Merrimack, and thence to Newburyport, a voyage of about eighty miles.

In this same month a small quarrel developed when it transpired that Margaret Fuller had taken Sophia aside in order to persuade her to sublet part of the house to her sister and Ellery Channing.

"And you agreed?"

"She made it very difficult not to. They are homeless and reliant on good will, just as we were when we needed a home."

"She pointed all that out, did she?" Mr. Hawthorne was appalled by the woman's moralistic guile. "But, Sophiechen, this is our Eden, we cannot have it shared."

"I didn't exactly say, Yes they could move in. I just agreed that someone should help them out in their plight."

"I shall get word to Emerson – it won't be us. Our Paradise is not to be disturbed. Have you ever met Ellery? It would be insufferable."

Mr. Hawthorne described Ellery Channing in his Journal:

> One of those queer and clever young men whom Mr. Emerson is continually picking up by way of Genius. There is nothing very peculiar about him – some originality in his character but none in his intellect. I like him well enough, but, after all, these originals, once one has met a few of them, become more dull and commonplace than those who keep to the more humdrum pathways of life.

A fortnight after Miss Fuller's tactical attempts on behalf of her

118

sister, by which time it had been broadcast that Mr. Hawthorne had vetoed the suggestion, she arrived at the Manse again, this time with her sister Ellen in tow. Mr. Hawthorne had been upstairs writing his Journal and resting a body which was aching from the effects of his first solo voyage in the *Pond Lily* the day before. Sophia, having been to the morning service, had only just arrived home, and he had not yet gone down to greet her when he heard the sound of arriving visitors. Recognising the voice of Miss Fuller he remained in his room, silently and not-so-silently fuming. He rushed air through the back of his throat, stacked some books heavily on his desk and strode energetically in as many directions as the space of the room allowed. Having heard that Miss Fuller's sister was due to arrive by stage that day, he made the assumption that this visit was an outrageous attempt at last-minute persuasion. Turn up with the helpless young creature, present one young wife to the other, and let the Sabbath spell do the rest. Sophia would have to stand firm, and do it by herself. It would be impossible for him to suppress his indignation.

In fact, Miss Fuller's motive for her call was somewhat more undercover. Her sister Ellen had arrived by stage earlier than anticipated, at a time when Ellery was paying a call upon Caroline Sturgis. The visit to the Hawthornes was a way of playing for time, and Nathaniel had to eat humble pie an hour later, when, hearing their departure, he stamped down the stairs and thundered, "I suppose that woman was going to deposit her sister with us, baggage and all. What woeful tale did she tell you?"

"It wasn't like that, dear. Miss Fuller brought her sister to meet us. Actually, she whispered in my ear that there was a problem with Ellery, who wouldn't be free to greet Ellen until later on. They have gone on to Emerson's place now."

"Agh, she was just being subtle. Hoping you would offer an unsolicited hospitality out of seeing the young thing in the flesh."

"Is that what *I* am?"

Mr. Hawthorne grunted a question mark at her.

"A young thing in the flesh?" She gave her husband a wifely cuddle. "You shouldn't dislike the woman so. Besides, all clever people have their vexing ways." She dug her thumbs meaningfully into his ribs and then darted away. They pursued one another through all the ground-floor rooms and then out into the garden. The game of chase ended with them playing catch with over-ripe, wind-fallen peaches.

At the end of the month Mr. Hawthorne went on a short walking excursion with Emerson, which involved an overnight stay, the first night apart for the newly-weds. It is not represented in the Journals as an exciting event, the word "pedestrian" used with a dual ring. Both men had been over-conscious of the fact that one another would be expecting interesting conversation, the result being that as they set out towards Harvard, their bedding-place, each of them withheld the offhand remarks that give a dialogue its impetus. Mr. Hawthorne saw some fringed gentians growing by the roadside and wanted to stop and examine them. Instead, he took mental note of the spot so that he could, if they returned the same way, bring them home to his wife, all the time walking on, alongside the taller man, as if nothing had caught his eye.

At length Mr. Emerson launched himself, with no apparent pretext, into a series of general reflections, such as those which his *Essays* and the bulk of his reputation are based upon. Many of them Mr. Hawthorne recognised from a collection published the year before. Others were fresh to his ear. Neither variety prompted more than the odd nod or grunt.

"This little journey I don't count as travelling. It merely represents closer examination of our locality. I wish I was less travelled than I am, though I leave Concord but rarely. The wise man stays at home with the soul. But the mind is as restless as the body. There is too much travelling of the mind. Too much imitation. I commend your stability. I do not detect much of the fidget in you. It is the kind of influence Ellery needs, if he is to become the American poet he desires to be.

"Where does this chronic feeling of missing out, of needing to get back in touch, issue from? I feel it myself. On a walk such as this. Here we are, two tramps on a small country roadway. And yet Nature still seems elsewhere. Each new landscape disappoints, partly through unresponsiveness. And so it is with friendships, although it has seemed to me lately more possible than I knew to carry on a one-sided friendship. Does this sun above us worry that its rays fall into ungrateful space? No, every man alone is sincere. Let him plant his influences where he will, and not care whether they are acknowledged or not."

It was a relief to Mr. Hawthorne that they took separate rooms at the hotel and that they retired early after their arduous journey. Over supper they determined to visit and breakfast at the nearby

120

Shaker village and this was really the sum total of their table talk. There was still a little twilight left when they went to their rooms. Mr. Hawthorne, sitting on the bed, had eased off his boots and was massaging a socked foot, when there came a sharp tapping at the window. Looking up, he saw a small bird, seemingly demanding admittance. After cocking its head once or twice to and fro, the visitor took wing. The incident had an unsettling effect on Mr. Hawthorne, for he could not escape the notion that the bird had been a spiritual visitant, with some urgent message to deliver. As he slipped into the narrow bed, struck by the unfamiliar tightness of the bedding, all manner of fears for Sophia's well-being came to molest him. She was frightened out of her wits in the empty Manse; the dead owl, impaled on its pole, haunted her efforts at relaxation; the thud of late-falling fruit provoked one of her cannonading headaches and she sensed herself trampling through wasp-ridden piles of decaying apples and pears until her legs were puffed and hillocked with stings and covered in an acid lotion of frothing and putrefying juices; a black-coated, bearded horseman galloped into the garden out of Sleepy Hollow; he broke into the house and . . .

Another fear, less irrational and therefore more potent, that disturbed Mr. Hawthorne's night, was the worry that he would return home and find Ellen and Ellery Channing, who had still not found a permanent dwelling, finally foisted upon them. This fear quite spoilt the excursion's second day, and at the Shaker village he contributed not a jot to the theological discussion that Mr. Emerson held with two of the brethren, and he quite forgot, on the return journey, to look for the crop of fringed gentians growing by the roadside.

*   *   *

Towards the end of November it was beginning to become apparent that they would have to share their Paradise with at least one other. Sophia was expecting a child. The pregnancy, had it come earlier, may indeed have been actively resented – the couple enjoyed so much their summer solitudes – but as it was they sat down to their Thanksgiving Day feast with the warming sense that a new family was gathered round the table. Mr. Hawthorne needed some such notion for he loathed the winter and the symbolical retreat of verdure. Earlier in the month, for economy's

121

sake, they had had three stoves installed in the house, so there could be no open fires to cosify the bleak days ahead. Soon afterwards he had become acutely depressed, and actually wept when he had discovered some fringed gentians in the meadow. They were blighted and withered and quite unfit for picking.

Sophia's announcement transformed his impression of the season, so that he was able to identify with the pregnant hibernation of the natural world. It was an identification which induced both mental and physical vigour. He began at last to write with some regularity – between two and four hours each day. The sawing and splitting of wood for the three stoves completed the sense of satisfied well-being.

It quickly developed into the most bitter winter the region had suffered in twenty years. The lakes froze over and the road to the Post Office was snowbound for the duration. It was a joy to have the dreary brown-ness of mud and bark covered with clean brilliance, and a double joy that callers no longer disturbed their solitude, although at times Mr. Hawthorne wondered whether his wife, used as she was to the sisterly society of Salem, was as happy in their solitude as he. She gave every indication of so being, but her condition dictated a cessation of the childish pranks which had thus far marked their honeymoon period.

Sophia went to watch her husband skating on the frozen river with Mr. Emerson and Mr. Thoreau. Wrapped in his dark cloak, he moved like a self-impelled statue, stately and grave, and, of the three, cut far the most impressive figure, despite the showing off in which Mr. Thoreau indulged, figuring dithyrambic dances and making Bacchic leaps upon the ice. As for Mr. Emerson, his was a pitiful aspect, pitching head foremost, half lying on the air, as if he were too weary to hold himself erect. In such manner did he coast in to Sophia, stumbling on the broken shoreline ice, and having to steady himself on a low-hanging branch.

"Your husband, madam, is a tiger, a bear, a lion. He is such an Ajax. Who can cope with him?"

Sophia blushed. Their expected event was a secret and these unsolicited commendations of her husband's masculinity produced an involuntary tightening in her groin.

In order to ensure Sophia adequate rest through her pregnancy the Hawthornes employed, with the financial assistance of the Peabodies, a serving girl by the name of Molly Bryan. Her wages were three dollars a week. This compared with rent for the Manse of a hundred dollars a year – but even this did not make it the cheapest abode in Concord. Three years previously, after the closure of his Temple school, Bronson Alcott had moved into a cottage called the Dovecote at a rent of just fifty-two dollars.

Mercifully for the newly-weds who, as we have seen, had little hunger for pestering visitors, Mr. Alcott had been away in England, on a journey financed by Mr. Emerson, during the early summer, and when he eventually returned in October it was in the throes of a vision and in the company of two English educationists. These two acquaintances did not go down well with Mr. Alcott's daughter, Louisa. She was now ten years old and had developed mock-romantic affection for Henry Thoreau, with whom she spent a considerable amount of time. But on her father's return Mr. Thoreau was waylaid by Bronson and his English friends in long contemplations of their proposed communal venture, leaving Louisa to run to her mother with the complaint: "Mama, they have begun *again*!"

Louisa's mother had to contain her own exasperation, especially so since it was at this time, influenced by the Englishman Charles Lane's celibacy, and by Doctor Sylvester Graham's theory of "semen retention", that her husband withdrew from their customary, once-monthly sexual indulgence. Notionally, at least. This was emphatically *not* the type of self-denying act Abba had in mind when she wrote in her Journal:

> A woman may perform the most disinterested duties. She may die daily in the cause of truth and righteousness. She lives neglected, dies forgotten. But a man who never performs in his whole life one self-denying act is celebrated by his contemporaries, while his name lives on from age to age.

If Mr. Hawthorne was brought into the discussions regarding the planned commune there is no evidence of his contribution.

Some time during the early part of the New Year Sophia suffered a miscarriage. It was several weeks after the event when Mr. Hawthorne wrote the following passage in his Journal:

> One grief we have had . . . Nor did the grief penetrate to the reality of our life. We do not feel as if our promised child were taken from us forever; but only as if his coming had been delayed for a season; and that, by and by, we should

welcome that very same little stranger whom we had expected to gladden our home at an earlier period.

It would be easy to dismiss such forbearance as verbal bravado, or a reflection of the need to protect his wife's sense of failure. Love had seemed to work a miracle upon her, a physical miracle, but here once again was evidence of her frailty. And yet the reaction is entirely consistent with Mr. Hawthorne's temperament. We have already heard, at a later date, Mr. Melville referring to his friend's fatalism, and we must stand as perplexed by it now as he did then. For it has no obvious source; certainly not in the well-spring of religious orthodoxy. Mr. Hawthorne was not a devout man. His fiction is full of protagonists stepping from the narrow way at their peril. If life is so precarious, and if one false step can effect a fall from grace, wherefrom comes the inner calm? This is an entanglement we must seek to unravel, and it would seem to be highly significant that, at the beginning of March, two weeks before making the Journal entry just quoted, the Hawthornes, in company with Miss Molly Bryan, abandoned the sad associations of their Manse bedroom and took the stage back East. More significant again is the fact that Mr. and Mrs. Hawthorne parted ways in Boston, so that it was only Nathaniel who journeyed on to Salem, resuming for nearly a fortnight the same life in which more than ten years of his youth had flitted away like a dream. Far from there being any sense of withdrawing from a hurt just suffered, he speaks of it being good to get apart from his "happiness", for the sake of contemplating it. Sophia, meanwhile, was wise enough to avoid the Charter Street residence, where she would surely have been treated as an invalid. Instead, she convalesced with the Sturgises and invited her parents to visit her there.

* * *

Before they had time to establish a springlike New Era in their Concord retreat, the two lovers were parted again, and Mrs. Hawthorne was on her way back to Boston, this time with the purpose of attending a family wedding.

> A wagon came about eleven o'clock to carry my Dove to the stage-house. I helped her in, and stood watching her, on the doorstep, till she was out of sight. Then I betook myself to sawing and splitting wood.

Mr. Hawthorne went inside. Molly brought him his dinner. He lay down and read the *Dial*, fancying to spend the whole term of his wife's absence without speaking a word to any human being. That same afternoon he broke the resolution by receiving Mr. Thoreau and learning of his purpose to leave Concord and Mr. Emerson's hospitality, not, as might be supposed, to join the imminent beginnings of Mr. Alcott's commune, but to become an independent tutor at Staten Island. He stated his wish that he might be allowed to accompany Mr. Hawthorne on one last voyage in the *Pond Lily* and the two of them made plans for the fulfilment of this desire; in return for which favour Henry assigned his prized musical box to Nathaniel's good keeping.

The pattern of the following afternoon was identical. Mr. Hawthorne dined, lay down with the *Dial*, got up to receive a caller. This time it was Mr. Emerson, and the two of them talked mainly of Margaret Fuller, Emerson apotheosising her as the greatest of women. They spoke also of Ellery Channing who was soon to have his first volume of poems published. Of Mr. Thoreau's impending departure Emerson seemed well pleased, for it appeared that he had suffered some inconvenience from having the long-nosed pencil-maker as a lodger. And they talked of Brook Farm and the desirability that one day its history should be written.

Late in the evening, his body weary from further chopping of wood, and his heart pining for his dear Little Wife, Mr. Hawthorne sat in the Grandmother Chair winding and re-winding Mr. Thoreau's musical box, until the peculiar sweetness of its melody evaporated and he might almost have thrown the little machine clear into the garden. As darkness fell and his loneliness and sombreness merged into a distinct sense of misery, Molly, with a knock and a cough, emerged with a letter from Sophia. Mr. Hawthorne snatched open the envelope, called Molly back to take her portion of the letter – which she received with broad-smiling delight – and then read, re-read and re-re-read, quadruply, quintuply and sextuply re-read, his good wife's fairy penmanship.

Next evening, after a day spent grappling with a new story idea, he wandered to the river, with the purpose of seeing how well the *Pond Lily* had weathered the winter. There were still large masses of ice floating down the current and at a point near the old bridge a solid tract of it stretched across the entire breadth, so that the broken pieces, when they struck the barrier, were forced high out

125

of the water, above the main sheet of ice. Mr. Hawthorne stood on the river bank, enthralled by this natural drama, and doubtless seeking to make out of it some metaphysical significance.

The boat seemed in such poor condition, and so full of water, that he made no sort of thorough examination, so that he was somewhat embarrassed two days later when Mr. Thoreau simply emptied the water out and declared her fit for voyage. On the return row they disembarked from the boat and boarded one of the large cakes of ice which were still floating down the river and were borne along by it right up to their landing-place, towing the *Pond Lily* behind them.

Sophia did not enjoy her sister's wedding. She had been irked that the sudden announcement of it had come so soon after their previous trip to Boston, but her annoyance had been as nothing compared with Elizabeth's, who was positively affronted at the secrecy with which the pair of them, Mary and Horace, had conducted the affair; and told them so to their faces.

The two victims of Elizabeth's displeasure had exchanged letters during Mary's stay in Cuba, but on her return there had been no outward flow of feeling, and once again she had had to settle for the role of silent admirer. Their parting look, on the Boston wharf, had become, to Mary, mythical, and to Horace, a radiance which had been sublimated first by his work as a lawyer and then by his appointment as First Secretary of Education for Massachusetts. Mary felt unable to approach him through his legal work, but his schools appointment opened an opportunity which she was quick to seize. She was, by this time, running a small school for very young children, and she offered Mr. Mann use of her premises for any research that he might wish to undertake. In the event he began by using Mary as menial labour, having her return to the school house after hours as copyist during the preparation of one of his annual reports. For some time yet the relationship maintained a professional distance, so that when the blossoming of affection finally occurred, and in a way that took all close acquaintances aback, it cannot but puzzle the interpreter. What led Mr. Mann to hold back for so long? What was the eventual cause of his opened heart? Considerations include the continuing memory of his first wife, and his professional obsessions. The schools-secretaryship became an all-consuming mission. He was in the business of transforming the world by perfecting rising generations. His salary was only fifteen hundred

126

dollars a year, a pittance when compared with legal fees, but job satisfaction was total. It was work his young deceased wife could be proud of, as she looked down upon him.

It appears that eventually his close friend Dr. Samuel Howe managed to persuade him that the punishing work schedule was ruining his health. What he needed was the possibility of sexual release. How about his female copyist? She seemed plenty interested. If this seems too crude a tack to take with the prudish Mr. Mann there is yet, in that same prudery, the eternal battle to keep lust under control. Howe had booked a boudoir on the May Cunarder for himself and Julia. He urged Horace to join them for a double honeymoon.

When Mary was asked if she could be ready to be married by the middle of April she said that it was all very sudden; she thought she might just manage it. She pretended to take it coolly right up to the crossing, insinuating to her family that plans had been laid way in the past, that it had been a well-kept secret. There was a good deal of amazement, both disbelieving and shocked, in the family reaction, and Mr. Mann was irked to find that his prospective entry into the Peabody circle was not more welcomed. Mary was thirty-six years old. He had known her for a decade. And yet they looked askance at him as if he had taken advantage of a young whippet. He spoke to Howe about it. The advice was marry and run.

When Sophia had returned to Concord and was asked how it had all gone, she said that it "had rained unmercifully right up until the boat had left the wharf, when suddenly the sun broke through. Oh Nathaniel, I felt such pity for my sister. The rushed and inefficient arrangements . . . even the service had to be delayed half an hour, waiting for two of Horace's nieces, who never did turn up. Mary had a grasscloth dress on, not quite white, it looked horribly drab and unornamented except for a pretty lace collar but no other decoration. And in her hair she had a ridiculous gold chain, much too heavy, it looked more like brass than gold. And the rain flattened her hair so that the chain slid too far down her high forehead. You can't imagine how unremitting the rain could be. Mama and Papa would not come to the wharf, fearing the storm. I remember our own departure together for Cuba. Such a family sendoff we were given. Poor Mary. I do hope she will be happy. And then the boat was scarcely out of throwing distance when the sun came out. It was too cruel!"

127

Nathaniel, seeing things from Mary's point of view, interpreted the sudden splash of sun differently. "Perhaps it was fitting that her family coastline should remain soaked in sombre hue until she was undeniably independent of it. The burst of sun which you described came as all the cares of her old life fell away. She was free. The sky was blue."

Sophia gave Nathaniel a sceptical look. She wanted to argue it out with him, but could not be sure that he was not mocking the explanatory wizardry of literature. In the end she smiled, and when he smiled back she knew that he believed her account to be the correct one.

Dr. Howe, knowing his friend's propensity for seasickness, prescribed generous tipples of brandy, in which Mary shared, so that their wedding night, in their private stateroom aboard the *Britannia*, was an entire success and Mr. Mann felt many of the tensions of the past years soothed out of him. When he woke in the morning his hair was still white and his mouth exceedingly dry but at dawn he strode the deck alone as if he were a young sailor on a maiden voyage, and he tried to communicate with his first wife, returning to Mary with the conviction that their liaison was condoned and had received a heavenly blessing.

They reached London in early May and Mary was disappointed the voyage could not have lasted twice as long. She enjoyed Julia Howe's company and Horace seemed influenced by the doctor's blither view of the world. Once on land, however, the extravagance of their journey had to be justified, and so began the informed, but never-ending, inspection of foreign schools, in England, Scotland, Germany, Holland and France.

Mr. Mann found it impossible to take a casual view of this endeavour and Mary soon became concerned when she noticed observable signs of overwork. He slept badly and had midnight fevers. A muscle in his cheek jumped uncontrollably. She could not influence him to take more rest and so she sought instead to lighten his load by helping him with the detailed recording of his observations. It might have been dispiriting, to have one's honeymoon diminished by professional interests and to have one's relationship advancing so little distance from the pre-marital pattern, but the continual changing of beds protected against any reduction in sexual ardour and Mary conceived a child halfway through their tour.

On June 9th occurred Sophia's first wedding anniversary, and Nathaniel left the following note for her in their joint Journal:

Methinks this birthday of our married life is like a cape, which we have now doubled, and find a more infinite ocean of love, stretching out before us. God bless us and keep us; for there is something more awful in happiness than in sorrow – the latter being earthly and infinite, the former composed of the texture and substance of eternity, so that the spirits still embodied may well tremble at it.

On this day, or very close to it, Sophia conceived for a second time. The eventual delivery of the two Peabody grandchildren was separated by a mere six days.

Mr. Hawthorne had spent the spring and early summer investing a significant amount of toil in the vegetable plot, which this year he was able to plant out and plan from scratch, and although he had to wage continual warfare on the squash-bug, it remained soul-renewing work, so that when he received a letter from his sister Louise informing him that Beelzebub, the Hawthorne family cat, was dead, he was able to vent his grief on the vermin, for whom he devised an ever-increasing range of booby traps.

Dr. Peabody came to stay for a week and niggled Nathaniel somewhat by pointedly renovating the garden tools and assigning them a new storage place, as well as preparing a fresh batch of clay for his daughter to sculpt. Although done from paternal regard this could not help but reflect badly upon Mr. Hawthorne's own management of the garden and servicing of his wife's talent.

*　　*　　*

In early October 1844 Mr. Melville arrived in New York aboard the frigate *United States*. He had been absent for nearly four years and had to spend a further ten days breaking and clearing out the ship before he could be discharged. Time enough for his family to be warned of his arrival and for Gansevoort to give him written advice regarding the making of his appearance presentable. There are no recorded reminiscences of his home-coming. Indeed, it appears that Gansevoort's high-profile campaigning for James Polk, the Democrats' presidential candidate, rather overshadowed the return of the prodigal son. Gansevoort's new mission had begun in August when he had straightway hurled himself into a rigorous twice-daily defence of the party platform in front of small and mass meetings (audiences ranging from a few dozen to as many as two thousand), his speech never lasting less than two hours and on one occasion going on for four.

He was described in the press variously as "this powerful and indefatigable champion of Democracy", as one who "probably has no superior as a political speaker in the country", as an "eloquent and powerful speaker with high-toned moral power". Such praise and such success with his audience bred hopes for political office following Polk's triumph in the November election. But despite recommendations from influential figures in the party the new President would not make the hoped-for appointment. It would seem that Gansevoort, at too early a stage, developed a sense of his own importance, and this had sent danger signals to the new incumbent. Even in September he had been writing personal letters to the party leader and although these letters started innocently enough, as progress reports from the campaign front, they developed into critical analyses of party organisation. The pressure to give him some form of reward continued unabated through to the early summer of 1845, and included this letter in Gansevoort's own pen of May 7th, expressing a transparently phony acceptance of the go-by:

> Although the entire failure of my application (for public appointment) has injured me more seriously than you can imagine both in the present and in the future and has fallen upon me with stunning force, yet having full faith that your personal feelings were throughout kind and friendly, and entertaining no doubt but that you have been guided in your decision by enlarged views of what you deem to be sound policy. I acquiesce in the result without a murmur.

This was after the failure of a month-long rain of epiphanies which included: "There is no one among us whose individual efforts contributed more than his to our gratifying triumph" / "He is a bold, fearless and eloquent champion" / "No one sustained himself better in the great questions" / "I know of no gentleman who in the same space of time, has, by the exercise of superior cleverness established a more sure foot-hold in the confidence and esteem of the Democratic party in the city of New York". The litany of praise is impressive and it begs the question, why was Gansevoort ignored by Polk? If the young man's talents had been so outstanding it would surely have been worth a presidential aide having a heart-to-heart regarding those over-zealous presumptions of the campaign. There must have been another inhibiting factor and we can be fairly sure that it was Gansevoort's history of mental disability. His indiscretions could all be attributed to an over-stimulated system, and public life could only be expected to exacerbate them. The President should have stuck hard to his policy of neglect, but in mid-June he bowed halfway to the lobbying of Gansevoort's supporters and appointed him secretary to Louis McLane, the American Ambassador in Britain.

Throughout this time, encouraged by family reaction to oral accounts of his experiences, Gansevoort's adventuring brother had been writing up a romanticised record of his Polynesian captivity. By the summer of 1845 the manuscript was fat enough to pack off with Gansevoort, aboard the *Great Western*.

The professional life of the would-be politician was a disaster from the start and Louis McLane had early cause to complain of being lumbered. In mid-September he wrote to James Buchanan, Secretary to the President: "There being an impression that the place at Constantinople is about or ought to be vacant, would it not be possible to send Mr. Melville there?" Three weeks later the plea is more urgent: "Next to restoring me to my home the President could not confer upon me a greater favour than to give some suitable office to Mr. Melville." And again in November: "Not doubting that this letter will be shown to the President, I venture in all confidence with him and yourself, and with no one else, again to prefer an earnest request that in some way or other he will suitably provide for Mr. Melville, out of this legation." In December Buchanan wrote back saying that the President refused to transfer Mr. Melville. McLane was not in the country to receive the reply. He was on a visit to France and had left Gansevoort to stand in for him at diplomatic dinners where the understudy took the opportunity of making embarrassingly long speeches in support of the American President.

He conducted his offices as literary agent with greater success. Soon after arriving in London he showed his brother's manuscript to John Murray, publisher of many travel books. Murray liked the book, but was suspicious. He did not believe it was the work of a novice. He did not believe the story was an honest recollection of a traveller's experiences. Gansevoort gave him assurances on both counts and Herman provided three new chapters in an effort to balance the more romantic episodes with some hard social observation. Murray took over a month to make up his mind, but on December 3rd the deal was finalised. After insisting on a few editorial omissions, for which Herman had given carte blanche permission, he paid a hundred pounds for the right to print a thousand copies.

Gansevoort immediately became caught up in a whirl of proof-reading and negotiating for American publication. On January 6th of the New Year, with McLane still away, Washington Irving, at present Minister to Madrid, called into the diplomatic office. He came again the next morning, at 10 a.m., to take breakfast and to meet his old friend John Murray. Murray went away at noon; Gansevoort took up the proofs of his brother's book and read aloud selections from the early chapters. Mr. Irving declared them "exquisite" and said the book was assured of public success.

The proof-reading continued through two or three revisions, with Gansevoort working four or five hours at a stretch. The book was ready for publication by the end of February, the successful culmination of his efforts on behalf of his distant brother leaving Gansevoort pretty well exhausted and the resulting approbation for the book (tempered only by the doubts which Murray had foreseen concerning its authenticity) had the effect of highlighting his own sense of professional failure. His indiscretions at the dinner table became more frequent and less excusable. He began to speak of the President in a mincing, ironic tone, and to give the impression that his efforts alone had secured that man in the highest office.

Through March he had dutifully sent off to Herman bundles of reviews and on April 13th he enclosed a copy of the arrangement with Wiley and Putnam for the American publication of *Typee*. Along with the enclosure Herman received the first indication that his brother's nervous condition was dangerously insecure. He wrote: "My thoughts are so much at home that much of my time is spent in disquieting apprehensions as to matters and things there. I sometimes fear I am gradually breaking up. I think I am growing phlegmatic and cold. Man stirs me not, nor woman either." There was a second enclosure with the letter, in addition to the legal paper. It was a handwritten quotation from *Measure for Measure*. The lines of Death beginning: "Ay, but to die, and go we know not where / To lie in cold obstruction and to rot / This sensible warm motion to become / A kneaded clod."

Four days later Gansevoort was threatened with a total loss of sight and was advised to withdraw immediately from his official duties. On May 4th Louis McLane wrote once again to James Buchanan: "For the last month he has been confined to his house, with what he represented to me as an affection of the eyes, and a consequent loss of sight! From his physician, however, I learn that his sight is not materially affected, and that his disorder is in some degree connected with the brain, and a state of nervous derangement, which if it should now come would not surprise me. I have never seen him since he came here that he was not in a mood painfully extravagant as to all Men and all things, and now at this day if I had no option but to remain here, I would myself face a departure. So it is I have discharged my duty and leave it to others to discharge theirs. Be assured of one thing: the P. will suffer more from his continuance here than I will."

Even if Gansevoort's illness had been, even in part, a physical plea to be returned to his family, Mr. McLane's letter arrived in America too late to effect an official suspension of Gansevoort's duties. He died at his lodgings in London of "cerebral anaemia", on May 12th, aged thirty years, six months and six days. In one of the ironies that the speed of modern times has almost eradicated, Herman wrote to Gansevoort on May 29th believing him to be on the way to recovery. Mr. McLane's letter of condolence to the Melville family, posted on May 18th, had not yet arrived. Herman's letter began, "I think I see you opening this letter in one of those pleasant hamlets round about London, of which we read in novels. Remember that composure of the mind is everything. You should give no thought to matters here until you are well enough to think about them."

His brother's death, and its associations with his father's loss of reason, would reap their morbid fruit in due course. In the meantime, just as Gansevoort had on the earlier occasion, Herman assumed the forthright role of head of the family and in early June wrote letters requesting the President to make an extraordinary contribution towards his brother's funeral expenses. The request was authorised to the extent of fifty pounds in English money. Herman went to New York to collect the body, which had been despatched on board the *Prince Albert*, and, transferring it to the *Henry Hudson*, travelled with it up-river to Albany, and within twenty-four hours of arriving there the funeral had been taken care of.

Less than twelve months after his return as an impecunious, renegade sailor, Herman Melville found himself a published author of some acclaim and notoriety, the acknowledged representative of a widowed mother and several younger brothers and sisters, and, despite his family's financial misfortunes, must also have been accounted a very eligible bachelor. But before we follow the course of his subsequent romance and engagement, we need to discover why, during the passage of Gansevoort's body across the Atlantic, the Hawthornes' second child, Julian, was born in Boston and not in Concord.

*   *   *

In June 1844 Margaret Fuller visited the Manse and ended up staying the night. Una was six or seven weeks old and not yet in any kind of routine. Sexual relations between the parents, the curtailment of which had hit Mr. Hawthorne very hard, had not yet been re-established to any satisfactory degree. As his Journals avow, he was a man sensitive to detail beyond the common measure and he found difficulty adapting to the post-natal alterations in his wife's physique.

"But, Nathaniel, she asked especially to see the baby, and wants to give me an afternoon's rest."

"Oh, yes, her visit would have to be of importance." Nathaniel had complained to Sophia about issuing the invitation before consulting with him. Miss Fuller was due to arrive at three, and would be staying for a late evening meal. Violations of their territory still enraged him, but to show Sophia that he was not seriously cross with her he chuckled and said, "I suppose you're trying to nurture maternal instincts in her, eh? Not much hope of that."

"She seems very interested in children. She often . . ."

"So was Jesus – interested in children."

"Nathaniel! That is a tasteless remark."

He sat still, with an impish smile, denoting a roguish sense of humour the world would never know. He took regular pleasure in offending his wife's highly-honed sense of good taste. When, in later years, she took to expurgating parts of his Journals, she defended herself on the very proper grounds that at times her husband wrote less than seriously and any emendations that she made were only the same ones he would have made himself before addressing his words to the wider public.

Molly came in with Una and handed the baby to Mrs. Hawthorne.

"She's a cherub, miss. Not a whimper when I dressed her. Just

134

gurglegurglegurgle, didn't you, precious?" Molly leant forward, looking closely at the baby in its mother's lap.

"Thank you, Molly. I don't think *Mr.* Hawthorne is quite so enamoured with her this morning."

Nathaniel had been up for a long stretch in the middle of the night, rocking Una's crib. Several times he had cursed the old boards of the Manse for disturbing the shallow slumber of the child. Finally, he devised an elaborate pathway of stepping-pads using spare bedding to muffle their creaking. After several attempts and rearrangements he had managed to creep back into bed without making a sound.

Because of the lost sleep he worked during the afternoon, which had the advantage of absenting him for part of Miss Fuller's visit. The two women sat in the garden beneath his window, the baby perversely asleep in the shade of an elm.

"You are lucky to have the Irish girl. No woman was ever intended to bring up a brood of children single-handed. Look at poor Abba Alcott, weighed under with the demands of her herd. It was no better for her at Fruitlands. The men only talked. There has to be a new and general principle of sharing. Men must give up some of their domain and bear part of the burden which has been ours alone for too long. Don't you feel that more than ever, now that you're a mother?"

"I am overjoyed to be a mother. And Una couldn't wish for a better father. She'll say so herself, just as soon as she can talk."

Mr. Hawthorne put down his pen and mimed applause for his Clever Little Wife. Hearing the female conversation drift into more benign subject matter, he eased the window closed and returned to his story.

Before supper he was left alone with Miss Fuller while his wife fed Una.

"There," Margaret said, when Sophia had left the room. "You have a firm-headed young wife, Mr. Hawthorne. She has put me in my place once or twice this afternoon. Most young mothers are merely rigid – confined within society's expectations of them. But Sophia seems an ardent apostle for established principles."

Mr. Hawthorne sipped his port. "There *is* something time-honoured about our way of life here."

"And how about Sophia's art? Will she find time to paint and sculpt now the baby's here?"

Mr. Hawthorne saw the artfulness of this enquiry and wished he

135

could muster something of his wife's innocent certitude by way of riposte. "There will be less time for that I expect." The resignation in the face of this reality was honest, but he knew it was exactly what Miss Fuller wished to establish, and would encourage further point-scoring tactics across the supper table.

Halfway through the meal Sophia let it be known that Miss Fuller had asked to stay the night. Molly had already made up a bed.

"We feel a certain sympathy for one another in body if not in mind. I have been telling Sophia about my headaches. One's health, I think, is of great interest as connected with one's mental life. I feel there has been a crisis in my constitution."

"Margaret cures *her* headaches by immersing herself, her head that is, in cold water."

"The water must be *very* cold. And the head must stay wet for as long as possible. It is not a cure to be recommended in mid-winter, but at this time of year . . . Do *you* suffer at all from infirmity?"

She looked at Nathaniel, but Sophia smiled. He had the uneasy impression that, after closing his study window, an unexpected bonding had taken place between them.

"No, he's as robust as they come. Mr. Emerson called him a tiger last winter, when he saw him skating down the river. He did have a lame foot as a child, though."

"How interesting. What caused the injury?"

"It wasn't an injury so much as an unexplained weakness of the joint. Papa tried to cure it, but to no avail. It forced a solitary, inactive life upon him."

"That is most interesting. And presumably it cured itself?"

Nathaniel nodded. "Most, most interesting. I really do believe that bodily afflictions could tell as much as dreams if only we paid them heed."

After the meal, Nathaniel walked outside to smoke a cigar. The sky was clear and twilight lingered late. He had worked less hard at the vegetable plot this season and some of the dug-over space was unplanted. The dark presence of the overhanging elms provided a fitting backdrop for his present mood. He continued to hold an instinctive distrust for Miss Fuller and feared for the sinister enchantment she might cast over Sophia. Since the birth of Una he had felt more than ever the requirement to protect his happiness. As a couple, the business of cutting themselves off from the world had been both natural and attainable. As a parent he

136

could see the world encroaching ineluctably. If only the magazines paid more, and more promptly, it might be possible to pursue this mode of life indefinitely. But he could not long, with easy conscience, rely upon the financial aid of Dr. Peabody in the support of his wife and child. He stubbed his cigar on one of the bean posts and threw the butt with such force as was released by the letting-go of an angry tension.

Mr. Hawthorne retired early, explaining the lack of sleep enjoyed the previous night.

"I'm glad to hear that Sophia doesn't have to woo the child single-handed."

He gave Miss Fuller a smile full of sugary graciousness, and closed the door.

While Sophia gave Una her midnight feed, Mr. Hawthorne got up from the bed and stood by the bedroom window.

"We didn't let Una cry overlong, did we?"

Sophia shook her head sleepily. "Why?"

"Our guest is still up and taking a second tour of the garden."

"Oh, dear, she must be suffering one of her headaches. Is her hair wet?"

"I shouldn't wonder, now I think of it, that this is not her common custom. Turning the elms into praying monastics. I swear she is casting a spell down there. All that we stand for is anathema to her."

"She is very jealous of Una here. And jealous of us both, if the truth be known. I wouldn't be surprised if one day a handsome, charismatic man sweeps her off her feet and forces her to denounce the silly prescriptions she gives to women now."

Nathaniel was glad to hear his wife speak like this.

*   *   *

The Presidential campaign, which so mortally consumed Gansevoort Melville, was of no consequence to the Hawthornes. Una continued to be a difficult child and, despite Molly's assistance, Sophia found herself tired out by the early evening. Nathaniel put on weight and retreated further into his writing. The passionate peak of the relationship was incontrovertibly over, a fact which Mr. Hawthorne resisted both in theory and in practice. The couple, who were keen to have more than one child, took no measures to delay another's conception, but Sophia did not

137

become pregnant again until after their departure from the Manse. The orchard, in the autumn of 1844, was less bountiful than heretofore, and Nathaniel had premonitions that their Eden had become sullied by an unpardonable sin. In his self-critical moments he blamed his own carnal cravings; in paranoid moments the culprit was most definitely Miss Margaret Fuller and the midnight spell she had cast beneath the silhouetted elms.

One evening, early in 1845, with Una upstairs and ready for her cot, though still too perky to be put inside it, the mother and father stood their ten-month-old girl on the bedroom windowsill and showed her the icy branches of the trees. Soon after Sophia's miscarriage two years previously, she had taken off her wedding ring and scratched into the window pane: "Man's accidents are God's purposes."

Nathaniel held Una at the elbows and helped her in her leg-strengthening exercises, bending at the knee, and pushing against the sill. Passing the child to his wife, he asked Sophia for her ring. She gave it to him, saying, "What are you going to put?"

"Something nasty about Miss Fuller."

"No, Nathaniel. Don't!"

"Yes, the truth must be recorded. It is my task in life." He began to scratch, in capitalised letters:

> UNA HAWTHORNE
> STOOD ON THE WINDOW
> SILL JANUARY 22ND 1845
> WHILE THE TREES WERE ALL
> GLASS CHANDELIERS A GOODLY
> SHOW WHICH SHE LIKED MUCH
> THO ONLY 10
> MONTHS OLD

"You tease. Isn't your Papa a tease? Go on, give him a smack." Sophia manipulated Una's arm, so that it tapped Nathaniel smartly on the ear. The baby giggled. And Sophia repeated the action. After five such smacks Una's chubby face was shaking in uncontrolled amusement, and the business of calming her before bed had to begin anew.

A sombre and indelible event took place on the night of July 9th, in their last summer at the Manse, and on the very day of their third wedding anniversary. At half-past nine in the evening,

Sophia having already gone upstairs, there came an urgent knocking at the door. Mr. Hawthorne opened it.

"Your boat. Can we use your boat to get at a drowned girl?"

Nathaniel responded swiftly, grabbing a jacket and explaining to Sophia that he had to go out with Ellery to search for a missing person.

The two men ran to the river. Ellery took the oars, Nathaniel the paddle, and they set off towards the bridge. There were lights on the bank marking the spot where a bonnet and shoes had already been found.

Miss Hunt, a girl of nineteen years old, of some education and refinement, but depressed and miserable for want of sympathy, had been seen at the river-bank between five and seven in the morning. She was a schoolteacher and had not been at her classroom during the day.

Two onlookers from the shore's edge came into the *Pond Lily*, bringing with them long poles with hooks on the end, and the search commenced. They caused the boat to float back and forth past the spot where the bonnet had been found, carefully probing the bottom with the poles. Once or twice the hooks caught in bunches of waterweed which, in the starlight, looked like light clothing. All this time the persons on the shore shouted out advice to search higher or lower, this way or that. Nathaniel paddled the boat again, past the point where she was supposed to have entered the water, and then turned it, to let it float broadside down the deepest part of the river.

They had drifted a little distance past the group on the bank when one of the men who had joined the boat cried out, "What's this!" And heaving up his pole with difficulty he added, "Yes; I've got her!"

He drew her towards the boat and grasped her arm, while Nathaniel steered into the bank. Some men with lanterns stepped into the water and drew out the body, which was rigid; as stiff as marble. They put her down under an oak tree and held three lanterns above her. Nathaniel found the illuminated spectacle dreadful to behold. Her arms had stiffened in the act of struggling and were bent before her, with the hands clenched. When the men tried to compose her figure, her arms returned to that same position. One put his foot upon her arm for the purpose of straightening it by her side; but in a moment it rose again. It seemed as if she would keep the same posture in the grave.

139

The pole had injured one of the eyes when it first struck her body and now blood began to stream from her nose. Two of the men fetched water and began to rinse it away from her face, but it flowed and flowed. An old carpenter said, "That's always the way it is. She'll carry on purgin' up to the burial. And, mark me, she'll be a darn sight more gruesome in the morning, all swelled up and pasty white."

Meanwhile, others had gone in search of rails with which to make a bier. When these had been procured, some boards and broken oars were laid across and Mr. Hawthorne took part in bearing the corpse from the bank of the river to her father's house across half a mile of pasture. The men who had waded into the river made squelching sounds as their sodden boots trod the ground. This was the only noise accompanying the otherwise silent midnight procession.

At last they reached the door and an old grey-haired man showed them into the kitchen, where they deposited the body upon a large table.

Rowing back up the river, Ellery told Nathaniel what he had known of the girl.

"One friend would have saved her," he said.

Nathaniel paddled in a trance, and then spoke, as if rehearsing a sentence for the page: "A severe penalty for having cultivated and refined herself out of the sphere of her natural connections."

It was the last memorable experience of their life at Concord this time around. News that the owners of the Manse wanted to re-occupy it did not come as too great a blow, although the experience of watching carpenters move in and proceed to strip the edifice of its time-honoured layers of moss and ancient woodbine, and to shave the wood back to a pristine whiteness, was painful to behold. From the point of view of their own future they had for some time realised that a change in their circumstances was both inevitable and desirable. Nathaniel had been forced to borrow a sum of money from his friend Bridge, and to pursue a claim for damages against George Ripley in an effort to regain a portion of his Brook Farm investment.

Something beyond a penalty for refinement had been paid out by the young woman drowned in the Concord river.

*   *   *

If Nathaniel had felt bad in 1842, returning to Salem a penniless suitor after the Brook Farm failure, he must have felt a good deal worse in that autumn of 1845, forced to return to Castle Dismal a second time, penniless again, and with a wife and young baby in tow. Soon after Una's birth he had written to his friend George Hillard, saying, "The spirit never can be thoroughly gay and careless again . . . I have business on earth now and must look about me for the means of doing it." His writings had been given a chance for three years, and miserably failed to support them. It was not immediately obvious what the new "means" were likely to be, though we can be sure that Elizabeth Peabody and others were busy pulling strings.

The return to her home town was a cruel blow for Sophia too, redolent as it was of her sickly years. There was no real danger that she would resume the life of an invalid but she would have preferred to have come back brandishing her new health and independence, not offering herself once again to the puritanical gloom of the town. To make matters worse, the Hawthorne sisters, particularly Elizabeth, were far from welcoming, and made it plain that they resented having their privacy disrupted. Sophia's own family, now living at Herbert Street, Boston, were simply too pressed for space, and any offer of refuge from that quarter would have involved a curtailment of Elizabeth Peabody's bookshop business.

Una, now eighteen months old, reacted badly to the electrical charge in the West Street air. She had tantrums at mealtimes, so that Sophia was not able to eat until Louisa had finished and could hold the child on her lap. During one particularly trying meal Sophia excused herself from the table without eating, handing the whining Una to Papa. Nathaniel finished his own meal with one hand and then left Una with her aunts and grandmother.

Sophia was weeping in their upstairs parlour. When he came into the room she sniffed and tried to be brave, leaned against him and fingered the lapel of his jacket.

"Phoebe, Phoebe," Nathaniel muttered – at a loss for other words. Putting his hands on her shoulders, they stood thus for several moments, swaying as if in time to some ethereal music. Slowly he bent his cheek to hers and with the rough edge of his day-old beard rasped away her tears. Their lips met and then all the passion pent up within the anxieties of the last months – the cares of parenthood, the financial worry, their eviction from the

141

Promised Land, this cold and cheerless haven – was let forth in ungovernable sexual ardour. He possessed her, as he might have possessed, in Truth or Fancy, one of the serving girls of his bachelor days, her shoed feet rooted to the carpeted floor, his strong forearms pushed up beneath her skirts. Sophia let go of his neck with one hand, pulled the grips from her hair and, throwing her head back, let it fall free and blow in a warm Cuban wind of the mind.

This re-awakened sexuality was the saving grace of the month or two spent at West Street and Julian was conceived in these, his father's boyhood rooms. In the end it was Nathaniel who found the atmosphere insufferable and in the New Year he took his family (Sophia by this time knew of her pregnancy) away, inwardly vowing that they would never return. The move, to Boston, was made possible by the news that President Polk had nominated Mr. Hawthorne for a position in the Custom House. Perhaps the assumption was that the appointment, when it was confirmed, would be to the same Custom House in Boston he had left before his marriage; at any rate, he was eventually asked, in April, to take up duties at the Salem Custom House. Quite whom he had to thank for procuring this position is unclear. It is ironic, though, that the President should respond so positively to lobbying in favour of a man who had done nothing in the election of 1844, whilst Gansevoort Melville, who had done so much, and expended more than a fair measure of his life-force, should, at the same moment, be on the brink of his fatal illness, alone and discarded in London.

Once settled in Boston, Sophia began having regrets that she had not made more of an effort to court the favour of the three Hawthorne women. Louisa had at least shown an interest in Una, and it was to her that she now began writing a series of conciliatory letters.

> I regret very much that I had so little intercourse with Elizabeth. I think we could have enjoyed each other very much. But now the time is past and I do not see as we can ever have another chance to become acquainted as my husband will never go back to Herbert Street, he says, under any circumstances.

The conciliatory air of such passages was perhaps defeated by their frankness and it is not surprising that no real exchange of

142

letters was forthcoming. Although Sophia did press home her endeavours at the beginning of June, as her confinement reached its end, with the following appeal:

I write especially now, to ask if you will come after my confinement to have an eye upon Una. I should much prefer your coming to having Anna Alcott, and if you can come I will not write for her. Otherwise, I suppose I must. Anna will be tender and trustworthy but I fear I would not induce her to obey and could not manage her about going to bed and bathing. Una, besides is extremely fond of you and likes to be with you. I think your mother cannot object for the sake of her new little grandchild, as well as for Una's sake. Aunties are always in requisition in such emergencies.

Julian was born on June 22nd, Nathaniel informing his sister that "a small troglodyte made his appearance here at ten minutes to six this morning" and repeating his wife's appeal.

In view of the misery caused by the brief sojourn at Herbert Street it is unclear what had led Mr. Hawthorne, in the summer of 1845, when he knew that eviction from the Manse was imminent, to decline a clerkship to the Charleston Navy Yard at a salary of nine hundred dollars. It was George Bancroft who offered him the post, having been approached once again by Horatio Bridge. Bancroft had been appointed Secretary to the Navy immediately after Polk's election success, and was living in Washington, where the death of his six-year-old daughter Susan (his only child by the second marriage) was to leave him for once in his life little desire for the social round. He concentrated on his writing and his official work, establishing a naval academy and outlawing the casual flogging of seamen by officers.

Mr. Hawthorne did spend a fortnight in Portsmouth, a naval yard on the north coast of the state, just below the borderline with Maine, but he cannot have been impressed with what he found.

On March 10th 1846, to celebrate the previous day's winning of 585 dollars in damages, the Hawthornes took tea at a restaurant near the Tremont theatre, still notorious for the audacity it had shown in 1843 by breaking from the Sabbath observance and including a Saturday night performance in its programme. They sat near the street to watch the passers-by. While scolding Una for taking liberties with the sugarbowl Nathaniel had his attention drawn by Sophia to a family group walking by on the other side of the street.

"Do the Shaws have more than one son?"

Mr. Hawthorne shrugged.

"We never did go walking with Mama and Papa. You wicked man, you used to steal me away by myself."

"With Elizabeth, you mean!"

Sophia silenced him with a frown. "None of your barbed remarks about Lizzie."

The Shaw group had stopped outside the theatre to examine the postings.

"I expect that fellow's a client, rather than a suitor. Look how deeply he and the judge are in conversation."

Two days later Sophia thought she saw one of the Shaw sons a second time. She was out walking Una, taking a look at the Charles River, when he passed her by, and bade her a good day. He was evidently returning home, for he had a case with him, which he carried sailor fashion on one shoulder. "Man with funny sack of doal," Una said. And then resumed the singing of her favourite rhyme:

> Bobby Shaftoe's gone to sea
> he'll tum back
> and marry Nona!

She sang it over and over again, and each time she came to her name at the end Sophia leaned forward and tickled her in the tummy.

Later in the year Sophia saw the man a third time. He was again walking with his sister. This time they were alone. It was early December and both wore new and fashionable coats.

*   *   *

The young woman was indeed Elizabeth Shaw, but the man was not her brother, it was Herman Melville.

Judge Lemuel Shaw, Chief Justice of the State of Massachusetts, had continuously shown the Melville family every consideration. His daughter Elizabeth might not have been a great beauty, nor did she have a singular personality, but we can sympathise with Mr. Melville's conservative choice of marriage partner.

The March visit to Boston came immediately after the publication of *Typee*, which was dedicated to Lemuel Shaw. Although he had not really been one in practice, all his benevolence having been administered from a distance, Herman certainly seems to have considered Judge Shaw as something of a substitute father. The prospect of marrying into his family would have recommended itself on several counts: firstly, it would legitimise the father–son relationship; secondly, despite his improved eligibility as a bachelor, consequent upon the reception of his first book, Herman could scarcely expect to strike a better match for himself than to marry into the family of the Chief Justice of the State; thirdly, having outraged his family by first running away to sea and then publishing an account of his experiences, the veracity of which was openly debated, marriage into a stalwart Boston family might go some way towards restoring his credibility; fourthly, he had already begun to work on the sequel to *Typee*, and the prospect of a short, straightforward courtship, followed by a marriage where means of livelihood were not likely to be an overriding problem (such was his naïve view at the time), must have added attraction and lustre to his image of Elizabeth Shaw.

When he arrived in Boston on March 4th 1846, it was as a young man in his twenty-seventh year, flushed by the imminent publication of his Polynesian narrative. The book was already out in England and this same day a steamer set sail across the Atlantic, carrying copies of the new volume for Mrs. Melville and Mr. Bancroft, together with six newspaper reviews. Herman's sister, Helen, had intended accompanying him on the trip – indeed arrangements for the visit had initially been made with Helen in mind, possibly with a view to making a match between her and the Chief Justice's son, John Oakes.

"Helen, I'm afraid, was indisposed and not quite up to the journey. She hopes to be able to come at the weekend."

Mrs. Shaw (the Judge's second wife – Elizabeth's own mother had died during childbirth) smiled. "Do you know Boston well, Herman?"

"Not as well as I know New York."

"John and Elizabeth will be glad to show you round, I'm sure. My own two sons are away at present."

They were drinking tea and eating cake in an opulent parlour.

John was at work. Elizabeth kept sipping from an empty cup, too shy to speak, too nervous to sit still. At mention of her name she blushed.

"I expect you would like a rest before supper. I know my husband is eager to listen to your sailor's yarns."

Herman put his cup and saucer on to the tray. "I have dedicated the book to him. It should be out in a fortnight."

"Oh, yes, the book." Mrs. Shaw stood up, to show the visitor to his room. Elizabeth remained seated, staring into her lap. "Your mother mentioned that Gansevoort was doing something about a book, over in London. It seems a pity the President could only find him the Legation. I'm sure he's destined for higher things. Your bag, by the way, will already have gone up. My husband expects to be home soon after six. He is often delayed but knows you are arriving today. Do come down if there's anything you need."

At twenty-to-seven a domestic tapped on the door, opened it, and informed Herman, who had been resting on the bed, that he was invited downstairs to join the Judge in a drink.

"Hello, Herman! Good to see you. Very good. Have some whisky?"

Judge Shaw enquired after all members of the Melville family, particularly after Thomas' widow, and the children. He shook his head. "A sad business that. I had only just received a letter from your uncle. About Henry – and there's another woeful business – how he needed certifying. And then by next post – t', t'. Very sudden. And on your birthday, I understand. They've left Galena. Is the mother all right financially?"

Herman drew in some breath and made ready to deliver the speech he had been practising upstairs in which, prompted by an instruction from his mother, but also with sincere personal feelings of gratitude on his own part, he would thank the Judge vehemently for all the assistance he had given the Melville family.

"Permit me to say, sir, how greatly moved the whole of my family has been by your generous support over the past troubled years. I . . ."

The Judge brushed aside further appreciation and took Herman's empty glass. "One more before the meal, I think."

John Oakes arrived home and was invited to join them in a drink. He declined and went to his room to change for supper.

"John is a little older than you. In years. But he's never been out of the country. My professional life has kept me too busy for foreign tours, and my son was not born, it seems, with an adventurous spirit. I'm glad in a way, and Mrs. Shaw certainly is, even though he's not her own. Your absence at sea must have caused your family considerable worry."

Herman was not at all sure that it had, but he said he supposed it did. They were called then, into the dining room. Herman was seated next to Elizabeth, John next to his step-mother, with Lemuel at the head of the table. Mr. Shaw said grace and the meal commenced with soup.

"John, this is Herman Melville, Helen's brother. Helen hopes to join us at the weekend." She looked to Herman for confirmation.

Judge Shaw, breaking bread on to his side-plate, mentioned Herman's forthcoming book. "Something about your whaling adventures, I suppose."

"No. I've left that for another."

"I see. You intend becoming something of a regular author then?"

"I have hopes of so doing. This first book I have dedicated to you, sir."

The Judge put down his spoon and patted his lips with a serviette. "That is most kind. Most kind. But will not your own family, your mother . . ."

"The kindness has not been mine, and my mother more than anyone, is aware that, indeed she . . ."

"No more gratitude, please. Your father was a good man, who deserved better success in this world. The least I can do is ensure his family suffer no unnecessary discomfort. Now, can you give us a foretaste of this book that's been dedicated to me?"

Herman told them its title, gave them a rough outline of the four-month-long adventure it set out to recount and hinted at the controversial content of his attitude towards the missionaries. Mrs. Shaw sought to draw him out on the subject of his own point of view as regarded the uncivilised parts of the world. He chose to base his reply upon a passage from the book.

"Look at Honolulu – a community, we are led to believe, of disinterested merchants and devoted self-exiled heralds of the Cross. Ah, but I have been to Honolulu. I have seen the natives civilised into draught-horses and evangelised into beasts of burden. Why, I saw a missionary's wife, taking her daily airing in a go-cart drawn by two of the islanders, clobber the men on their skulls with the handle of a huge fan, urging them to pull her out of the loose soil of a wheel-rut. Is this uplifting behaviour? Let the savages be civilised. But civilise them with benefits and not with evils."

"In the earthly execution of a spiritual cause there are bound to be falls from grace," Mrs. Shaw observed.

"Madame, I grant as much in my book. I am afraid, however, that my little example sets the rule and not the exception."

"Come, now – isn't it the loose morals of these savage peoples which, in the end, is their undoing?"

"The looseness of the marriage-tie has made some of the islands vulnerable to European diseases, yes. But on which side lies the blame? And in Typee itself, the social organisation, though different from our own, was strictly adhered to. Each man had just one wife, though a woman was allowed four or five husbands, which fact alone speaks for the gentle disposition of the male populace."

The Judge, indicating to a maid that they were ready for the main course, said, "I think, my dear, that we should allow Herman to put all his evidence in front of us before we make a judgement. He has been there and we have not. I am sure he has written honestly, and will send us a copy of the book."

Herman confirmed that he would send them a personally signed copy as soon as one was available. The next course characterised itself by greater concentration upon enjoyment of the food, with just a little family conversation. During dessert it was pointed out to Herman that John would be working again the next day, but that Elizabeth could begin to show him around the city. Elizabeth, who had hardly spoken since Herman's arrival in the house, now merely nodded her head, and sipped her glass of water.

After the meal, the gentlemen availed themselves of drinks and a cigar, John and his father talking about a local political issue which eventually brought them round to mention of Gansevoort.

"If your brother is making as big a name for himself in London as he did on this side of the Atlantic during last year's election I should think it would be a wise move for him, on his return, to stand for office. He is politically ambitious, I take it?"

"Well, to tell you the truth, I saw so little of him after my return, that it is some five years since I can claim to have *known* my brother. He is a good bit changed since then. We have gathered from his letters though that he does not see eye to eye with the Ambassador in London."

"Expect the fellow recognised he's out-qualified. Uncomfy feeling that. Get it myself sometimes. Is the cigar all right, Herman?"

"Yes, thank you, sir."

"Do they use tobacco in the South Seas?" John asked the question with the formality of a schools examiner.

"Certainly, but in pipes, not rolled. And they pass them round from hand to hand. They regarded my systematic smoking of whole pipefuls of tobacco as something quite wonderful."

The Judge departed, at the end of his cigar, to study some papers, and John Oakes did not offer Herman a further drink. He was a young man with little to say for himself, and although Herman was loquacious about specific matters he was not disposed to fill a silence with pointless remarks. Instead, he went to his room, and read for nearly two hours, savouring the pleasure of reading a good book in a strange house.

* * *

The next day Elizabeth walked him around Boston. She showed him the Common, claiming to remember, as a young child, seeing a herd of cows pasturing there; Beacon Hill, with its fine bow-fronted houses; the sixty-foot-wide Charles Street, laid out at the end of the last century; and the Back Bay, where the area known as Fenlands had been recovered from the swamps. It was a strange experience for both of them, and one they must have remembered subsequently with some curiosity. Mr. Melville, with his reputation as newly-published author, his history of naval adventure, and his easy way of speaking with her father, was too formidable a figure to be considered realistic material for a love match, whilst Miss Shaw was too self-deprecating a companion to arouse, of her own accord, romantic aspirations in the male mind. And yet, it was during this uncomfortable, self-conscious tour of the city, that the idea of making Elizabeth his wife first planted itself in the bachelor's mind. Foot-weary at last, and having stopped for a cup of tea, it was as they sat across from one another at a small table, with Elizabeth efficiently sorting the cups and pouring the drinks, that his mind played with the prospect of their being betrothed. Both playful and fleeting though the first visitation of the idea had been, and though they resumed walking with the same awkwardness between them, it would prove impossible for Herman to look upon Elizabeth with disinterest again.

They arrived back at the house in time for a late, informal luncheon, after which, genuinely footsore, Herman bathed and attempted to settle lazily with the same book he had enjoyed the previous night. Finding himself re-reading the opening paragraph of a new chapter over and over again, he looked away from the printed page to allow the thought that was distracting him to reveal itself. Elizabeth once again turned the cups the right way up and poured the tea, then pushed the sugarbowl towards him.

He was curious to know what it was about this very ordinary young woman that had found a way of intruding herself upon his thoughts and he was astute enough at self-analysis to see immediately what it was. He was comfortable in this house and had not experienced the same secure sense of being within a firmly established family home since his happy childhood had abruptly ended in exile from their Broadway residence. His uncle's home at Albany had been secure but cold, whilst the Pittsfield household had been warm but anarchic.

By the time Helen arrived at the weekend, Herman was glad of the shift of focus, for he was by this time actively courting the Judge's daughter. His tales at the dinner table, culled again from the Typee experiences, were addressed to the whole family but with more than proportional eye contact with Elizabeth, who could not quite believe what was going on and in the first instance, ascribed the guest's fulsomeness, as compared with his silences during their walk, to too copious a supply of liquor before the meal.

On the third day, during a morning of inclement weather which kept him from prowling the city alone, he found Elizabeth and asked if she could give him permission to look at her father's library. It was something the Judge himself had alluded to already in a casual way designed to make Herman feel ready to browse as he was inclined, but Herman preferred, for obvious reasons, to make a formal approach.

Elizabeth showed him the room. It was not a large library, the Judge keeping the majority of his law books in his office, and it was plain that he would not need Elizabeth's further assistance, so he detained her with a general question.

"Do you read?"

"I shall read your book, when you give it to Papa."

"Parts of it will be a little stale. I told the good bits last night."
He smiled. And she smiled back.

"I'll see you later, then." It was not what he had wished to say, for it made Elizabeth withdraw with the impression that the reason for her aid had been nothing more than requested.

He spent twenty minutes or so in the library, finally selecting a volume of naval history. He met Mrs. Shaw in the hallway and she told him that a message had been received saying Helen was well again and would be arriving on tomorrow's stage. Herman showed her the book and Mrs. Shaw put her hand on his fore-arm, as if she were about to say something in confidence. "Lemuel would have loved to have been a seaman; loved it. That's why he gets on so well with you."

The Judge had a dinner engagement that night and John Oakes was attending a committee meeting of the young men's social club to which he belonged. Herman, terrified that he might be called upon to act as head of the table, to say Grace, and make unsolicited conversation, decided during the afternoon that, despite the possibility of appearing to snub Elizabeth, he must make his excuses for the evening. So he quickly found Mrs. Shaw and told her that he would be out for dinner that night and apologised for not having warned her sooner.

"Quite all right. With Lemuel out we were only having cold meats. Will you be late? John, I doubt, will be in before midnight, so the house will stay lighted until then at least."

Herman said that would be quite late enough for him, and then, turning to go back to his room, he saw Elizabeth had been listening behind them.

By the time the Hawthornes spotted the Shaw family outside the Tremont theatre, the weekend was over and it had become abundantly clear that whatever romantic hopes had speeded Helen's recovery, a love affair with John was not even a remote possibility. He had made himself busy for much of Saturday and Sunday, with business arising from the committee meeting, and on the Monday had refused to take time off work. There had been a furious argument before breakfast, which Helen had been unaware of, but the general atmosphere was sufficient to provoke a slight relapse in her health, so that she stayed in when the others went for a walk which took them past the Hawthornes' celebratory tea.

In fairness to Helen, lest she seems to have been suffering a surfeit of unladylike presumption, it needs to be said that a previous visit to Boston, around Christmas-time, had quite

151

legitimately raised her hopes. Although there had been no subsequent correspondence a certain relationship *had* seemed to have begun, and the abrupt retreat of John Oakes now must have been due in part to a realisation that the signals of his earlier friendliness had been misinterpreted.

The effect of all this was to make more realistic the tentative beginnings of Herman's and Elizabeth's relationship. Still Judge Shaw commandeered the conversation and, from the morrow onwards, when Helen was again recovered and resigned to John's inattentiveness, Elizabeth spent most of her time with Herman's sister. This was to be no bad thing, for when it came time to depart Helen was heard to say to Elizabeth that the hospitality of their family ought, at some future date, to be reciprocated in Lansingburgh, and Herman beamed his assent to that suggestion in a goodbye smile.

*　　*　　*

There were not many beaming smiles to greet him at the family home, for he came back to the news that his youngest brother – Thomas, aged fifteen – had left to join the crew of a whaler. Mrs. Melville was ready with the blame.

"Now look what your fireside tale-telling has led to!"

And with the tears,

"Poor Tom! However will he . . ."

"Unless he lies about his age, mother, they might not take him. He's three inches shorter than me yet and not the stoutest looking youth in the state."

"They'll take him, right enough. You know that as well as I do. And take any lies he cares to spin them, without question."

Herman was himself distraught at the news. Although he resented his mother's imputation and could not recall similar maternal concern at his own seagoing apprenticeship, he was indeed worried that Thomas' might have been influenced by his own adventuring. And such a worry cast a pall over American publication of *Typee*.

The book came out on March 17th. On March 19th Herman posted off an inscribed copy to Judge Shaw together with a thank you note.

Remember me most warmly to Mrs. Shaw and Miss

Elizabeth, and to all your family, and tell them I shall not soon forget that agreeable visit to Boston.

The book was taken up and reviewed by all the notable names. The earliest American review appeared in the *Salem Advertiser* on March 25th. It was written by Nathaniel Hawthorne:

> The book is lightly but vigorously written; and we are acquainted with no work that gives a freer and more effective picture of barbarian life etc.

Other reviewers included Margaret Fuller, George Ripley and Walt Whitman. The book's success, and the publicity generated by the spontaneous declaration of Richard Tobias Greene, Melville's fellow adventurer, were somewhat overshadowed by the death of Gansevoort, and Herman, instead of attending to the rewards of his accomplishment was forced to spend much time in the correspondence with Mr. McLane.

"Toby" turned up in Buffalo, with a timely corroboration of the Typee story, insofar as he had been involved in it. Timely, because Melville's American publishers, Wiley and Putnam, were pressing him to delete what they saw as the romantic, contentious episodes, and to prepare a revised edition for the autumn. It was during the negotiation for this expurgated edition that Melville first met Evert Duyckinck, who was one of Wiley's chief editors.

These concerns took up the months of June and July respectively, but were possibly ameliorated by the amorous attentions of a mystery lady in New York, whom he was on close enough terms with later in the year:

> DECEMBER 1846 – In passing through town some ten days since I left the ms of *Omoo* with a particular lady acquaintance of mine, at whose home I intend calling this evening to obtain it. The lady resides up town.

It is easier to identify with Mr. Hawthorne's erotic life than it is with Melville's, but it is just possible that, during this period of late summer and autumn, while he consolidated his courtship with Elizabeth Shaw, Melville was consorting elsewhere as well.

Miss Shaw had been invited to summer at Lansingburgh, ostensibly as a friend of Helen and also to give Mrs. Melville added female support during her protracted period of mourning for Gansevoort. She arrived on August 31st, picked up at Greenbush by Herman. It was the first time the young woman had journeyed away from home on anything other than visits to close relatives in Boston, and this buggy-ride through the fields of Massachusetts, which were golden with sun-scorched bounty, gave her just the same sense of freeblown emancipation as Sophia Hawthorne had experienced when setting sail for Cuba.

It is difficult to give a modern approximation to this feeling. Children, particularly girls, make their bid for freedom at an earlier age today. On the other hand, there are grounds for arguing that family life is more claustrophobic now. There are fewer relatives to visit and children are not often sent on holiday by themselves, as happened very frequently in the nineteenth century, and in the early part of our own. But more important is the ease with which the adult world of today is trespassed by the young. It is a spurious ease of course, but delusion generates its own authenticity. If we cannot truly share the thrill of this twenty-four-year-old young woman riding beside Mr. Melville and sensing that at last she was being transported across a mystical boundary which Destiny had been holding back for her and her alone – the sense of personal destiny being yet another aspect which might distance us from her experience – we can at least keep company with her.

The Melville household, when it was fully gathered, consisted of Maria aged fifty-five, Helen aged twenty-nine, Augusta aged twenty-five, Allan aged twenty-three, Catherine aged twenty-one and Frances aged nineteen. Herman's presence, with his continual trips to New York and Boston, was still very much a wayfaring one, and Allan the fifth-born was too much the junior to Helen to exert much masculine command over the establishment. So, for the first time in her life, Elizabeth entered a world dominated by the female gender.

In the small house she had to room with both Helen and Augusta so that, during her entire stay, her most private moments were those occasions when Herman managed to be alone with her. His romantic interest in the visitor had already been communicated to Helen and he did not mind the speed with which it was transmitted to the three other females since their jokey insinuations counteracted the necessity of casting himself in the role of suitor, although Elizabeth had already regarded him as such, following the solicitous attentiveness he had displayed in the course of their first buggy ride.

Even supposing there was no liaison with a mystery lady in New

154

York still we can state, with some degree of certitude, that Melville, during his days as a prisoner in Tahiti, and the months spent as a beachcomber in Honolulu, had satisfied that physical curiosity as regards womankind, which otherwise dominates a first relationship. Had he been as highly sexed a character as Mr. Hawthorne this would have made no great difference. Such was not the case. Elizabeth stirred no wild feelings of lust in him.

Mrs. Shaw, having perhaps been more perspicacious than either Elizabeth or Herman might have supposed, and at any rate intrigued by her stepdaughter's painstaking reading of Mr. Melville's *Typee*, had taken it upon herself to issue certain caveats regarding the financial status of the Melvilles in general and the prospects for a freelance author in particular. Although she had shown Herman every courtesy during his stay, the truth was that she regarded her husband's continuing patronage of the family as unnecessary – there was no blood relationship, and in darker moments she imagined that Lemuel's generosity betokened the atonement for some wrong done in the past.

Elizabeth was never a serious reader, but it is true that she had pored over *Typee* with the kind of attention a conscientious student gives to a set text, returning to key passages and marking the book, not in her father's autographed edition, but in her own copy, bought out of personal spending money. At first she had found the book difficult to enter and she did not care for the informative social picture of Typee life which the author amassed – she was much more intrigued by what the book only half-said, or left unsaid, regarding the writer's day-to-day relationship with the natives, and she underscored this sentence with a triple line:

> At any rate, I have more than one reason to believe that tedious courtships are unknown in the Valley of Typee.

There was to be no tedious courtship in Lansingburgh either. Herman was busy much of the time with the writing of *Omoo*, leaving Elizabeth to the overt purpose of her visit – being a companion for Helen and giving assistance in the domestic management of the household while Mrs. Melville continued to languish.

The older woman was neither cold nor austere in her mourning – her character was very different from that of Mr. Hawthorne's mother – rather she was piquish and cantankerous. Her daughter did not run the house to her liking. Elizabeth was ordered about as if she was a hired skivvy. She, who was supposed to be exhausted and incapacitated through grief, wandered the house finding fault, and complaining that Herman, who might now have taken upon his shoulders the provision of the family, shut himself away writing *stories*.

"My mother hates me," Herman confided to Elizabeth, during their first time alone together since her arrival. It was late afternoon and he had been writing all day. There had been rain in the morning – indeed there had been such a squall and downpour that it seemed as if all trace of summer would be blown and washed away – but now the sky was blue and the sun shone with a pleasing warmth, so that one would almost agree with the fellow who maintains there are only three seasons, summer, winter and a transitional. Autumn days in March and April. Spring days in September and October. In equal quantity. So this fellow argues.

Their walk took them through a field of young bullocks and, having to cross a stile near the region of their feeding trough, Elizabeth began to slide in the soft much-trodden mud. Herman held out his arm so that she might steady herself. It was their first physical contact and it came immediately after his remark about his mother.

"Are you all right?"

She looked white but it had not been the lost footing which had unsettled her so much as an apprehension that the bullocks, moving behind her, were ready to butt or stampede. The city dweller of the nineteenth century, especially the female, was even more country-shy than their modern counterpart.

"Here, I will hold your hand. From now onward." Such was the punctuation of his words as she heard them, the "from now onward" resonating with a separate, self-contained meaning.

"Did you know your own mother?"

But the question came as Elizabeth was actually putting her foot over the stile, and managing to get it hopelessly tangled in the ruffles of her petticoats. Colour gushed abundantly once again upon her cheek.

"Are you sure a hand will be enough or do you need carrying?"

The two of them walked on with smiles on their faces and Herman did not attempt a third time to talk of mothers, either his or hers.

They called at one of the farmhouses and collected a dishcloth full of the creamed cheese which Mrs. Melville had been promised.

156

"Is your mother bearing up now, Herman?" asked the mistress, as she knotted the muslin. The milkmaid who had fetched the cheese in a sort of long-handled tureen was well known to Herman. She had flirted with him often on his walks past the farm and he frequently stopped to watch her at milking.

"Your mother, Herman. Is she at all better? Doing any more?"

"Yes. Oh, I think so. Miss Shaw – this is Miss Shaw from Boston – how would you describe my mother's mood, her, well, her recovery?"

The milkmaid, in full view of Elizabeth, appeared to be massaging her own bosom.

"I – I really don't – she seems – certainly she has energy – but it was such a great – such an enormous – loss."

In after-images of this stumbling reply Elizabeth fancied she saw the milkmaid going to excess, and plastering herself with the cream cheese.

Herman had turned round immediately Elizabeth began struggling for words and the milkmaid brushed the tips of her fingers down across her skirt, as if to straighten out some unsightly rucks in her clothing, before taking the long-handled vessel out of the room. Backing away as she closed the door she gave Herman a look of jealous, inverted snobbery.

"Well, thank you for this. The evenings are turning damp and I must get Miss Shaw home."

They walked briskly back, without holding hands. The milkmaid had been nothing to him – he had never succumbed and would never have succumbed to her willing wiles. Similarly, Mr. Melville would have recoiled from any form of forwardness during the courtship.

To begin with, Elizabeth had attributed at least part of the domestic chaos at Lansingburgh to her own arrival but when she had been there a week and the débâcle did not abate she began to recognise it as the normal condition of the household. Herman, at an early point in the day, withdrew to his writing room – not his own bedroom which he shared with Allan, but Tom's tiny room, a venue which, in the circumstances, did not find favour with his mother.

"Many a mother would have made that room a shrine until the youngest born's return. My oldest and youngest have gone from me in the space of a few months. And he sits up there rubbing salt into the wound. Tell me more about your brothers, dear."

Mrs. Melville had mixed motives in these requests for family information, which Elizabeth had already given, repeatedly. She wanted, self-pityingly, to highlight her own miserable family status; she wanted, by implication, to chastise her own children, and particularly Herman, for not following an orthodox business career. She wanted to lament the absence of a male hierarchy in the Melville line. Thomas was dead, but had not been much use while alive. Everything she said stemmed from a single, bitter regret. She wished she had never married Allan, for the vacillating Melville heredity had quite ruined the Gansevoort line, which went back, via the Orkneys, to the Kings of Norway.

It was all nonsense of course and Elizabeth at this time was proud enough of her own sex to see that Mrs. Melville's derangement was by no means inevitable, and that she was the one to be directly blamed for the lack of domestic discipline. She did dominate the household, but it was her disruptiveness which held sway.

Elizabeth could not help but admire Herman's determined detachment from such an atmosphere. So busy was he with the writing of *Omoo* that Allan became his new business agent, pressing Wiley and Putnam for a statement of the author's earnings to date. On October 7th, after the sale of seventeen hundred copies of *Typee*, these stood at 86.26 dollars. The majority of these small earnings was being spent as fast as they accrued, as a later statement testified.

February 8th 1847

797 paper copies sold

387 cloth copies sold

	661.94
less expenses	439.18
$\frac{1}{2}$ to Herman Melville	222.76
	111.38
less book orders	103.57
	7.81

Therefore, at the time of writing *Omoo*, Herman was fully aware that his existing earning power was something in the region of a hundred dollars per annum. He could not court Elizabeth with any confidence on that, so his industry throve on several desperations: the desperate need to prove to himself that he was no one-book wonder; the desperate need to put more copy on the market, fast, while his name was fresh; the desperate need to prove his commitment to Elizabeth, and through her, to his prospective father-in-law, Judge Shaw; the desperate all-consuming need to cancel his mother's opinion of him; and the desperate psychological necessity of keeping up an occupation which provided blessed refuge from the demands of a dislocated family.

And so the autumn went on. One day – it was mid-morning and she had come upstairs to attend to a bruised finger sustained while moving furniture at the directive of Mrs. Melville – Elizabeth found herself alone in the bedroom. A tree, which grew close to the wall of the house, was being buffeted by a harsh October wind. She unfastened and opened the window, the better to hear the mystical element rushing through and stirring the branches. It was a noise that reminded her of the sea, and thus of home, a nostalgic reference which ushered in one of those rarefied moments of decision that the existentialist seeks to universalise.

A sudden intensity of the gale shook even the heaviest of the tree's branches and Elizabeth shuddered at the choice which confronted her. Young women of her era, however romantic the attachment to their suitor, liked to feel comfortable with the family they were marrying into. Elizabeth sensed some kind of curse hanging over the Melvilles and could not believe that the adversity would stop at the deaths of father and eldest son. And yet the idea of a spinster's life at home, or even of marrying into a similarly stable Bostonian family, seemed to be ridiculed by the zealous flurry out-of-doors.

The act of determination was neither easy nor pleasurable; as a Christian she felt betrayed by the overpowering sense of loneliness that accompanied the decision. The majority of our choices we comprehend only in recollection. We seem to have been taken down one road rather than another by the natural momentum of our lives. But there do come moments of stark choice, when we feel utterly alone.

Having dipped her thumb in a jug of cold water, she lightly bandaged it, then shut the window. She paused on the landing to stare at the closed bedroom door behind which Herman worked. On the stepping of the stair her decision was made and Mrs. Melville, had she been less self-centred, might have noticed the subtle shift in the register with which the guest voiced her communications for the rest of the morning.

By the time Elizabeth took her leave of Lansingburgh on November 1st, the romance was more or less common knowledge

159

amongst the Melville family, although no one made overt reference to it, neither did Elizabeth or Herman display anything more than polite affection for one another in front of others or, for that matter, in moments of privacy.

*   *   *

For the remainder of the month Mr. Melville, writing the final third of *Omoo* and preparing the entire manuscript for presentation to his publisher, escalated his detachment from the family circle, with the result that his mother and sisters began to speak about him as if he were absent from the house. Mrs. Melville, who, in her protracted state of emotional dishevelment was increasingly reliant upon consignments of sherry and gin obtained by virtue of a romantic attachment enjoyed by her other son Allan, refused to acknowledge the labours of the one who locked himself away.

"He thinks he can hide his crime by never showing himself, does he? Not that we want to see his face again anyway. Great riches *he* brought back from the South Seas, I must say. But if only young Tom would walk through that door, our spirits might rise again. At least that Judge's daughter is off back to her home. Silly bitchock. Fancy mincing around Herman for an entire two months. I shouldn't wonder if seagoing hasn't entirely blotted out his family instinct. I remember your father telling me about sailor friends he knew. Some things you wouldn't credit, but . . ." She muttered like this to herself, out of earshot.

At the end of the month Herman went to New York and spent an evening or two at the home of his female acquaintance, leaving her the completed manuscript of *Omoo* to look over.

The reception of this second novel, published in April of 1847 (at the beginning of the month in London, and the end of the month in New York), was a vital part of Herman's courtship. He had begun the New Year determined to end it a married man. In February, while negotiations for publication were still in progress, he had travelled to Washington, and, calling upon Senator Dix, had put himself forward for a post in the Treasury Department, an act of self-advertisement which proves how much he hankered after marital status. But Treasury posts, like those in the Customs House, were party political prizes, and Mr. Melville had as yet displayed no allegiances worth speaking of. His personal presentation was backed by written entreaties, but Mr. Dix replied,

"You know in the lottery of political life it is impossible for all to secure prizes. There is little encouragement in this line for any one just now."

It is hardly surprising then that when at the end of March Mr. Melville drew bills on J. R. Brodhead to retrieve the sum paid by John Murray for the English copyright of *Omoo* he deducted nearly five pounds to "provide for any little outlay which may be occasioned by your granting me a little favour I have yet to beg of you"; the favour being the collection and despatch of reviews and notices.

In they came, from home and abroad, throughout the month of May. Walt Whitman's judgement was fair and typical: "We recommend this narrative as thorough entertainment, not so light as to be tossed aside for its flippancy, nor so profound as to be tiresome." The New York edition sold three thousand five hundred copies in the first week and there was also renewed interest in *Typee*.

The author, keeping to his Lansingburgh retreat, must have felt a mounting sense of elation. Even his mother, albeit that young Tom had still not surfaced (naturally, she feared him drowned), gave temporary recognition to the elder of her middle sons. The sisters doted on their famous brother, pressing and mending his clothes with a special assiduity. Helen, who was to become as devoted a copyist as Mr. Hawthorne's sister had been in an earlier day, began now by writing out fair transcripts of the reviews, particularly those from London, to post to friends, and to pass around the village.

By the end of May, Mr. Melville had been sufficiently cosseted and felt sufficiently sure of his authorial standing to set out for Boston with the purpose of making official the contingencies discussed with Elizabeth in March; contingencies which had rested upon the success or failure of *Omoo*.

Arriving at the Shaw home on Tuesday June 1st, Melville felt brim-full of confidence, and instead of retiring to his room until the arrival home of Judge Shaw he asked Mrs. Shaw if he might sit in the drawing room and help himself to a drink. It was past five o'clock. The day had been sultry. He would take a gin with a cut of lemon.

He was left there for the better part of an hour before he heard the Judge step into the hall; the sounds of a muffled greeting; then the drawing-room door opening.

"Herman! Good to see you. Let me change, then I'll join you in that drink."

Herman himself went upstairs to change for dinner. He had not yet seen Elizabeth, her absence being part of a pre-arranged plan. John Oakes was now married and the two Savage sons were again away from home.

When he re-entered the drawing room the Judge was already at the sideboard in a fawn sunjacket, pouring himself a whisky. "Same for you?"

"I have a glass. Was drinking gin actually."

"Oh, well, if that's what you're taking. There. And a toast to the continuing success of *Omule*. Very well done."

"Sir," Herman began, as they took their drinks across to the soft chairs, "I have come to your house . . ."

The Judge coughed, and had to bib some whisky from his chin, and from the knees of his trouser leg.

"Easy on, dear boy. You're not in church."

Unabashed, Herman began again. "I have come here today to ask for Elizabeth's hand." The Judge was still fidgeting with his handkerchief. "In marriage," Herman added.

The diversion with the handkerchief was both guileless and beguiling. It was not premeditated but it was one of those instinctual actions which had become a part of the legal man's professional theatrics. He continued to fold and refold the piece of cloth, while responding to Herman's announcement.

"I have every wish that you and Elizabeth be wed. It would complete, shall we say, my own obligations to your poor father. And I have no doubt that Lizzie wants you for a husband. She has watched John Oakes be married and is itching to set up home herself. So that what I have left to say – if a note of reluctance creeps in – you must lay it all to the special feelings a father has for his only daughter and a need to make her dead mother rest easy with the future. Do you believe in the hereafter, Herman?"

The Judge looked up from his handiwork. Herman's confidence was suddenly gone. A sip from his gin retrieved none of his self-assurance, and he wished now that he had chosen a drink of darker hue and richer body.

"I mean, not just Heaven. But the ability of those in Heaven to see and care about life here. Do you believe in that?"

Herman answered unsurely. "I suppose I do."

"I have then to execute the cares and responsibilities of three parents. My first wife's, Hope's and my own. In addition, I am only three years off my allotted span of seventy years. To put it plainly, I want to pass my daughter not only into a lover's arms but into the care and good management of a well-situated guardian. I have heard that your latest book has been successfully received but I would like you to give me some firmer notion of the monetary return that regular authorship might be expected to furnish you, especially since both you and I know how hard pressed your own family circumstances have so unfortunately been. I would like to know, in short, how immediate are your prospects of being able to set up a home.''

"Well, besides the return from the books – and that is rather difficult to gauge – er, *Typee* didn't make me very much, I feel bound to say, but then *Omoo*, *O–moo* by the way, the sales from that are carrying off a certain number of unsold *Typee*. I made, for instance, a hundred and fifty English pounds from the copyright of *Omoo*, but then, as I say, besides the book, I am very friendly with Evert Duyckinck who has just brought out a new literary gazette, and he has asked me to write for that. Nor would I be averse to taking some government office . . .'' As he spoke Herman realised how inadequate it all sounded and how little honest attention he had given to the precise shape which his future with Elizabeth might take.

Judge Shaw finally put his handkerchief in his pocket. "I'll confess something to you, Herman. Lizzie has already hinted to me that this is the way things between you were going. She even mentioned having the wedding on your birthday in August. Is that what you've been planning?''

"Sir, we have spoken about the future in endearing tones. I hope you won't consider us guilty of presumption.''

Having first reached across for Herman's empty glass, Lemuel approached the drinks sideboard to fill them. He carried on the conversation with his back to Herman, who, in turn, had his back to the sideboard. Both men spoke with raised voices.

"You're getting crusty with me. It's my own fault. I've made you feel that I'm about to say 'No.'"

Herman certainly felt he was being toyed with. His head began to freeze over with the pins and needles of nervous tension – a sensation he tried to alleviate by stroking his forehead with the knuckles of his right hand.

"I only wanted to make it quite plain that we have not taken your . . .''

"My permission for granted. I know.''

"Your blessing I would rather say, sir."

"You have my blessing."

The Judge returned with the filled glasses. "Yes, you have my blessing," he repeated, as he sat himself down again. "You must forgive all that former preamble. Just playing the paternal part, though there *are* details, financial details, which we shall have to sort out. How long are you here?"

"Till the weekend."

"That's fine, then. For tonight we shall celebrate in principle. It shall be an engagement dinner. Just the four of us, I'm afraid. And anyway, how could I have said 'No', after you had dedicated your first book to me."

"Believe me, there was no subtlety in . . ."

"Now don't get prickly again. And as for what I had to say about the hereafter there is of course one other resident of Heaven who ought to derive some pleasure from the result of these masculine negotiations. Don't you feel there's something primitive about my controlling a daughter's future? Even if the control is only ostensible. No wonder there are stirrings from the weaker sex. I fear we're seeing only the first of it. Have you heard mention of the Peabody woman? But we were about to remember, my dear friend, your father. It is rather fitting that I should take over his paternal responsibilities in a legal sense; it will complement my existing obligations."

The Judge, vitalised by the liquor, and by the poignancy of his acceptance of a future son-in-law, began to speak of Providence and of how his rather silly attempt at paternal rectitude had merely mirrored the eternal pretence of man's control over Destiny. It was just such a theme to which Herman would have warmed had he been able to recover more quickly from his nervous discomfiture. As it was, he welcomed the monologue for the opportunity it gave him to achieve a more confident bearing before confronting Elizabeth with the embarrassment of a formal announcement.

*   *   *

The theme of predestination assailed him again on the last night of the honeymoon when he sat alone and cold on the deck of a returning canal boat. Elizabeth, tired of having to bob her head down every time the helmsman called "Bridge", and worried that

164

she might catch chill from the fog, had chosen the heat and bad atmosphere of the ladies apartment below deck. It had been a decision prompted by Herman's own entreaties; nevertheless, a sense of desertion made wistful the musings which, together with the physical discomfort, kept him awake the entire night.

There was also the ironical and inescapable contrast between his earlier career as a sailor, hauling in a whaler's mainsail amid Pacific turbulences, and his present position as a recumbent passenger upon a freshwater pleasure boat.

The wedding had taken place on August 4th, a Wednesday. His twenty-eighth birthday having fallen upon a Sunday, it had not proved possible to arrange the wedding then. During the two months following his interview with Judge Shaw, he had written a series of satirical articles for the American *Punch*, entitled "Authentic Anecdotes of Old Zack", hoping to be able to demonstrate the scope of his earning capacity. Unfortunately, it was work for which payment was a long time coming, yet it had kept his mind unencumbered by the details of the wedding arrangements. These were left entirely to the bride's family and Herman gave Elizabeth liberty to plan a honeymoon agenda consistent with her father's financial provision. The rest of the time he spent in therapeutic hoeing of the family bean patch.

He travelled to Boston two days prior to the wedding, in company with his mother and two of his sisters – the oldest, Helen, and youngest, Frances. These four were accommodated at the bride's house, so that the day before the wedding was an uncomfortable time during which no one felt at their ease. Herman, not wishing any sign of family rancour to display itself, and positively wanting to cut the figure of a considerate eldest son, treated with ingratiating indulgence his mother's incapacities which she, as a guest in her chief benefactor's house, made once again the core of her emotional bearing. Mrs. Shaw, although not naturally disposed to sympathise with such an over-dramatised fragililty, and with all the affairs of the morrow to cater for, nevertheless treated her senior guest with meticulous patience and propriety. More difficult to deal with was the spectacle of Lemuel making himself ridiculous by an overbearing courtesy. He gave up to Mrs. Melville his own favourite chair. He waited on her personally, bringing cup after cup of tea and, later in the day, a bountiful

165

supply of madeira. He listened attentively to the explanation of her continuing despondency – the loss of husband compounded by the loss of oldest and youngest son (she was adamant that Tom had perished and Herman, for once, did not dispute her pessimism); the failure, so far, of her other sons to put the family finances on any kind of a footing; her own health, which she felt to be mortally afflicted by every one of these griefs. Not once, during these conversations, did she refer to the joyous prospect of the ceremony which had brought her into this household, but rather she seemed to imply that her life was about to be unbuttressed yet further. Her whole demeanour intensely angered Lizzie, almost to the point of tearful tantrum (she did weep, but quietly and alone in her room) so that her day was spent having to rein in any public display of bitterness. Helen, on the other hand, had to spend the day fighting a profound boredom, staying beside her mother out of a sense of duty and having to listen to the familiar litany of gloom. Only Fanny really enjoyed the day, spending much of it out of doors with the two Savage boys, the youngest of whom, Samuel, not yet quite fourteen, created an excuse for the older pair to be prankish and silly.

After dinner, at Maria's suggestion, they played cards, the Shaws against the Melvilles, with Lizzie being allowed to sit out and prepare her mind for the ceremony. The two Shaw boys, who were partnering one another, had been excited into a silliness that would not lie low and Herman, partnering Frances on the same table as they, felt somehow implicated in their immaturity. There was giggling and ridiculous card play, such as beating a partner's Queen with a King. This particular gambit was no doubt intended as an insistent reference to the wedding, but Herman found it unfunny, and was thankful that although Frances laughed with the boys she played her own cards more sensibly, with the result that, on this table, the Shaws received a thorough and speedy trouncing.

It had been intended to change tables at the end of a dozen hands but the senior group was delayed by more considered play, and by the demands of sustaining a conversation regarding arrangements for the journey to and from church.

Herman took a walk in the garden. It was pleasurable to remember, as he slumped back on the bench of the canal-boat and pulled his waterproof tight about his neck, that ten-minute stroll of just over three weeks ago. The sun had all but disappeared but a

166

number of insects hopped and hovered on the still warm and luxurious air. Both Mr. and Mrs. Shaw were keen gardeners and they employed additional help to care for the blooms in their prolific borders. It was to be the memory of this garden, and the influence of Elizabeth's inherited love of flowers, which would, in later years, turn Herman into a dedicated grower of roses. For the moment, it was the time of year, and the time of life, for plants with more resplendent sprays. He stopped beside a clump of orange blossom which Elizabeth had told him was the emblem of married love. The buds were half closed but the perfume was heavy and reminded him of the warm cleanness of Elizabeth's hair after she had been sitting some time in the sun. Walking towards a group of fruit bushes he noticed that clover was beginning to attack the lawn and he contemplated searching for a four-petalled stem so that he might be able to return to the house and make a declaration of good luck; but the sudden thought that this would identify him yet further with the immaturity of Frances, who had earlier made daisy chain necklaces with which to lasso Samuel and Lemuel Junior, put a veto on the notion. The fruit bushes were in full and generous leaf. He bent down and parted the verdant curtain to spy upon the bashful world where bunches of berries hung precariously from threadlike stems, each agglomeration threatening by its fulness and readiness to break away from the restraining filaments.

Mr. Hawthorne might have returned to his room and made a note in his Journal about such an observation, describing it so as to draw a human or emotional analogy. Melville, as has been mentioned before, never kept a Journal, except while out of the country. Had he done so it is unlikely that this twilight walk in the Shaws' garden would have warranted anything more than a short matter of fact statement of the event; certainly he would not have dwelt on the recollection of sensory perception nor would he have teased out clever conceits for instructional effect. For the moment Mr. Melville let the branch of the fruit bush spring closed and then straightened back up to look down the ever-murkier garden. He noticed that just one of the upstairs rooms was lamplit. It must have been Elizabeth's and he was about to make some mental estimate of what might be going through her mind on this wedding eve when a powerful rush of *déjà vu* eclipsed such a thought. It was one of those occasions when more than just the immediate instant becomes familiar and something known before; the feeling of precognition leaks backwards so that those things which one has just done, and done with no special awareness, are appreciated anew, as having also been charged with whatever tidings from a hidden world *déjà vu* carries with it. In this case, the card game, the garden, and Herman's position in it, the thought about the four-leaf clover, and, mysteriously, the ring on Judge Shaw's finger, were all implicated.

The next morning, while Elizabeth attended early communion at James Freeman Clarke's church, he escaped the excitement and bustle of the household by taking a walk in Boston's streets. Chancing upon a small square he leaned against one of the central trees. The houses, obviously inhabited by families of means, reminded him that his future circumstances were wholly uncertain. At the end of the honeymoon they would return either to Lansingburgh or Boston, and only then make a decision as to their future. The thought of independence frightened Herman and he did not know why. All he did know was that he was considerably more fearful now than he had been before any of his ocean sailings. The dimensions of this fear had become more clear to him as he drifted along the Otter Creek that misty night later in the month. He was afraid of himself – a profound apprehension, stemming from an awareness of incapacity, put at nought the short-lived confidence of literary success. As a bachelor he had been free to nurture every opinion of himself. Yes, if he chose, he might be that successful businessman, that authoritative father, that owner of property, that considerate husband, that cigar-smoking holder of public office. But what he was beginning to see now was that the act of choosing could not alone perform a transformation – his marrying would not suddenly change his character. However, his uncertainties were balanced by the experience of foreknowledge in the garden, which seemed to be telling him he had chosen correctly. And all of this knitted in with the words of Judge Shaw to which he had only half-listened. We seem free to choose; we make certain motions in unrealistic directions; in the end we are propelled towards the inescapable.

He pushed himself away from the tree with the back of his heel and, noticing that there were patches of clover in the grass, began to walk along with the same hands-behind-back, bent-over gait he had adopted as a beachcomber in Honolulu. But searching for a four-leafed clover required a closer manner of inspection and he soon dropped down on his knees so as to finger apart individual stems. The exploration met with such prompt success that he sat back on his haunches twirling the fortuitous find between thumb and forefinger, and watching the symmetrical umbrella-span of its petals rotate back and forth with such glazed appreciation that an onlooker might justifiably have questioned the soundness of the bearded man's mind.

When he stood up he had to loosen the trouser cloth away from his knees, before walking briskly along with the clover stem cupped in his hand.

Elizabeth had arrived in her parents' hallway only moments before Herman's return. When he came in she was still unpinning her bonnet and telling Helen about the well-wishers she had met at church.

"And Dr. Nourse was there, with Lucy, Herman's aunt – oh, Herman, your aunt was at church, and look what she presented me with." Elizabeth picked up from a small hallway table a darkly bound Bible. "But what has happened to your knees?"

"They have been gathering good fortune." He held out an open hand.

Elizabeth picked off the clover stem and counted the petals. "It has! It's got four! Helen, look." She passed the clover to Helen. "Herman, you clever man." She kissed him on the cheek.

Helen told her brother to go away into the drawing room, that the groom wasn't to be so familiar with the bride on the morning of the wedding and that anyway Allan had arrived.

"Give it back to me," said Elizabeth. "I shall put it in damp blotting paper and pack it in my valise. It must come away with us. And my new Bible." She hugged both, with crossed arms against her chest, as she climbed the stairs to her room.

*   *   *

The four-leaf clover was still in Elizabeth's suitcase over three weeks later. In each of the rooms that the couple had stayed at, the blotting paper had been unfolded and the talisman of serendipity put on display. The dampening and redampening of the paper could not prevent its natural shrivelling, so that on its last appearance in Montreal, since the incongruity of its dilapidation disturbed him, Herman had urged Elizabeth to dispose of it. His wife had argued that it ought to accompany them until their honeymoon was over and they were safely returned to

Massachusetts before she would think of discarding it (though she secretly intended keeping it for a much longer period.)

A dog barked somewhere beyond one of the river banks. The boat, negotiating a bend, met with a little turbulence, so that a mother, coming up from below decks, with a fretful child, had to steady herself on the Melville trunk, which Herman was using as a footrest. Recognising the woman from earlier in the voyage, and knowing that her husband had some time since retired to the gentlemen's compartment, Herman said, "Your husband has gone below. Would you like me to fetch him for you?"

The woman shook her head silently, and turned, with the child more fractious than ever and kicking its feet against her.

They had not been pleased with their rooms in Quebec, but otherwise this was the first tourist discomfort they had had to endure. On the evening of the wedding day they had travelled by train to Concord, New Hampshire, and the next morning continued to Franklin, the terminus of the Northern Railroad, before taking a stage to Center Harbour, a romantic spot at the extremity of Lake Winnipesaukee. Their two-night stay in this picturesque spot was spoilt, in the scenic sense, by dull cloudy weather, but it was here that they began to relax and to feel properly husband and wife. They spent much of the time in their lodgings, sitting beside rain-spotted windows, writing letters home to Boston, and remembering amusing aspects of their wedding day.

"Did you see what Hope had done to my father's hair? Pulled it all back and brushed it till it was sleek. His growlish, ragged look was quite undone."

"I'm not sure about that. There were still those aggressive bags under his eyes and hard cheeklines." Herman drew a forefinger under each of his own cheekbones.

"Herman!" Elizabeth tapped his knee. "Just because you've captured me now doesn't mean you can be rude about my father." She let forth a short, throaty laugh, through pursed lips. "I suppose he can look rather terrifying." Moving the wedding ring up to her lower knuckle and back again, she added. "You were a brave dear going to him like you did."

"He made me feel it too. Toyed with me a bit."

"Did he really? I expect it's his habit. Putting the accused ill at ease, before letting them off lightly."

"Have I been let off lightly?"

"There are worse than me, aren't there?" She sat with her hands in her lap, head bowed and eyes upturned, inviting a kiss.

Instead, Herman pushed gently on her elbow. "Come, there are copies of the *Home Journal* in the lounge and I feel like a cigar."

They left Lake Winnipesaukee on August 7th and took the stage to Conway, at the south-eastern edge of the White Mountain Forest. There began a period of seven days during which they wrote no letters home and enjoyed a spell of improved weather by leading an outdoors life amongst the mountains. It was also a period both of deepening affections and incipient irritations.

Elizabeth, having led a cosseted life, and with a tendency to asthma, was not up to walking as far as Herman would have liked. She was predisposed to under-estimate her own constitution and had none of Sophia Hawthorne's determination to squeeze out every drop of vitality that her body would begrudgingly allow. When Herman climbed to many a high point on his own, and waved to the small figure of his resting wife below, he could not help feeling the same sense of sulky desertion that so shrouded him now, while he recollected these emotions on the canal boat. The sense of desertion amounted to a failure of comradeship and it was a foretaste of that which would cloud the early years of their marriage.

In like respect Elizabeth considered Herman lacking in solicitous patience and a little self-indulgent in refusing to let her incapacities thwart his own more energetic impulses; and so, as he raised himself up in masculine triumph on yet another high plateau, her response would be both reticent and resentful.

Elizabeth's love and knowledge of flowers, both wild and cultivated, was a blessed source of confidence to one who, in every other respect, felt intellectually inferior to her partner. Herman was perfectly happy for her to brandish this particular advantage and they spent many a restful half-hour, on a grass bank or against a broad-trunked tree, with Elizabeth naming each flower in sight, and elaborating on its identifiable characteristics. Whenever distance caused her to doubt a classification she would dispatch her vigorous husband to fetch back a sample of stem, flower and leaf.

At their lodgings Herman displayed complete satisfaction with the company of his bride and made no attempt to fraternise with other holidaying guests. Indeed, Elizabeth, whose father always had a sociable word to pass with strangers, was somewhat surprised by Herman's indifference. She had supposed that his foreign travel would have made him as skilful a raconteur in public lounges as he was at private dinner tables; and that his chosen craft would have predicated a greater interest in the chance encounters of hostelry life; whereas, he was much more taken by the inanimate trappings at their stopping places, particularly the paintings, and he told her of a canvas remembered from his childhood home (one of those his father had brought back from Europe) a piece of which he had always fancied eating, so grilled and basted did it look.

Surprisingly, they did not otherwise touch upon one another's childhood memories – this was to come later, when they were beginning to set up home. In fact they did not talk at all to any significant degree. Much of the time Herman smoked and Lizzie read a magazine. Such silences – not the eye-gazing silences of enraptured doting – were testimony to a conjugal precocity.

Herman put his feet back up on to the trunk. He had taken them off when the mother stumbled into it. A hip flask would be very welcome. Lizzie drank nothing but the odd, ladylike dessert wine and he had tasted little hard liquor since just after the wedding. Yes, a hip flask would be welcome. They had been given one as a wedding gift but had left it behind. It was, if he remembered correctly, a quarter-pint flask, just right for the pocket. The mists off the river made him cold, and further memories of his honeymoon made him colder. A hip flask might be filled with spiced sailor's rum, or neat whisky. He did not think gin, to which his family was partial. He was numb with cold and he thought numbly about alcohol and about the austere cities of Canada.

They passed from the lush mountains of New Hampshire to the Convents, Cathedral and Parliament House of Montreal and the cold garrisoned walls of Quebec, in which city they stayed at a great rambling castle of a house, full of tawdry decorations. It was here that a reciprocal irritability made itself felt.

The weather was dreadful. The stone ramparts of the city never once dried to a granite brightness but were permanently sluggish and oozy. Herman, prevented from making exploratory rambles around the town, and with nothing to read, was reduced to going on petulant tours of the hotel stairways and corridors, sneering back at the ugly portraits of British officers. There were contemporary examples of such officers staying at the hotel – indeed, it seemed to be used as something of an overspill barracks and there were no other women in the house, bar servants. These English officers were prone to raucous behaviour in the dining room, which offended Elizabeth. She wanted her husband to remind them that there was a lady present, but he refused. She could not see why they had to spend so many nights in such an unsuitable place, but Herman seemed to take perverse pleasure in it.

Their room, in which she was left alone while Herman scowled at the paintings in the hallways, frightened her. There was too much old and fussy ornamentation, and the wood panelling spoke of hidden passages. She became prey to stupid suspicions. She saw Herman sitting at a table amid the English officers, telling them sea stories and laughing at his dainty wife. Or she saw him disappearing into doorways with pinafored serving girls. She did not know which of these imaginings should cause her most pain, and wept equally at them.

She wept again in the hold of the canal boat – a slight self-pitying weeping with part of her skirts held up to her face, muffling her sobbing and filtering out the unsavoury air. She perceived the honeymoon journey (despite the fact that this last leg completed the course of a parabola) as a leave-taking along a straight, well-laid avenue, the house of her childhood receding into the past; and on the other side of fortified battlements (forbidding return) stood a small shabby weatherboarded house with a black-shirted woman of middle years at the gate. Herman was taking her home to his mother. He had no plans for an independent life and when she had tentatively asked what was to become of them he had had the audacity to quietly pick up her Bible, turn to a New Testament passage forbidding thought about the morrow, and hand it back to her.

At three in the morning she gave up any further attempt to sleep. She wanted to return to her husband, to lean on him and will his presence to force away her fears. But she was afraid that he would be sleeping soundly and that her place below would be taken as soon as she moved. Beneath her, the mother who had made a brief appearance on deck was suckling a child. Elizabeth, suddenly aware of its gulping, felt even less certain of the wisdom of her decision made at the Lansingburgh window those several months ago, when the autumn blast drowned out all heavenly counsel. Through the folds of her skirt she clutched at her Bible, a verse or two of which she had read while the lamps had still been burning. It was of solid, regular and reassuring shape and the sense of touch which its hard outline produced beneath the linen was not without erotic appeal.

Finally, she dozed with such a despondent weariness that Herman, seeing all but his wife emerge from the hold as the canal boat approached the dock at Troy, went below and had to shake her awake with the intelligence that they had arrived.

"Are you all right? Are you well?"

He was more than a little alarmed by the vigour with which he had to rouse her, and by the blotchy swellings on her skin when she lifted her face to him.

"Herman! What time is it?"

"Five. We are pulling in to the dock. Are you well, Lizzie? You look feverish."

"It must be the air in here. Are the others gone? Is the boat docked?"

"On deck. We are just pulling in. Come on. You can sleep some more when we get home."

As Elizabeth swung off the bunk ledge they felt the boat knock into the dock. She was thrown into her husband's arms and her Bible fell out of her skirts. He kissed her, then bent to pick up the book. But it was only when they were on the deck and he was ready to begin lifting the trunk that Herman handed the Bible back to his wife. Even then, it was at the last minute, when the baggage handlers were beginning to shift passengers' luggage in earnest and she and Herman were on the point of disembarking, that Elizabeth suddenly flicked her thumb across the leaves of the Bible, their golden edge temporarily giving way to a blur of print, and then tipped it up, with front and back covers in either hand. When nothing but the cloth book mark which was attached to the top of the spine fell out, without explanation she fled back to the ladies' compartment and scrambled on the floor beneath the ledge she had occupied. Once-crowded and recently-vacated rooms or gathering places, such as theatres or classrooms, have a peculiar atmosphere. Though there may be not another soul therein, they never seem quite empty. It is as if a second, less visible company is filing out on the tails of the first, and having its own more leisurely tidying and gathering to do on the way. Just so it seemed to Elizabeth who, paranoid with an accumulation of travel-weariness and the fears and tremblings of her Canadian stay, picked up from the floor the keepsake which she had been unwilling to abandon, and then fled the cabin as if a hidden hand might forever detain her there.

*   *   *

Later, succumbing to her exhaustion, she retired to one of the Lansingburgh bedrooms, stretched herself fully clothed on a bed which was normally shared by two of Herman's sisters, and contemplated her "homecoming".

It had been just six o'clock when she and Herman walked up to the house, and they had had to knock repeatedly to wake the occupants. At length it was Frances who came to the door and, instead of greeting them instantly, fled back into the hall, shrieking, "Mother! Allan! They're *here*! Lizzie and Herman have come!"

Herman had followed her in but Elizabeth stayed, through no reason other than a mild embarrassment, on the porch. Frances, having been warmly hugged by her brother, repeated her call, this time to her other sisters.

Allan was next down the stairs, hurriedly dressed in shirt and trousers, but with nothing on his feet.

"Hello, Herman." And then, looking towards Elizabeth, still standing ill at ease in the doorway, added, "I heard you knock and holler but I didn't want your new wife to see me in my pyjamas."

"What's that excuse Allan's giving you?" Helen came slowly down the stairs, properly dressed, and her hair hurriedly bunned. "The only reason he wasn't down to the door first is he's out every night courting Miss Thurston."

"I've got some news for you later." Allan nudged Herman in the side.

And then the four Melvilles who had collected at the bottom of the stairs – Herman, Helen, Allan and Frances – looked up in silence as their mother began to descend. She said nothing until she had reached the bottom of the stairs.

"Helen, Frances – go and do something about breakfast. It's not you that's been away."

Mrs. Melville Senior issued this instruction without her usual brashness and Herman immediately noticed, in her descent of the stairs, and her general demeanour, a degree of composure of which he had not previously thought her capable. To begin with he felt sure – and her next utterance convinced him of this – that she was sustaining it only with a theatrical exertion of will power.

"Oh, look! Your young wife is waiting at the portal. She wants you to carry her over the threshold, Herman. How perfectly charming. Helen, Frances – do come back one moment. Ah, Augusta, Catherine – just in time."

The two other Melville daughters came downstairs and joined

the throng. Elizabeth, acutely embarrassed by the attention that was thus focused on her, began to swoon. Herman rushed to her side and let her fall into his arms. The onlookers applauded. Herman carried her into the house and put her down in front of his mother. Elizabeth was still dizzy. Her face was drained of colour. She slumped sideways into Allan, who gently pushed her upright, as if he were steadying a ninepin. Mrs. Melville Senior instructed Helen and Frances a second time to go to the kitchen.

"The poor girl's worn out with travel. Herman, take her through and let her stretch out on the couch."

Still his mother was calm and authoritative, and Herman responded obediently.

Left alone in the front parlour of the house, Lizzie at first refused to lie down on the couch.

"I was only dizzy, Herman. I never meant you to sweep me off my feet like that."

"It's a little soon for that kind of regret, my dear. Here, I think you could at least put your legs up." He pushed two cushions against the higher end of the couch and let Elizabeth sit on it lengthways. "My mother doesn't appear to be in any mood to be gainsaid this morning."

There was a knock on the door. Lizzie instinctively put her feet down on the floor. It was Allan; he brought in some of their baggage.

"Well you two – is it to be recommended then?"

Lizzie looked up at Herman. "Not the canal boat."

"No, that *was* a mistake. But you should get up to the White Mountains some time."

"Marriage, dolts! Not the dashed itinerary. This is your last chance to warn me off it. I'm to marry Sophia next month."

He added nothing to the announcement, but stood before them looking the part of a smugly successful suitor.

Allan was always more debonair than Herman. He sported a full beard, closely trimmed, at a time when his brother was still shaving the upper lip. Out of doors, he wore a wide-brimmed hat, and carried a cane. Even at this early hour of the morning he had, by now, put on a new pair of shoes and a jacket with a fashionable slanting breast pocket.

"That was quick work, you young rogue."

"Definitely not. We have known each other for several summers."

176

"I meant there wasn't a glimmering of this when we left three weeks ago."

"No – well – it must have been your influence then. So, no words of warning?"

Elizabeth stood up and smiled. "You'll have to ask Herman that in confidence, man to man, when you're alone together. Congratulations, Allan. I shall be delighted to have married relations."

"Haven't you had those already?"

Elizabeth blushed, and Allan, turning to Herman, apologised for the witticism. And then, looking back to Elizabeth, he said, "Mind you, you've been brought up on the risqué judging by your father's conversation when he was here a week ago."

"My father?"

"Yes; he wouldn't have mother and Fanny travel back on their own. They had stayed in Boston till last weekend. He stopped here two nights and went back on Monday. Did us all a power of good. A great rumbustious talker. Don't you think mother seems much better for a spate of socialising?"

"Yes, she does. I dare say she's looking forward to a second wedding," Herman responded.

Elizabeth, once again growing pale, dropped back on to the couch.

She had had breakfast and a hot drink brought to her, which she had consumed in solitude, the others considering that the presence of an inquisitive company would be too much for her. Herman took his breakfast out in the garden, the night mist having cleared to make a sunny start to the day. Chairs were brought out so that his brother and sisters could ask him about his recent travels. Mrs. Melville, in another display of maternal composure, busied herself preparing the newly-weds' room, so that Elizabeth might retire and repair herself.

When Elizabeth awoke she experienced the disorientation that commonly accompanies waking from an exhausted sleep, especially when such a sleep takes place on an unfamiliar bed and at an unfamiliar hour. For quite some moments she forgot that she was married, forgot that she was anywhere other than in Boston, forgot that she was anything other than her father's daughter. She forgot that she was now a woman and instinctively began to roll the soft lobe of her ear between her thumb and forefinger, as she had done when trying to get to sleep as a child. The position of the window was different in her Boston room and it was this which first stirred the process of remembering, of re-identification. But even then the recognition was indistinct, as of a holiday room vaguely recalled. Then she saw, through this window not in its rightful place, the same tree as had been the atmospheric prop of her momentous decision the previous autumn. It was greener than it had been then, and unbuffeted by any zephyr. Her mind too was calm, unpanicked by the slow clearing of her bafflement.

Looking at the treetop, she gradually discerned the sound of voices coming from somewhere at ground level near to the house. They were men's voices and although the words were indistinct she recognised the pitch and delivery of Herman's, but she did not perceive it as the voice of her husband. Not until her eyes traversed the floor of the room was she properly drawn out of this relaxed and rather comfortable semi-waking state.

She saw the trunk and other baggage which had been placed in their room, and these, whether it was that she had simply become more awake, or whether it was that they were such recent indicators of her true position, the sighting of these instantly cleared what puzzlement remained.

She swung her legs off the bed, and went quickly to a bureau mirror, almost as if to corroborate beyond doubt her rediscovered identity. It was she – the same, unsatisfactory, almost non-existent chin, the narrow mouth and pursed lips; she yawned widely, to dispel the image of her most hated features.

Standing at the window she could see Herman and Allan now strolling in the grounds of the house and continuing their conversation. Neither voice was audible but Allan repeatedly and emphatically jutted his head forward while he spoke and Herman, stopping to reply, would tamper with the dead heads of some tall grasses.

It wasn't long before she discovered the nature of their conversation. Looking down again in the mirror to put her hair straight, she went downstairs to discover, from a clock in the hall, that she had been asleep only a short while. It was not much past nine o'clock.

She found Catherine and Frances preparing vegetables in the kitchen.

"Mother thought you'd be in bed until midday at least," the youngest said.

"Oh, no; I did sleep on the boat. It's Herman who was awake

178

the whole night, and sitting in the fog. Thank heavens it's a warm sunshiny day today."

"Herman said he quite enjoyed the canal boat."

"Oh, it was abominable! He was teasing you. It was horrible to be parted but I think I might have become seriously ill had I stayed on deck."

Catherine asked Elizabeth if she'd had enough breakfast and said that she was making some tea and would get out some thick biscuits that Frances had made. "You're good at biscuits, aren't you, Fanny? Can you cook, Elizabeth? I expect you and Sophia will want to experiment together."

"Sophia?"

"Yes – Sophia Thurston. Allan's . . . Oh, of course, Herman won't have spoken to you yet. Only, Allan's got some plans. You'll hear."

Elizabeth drank her tea and ate her biscuits in puzzled silence, while the two younger girls went about their business, and then, when the domestic help arrived, notified her of the additional numbers for lunch.

Elizabeth finished her tea and went to look for Herman in the garden. He was sitting with his brother on the trunk of a felled tree, and as she walked towards them, Allan stood up, turned to say something to Herman, and then walked back to the house, passing Elizabeth on the way.

"Fine morning, Elizabeth. Feeling refreshed now?"

"Yes. Yes, thank you."

Herman, when she reached him, made no such enquiry, and seemed to have things on his mind. She sat next to him without a word, willing to give him time to speak. In due course he did.

"Do you like New York?" Elizabeth turned her head very slowly. "Only Allan's got some plans about setting up house together." He stepped down from the tree and brushed his palms along the back of his trousers. "I don't know if they'll come to anything," he added.

*   *   *

The house selected by Allan, but purchased mainly by way of a large loan made to Herman by Judge Shaw (a loan which Elizabeth and Herman would later view as the result of a coup engineered by Maria during the days of their Canadian

179

honeymoon), was at 103, Fourth Avenue, a street which led into the top end of Broadway, at Union Square. The house was occupied by both sets of married couples and also by Maria and the Melville sisters, the Lansingburgh place having been abandoned as part of the deal.

A letter written by Elizabeth to her stepmother two days before Christmas reveals the extent to which, after three months occupation, the house had settled into a daily round.

> Perhaps you will wonder what on earth I have to occupy me. Well in fact I hardly know what myself, but true it is, little things constantly present themselves and dinner time comes before I am aware. We breakfast at 8 o'clock, then Herman goes to walk, and I fly up to put his room to rights, so that he can sit down to his book on his return. Then I bid him goodbye, with many charges to be an industrious boy, and not upset the inkstand.

Elizabeth's suggestion of whirligig industry during the rest of the day is less than honest. There was only a small part of the house that she could legitimately consider her own private domain and, as for the rest of it, the Melville sisters looked after that, under the scrutinous maternal aegis. Allan did not work at home so that Sophia, his wife, joined more closely in the general domestic management than did Elizabeth.

"Whatever I am about, I do not much more than get thoroughly engaged in it than ding-dong goes the bell for luncheon." This was correct only insofar as she engaged herself in tasks which had no finite end, such as arranging a vase of flowers or altering the layout of hairbrushes on the dresser. She was hardly rushed off her feet. It was during one such "hectic" morning that she wrote this letter.

> After luncheon, at half past twelve o'clock, Herman insists upon my taking a walk every day of an hour's length at least. By the time I come home it is two o'clock and after, and then I must make myself look as bewitchingly as possible to meet Herman at dinner which is at four.

Again we can sense Maria's stipulation. You go and make yourself look sweet. I'll run the show downstairs.

> After dinner is over, Herman and I come up to our room and enjoy a cosy chat for an hour or so. Then he goes down town for a walk. Looks at the papers in the reading room and returns about half past seven or eight.

180

So Elizabeth's day was a tantalising mix of interludes, with and without Herman. Everything was geared to the "with", so that inbetweentimes she felt languid and supernumerary.

> We all collect in the parlour in the evening and Herman listens to our reading or conversation, as best pleases him. Tomorrow night, for a great treat, we are going to the Opera, and this is the first place of public amusement I have attended since I have been here, but somehow or other I don't care much about them now.

It is a sad letter, and it compares badly with the vivacious epistles Sophia Hawthorne sent home from the Old Manse.

Herman once again demonstrated his ability to isolate himself in a crowded household. He was married, yet maintained much of the independence of a bachelor. If, later, he was to see smoking as a means of asserting masculine solitude, writing and the need to shut himself away were open to similar analysis. He took his evening stroll to the reading rooms not solely or even primarily to acquaint himself with the news, although he took a ready interest in the press, but to partake of that anonymous masculine society which we see depicted in prints of the period. Looking at these prints now it would take a cool eye to declare that, whatever benefits have accrued from the greater commingling of the sexes, there was not something beneficial and restorative in such hand-in-pocket, cigar-in-mouth, cock-hatted company.

I look at one such as I write. Three speechless gentlemen occupy three rocking chairs. They read their papers, they smoke, they use the spittoon. They say nothing. And yet it is not merely the artist's sense of form which suggests there is some kind of communion between the three. I can believe that not one of them could have read their paper either in solitude or the company of their respective wives, assuming them to be married, with the same detached immersement. It is probable that the opportunity for such silent, smoky intercourse persists only in the older London clubs or amongst the more traditional followers of the game of cricket.

The visit to the Opera proved to be more vivifying to Elizabeth than she had forecast, with the result that they led a more sociable life up until the middle of the following February when, after a grand and notable Valentine gathering at Waverley Place, Herman declared that the late nights must stop, for they were proving injurious to the progress of his new book.

At the end of January, Elizabeth's brother Lemuel Junior came to stay. After several days' sightseeing they took him to a fancy dress ball. Herman, sitting in his room a month later, with a volume of Rabelais open on his desk (he had lately become a member of the New York Society Library) and one of Babbalanja's speeches in mid-draft, recalled his wife's excited adjustment to her brother's costume. On several occasions since then he had tried to analyse why Elizabeth's gaiety had hurt him so, and to probe the perverse mechanism in his own personality that had prompted this cold withdrawal into his work.

Lemuel Junior had been dressed in their own rooms, away from the rest of the household. He had been stood in the middle of the room while Elizabeth, trying to give him a regimental appearance, attached a strip of coloured ribbon to the outer seam of his trousers. She knelt, took pins from her mouth, stood up, stepped back to survey the effect, made quick tugging and smoothing movements with her hands, asked Herman if the ribbon were straight, ignored his assurance that it was straight enough, unpinned the ribbon and began all over again.

"This reminds me of my first dressing-up party. It was John's twelfth birthday and lots of Papa's friends came. It was really a grown-ups' party and my gown was bought from *the* most fashionable shop in Boston. I was so cross, though. I grew so fast I only did wear it that once. Now that side's done. I think it's more crooked than before but it'll have to do. This other piece of ribbon's a slightly darker shade. Do you think it matters? I don't. No one will see both sides of you at once. Don't turn round. I'll crawl over, then you can talk better with Herman."

He had never heard his wife babble so. Lemuel Junior turned to him and said, "Quite a little seamstress, isn't she?" The remark intensified Herman's irritability. It was plain that Elizabeth had adopted, since meeting him, a reserved seriousness which in some ways was counter to her nature. She was in awe of his intellect and his adventurous experience, and instead of countering it with the fun-loving enthusiasm of which she was now clearly capable, she had emphasised her Christian forbearance, so that now, in these late winter evenings, while the rest of the household played whist and her husband read Thomas Browne, she would turn over pages of the Gospels and write to her stepmother saying that the end of their brief spate of social life was no sacrifice to her and that she really was quite as content as Herman to stay at home. Herman had read these letters and now, as he remembered that first party, knew them to be hogwash.

As he had watched her shuffle over the rug, pushing the needlebox ahead of her, he had felt a receding feeling, as if he, on the soft sofa, were being pulled backwards on its smooth castors, whilst the angular profile of Lemuel Junior remained fixed in size, and only the bent busy figure of his wife diminished in keeping with the laws of perspective. Then, seeing his feet a long way off from him, he realised that the sofa had neither moved nor been part of his sensation, but only his head and sight had backed away so that the perception of his body had become elongated. This far-off feeling was to come to him often and always when right perspective had returned, as if the interlocking cylinders of a telescope had been snapped shut, and his body was once again its customary length, he felt the moody residue of isolation.

"There. That's you finished, Lem. I put the epaulettes on your jacket earlier. Allan's broader than you but it should hang reasonably. You'd better find Sophia and ask her for it. I should leave the trousers on now." She had been packing needles and cotton away whilst saying this; now she stood and looked her brother up and down. "My, you look grand. I wish Herman would have gone like that."

Herman gave a quick sardonic flex of his cheek muscles at this remark. Often, at the inception of one of his withdrawn states of mind, people would start talking about him as if he were not present.

"Herman doesn't like playing soldiers," he said aloud.

Lemuel Junior, sensing difficulty, took immediate leave of their room, and went to find his jacket.

"Then how *shall* we fix you up? We have to decide and I can't . . ." She paused as her husband suddenly drew himself erect and went to the window, standing with his back to her. "Until you decide how you're dressing I shall not know what to do to complement it. Please, Herman."

Still staring out of the window, Herman said, "I shall go as I am. If you *must* dress up, go as Lemuel's sweetheart."

*　　*　　*

Passing herself off as an independent *Miss* Melville proved so successful (she wrote to her mother that she had been "quite a

183

belle!'') that Elizabeth readily agreed to Herman's suggestion that she adopt a similar role for the Valentine party. Lemuel Junior was no longer with them, so it was decided that Elizabeth would play the part of Herman's sister. During the evening, while Lizzie was on the dance floor, Herman found himself in conversation with Bayard Taylor, the local Poet Laureate, employed on such occasions to hammer out dedicatory stanzas for the more note-worthy guests.

"Melville, Mrs Lynch has asked me to read out your Valentine. You had better take a look at it, but I'm sure you'll find it innocuous enough." He took a roll of papers from his side pocket, undid the length of cord which fastened them, passed three or four sheets from the top of the pile to the bottom and gave the next to Herman, who read the stanza quietly to himself.

> Bright painter of these tropic isles,
> That stud the blue waves far apart,
> Be thine, through life, the summer's smiles.
> And fadeless foliage of the heart:
> And may some guardian genius still
> *Taboo* thy path from every ill.

"Clever."

"Passed for public consumption then? The *Home Journal* wants to use them in its next issue. Is that all right as well?"

Herman, still holding the thick manuscript paper, did not hear the question. "Summer's smiles, fadeless foliage, guardian genius," he muttered, as if he were back in the schoolroom itemising the compositional features of the verse.

"Of course," said Bayard, "I assumed your wife would be here and that she would take the closing couplet as reference to herself."

"Are you suggesting my wife considers herself a genius?"

"No, but most wives of creative men consider themselves guardians in some way. Does your sister commonly accompany you at social gatherings?"

"Yes, she does."

"Good. I have my name on her card, but I am far down the list. I may have to wait a second occasion. Excuse me, but I have other verses to present."

Herman sat back and watched Elizabeth work through her card, allowing his glass to be replenished many times over with a

184

rich, sweet sherry. It was pleasant to be able to sit on his own, and not have to introduce his wife to boorish older ladies of New York society.

The floor was crowded and he caught only infrequent glances of Elizabeth. Once again she seemed a gay and different person and he could not help remembering the morose evenings they had spent in the latter part of their honeymoon, silently reading or actively avoiding one another's company.

Lighting a cigar, he started composing in his head a verse about smoking. He'd show that Bayard Taylor how to knock them out:

> More musky than snuff
> And warm is a puff: –
> Puff! Puff!

He woke the next morning with those and other lines pulsing in his head, together with throbbing hangover pain. He was late for breakfast and did not have time for his morning walk so that Elizabeth was unable to put the room straight before he went there to work.

When he appeared halfway through the morning, Elizabeth, who was hanging and putting away her party clothes, asked what was wrong.

"I'm not bright enough for it today."

"Never mind. I don't remember you missing recently."

"As a matter of fact I haven't been working well for some time. The late hours we've been keeping have prevented me from getting a full night's rest. And I can't afford to throw the days away. I have resolved that we must stop."

It was spoken as authoritatively as any nineteenth-century husband could have managed.

"I have some books to return to the library."

Leaving the house he passed his mother, who was polishing brass in the front entrance.

"Herman." She came up to him and laid the dusting cloth on his sleeve. "I'm so glad you're taking Lizzie out at last. She's finally beginning to bloom, don't you think?"

Herman withdrew his arm, and left the house, pulling the front door shut with considerable force.

*   *   *

Throughout his use of the library Herman was getting to know Evert Duyckinck very well and the acquaintanceship was such that Evert had been given chapters of the work-in-progress to read and comment on. For his part Evert was duly impressed by Melville's ravenous consumption of what he called loosely "old books", and wrote letters to his brother George to the effect that the author of *Typee* and *Omoo* was proving more than a sailor with a gift for spinning a yarn. His interest in Herman was aroused further after he had experienced at first hand the unliterary environment in which the writer passed his time. Invited to Fourth Avenue to make up a rubber of whist he had spent an evening devoid of intellectual conversation and Herman himself had been as silent as a mouse. Evert described it as "the longest rubber of whist I have ever encountered – like a calm at sea". Thereafter, his sympathies awakened, he made a point of being especially obliging to Herman, opening up his personal library and readily advising on the next set of stepping-stones in his leather-bound adventure. Herman always claimed that, for all his experience at sea, it was this period of intensive reading which constituted his proper education.

This massive over-consumption of heavy-headed matter passed immediately down Herman's arm and off the point of his pen. *Mardi* is an interesting book because it contains all or most of the themes he was to pursue with a controlling and creative purpose in *Moby Dick*, and many of those which were to make his later fiction so perplexing to his contemporaries. The speeches of Babbalanja in particular reveal the quick absorption of philosophical ideas and a facile use of mythological and geographical reference.

Letters from London continued to suggest that John Murray doubted the factuality of *Typee* and *Omoo*. Herman wrote furiously at the end of March that if that were the case Mr. Murray had better brace himself to receive a real romance.

> The reiterated imputation of being a romancer in disguise has at last pricked me into a resolution to show those who may take any interest in the matter that a *real* romance of mine is no Typee or Omoo, and is made of different stuff altogether.

By this time the manuscript was only six weeks off completion. Since the curtailment of their brief foray into society Herman had been working intensely both morning and night, giving up from the earlier routine not the solitary hours of his morning walk or evening visit to the reading roms but the night-time parlour hours with Elizabeth and the rest of the house.

She suffered this cold withdrawal for a month before Herman's absence from the parlour, and the table talk it provoked, spurred her into saying something.

Mrs. Melville Senior, was, as always, the first to chastise her son. "Has he hid himself away again, my dear? It is an awful shame. Sophia wouldn't put up with it from Allan, would you, Sophia?"

"Nor can she expect to have a famous husband one day," Allan said.

"Fame! A wife wants just enough success and money to mix with her own level of society. No more. And what kind of Fame do you get from books, may I ask? Posterity can keep its praise. We want a bit of affection today, don't we, Lizzie?" Maria came behind Elizabeth's chair and placed her hands on the sad girl's shoulders.

"Perhaps you could start helping Herman more. No, that sounds wrong. Sorry. I mean, act as his assistant. He'll be wanting a copyist of the manuscript." Helen's suggestion was a charitable one, for she had dearly enjoyed copying *Typee* and *Omoo* and identified much more sympathetically than her mother with her brother's literary ambitions.

Elizabeth left it a day or two and then one afternoon when the weather was wet, rather than go for a walk or return a call, she stayed with Herman. Her first effort was to ensure there was any conversation at all; her second to keep it on the subject of Herman's book.

"It's a long time since you've read me your day's work in the evening."

"Well, it's not the same book, Lizzie."

"I'd still like to hear it."

"You've never said."

"You know I would! I don't need to say."

Herman, already irritated, responded, "You *do* need to say. You hardly speak a word and I'm supposed to divine your every feeling."

"*I* hardly speak a word! That isn't very accurate. And, anyway, I'm your wife. You ought to be able to read me."

"Perhaps so. At normal times. But I am in the midst of filling other silences. You are going to have to appreciate that the getting-up of a book is all-engrossing. I need support, Lizzie. Do you think I am unaware of the murmurings belowstairs?"

Elizabeth felt momentarily jolted by guilt, but seized her opportunity. She knelt beseechingly at Herman's feet. "Then help me to appreciate. Why not let me copy your book for the printers. I'd love to do that for you."

"But Lizzie." He moved a heavy volume from off his lap and took her hands in his. "It is an arduous task, and very wearying. I couldn't ask you . . ."

"No, I am asking *you*."

"As you wish." He let go of her hands and patted them. "Let's begin."

Getting up, and moving to his desk, he fetched the piles of manuscript and explained that as the early chapters would be re-written she should start in mid-stream. "Here, this chapter's typical enough. We'll see how you get on. No spelling mistakes and one side of the paper only. Where will you work? I shall have to stay alone."

The start was inauspicious. Elizabeth's first page provoked violent criticism.

"The punctuation, Lizzie!"

"Show me."

Herman pointed out several errors but when Elizabeth checked them with the manuscript she found they were in the original also.

"That's not the point. Or rather it *is* the point. As copyist you must spot such mistakes. Remember that I am writing quickly. That page was easy. There were no deletions or insertions. Look at this next one. You see here. And there. That smaller phrase must fit into the line beneath. But nothing indicates where. Here, I will show you this time." Herman picked up a pen and made an upturned "v" between the two words in the lower line. "But normally you will need to decide for yourself."

Elizabeth continued to make mistakes but stubbornly refused to give up the task. Eventually Herman suggested she copy without any punctuation leaving him free to make a final revision and this method at least proved endurable.

The work was exhausting. *Mardi* was an enormous book and Herman's sense of urgency knew no bounds. He would have had Lizzie working all hours of the day and night until she had caught up with his own place in the first draft, were it not for the intervention of his mother, who imposed a strict limitation on the amount of time worked by Lizzie, notably by demanding her presence at certain times of the day in the kitchen downstairs.

The strain upon Elizabeth became worse when Herman declared, at the end of the first week in May, that the book was done. This meant that he was free to give full attention to overseeing the copying process and to making final revisions. He had already been in communication with Mr. Murray regarding its publication.

The philosophical ruminations of the book were disturbing to a young woman brought up to view life in terms of a straightforward and sentimental orthodoxy as regards social and moral law. As she transcribed the words "all men are possessed by devils" she did seriously wonder at the nature of her husband's inspiration. There were other sections of the book which she found more comforting, and indeed flattered herself into thinking that she might be responsible for their inclusion. Certainly much of the floral symbolism had come from her or from books that she had brought to Herman's attention, but she also liked to think that the author's partisanship for the Heart over the Head was attributable to the influence of married love. Nevertheless the accumulative impression of the book shocked her. It seemed to undermine the entire tradition of Christian teaching by questioning the degree to which diabolic and earthly instincts can be controlled or given spiritual direction. She had once heard Herman remark to Mr. Duyckinck, in the course of a discussion about the duties of literature, that since the Gospels presented so unworldly and unattainable a combination of virtues and therefore had the effect of ever convincing men and women of their own unworthiness all copies of such documents ought to be banned on the grounds that they caused unnecessary misery to many who would otherwise live quite happily and quite virtuously within their earthly limitations. The view had been put forward half in jest, but when she found Babbalanja repeating it:

> The prophet Alma came to guarantee our eternal felicity
> but that felicity rests on so hard a proviso that to a thinking
> mind but very few of our sinful race may secure it.

she realised it was something Herman had thought through more seriously.

189

Her summer cold or hayfever came earlier than usual and Herman was quick with husbandly concern.

"Do you think perhaps you ought to accompany Sam back to Boston and see if the change of air might benefit you?"

Sam was Lizzie's other half-brother and had been staying with them unobtrusively for just over a week.

"Oh, Herman, I *must* stay and finish the book."

"But it is probably the copying that has made your head thick already. I can get it through in time. You've helped me over the worst. And there's always Helen. Be a good girl, and I shall come and join you when I take my vacation in August."

"Mercy be! I can't be away from you that long."

"Well, I shall visit you every two or three weeks then."

"You shall collect me in three weeks' time, if I go at all, and no longer."

"It's agreed then."

"I'll see."

Elizabeth dabbed her reddened nose with a small unfolded handkerchief.

It was another ten days before she actually left for Boston. She had insisted on hurrying the copying through to a finish (in fact Herman held some chapters back so that her departure could be undertaken in good conscience) and on remaining in New York for her twenty-sixth birthday, which was on June 13th.

It was during these final days that their first child, Malcolm, was conceived. Intriguingly, Allan and Sophia's child was conceived in precisely the same week. His brother and sister-in-law continued to play the parts of a dotingly honeymooning couple, and the soft transportation in Sophia's eyes vexed Herman for it ever appeared that she had just broken away from a climactic swoon, while his poor Lizzie's eyes always bespoke of a frowning frustration.

*   *   *

Just as Mr. Melville prepared to pass several months of intermittent solitude and expectant paternity, the Hawthornes were spending their first summer in the tall, narrow house in Mall Street into which they had moved the previous autumn. This, for them, was the period of their greatest settlement, and if Mr. Hawthorne's term of office in the Salem Custom House had

190

proved more permanent (he was to be dismissed in 1849, once again in the wake of electorial defeat) it is conceivable that we might never have had *The Scarlet Letter* or any other of his full-length novels.

Una, four years, and Julian, two years, were having a particularly frisky morning and Sophia was disconcerted by Nathaniel's lingering in the lower chamber, rather than climbing the stairs to his third-floor study, as he more normally did on days when he had no duties at the Custom House. When they had moved from the tiny apartment in Chestnut Street it had been a "Paradise of Peace" to think of him alone and still, yet within her reach, just as he had been in their beloved Manse. It was now nearly three years since they had been evicted from that enchanted dwelling and she thought it such a pity that neither of the children would have a memory of their first delightful home.

Nathaniel was attempting to write in his Journal and although he was obviously distracted by the children's boisterousness she dared not suggest he remove himself to his den, since he had obviously taken a decision not to sequester himself away. Una persistently asked him how many babies she had and he replied, automatically, sixty-four. "Write it on my hand so I don't forget," she said. And he took his pen and scratched the figures on to her palm, making her squirm and giggle. "Una Hawsorne's got sixty-four babies, Una Hawsorne's got sixty-four babies," she went away chanting, and waved her hand in front of Julian's face, so that he ran across saying, "Me farver, me farver . . ."

Sophia called to Dora, that she might refrain from washing the breakfast dishes, and come and help with the preparation of the children. It had already been decided that she would take Una for a morning walk. While Sophia was away from the room making sure that Dora had heard her call, Nathaniel cried out. "No! No! Little boys must not pull." She returned to find them fighting over a picture book, although by this time Julian was crying profusely and making only the limpest of attempts to keep hold of the book. "Papa shouted at him. Tell him he is much too stern." And then Una turned to comforting her brother, casting reproachful glances at her cruel father.

Una had been dressed in a dark mousseline gown, a favourite of Mr. Hawthorne's, which to Sophia's mind showed up badly her fair complexion, but which he said did wonders for her auburn-shrouded "phiz". Such an ugly word, Sophia thought. His vocabulary, both written and spoken, usually most discreet, was prone to the odd lapse. Now and again she had pointed out coarsenesses of expression in his Notebooks and he had always accepted the criticism. It was, after all, the direction of his serious writing – towards refinement and delicacy. He scribbled away so quickly in his notebooks that misjudgements of taste were bound to occur. He was writing strenuously on this particular morning, in a chair which was really too low for the task, so that his shortness of temper with little Julian had not taken his wife by surprise.

While Dora was dressing Una in her purple pelisse and gaiters, and putting on her white satin bonnet, Julian rushed over to assail Mama, beating her legs and intoning, "I go with Nòna, I go with Nona." Customarily they did not ask Dora to take the two children out together, not wishing to subject her to the petty bickering which was bound, at some point, to blight the excursion. But on this occasion Mr. Hawthorne's strange and silent dilatoriness, and his most wilful expression, prompted Sophia into thinking that it would be best to let Julian have his way. Dora said she was sure she could manage both of them admirably. And so the two of them quickly set about adorning the little fellow – she taking the top half, putting on his black beaver hat with the ostrich feather and tying a silk cravat round his neck, while Sophia equipped his lower body in India-rubber overshoes and put mittens on his hands. While she was waiting, Una went up to her father's chair and said, "Papa, why do you write downstairs? You never wrote downstairs before." By way of answering he kissed her on the forehead and bade her be a good girl with Dora and not run away, nor annoy her mother by stepping in the mud.

Having waved the children off from the porch, Sophia went straight into the kitchen to finish the tidying away of the breakfast table, and to allow Nathaniel a period of solitude. When at last she was drying the final pieces of cutlery she wandered into the doorway of their little parlour to see if he might want a hot drink of chocolate. She half-expected that he would at last have stirred himself and climbed the stairs to his study, but no, he was still in the chair, his Notebook on his lap. One could have thought him dozing, so insubstantial seemed to be the grip upon his pen that it looked poised to fall at any moment. His head was inclined to one side, as if let drop by a complete relaxation of the neck. Sophia had been deluded into thinking as much before, but knew well enough by then the deep and all-engrossing reveries into which her husband would sometimes fall.

She went forward and knelt beside the arm of the chair. "My Noble Melancholy Lord, what troubles you? Are you sad?" He put his hand upon her shoulder and affectionately massaged her neck with the tips of his fingers. "Why do you write downstairs today? Are you weary?"

"So many questions, Sophiechen. No, I'm not sad. Not that at all. I have started historical labours, more current than any I have engaged upon in the past. Last night I had a dream. We were at a party, a gathering of some kind, and you announced with perfect composure that you were no longer my wife." Sophia had learned to listen to her husband's dreams with a mute sympathy. They chilled her to the bone and afterwards haunted her far more than they did Mr. Hawthorne. But if he had known as much he would not have been so free in declaring them. "And then your sister, Elizabeth, who was likewise present, informed the company, that, having ceased to be *thy* husband, I of course became *hers*, and turning to me, very coolly enquired whether she or I should write to inform my mother of the new arrangement. I woke from that dream in a cold sweat. No offence to Elizabeth, but the thought of changing you for her was a nightmare nevertheless." Sophia put her hand behind her neck and their fingers eagerly interlocked. "I awoke with a determination to give our present life, these present happy days, greater substance. We dwell in the shadow cast by Time, and only by picking out the details can we begin to discern the image of the present. And so this morning I have begun to record the daily routine and exchanges of Una and Julian, almost as a painter would his sitting models."

She sat up and grinned at him. "There, and your silly wife has gone and bundled them off with Dora, thinking you had a headache or malady of the spirit."

He raised his brow as if to say, Ah Well, and then, closing his notebook and putting the cap back on his pen, invited her on to his lap.

As he pulled her tight into his embrace she remembered the incident of their first quarrel. She had walked across an uncut hayfield, and with the proper indignation of a one-time Brook Farmer, Nathaniel had rebuked her vehemently. Later they lay down on a carpet of pine leaves in the lovely shade and, clasping him in her arms, there on the bosom of dear Mother Earth, she had told him she would not be so naughty again.

* * *

As Mr. Hawthorne himself was to confess in his long introduction to *The Scarlet Letter*, Literature, its exertions and objects, were now of little moment in his regard. And yet, although the introduction was written after his dismissal from the Custom House, so that the mind had had its opportunity to rationalise his change of circumstances, there does seem to have been a good deal of conscious savouring in the three years of workaday domesticity, as of a tenor of life to be tasted once only.

> It might be true indeed, that this was a life which could not, with impunity, be lived too long, else it might make me permanently other than I had been, without transforming me into any shape which it would be worth my while to take.

In the autumn he would sit for half an hour before bed, without light, except from the coalfire and the moon, so that all the familiar things – chairs, table, couch, bookcase – seemed to be remembered through a lapse of years rather than seen with the immediate eye. When retiring to bed, and after once closing the sitting-room door, Mr. Hawthorne would re-open it, again and again, to peep back at the warm, cheerful, solemn repose, the white light, the faint ruddiness, the dimness, all making him feel as if he were in a conscious dream.

And then, to the tender arms of Sophia, who busied herself when she could in the making of small tapestried shields which ladies used to protect their complexions from the glare of the coals. These she sold for ten dollars a time.

Mr. Hawthorne's meticulous recording of the children's manners and speech makes up the entire content of his Journal entries through the end of 1848 to the beginning of his mother's final illness in the summer of 1849.

Una embroiders the hem of a towel for Grandpa Peabody's birthday; Julian impersonates Dora and dusts the room; Una always tragic and imperative; Julian always comical and with a bodily vigour independent of the state of his spirits.

The elder Mrs. Hawthorne's failing health – her heart was

weakening – had forced her to give up her house during the winter. The sisters had moved to other towns so Nathaniel brought his mother across the few streets separating the Mall Street residence from his boyhood home. It cannot have been an easy decision to make, and the burden of it fell squarely upon Sophia, as she must have well known in advance.

On Sunday July 29th the Journal begins to make record of Mrs. Hawthorne's final hours. The day began with Sophia being called to the sick-chamber while she was in the midst of fixing Una's hair. Una, making a scene at her abandonment, was shut up in the drawing room until Julian, puckering up his little face in sympathy with his sister's bitter and continuous outcry, persuaded his father to let him go to the drawing-room door and release Una from her imprisonment. Having completed his mission he lay down on the couch saying, "Father, I'm so tired," while Mr. Hawthorne kissed Una's discoloured face until she began to smile. Seeing Julian get up for a moment, Una immediately broke away from her Papa and took possession of the couch, so that a dispute ensued which seemed likely to end in violence.

"Una. Come and sit on my lap."

She did so, and Julian took the couch, but a second later was beginning to bargain an exchange of places with his sister.

"No, Julian. You wanted the couch back. Now keep it."

"Father, my hair is all tangled. When will Mama come down? You brush it. Plea-ease."

At last Dora arrived and took Una away to finish the hairdressing. Julian, hearing the two of them prattle about various matters, put down the iron bar that he had been using for making musical sounds and ran into the little room to join the conversation.

Sophia, having heard Dora arrive, made a fleeting appearance downstairs, and Julian asked to be taken up to see Grandmama.

"No, Julian, not this morning."

"A kiss then." And while he was receiving it, "Please can I come."

"I said not this morning, Julian."

As his mother left him, Julian became sulky and tearful and so Dora, continuing to fix Una's hair, began to tell him a story.

Sophia communicated to Nathaniel that his mother had taken a turn for the worse and she felt certain these would be her final hours.

"Well, Father!" cried Una, coming out of the little room, with her hair properly combed and looking into the mirror with an approving glance. She was too late to have heard any of her mother's bulletin and yet seemed to sense that drama was afoot, for she said to her brother, "Oh, you don't know how sick Grandmama is, Julian; she is as sick as I was when I had the scarlet fever in Boston."

Later in the morning Una was allowed up to her grandmother's room and on her return did not fail to make the most of her privilege.

"It would be very painful for little Julian to see," she said, "for she is very sick indeed, and sometimes she almost cries."

Julian, going back and forth on a large toy farm cart, responded, "Why, if I were to see her I would stroke her, and she would be very quiet."

Dora, overhearing this, and fearing that such morbidity would upset the master, told the children to go out in the yard. "The black hen is there," she added, and this was sufficient inducement to make them race one another outside.

Julian began to stroke the bird's feathers the wrong way so that Una, with exaggerated sympathy, picked it up and began carrying it like a baby. But the hen committed an unspeakable sin on her apron so that she went running to Papa with a wrinkled nose and her hands held well away from the blemished cloth. Julian poked the bird with a stick to chase it away but after lunch the two of them were again playing with it, vying for possession and secretly petitioning it to make another of its messes on their clothes.

At last tiring of the bird they began putting it through the fence, daring it to escape. But as soon as it made to be off one of them would open the gate, run in pursuit, and come back triumphantly with the abominable fowl in their arms, until, with a squawk and unaccustomed acceleration, it made off beneath a bush, leaving both children hanging on the gate, themselves like two birds in a cage.

"Little Julian should not cry for the hen when he has so many good things that God gives him."

Una, having administered this advice, was called in to accompany Dora on a walk. Julian wept and wailed at not being permitted to go too, and Sophia, hearing the commotion, came downstairs and produced a set of tiny wooden dolls' furniture, which, though all broken to pieces, amused him the more for having to try and adjust them together.

It was two complete days since Mr. Hawthorne had set eyes on his mother. Although he loved her there had been, ever since his boyhood, a coldness of intercourse between them as is apt to come between persons of strong feelings if they are not managed rightly, and now, because he did not expect to be much moved at her passing, he was reluctant to visit the sickbed. But Sophia, fearing there might not be a further opportunity, insisted after tea that he climb the stair.

A Mrs. Duke was in the chamber but she left the room as Nathaniel moved to kneel down close by his mother and take her hand. She knew him, but could murmur only a few indistinct words, the clearest of which were an injunction to take care of his sisters. Tears gathered involuntarily in his eyes. He tried to hold them down but they kept filling up until he shook with sobs, in an emotional abandonment over which he was a long time gaining control.

Afterwards, he went to stand by the open window, and looked through the crevice of the drawn curtains. Una and Julian were again playing in the yard and their shouts and laughter coming up into the chamber made a strange contrast with its deathbed scene. He looked first at little Una, with her golden locks so full of spirit and life, and then turned to his poor dying mother. Between the two of them, standing there in the dusty midst of it, he seemed to see the whole of human existence at once. There had to be something beyond Death or the close of Life would surely not be so dark and wretched. We couldn't be thrust into annihilation in this miserable way.

Mr. Hawthorne's attempts at enforced optimism were put to nought by a remark of Una's which came distinctly into the upstairs room. The children were obviously discussing their Grandmama's condition and Una was heard to say, "Yes – she is going to die." She did not add "going to God" as she might have done when talking about the black hen and which would have been so hopeful and comforting uttered in that bright young voice of hers.

The next day Mr. Hawthorne's mother was still living but barely conscious. Una, continuing her fascinated interest in the old lady's condition, was at her most elfin and supernatural, continually teasing to be permitted to go up the stairs. Once she had been convinced that permission was not to be granted she persuaded Julian to pretend to be Grandmama while she played the part of Mrs. Duke, the sick-nurse.

197

"Will you have some of this jelly?"

Julian sat up to take the pretended jelly. Una pushed him back sharply.

"No. Grandmama lies still."

Julian smacked his lips, pretending to suck the jelly off its invisible spoon.

"You must not smack your lips so hard."

She pulled him from the couch and lay upon it herself. Lying perfectly still, as if in an insensible state, she then groaned and spoke with difficulty, moving herself feebly and wearisomely. It began to recall the scene of yesterday with such frightful distinctness that when, in the midst of it, she flashed a smile of glee at her observing father, he felt his stomach twist inside him.

They swapped parts again.

"You're dying now, so you must lie still."

"I shall walk if I'm dying," said Julian, and promptly began stamping about the room with heavy steps and a pop-eyed expression on his face which put Una into hysterical laughter.

Mr. Hawthorne sat by dumbly while his children made merry of their Grandmama's fate, knowing they meant no ill by it, but that even so other parents would have put a stop to it long ago.

The old Mrs. Hawthorne lasted one day more. The funeral was held on August 2nd after which Sophia, worn out by nursing and the uncertainty of the future now that her husband was unemployed, went to Boston to rest, leaving the children with Nathaniel.

*   *   *

In the space of two months, Mr. Hawthorne had lost his job and his mother. For a time he had trod the common path of earning regular money and enjoying the settled, sober gladness of a man by his own fireside. Now everything had again been thrown into uncertainty and at the age of forty-five it would not have been surprising if Mr. Hawthorne had proved incapable of handling such personal turmoil. He had never earned sufficient money from his stories to support his family, and his reputation had been diminished by a period of three years' inactivity. But he had two healthy young children and a wife he dearly loved with an enduring romantic affection, so that although he was briefly ill and mentally run-down during August, as the autumn progressed, uplifted and touched by the way in which friends began to rally to his attendance with suggested accommodation and financial assistance (Hillard organised a collection which raised a considerable sum), he started to write a new tale with a speed and purpose he had never known before, warding off morbid depression by creative energy. It was the hell-fired story *The Scarlet Letter*. Tradition has it that it started life as just another of his New England tales, and that his friend Fields, seeing an early draft of it in the latter part of 1849, urged Mr. Hawthorne to blow it out into a novel. It is strange that so many who have read the book have accepted such a claim, acknowledged by Mr. Hawthorne merely out of politeness. The real evidence is in the reading. The book could have been no other length. And there is plenty of other evidence that the writer knew, from the beginning, that he was in the grip of a more self-impelled inspiration than he had ever known before. When his sister-in-law Elizabeth Peabody asked him how the book would end he answered that he hadn't a clue and she found such an expression of artistic surrender utterly extraordinary. "The hell-fired story" – his own appellation – broke Sophia's heart when he read the final pages of it to her in February 1850, and sent her to bed with one of her cannonading headaches which, in the perverse flush of creative pride, he looked upon as a triumphant success.

*   *   *

At the close of 1848 Mr. Melville, bringing near to completion an agreement for the publication of *Mardi*, had received a five-hundred dollar advance from Harper and Bros. In addition Allan, on the expiration of the agreement with Wiley, had prepared a financial synopsis of *Typee* which revealed a profit of nearly seven hundred dollars, so that, at the turn of 1849, arriving at the Shaws' home, where they planned to stay for the rest of Elizabeth's pregnancy, Mr. and Mrs. Herman Melville had every reason to join the Judge in a toast to a prosperous and fruitful New Year.

Herman spent his time lounging on a sofa reading Seneca and Shakespeare, the latter in an edition of glorious great type. He also did a fair bit of commuting back and forth between New York and Boston, going home towards the end of January, for instance, to write the preface to *Mardi*. According to Appleton's *Railroad and Steamboat Companion* of 1848, there were four alternative routes:

199

one via Fall River and Newport; one via Providence and Storrington; another via Springfield and New Haven; and the last via
Worcester and Norwich. The first of these was largely by steamer,
taking the train as far as Fall River on the northern bank of the
Newport inlet, and thence across the water through Long Island
Sound. The distance travelled was 236 miles, only 50 of these by
rail. The fare was five dollars and passengers were delivered in
New York during the early hours of the morning. The second route
was probably the quickest and most direct, the train taking
passengers a distance of ninety miles by way of Providence to
Storrington, a harbour town on the eastern extremity of Long
Island Sound. After that it was again by steamboat, and the fare
was once again five dollars. Passengers preferring day travel
would have chosen one of the other two routes. The first half of the
third route formed the main freight link with Albany and was the
busiest of the four. Passengers left Boston from the Worcester
Depot in Beach Street and travelled 160 miles by rail to New
Haven, changing at Springfield. The final eighty miles was by
steamer and once more the cost was five dollars. An alternative to
this third route was to take the car only as far as Worcester and
then to change on the Norwich line, culminating at Allyn's Point.
The advantage of the last route was that in exchange for an extra
hour on the time of the journey passengers enjoyed the luxury of
the most splendid and commodious steamer of all the four routes
to New York. The fare was exactly the same as for the other three.

We know from Hope Shaw's diary that Mr. Melville arrived
back from his preface-writing expedition during the forenoon of
January 30th, and it seems likely, as he did not use the day line,
that for the sake of a longer steamboat ride he chose the Fall River
route, one of the pleasures of which was pulling into Newport,
Rhode Island, for the taking on and setting down of passengers.
Travelling back and forth on his own by this route during the first
quarter of the year it is probable that a certain travel-restlessness
was aroused in Melville; it is certain that he enjoyed the solitary
journeying. And the steamboat departures from New York in the
waning dusk of winter evenings, leaving behind the lights of
suburban Astoria, through the choppy waters at Hurl Gate, out
into the Sound, with Long Island to starboard, and the Connecticut shore to port, must, at the least, have stirred saline memories.

The journeys were not altogether without purpose. He liked to
be on hand for the final preparation of *Mardi*, the publication of

which was in fact delayed until the middle of April, having first had to wait for the English printing. (The copyright laws of that time did not protect American books from being bootlegged in England.) Mr. Brodhead's negotiations with the house of Murray had come to nothing early in the year. An influential subscriber to the list of books to which *Typee* had belonged had earlier made vigorous complaint to Murray about that book's unsavoury content, but that notwithstanding Murray was never going to have any editorial sympathy for the new work. "It is a *fiction*, and Mr. Murray says it don't suit him," was Mr. Brodhead's succinct report in his personal diary. It did not matter a great deal – except that the delay was to be regretted – for Richard Bentley was quick to accept the book, on the same terms Melville had originally demanded of Murray.

By the time all this was sorted out and, therefore, well before the hostile reviews began to appear, Lizzie had given birth to a son, named Malcolm. It is not a name which appears elsewhere in the family tree although one of Maria's Scottish forebears is reported to have been so named, and the most likely source of inspiration is Shakespeare's *Macbeth*, in which Malcolm, as the murdered king's son, is the focus of the play's corrective force.

The name had been chosen in January, at the beginning of the week in which Lizzie went into labour. Herman had attended a reading of *Macbeth* by Fanny Kemble at the Masonic Temple.

It was a long all-night delivery with Herman and Lemuel Senior keeping vigil by the brandy bottle. For several of the small hours of the morning they snoozed, fully dressed, in their chairs, Mrs. Shaw occasionally dropping in to report on progress, which she did by whispering in Herman's ear, hardly disturbing him, so that several times he received the information without even opening his eye.

Only two days later Allan and Sophia's baby, a girl, was born. When they heard that she had been called Maria, Herman and Lizzie winced together. Ever since the previous summer, and her coming home during the hayfever season, there had been a cooling of the relationship between Elizabeth and Maria Melville coupled with a corresponding domestic intimacy between Sophia and Maria. This both pleased and rankled Herman; pleased, because he liked as little interference from his mother as possible; rankled, because Lizzie seemed to have received a black mark for just that type of action in which his mother had herself indulged during his childhood summers.

It has become the established view that, in response to the reviewers finding *Mardi* quizzical or plain incomprehensible, and to poor sales, Melville set about, during the rest of '49, writing two further narratives more in line with *Typee* and *Omoo*, in a conscious effort to retain his popularity. The view has been bolstered, it is true, by several disparaging remarks that Melville himself made about the two books thus produced, *Whitejacket* and *Redburn*.

But on April 5th, before he had set eyes on a single notice of *Mardi*, Herman was writing to Evert Duyckinck and confessing that "it seems so long ago since I wrote it and my mood has so changed that I dread to look into it". It was spring. He was now a father. Much of the reading that has been regurgitated uncooked and undigested in *Mardi* had now been given time to ferment.

As he and Elizabeth finally travelled back to New York on April 10th, increased by a son and his nurse, a Mrs. Sullivan, Herman must already have been thinking about his next book. When they had boarded the steamer and Mrs. Sullivan had taken Malcolm to the warmth of the ladies' room, he stood with Lizzie on deck, his arms folded and resting on the rail. As Lizzie held his upper arm he squeezed her gloved hand against the side of his ribcage, and she leaned her head against his shoulder. In the dark of night there was no sign of the Long Island shoreline and they might as well have been plying a course due East, across the open ocean.

"Do you miss the sea, Herman?"

He turned and gently kissed her forehead; said nothing.

"You do then."

There were things he wanted to say: about travelling, about water, about skies and rough weather, about rooms and babies' clothing, about his work and being nearly thirty, about Malcolm and the house on 104th Street.

He kissed her forehead a second time; again said nothing.

"I will pray for you, Herman." She kissed his arm, then withdrew her hand and went below.

When she had gone Herman closed his eyes and listened to the rhythmic efforts of the steam-powered engine. He lifted one hand from the deck's rail and put it under his chin, feeling the gentle dip and rise of the sea's swell transferred to his skull so that his very brain seemed affected by a sympathetic surging and undulation. His wife had never spoken a remark of that kind aloud before, but she had often responded to his silences with an expression of such

202

sorrowful pity that made it obvious she regarded his incommunication as due to a hidden and unspeakable despair.

The reviews of *Mardi* were not all bad, but those that were were damning. Of these, the *Boston Post*'s is a typical example: "The whole book is not only tedious but unreadable. In a word *Mardi* greatly resembles Rabelais emasculated of everything but prosiness and puerility." Melville seemed well able to handle such criticism. "These attacks are matters of course, and are essential to the building up of any permanent reputation," he wrote to his father-in-law.

If anything Elizabeth was both more interested in and more affected by the reviews than Herman. Having understood little of the book while copying it she was secretly pleased when her own failure in understanding it was shared and admitted to by the critics. When her father and mother-in-law came to read it she was positively embarrassed at what they might make of it, and in a letter to Hope Shaw, otherwise consisting in a rather formal gratitude for her long visit home and the opportunity for recovery it had afforded her, together with a message of assurance to Mrs. Sullivan (who had returned to Boston once the Melvilles were settled back in their New York house) that Malcolm's scalp rash was due to overheating beneath his knitted bonnets, she also requested all overheard remarks about *Mardi* to be passed on to her: "When you hear any individual express an opinion with regard to it, I wish you would tell me – whatever it is – good or bad – without fear of offence – merely by way of curiosity."

Such curiosity betokened a concern for her husband's reputation that had become a little more than ordinary lovers' solicitude; there was an element of the neurotic there which, at a later date, Herman's mother would seek to manipulate.

If the sales of the book were disappointing they might have been worse. It seems likely that the extreme variation in the reviews encouraged the public to find out for themselves how good the book was, so that by September Harpers reported that two thirds of the first print run of three thousand had been sold. In the meantime Herman had been working with such diligence and productive energy that it is impossible to accept at face value that *Redburn* and *Whitejacket*, both written in the space of three or four months, were completed in a writer's sulk.

Elizabeth stayed with him throughout the summer, motherhood seeming to have improved her hay-fever. Neither *Redburn* nor

Whitejacket is a short book (Richard Bentley liked to publish in two, preferably three, volumes) and Herman, writing from morning until night in the crowded house, insisted she kept Malcolm, who was teething well out of the way. During the writing of *Redburn* Elizabeth accepted having a recluse as a husband with good humour. Her own time was more occupied with the baby to look after, and she had a point of contact with Allan's wife, so that there was no longer any need, nor opportunity, to spend lonely, dithering hours at her dressing table. Admittedly, she had every reason to believe that the quicker Herman finished his new book the more of the summer would be left for him to take her on picnics and excursions.

So that it was only when he immediately went on to a second book that the rancour and resentment that his mother had always felt for his occupation spread to Elizabeth. There seemed no good reason why he had to begin another book so soon. *Mardi* had not long been published. *Redburn*, which he had negotiated by post with Bentley, was not likely to be out before the autumn. The winter would be soon enough to start work again. But Herman was in no mood to be accused, however obliquely, of creating an excuse for himself to lead an antisocial life.

The writing of *Redburn* had done several things for him. The facility with which he had written it had been the main factor encouraging him to capitalise immediately upon a further outpouring of energy; the autobiographical remembering had reawakened his appetite for travelling, an appetite which did not encompass the possibility of a family holiday; it had made him nostalgic for the fraternal companionship of sailor for sailor, a nostalgia which was to increase during the writing of *Whitejacket*; the recollection of his first voyage to Liverpool had made him keen to set foot in England again and this time to visit London, the place of his brother's death, the city of Carlyle and so many others he had been ignorant of on that maiden voyage.

*   *   *

Herman had made up his mind, while halfway through *Whitejacket*, that he would make the journey to Europe alone, and as soon as possible after the book was done; but he said nothing of his plans until late August, during a weekend in Boston to which he had treated Elizabeth now that he was a free man again. He asked Judge Shaw, in the privacy of the smoking room, whether he might set about collecting one or two letters of introduction for a proposed visit to London, which had to be embarked upon for publishing reasons. When the Judge spoke further about it at the dinner table, listing aloud the men he thought approachable (Edward Everett Dana Junior, Charles Sumner etc.) Melville's embarrassment was lessened by his wife's loyal diplomacy.

Herman retired very late that night so that it wasn't until the journey back to New York the next day that Elizabeth was able to make apparent her extreme anger, which she did simply by informing Herman that she had things to say to him which could no more be said in front of strangers on a steamboat than they could in front of her own mother and father. She hugged Malcolm close to her, as if his father was not to be trusted near him.

"What interpretation am I to put upon it," she asked, when they were finally alone in their own rooms, "when no sooner have you stopped your punishing and unnecessary routine than you plan to set off gallivanting over the ocean as if you were still a bachelor without a care or responsibility in the world? I am your wife, Herman. You have a son just six months old."

Herman might have replied that the "unnecessary" routine had been occasioned by just the cares and responsibilities Elizabeth alluded to. He had a son and a wife to provide for and must therefore work harder than before. But he had long ago appreciated the appalling egotism that drove him in his craft, and had no real reply to Elizabeth's request for interpretation. What rankled was the suspicion that it was other people's interpretation of his behaviour that concerned Elizabeth. She didn't want to be seen as the deserted and passed-over wife.

His long delayed reply was short. "Lizzie. I need to go."

"You don't need to go. Mr. Brodhead has been handling things perfectly well. And anyway, you fixed up *Redburn* directly with Mr. Bentley. It is an unnecessary journey."

Herman shook his head and said, almost in a whisper, "Not that kind of a need."

"And what of *our* needs? Malcolm is just becoming more alert. These next few months will see an enormous development. You ought to be here for that."

"But there are many fathers whose business demands their absence. My own father was often away from home."

Herman could see from Elizabeth's facial expression that this

205

was no kind of answer, and if anything fuelled her case rather than his.

"Lizzie, be positive about this." He stood up and began to move about the room. "You can take Malcolm to Boston. You know how much you like it there, and when I get back we can perhaps think of moving house. What do you think of that?" He put his hands on her shoulders, trying to shake her gloom away.

"When?"

"Oh, I don't know, that will depend on how much these two recent jobs fetch for me."

"I mean, when will you come back?"

He walked away, and with his back to her said, "I am not entirely certain yet. A month or two will be enough I should think."

Six weeks later, and less than one week before his departure, Herman wrote to his father-in-law, thanking him for the letters of introduction, and adding,

> Lizzie is becoming more reconciled to idea of my departure, especially as she will have Malcolm for company during my absence. And I have no doubt, that when she finds herself surrounded by her old friends in Boston, she will bear the temporary separation with more philosophy than she has anticipated.

This, of course, is the kind of passage which says the opposite of its literal sense. It is quite clear that Elizabeth was *not* reconciled to his departure and that Herman had grave doubts as to her inclination to view the separation philosophically.

So that when George Duyckinck reports that "the morning (October 10th) was so wet and rainy that none of his friends went to the Hook" with Melville to see him off, it is likely that there were reasons beyond the weather for his lonely departure.

Waiting on the wet and windswept waterfront he was reminded of the stormy night he had spent with his father on the other side of the Hook, waiting for the river boat to Albany. The memory, setting off a complicated chain of neuron firings, gave rise to the following thoughts: he loved his father and identified with him now as he prepared to set sail for England; he wondered what kind of an adventure they might have had if they had crossed to this side of the dock and fled together, a runaway father and son, to the cities of Europe; he thought of his own son and Lizzie's accusation

206

as regards him; he thought of his mother and her strange irresist-
ible tyranny; he thought of the two books he had just completed
and the lack of satisfaction felt; he watched sailors disembarking
from a tugboat and although he did not envy them as regard their
condition and occupation there was still an independence about
their lifestyle that attracted him.

All such ruminations stemmed from the problems he was
experiencing adapting to the role of husband. He wanted to be a
good husband – more than anything he wanted to be a good father
– yet implicit in these two aims and bound up with the whole of
family life was a commitment to a time-consuming sociability
which at present he found both wearying and confining. Here on
the shoreline where the soft waters lapped the hard land, he was
poised between two allegiances, but somewhere, in the days
ahead, out on a new shore beyond the deepest waters of the ocean
might lie the kind of solution which the voyagers in *Mardi* had set
out to discover.

With just such high hopes at least temporarily in mind for his
journey, and with so mordant a leavetaking behind him, how
distressing it was to find that the sailing packet was to be delayed
for the third day running. Leaving his luggage to be installed upon
the tug he walked home in driving rain all the way up Broadway,
passing Delmonico's, Trinity church, and, at the top end, turning
off into the Bowery by the Astor Opera House, and walking the
rest of the way home beneath the shelter of the Harlem Railroad.

He spent the evening writing a letter to Evert Duyckinck in
which the phrase "I must spend my first evening of arrival at my
own fireside", composed casually and as betokening an absurd
humour, nevertheless seemed to conceal a didactic truth, so that
he copied it out again and again on rough paper, as if it were a line
from an obscure poet, the mechanical copying of which might
assist understanding.

The next day the weather was not noticeably better, and
Herman's farewell to his kindred no less grouchy, but the passengers (about thirty in number) were put into the tugboat *Goliath*
and at half-past twelve during a cold, violent storm from the West
set off for the North River where the *Southampton* lay at anchor.

*   *   *

To his great delight a proposed room-sharing with a sickly youth

207

of twenty, which the boy's father had tried to negotiate on the wharfside did not come off, and the captain of the vessel kept to his promise of placing Herman in the individual occupancy of a large state-room, the only passenger thus honoured. There was enough light in the room, from a thick bullseye window, which he could open in fair weather and he spent all that first afternoon glorying in his inhabitance and time and again looking out upon the sea through the thick, slightly distorting glass.

In the evening, after dinner and a walk upon the deck, he agreed to make up a whist party, but it was short-lived, for one of the number succumbed early on to seasickness. It was indeed a turbulent sea and Herman congratulated himself the next morning on being able to sleep soundly.

He was on the deck before breakfast, going to the mast-head and recalling "the old emotions". During this first full day on board he began to take note of the more interesting passengers and to see if there were any with whom it might be pleasing to strike an acquaintance.

The most interesting passenger was George Adler, a German–American scholar and author of a formidable lexicon. He was a shy man and Herman determined that later in the day he would approach him and try and work up conversation. Throughout the morning he kept noticing a lady with a copy of *Omoo*. She held the book open, but never appeared to be reading, rather it seemed she had eyes only for Herman himself, evidently having been informed of his identity. She was a comely woman and he exchanged eye-catching glances with her, until discovering that she was married to a Mr. Keese, also on board, a Scottish painter. He was, anyway, totally unbothered about her as a reader of his work and this lack of concern rather proved to him how worthless his writing had been so far. He couldn't care what she thought of the book, whether she was reading it at all, or just using it as a ticket of introduction. A new creative impulse was being born in him – one that paid no heed to the public. He had already written to his father-in-law:

> My only desire for "success" springs from my pocket, and not from my heart. So far as I am individually concerned, and independent of my pocket, it is my earnest desire to write those sort of books which are said to *fail*.

In the circumstances it was a foolhardy confession to address to a man who had served so long as a benefactor. Obviously this new view of his vocation was too strong to be kept in prudent check.

After dinner on that second evening on board Mr. Keese came over to his table and said, "Mr. Melville, the author?"

Mr. Melville, the author, dabbed at his beard with the napkin, replaced it in its silver ring, and looked up at the Scotsman.

"My wife has one of your books. We were wondering if you'd be so kind as to join our table. I believe we both know Mr. Twitchell."

"Asa Twitchell?"

"Yes. He painted your portrait a while ago. My wife has one of the preparatory sketches, by which you can judge she is quite an admirer. I am a painter myself. I have patrons in Albany. We are on our way home to collect more landscapes."

He had sat himself down on a vacant chair at Melville's table. Herman turned to Mr. Adler, who was eating with his back to him at an adjoining table. He then turned back to Keese. "Ah, I see Mr. Adler has finished. I have promised to accompany him on a walk of the deck. I mustn't keep him waiting. Another evening, perhaps?"

Mr. Adler, hearing his name mentioned, turned round in some confusion. Keese, deflated by being so unexpectedly "cut", let his white hands fall limply between his trouser legs. Instead of inviting Mr. Adler to join his table too, the neglect of which tack his wife severely criticised him for, he said instead, "You will of course autograph my wife's book during the voyage?"

"Of course." Herman's agreement was all the more readily given as it appeared to preclude any further invitations.

"Now, Mr. Adler, let us see how the wind blows."

Mr. Adler dutifully rose and followed Herman through the dining salon, Mrs. Keese giving them a smile and a nod as they passed.

The writer and scholar had spoken once beforehand – about Evert Duyckinck, a common acquaintance. Even so, Herman felt obliged to thank Adler for his complicity.

"That was first-rate. I don't think you gave that Keese fellow a moment's suspicion. Thank you. A fine piece of acting. And I am saved from a huntress."

"There you are, you see. A perfect example of Free-will dictating to Fate."

Adler was a philosopher as well as a lexicographer and already in their first conversation the name of Kant had been mentioned.

"Ah, only from our point of view, Adler. I have avoided, I grant you, by my own diplomacy, and with you as my henchman, a painful half-hour in cloying company. But, looked at from the other side, Fate can claim to have snatched the lady's opportunity from her. She did what she could but failed to get her way. It is always a fine line this, judging each circumstance according to Fate and Free-will. And even in the continuum of moral behaviour, is the good man justified in congratulating himself upon his rectitude or is it not the case that the person's constitution and natural instincts make them pious?"

"Causation, the great metaphysical bugbear."

Herman put his hand on his companion's shoulder. "Mr. Adler, let us make this a historical voyage. Come up beneath the mainmast and we shall tackle this bugbear together, till it's been finally and thoroughly picked out."

The sea was still high and although there was no rain the wind blowing across the open area of the middle deck made it necessary for the two men to shout.

"What accent did that man have that spoke to you just now?"

"Keese? He's a Scot."

"I thought he might have been. It was a Scotsman who denied the bugbear altogether."

"You'll have to tell me. I only know a bit of ancient lore. And Rabelais."

"Hardly a philosopher! It was Hume who denied causation."

Herman bellowed out this last statement in mimicry, roaring with laughter. There was something in the mispronunciation of "cow-sation" and the repeated consonant and vowel sound of "Hume who" which he found so irresistibly funny as to risk hurting his new friend, who thought he was laughing at the veracity of the statement, and not its expression.

"It is true, absolutely true," he said excitedly. "You have to know about this. Our lives go by a day at a time, and it is only because day follows day in quick succession that we interpret our experiences as being consecutively determined. There is nothing. No link."

"You are certain? You are sure?"

"Not me! Mr. Hume. The Scotsman."

Herman roared with laughter again. "But he is just a painter, the Scotsman. Come, the wind is cold; we shall continue talking on the move, and look, if there's no causation, we need not talk of

210

Mr. Hume, or any other name, just of ourselves, as we tread the deck this stormy night. Let us be Shakespearian characters with the whole instructive weight of God's Providence upon our lips. Act Four, Scene the Third."

The two men walked the deck and Herman, resisting further banter, entered deeply into the conversation, pleased to have found a companion interested academically in the same themes which bothered him to the quick.

"You are a Fatalist then, Mr. Melville?"

"No." Herman gave the word its slow and ponderous delivery, introductory of elaboration. "Fatalism presumes an irrevocable edict of Heaven concerning a particular event. A future punishment for a past sin with all intervening time irrelevant. This is a less gentle model than that of Providence, which posits a divine plan for the multitude of earthly events."

"I think perhaps you confuse your notion of Fatalism with that of Fate itself. The old philosophers recognised both Fate and Providence, the one being a channel for the other. Put simply Fate is subject to the natural law and the fixed plan must nearly always work through Fate. Only rarely will Providence change the laws of Fate to bring about a required conclusion. So the thinking goes."

"Mm, but the rarity of an event increases its mystery. The natural world is mysterious and unpredictable enough, as any of these sailors will tell you."

A group of deck-hands had just descended one of the mastheads, having made adjustments for night sailing.

"Unpredictable to *us*." Adler picked up the thread of the conversation after they passed polite and sympathetic words with one of the crew. "But in talking of Providence we are assuming an absolute foreknowledge."

"Precisely. And where does that leave freedom of the will?"

"It leaves us back – or brings us back I think the expression is – to causation." And this time Herman did not laugh at the pronunciation. "Does an event happen because it is foreseen? Or does it become foreknown because it has happened?"

"That distinction befuddles me, Adler. It is typical of philosophical avoidance."

"That is the way with philosophy." Adler shrugged and smiled.

Turning down the starboard side of the deck, Herman said, "Well, let us try a confrontation. The weather is wild enough for some elemental strife."

211

The wind indeed blew more strongly on this side of the boat, and the two men held on to the deckrail, making their way with a sidelong gait, and shouting their words out into the dark emptiness of the ocean.

"Foreknowledge is foreknowledge, however it is construed. And think on this, ye pulpit proselytisers, if there is no uncertainty there can be no accountability, so that which you also propound – the punishment of the wicked and the reward of the good – becomes ludicrous, because all has been bound by a single manner of occurrence. By the same token what is there to pray for?"

Adler, a little perturbed by the dramatic persona that Melville had adopted, felt it necessary to take on the counterbalancing voice of classical philosophical discourse, even though by nature he was much more comfortable in the questioning part.

"I shall have to say a word in Providence's defence."

"Come along then, my Socrates. We are all ears, the stars and me."

"Think of the word. A foreigner sometimes sees things better. Provid–ence. It is more to do with providing for the future than with seeing beforehand. But that was just a small thought. Listen, we have just seen some men climb down the mast. Did our seeing them make their mast-climbing necessary? No. They were ordered to it by a superior. And before that they enrolled upon the voyage. Neither of these conditions rested upon our beholding of the event. And yet we saw it. We saw it happen. Simply that. And so, Providentially, is it with the divinely observant eye. All things, past, present and future, are seen by God. But their being seen does not bind them to an immutable law. Those things which happen in the present as the result of Free-will are seen by God as future events – bound to be, but freely undertaken."

"This argument is too free. It catches all riposte. Free-will has too wide and too assailable a scope, if, whatever choice it makes, that choice is visible and has always been visible to Providence. Too lenient a God is it who inclines its knowledge to my desires."

"Too lenient? But you complained of the harshness of Providential law."

"Not the harshness. The hopelessness."

"Well, that hopelessness is answered once Free-will is allowed. The overview does not change, as you suggest, now here, now there, now today, again tomorrow, but with one glance. You can have faith again in Hope and Prayer."

"Well spoken, Atheist."

"I count myself a free-thinker and Abstract explorer, not an Atheist. As my countryman Kant discovered, it is all in the mind, and however we train ourselves to view the world, so the world becomes. And now you shall have to excuse me. I begin to feel sea-queazy."

Herman remained alone upon the deck for some time before returning to his cabin. He sat with his back against one of the rope storage units, sheltering from the wind, and in silent meditation began, with reference to this present voyage, thinking of Fate in terms of a personal destiny. In what sense had he been "bound" to embark upon the *Southampton*; and was the encounter with Mr. Adler part of the prescription? Lizzie and Malcolm seemed not to require concern. It was as if Providence had allotted them a marginal corner of his existence which he could very easily put to one side, and pursue his destiny as if they didn't exist. It was conversations such as he had had with Adler that shunted the mind along its pathway of discovery. Conversation and reading. Some found books dry, but with the right arousal they could open up liquid depths to plunge into.

Finally in his cabin he found he could not sleep, at least not deeply. In a light slumber he consistently imagined that Elizabeth was on board and that ministrations to his wife, who in this daydream was still pregnant, precluded any attempt to befriend Mr. Adler, whose aspect greatly intrigued him. Each time he woke from this illusion he was to feel a mounting sense of guilt and shame that his instinctive response to it – the imagined presence of his wife – should be one of open annoyance. And it also showed him the reverse side of the voyaging impulse – not one of discovery, either mental or physical, but one of escape, of desertion. It was one which he would learn reluctantly to accept as an instinctive reflex, having its roots in the desertion of the *Typee* experience, upon which the whole of his contemporary fame was based. He was a runner away.

*   *   *

At daybreak, with the light-headedness that comes from the lack of deep sleep, he went on deck and persuaded some of the sailors to let him climb halfway up the mast-head, to display some old-time gymnastics. It was a sunny morning, but large puffy clouds were gathering in a quick breeze. They had the appearance of strange

213

and mocking faces, leprously swollen and sneering. The sun went behind one such shape and in the dizzying lessening of the light Herman perceived that the clouds, instead of being blown in a single crosswise direction, were converging upon him from all four quarters, and in their advance the looming features became hollowed out and cadaverous.

Herman descended the mast and without thanking the crew or saying a word to any of the spectating passengers he went to his room and fell upon the bed; but, still breathing deeply, he rolled off on to the floor of the cabin and lay gently knocking his forehead against pulled-up knees. The large droplets of rain already spattering against his bullseye window were as the pickaxe knocks of goblin spirits trying to force admittance to his cabin.

There follows an episode which is so extraordinary that for once I must resort to the orthodox biographer's technique of quoting from source. It is necessary that we should hear Herman's first person account of what took place that afternoon, because it is from the narrative tone that we can make certain deductions about the reported event.

> After dinner the rain ceased, yet it still blew swiftly. I was walking the deck when I perceived one of the steerage passengers looking over the side; I looked too, and saw a man in the water, his head completely lifted above the water, about twelve feet from the ship. For an instant I thought I was dreaming; for no one else seemed to see what I did. Next moment I shouted "Man overboard" and turned to go aft. The Captain ran forward, greatly confused. I dropped overboard the tackle-fall of the quarter-boat, and swung it toward the man, who was now drifting close to the ship. He did not get hold of it, and I got over the side, within a foot or two of the sea, and again swung the rope towards him. He now got hold of it. By this time a crowd of people – sailors and others – were clustering about the bulwarks but none seemed very anxious to save him. They warned *me*, however, not to fall overboard. After holding on to the rope, about a quarter of a minute, the man let go of it and drifted astern under the mizzen chains. His conduct was unaccountable; he could have saved himself had he been so minded. I was struck by the expression of his face in the water. It was merry. Running to the taffrail we saw him again, floating off – saw a few bubbles, and never

214

saw him again. No boat was lowered, no sail was shortened, hardly any noise was made. The man drowned like a bullock. It afterwards turned out that he was crazy and had jumped overboard.

Apparently, Melville had witnessed another such drowning ten years previously, on his maiden voyage. And only a few months beforehand he had recounted this first instant in the writing of *Redburn*. It is possible, therefore, that the event described in his Journal was the product of visionary recall brought about by a state of nervous exhaustion, engendered by a summer of intense overwork. Certainly the suicide is insufficiently corroborated by other evidence, and the rôle of other passengers and crew, as reported by Melville, is surely wholly unbelievable. For the most part they stand mutely by with that eerie silent gloating which onlookers in a dream often possess. The exhortation to Melville himself not to fall overboard might suggest that the vision was so real as to provoke an actual rescue attempt, which would indeed explain why the only anxiety expressed by others was for the rescuer.

Secondly it is possible that neither suicidal drowning took place – that the first was included in *Redburn* as a fictional dramatising of autobiographical experience and that the second was attributable to the hallucinatory power of that fictional invention.

But perhaps it is more likely that while the first episode was an invention (after all, its only mention is in the pages of a novel) the second actually happened. Writers often experience that their imaginative contrivances prefigure real events but they almost never fail to remark upon the unexpected parallel.

I must not be dishonest; I find such multiple propositioning tortuous and there is a sense in which I have presented this short episode as if I were writing a conventional biography to prove the advantages of an assertively fictional approach. But there are areas in which the novelist hesitates to make too confident proposals in regard to historical characters – and it is with Melville's mental stability that I feel the greatest hesitation and uncertainty.

Immediately following the reported suicide there was an intensification of the storm and the ship began rolling and pitching in an amazing manner, so that all sorts of nausea-noise was to be heard from the state rooms. Herman, it seems, and one crazy Englishman whose mad feelings found something congenial in the

215

riot of the raging sea, were the only passengers to take to the deck. The madman kept claiming to see steamers and was apparently afflicted by delirium tremens, consequent upon keeping drunk for the last two months. Did he exist, or was it Melville himself who was guilty of extravagant outbursts in front of the second mate?

The storm lasted all weekend and on Monday, with convalescent passengers beginning to ease themselves back into the voyage, Herman reports that he "drank a small bottle of London stout for dinner and think it did me good". There is something pathetic and unmanly in this statement, and it is most uncharacteristic of his general attitude towards alcohol. As, by his own admission, he had been untouched by the seasickness, it is to be presumed that he took the stout as a sort of nerve tonic.

Before the voyage was a week old he started to mention Elizabeth and little Barney, the nickname for Malcolm, in his Journal. But the inclusions are strangely stunted (sometimes the interpolated "Where dat old man?" – purportedly an example of Malcolm's baby talk, but hardly the type of sentence an eight month old would articulate) as if they had been inserted as afterthoughts or out of a sense of propriety. Although Allan claimed to have discerned from Herman's letters home to Elizabeth (she read parts of them aloud) that Herman was homesick from the start, it does not appear that way from the Journal, for once the storm was past he began to discuss, with Adler and a cousin of Bayard Taylor, the possibility of turning this European jaunt into a Grand Tour. Together they sketched a plan for going down the Danube from Vienna to Constantinople; on to Athens by steamer; to Beirut and Jerusalem, Alexandria and the pyramids. And the one small bottle of stout was passed over in favour of tumblers filled with whisky punches or mulled wine.

Adler continued to evangelise about the German idealists, addressing the other two as "Gentlemen".

"Gentlemen, if, in accounting for this world, we put forward the hypothesis . . ."

Taylor and Melville, drinking more heavily than the German, were often in teasing mood, compelling Adler to elaborate his metaphysical abstractions until they fell prey to every kind of contradiction. But Herman listened and learned, and took particular note of the philosophical system of Hegel, not finding much that he could agree with in the notion of historical improvement, but liking the identification of the abstract with the particular. If he had been alone with Adler he would have developed a more serious debate, trying to link Hegel's system with the ideas of Providence and Free-will discussed at the start of the voyage. If it is in the unfolding of actual events that any abstract or divine purpose is to be construed, then presumably the Individual Will is intimately bound up with such a purpose.

"Yes!" screamed Adler. "You see, gentlemen, it is not necessary to account for . . ." Melville and Taylor each choked on a mouthful of whisky punch at this familiar preamble. "It isn't necessary, I say, to account for a personal God by theology or theological interpretations of the scriptures. Philosophy has proved it an inescapable condition of existence. In fact, for a full relationship with the Godhead or Abstract Principle one should not retreat from life, in a monastery say, or a sect, but take a full part in the affairs of the world, particularly in domesticity. One should not live alone. One should have a wife. Have children."

"That proves it, Adler," said Taylor. "You must come to the East and find yourself an Egyptian princess."

The German blushed. "These are Hegel's views. I am more inclined to the scholastic way."

Such evenings, with their mixture of serious and jovial chatter put Herman into excellent spirits, so that he suddenly seemed recovered from the nervous exhaustion which had been evident during the weekend of the storm. He even promenaded with one or two of the ladies and played shuffle-board with them. He read a copy of Lamb's essays, found in the ship's library, and he relished the superb meals provided in the ship's dining salon. In fact, he couldn't help thinking that if it were possible for men, women and children to live in a community, then on board a sailing packet would provide the environment most likely to make a success of it.

*   *   *

Nearing the end of the voyage the ship became encalmed in the Channel for two days and Melville and his companions, impatient to set foot on English soil, disembarked at Deal, leaving their luggage on board, to be carried around the Kent and Essex coasts and up the Thames estuary.

They put foot on shore at 6 a.m. and walked the country road between Deal and Sandwich where they breakfasted at a tumble-down old inn and then took the train to Canterbury. They visited

217

the cathedral and went to the theatre to see a farce. They spent the night at an "odd hole", all three of them sharing a single room, before taking the third-class cars (which in those days were exposed to the elements, and in November gave a devilish cold ride) to London Bridge. Securing three separate rooms in the same West End hotel, they immediately embarked upon a hungry round of concert-, theatre-, and gallery-going, very often in one another's company, although gradually Herman's business interests (the now imperative need to sell *Whitejacket* for a generous advance in order to finance the proposed Grand Tour) and the letters of introduction that he had brought with him drew the author into more indigenous company.

His first forays were unsuccessful. Both Mr. Bentley and Mr. Murray were out of town on Thursday, November 8th, so, sending a note to Bentley for a meeting the next Monday, at noon, Herman, by inclination rather than necessity, dispensed with the company of Adler and Taylor, and spent time tramping round the city in the wonted way.

On Saturday, the day after the Lord Mayor's Show, he sauntered through the Temple courts and gardens, down Holborn Hill, past Pryor's the Umbrella Manufacturer, and through Cock Lane to Smithfield, Charter House and the rear of Guildhall, where a crowd of beggars was queueing to receive the broken meats and pies left over from the grand banquet.

Continuing his walk down King William Street and past the Sun Coffee House in Fish Street, he came out at Tower Hill and then went down to St. Katharine's and the London Docks. He crossed the river, and back again, by the Rotherhithe ferry, returned to the hotel and, after dinner, took Adler out and enticed him into stopping at a penny-theatre.

It was on this day, the first of elected solitude, that Herman began to grow homesick and sentimentally unhappy. The historical and literary associations of these old streets, summon them as he may, seemed powerless to deliver any kind of mental thrill. The rather pointless crossing back and forth on the Rotherhithe ferry mocked his manhood and the whole of his adventurous experience and reputation. What fascination or strange desperation for something to do had enticed him to cross the calm waters of a city river? It was as if the boyish wish to set foot on any boat, however small, in pond or on river, lived on redundantly, despite his having reached man's estate and experienced the rigours of ocean sailing.

And in this, the episode was exemplary of a weird imperviousness that characterised his mental and emotional armoury, and made him doubt his general level of maturity. He was not as resistant as he would have liked to suppose to the perennial suggestion of his mother's that no man could consider himself truly a man who did not apply himself in some capacity to the world of commerce and the direct manufacture of material wealth for home and country.

Inherent in his fast-approaching friendship with Mr. Hawthorne was to be the relationship of an adolescent to a grown man, with the latter holding (and with-holding) the key to maturity.

For the moment his companions were not in that calibre. They were of the same generation as himself, sharing in the sense of being lost in a world of unreachable limits, both geographical and imaginative. In fact Herman felt himself, justifiably, to be the superintendent of the triumvirate. Upon his publishing negotiations rested the viability of the Grand Tour. And upon poor Adler, shaking with an absurd moral panic at the penny-theatre, rested all of the more travelled man's worldliness.

After spending Sunday as a regular tourist at Hampton Court, Mr. Melville was received by Mr. Bentley at the New Burlington Street publishing house and offered two hundred pounds for *Whitejacket*, which Herman found a liberal enough offer, but unfortunately there was no prospect of an advance. He told Bentley he would think the matter over, but once outside he quickly consulted his streetplan and headed for Albemarle Street, to try and extract an advance out of Mr. Murray. But Murray was again out or, expecting difficulty with the once-rejected author, made appropriate excuses.

In a mood of depression that suggests Melville suspected he was being given the cold shoulder he walked straight across the city, making for his hotel in the Strand, but drifting too far north, and, finally, in a resigned loss of way, ending up at St. Paul's Cathedral where he sat for an hour in a dozy state listening to the chanting of the boys' choir.

In his Journal he confesses to a feeling of "homesickness and sentimental unhappiness". He was probably suffering from that special tristimania that a married man must invariably feel when, after living a life of uninterrupted companionship for a year or two, and particularly after having become a father, he attempts, even for a day, to live again the single life, to be the lone wolf treading jauntily and hungrily along the wooded way. Inevitably, if the ties

219

of companionship are true, he will sense a door having been irrevocably closed on the life of independent expectation so that all he derives from the effort to get past it is the sense of guilt and betrayal that emanates from the attempt.

The next day Melville witnessed the public hanging of Mr. and Mrs. Manning in Horsemonger Lane. Returning to his room at 4 p.m. he described it as "a most wonderful, horrible, and unspeakable scene". It is interesting that the following day Melville makes it clear that he has dropped all plans of making the Egyptian tour, and we can readily imagine that there was something in the horrific spectacle of observing a man and wife going to their death which had compounded those feelings of homesickness already afflicting him. "The man and wife were hung side by side – *still unreconciled to each other*". As he recorded this phrase Melville reflected upon his parting from Elizabeth and the lack of reconciliation in that series of false-started farewells. "What a change from the time they stood up to be married together!"

The youngster McCurdy, who was continuing to hound the older set, called into Melville's room while he was finishing this Journal entry. Herman was bored "terribly" (he added the statement while McCurdy was still talking) and pointedly began to write a letter home, enclosing a broadside of the hanging for his father-in-law.

On Wednesday 14th, for the third time, Herman called at Murray's Albemarle Street firm, a four-storey building close to the Piccadilly end of the street. A lamp was burning in its holder, set in the glass arch over the main entrance. The footman walked to the far end of the hall, knocked, and opened a door.

"A Mr. Melville to see you, sir."

There was a sound of some papers being re-arranged, and the footman, with a quizzical nod and smirk aimed at Herman turned off into the dining room, the noise from within making it apparent that servants were still clearing away lunch.

Herman stood awkwardly, not knowing whether he was invited to go up to the room at the end of the hall or not. The sound of ladies' conversation began to fill the top of the stairwell, but he was saved from any embarrassing encounter by Mr. Murray at last appearing in the doorway of his study.

"Mr. Melville; do come this way."

Herman was shown into an extremely tiny room with a domed glass skylight and a hanging lamp suspended from its centre.

Burning coals glowed in the grate at his left-hand side as he opened the door. The heat in the room, and his nervousness brought Herman out in a perspiration which he knew must be visible on his face. Murray asked him to sit; not without a critical glance at the green jacket that had already been the cause of much head-turning as he walked the London streets.

"I believe you've called before. I'm so sorry I was out."

It had not escaped Herman's notice that in the week that had elapsed since his first call at Murray's, no attempt had been made to contact him at the hotel, the address of which he had naturally left with the footman.

"It is always a great pleasure to meet one of our transatlantic authors. Mr. Irving, a countryman of yours, is a frequent visitor here. No doubt you know him. He has sat in that chair many times, though normally we would go up to the drawing room. We shan't today – it was ladies' luncheon day and my wife is entertaining."

Mr. Murray paused for Herman to make some indication of the purpose of his visit; none was forthcoming.

"I understand you have returned to the travelogue style which made us take *Typee* and its follow-up. Bentley feels he has made quite a catch, I know. But we could never have taken that third book of yours – Murdi, or Murki was it? Though we don't want to go into that now."

"No, and I don't think *Redburn*, which I offered straight to Bentley, would have interested you either, the travel experiences being a mite too coloured up and heightened for your taste. But I have brought a fifth book with me, entitled *Whitejacket*."

"*White* jacket you say?" Murray arched his brow and took a second, quizzical look at Mr. Melville's jacket.

"Yes. Has the title been used before?"

"No, no. Carry on."

"Mr. Bentley has made a provisional offer of two hundred pounds, but all things being equal I am still keen to maintain the link with you, and I do believe, sir, that this book, a factual account of life on board a United States frigate, will be much more to your taste than even *Typee*. The point of my call is therefore to ask if you will take a look at the proofs. I have them at my hotel and could bring them round whenever you are free to look at them, although naturally I am not away from home for long and wish to settle this matter at the earliest opportunity."

221

"Quite so. Of course, of course." Mr. Murray perceptibly relaxed. He had anticipated a more complicated request, perhaps even a complaint against previous treatment. "I understand your urgency. And the copyright matter is the very devil for you Americans, ain't it just?" He stood up. "Well, we have your address. I shall send over this evening for the sheets."

"Thank you, sir."

Melville stood up and buttoned his green jacket. Outside he noticed that one of his lapels bowed outwards and he had to correct the buttoning staring all the while at the chiselled lettering of Albemarle House on the other side of the street.

On his way back to the hotel he bought two books (Beaumont & Fletcher, Ben Jonson), the first of many second-hand works he was to acquire during his stay. In the evening he went out to dinner with Taylor, Adler and McCurdy, and he and Adler declined finally and irrevocably to join the other two on their Eastern tour.

When, three days later, having already seen Taylor and McCurdy off on their adventure, Herman declares in his Journal that even the extent of his European trip is in question (due to lack of success with the advance) – "I shall not see Rome – I'm floored" – it is with no impression of disappointed conviction. Rather does he seem at last to enjoy his spell abroad, relishing the sensory pleasures that were so much a solace to his nervous disposition: chops and pancakes washed down with stout and scotch ale; cigars lit, and pipes puffed.

Murray had decided it wouldn't be in his "line" to publish the book, and Longman's had left a rejection slip on the blackened boots outside his room, so he was still hawking it about and plying his letters of introduction. He was able to write home that, at Windsor, he had seen the Queen go by in her carriage, that he had bowed to her and would commend to her the use of Rowlands Kalydon for clarifying the complexion. He spent a rattling good evening among cockney literati, mostly writers from *Punch*, and stayed out until 2 a.m.

On Friday November 23rd he was invited to dine at Albemarle Street, a gesture which was perhaps thought owing to him. He arrived in his usual green jacket to find the footman togged up in belled breeches and tights, revealing a despicable pair of sheepshanks. Shown upstairs to the drawing room where guests were collecting before the meal, Mr. Murray at once abandoned him to a galvanised ghost of a fellow who was got up in the style of Walter

Scott with a prodigious white cravat. He gave Herman the tips of two skinny fingers to shake. There were about seven men and four lean women present, mostly sitting on couches and chairs.

But if the society were stuffy the room itself was wonderful, with pictures of Coleridge, Southey and others hanging on linkchains suspended from a brass rail. When Mr. Murray finally came to speak to Herman he pointed out the white marble fireplace where a fire was in full flame. "It was in that grate and in just such flames that my father consigned to ash the autobiography of Lord Byron. The portrait above the mantelpiece was there then, so the destruction took place in full view of the Lord, you could say. That was in 'twenty-four, a quarter of a century ago."

It is ironical that Melville, who was rather affronted by this story, and felt that the burning amounted to vandalism, was in due course to touch a taper to many of his own papers, while Mr. Hawthorne, who countless times railed against the preservation of relics, kept just about every scrap.

A quarter of a century might have elapsed since Lord Byron's death, but he was still much talked about, and as they went through the curtain that separated the drawing room from the room which led on to the stairway, Herman was informed that downstairs he would see the window through which had been passed to a clamouring public the latest Cantos of *Don Juan*.

The Byronic presence was still very much in evidence a century and a half later when, late on a Shrove Tuesday afternoon, I sat just outside the drawing room while a contemporary Mr. Murray poured me tea. For the serious, exploratory biographer such an afternoon would have been part and parcel of research; but for me, opting not to walk in my subjects' physical footsteps, but to keep to the suppositional mode, it was a singular event. Mr. Murray was very gracious; he showed me original letters written by Herman and his brother Allan. I cannot pretend that it wasn't a great thrill to hold these folded papers in my hands – the delight was real enough, but inapplicable; so that as I come to write of this evening dinner (fulfilling an intention long ago marked on a six by four inch card headed "Scenes") I find that the early hopes of recreating the conversational and dramatic conventions of the dinner table have been scuppered by the force of personal memory.

At the time of my visit the publishing house was undergoing minor interior refurbishment. The stairwell was draped in decorators' dustsheets. Mr. Murray led the way down and into what had been the dining room: on the ground floor at the front (here were those famous windows). If the drawing room and accompanying rooms on the first floor had been little altered since the first half of the nineteenth century, the same could not be said of this present space, which was very much the office. Perhaps not quite an office of the 1980s (there were no computer keyboards or visual display screens), but there were typewriters, filing cabinets and boxes of books. A quiet undemonstrative man who reminded me of Bartleby, putting on an overcoat and picking up a pile of mail, was preparing to go home. He lingered a while, politely, for Mr. Murray to introduce me, and he smiled at the reminiscence, probably heard many times before, of a previous Murray "mustering" the Colmans for dinner.

I do not regret my visit. It was an invigorating excursion, but instead of coupling me with the past I find it isolates me from it so that the best thing I can do is quote briskly from the Journal, and move on. It is a fault of much itinerant biography, and now I know the mechanics of the weakness: an old haunt of the subject's is visited (a dwelling, or the scene of a special event or inspiration); a contemporary description is given; perhaps an anecdote relating to the researcher's enquiries; finally, a direct quotation. But the present and the past remain unbridged and the materials for making an imaginative leap are withheld.

> At dinner the stiffness, formality, and coldness of the party was wonderful. I felt like knocking all their heads together . . . I sat next to Lockhart, and seeing that he was a customer, who was full of himself and expected great homage; and knowing him to be a thorough-going Tory and fish-blooded Churchman and conservative, and withal editor of the Quarterly, I refrained from playing the snob to him, like the rest, and the consequence was he grinned at me his ghastly smiles. Oh conventionalism, what a ninny thou art to be sure.

Not so much a ninny the following night, when Herman proved that he was well able to enjoy and sparkle in the company of high society. He had been invited to dine and stay the night by Joshua Bates of Portman Square. The stage took him up Regent Street, along Oxford Street and dropped him at the Baker Street turning. Herman picked his way through the fog towards a distant illumination, towards which same beacon other, shadowy figures were heading.

Mr. Bates was standing just behind his footman, welcoming guests as they arrived. In the drawing room Herman drank his sherry in the company of a moustachioed Viennese. At the table he was partnered by a nephew of the aristocracy and by an American merchant. There was a baron opposite him and a lovely young girl who proved to be the daughter of Count Chaumier, the sea novelist. The atmosphere was rich with the varying accents of foreign tongues and with the free gesticulation of uninhibited intercourse. Herman spoke to the American about his father's connections with England. He spoke loudly so that the novelist's daughter, who was staring his way, would be able to hear. The meal consisted of a series of mysterious dishes. Miss Chaumier said many of them were French. Her eyes sparkled as she sipped juice from a spoon, or ate flakes of fish from a fork; but Herman became disinterested in the playful flirting when it became apparent that the American had been acquainted with Gansevoort.

"Yes, certainly I knew Gansevoort." And pressing a napkin to his lips added, "I did not mention it sooner for fear . . . well . . ."

"I would like to hear a little of how you found him." Herman, scraping the last crumbs of meringue from the bottom of a porcelain bowl, turned sideways on his chair, and lowered his voice. "Something of his frame of mind in those last days. Did you see him then?"

"I saw him not long before his end, yes, but he had rather shunned society while here. There were differences, as you no doubt know, at the Legation, and these had rather sapped his social confidence." The American shook his head, as if marvelling once again at the quick demise of a promising talent. "I tried to entice him into business. For I recognised the qualities of enthusiasm and exhaustive endeavour that had marked his early reputation. But it seems an unpropitious family history had turned him against commerce for ever."

"Yes, our father was a bankrupt, you see."

"He did tell me that."

"And Gansevoort had a business failure in the fur trade before entering politics."

"That he kept from me, but I guessed at something along the line."

"Was he very reclusive?"

"He did not appear to have many friends, particularly of his own generation, and his infrequent forays into society during the last months must have enforced many lonely hours in his rooms. I have often wondered whether such isolation contributed to his derangement."

Before leaving the table Herman accepted an offer from the American to accompany him back to town in his carriage. Thoughts of Gansevoort kept encroaching on the rest of the evening but did not entirely spoil the enjoyment of after-dinner drinks. There was a short entertainment and a little dancing to the piano. There was a further bout of innocent flirtation with Miss Chaumier. And there was Herman's excuse and apology to Mr. Bates at the leavetaking.

"Not at all, my dear boy. It was only that we did not want to have you set upon by street ruffians. Very glad that you have a safe escort. Mind you take Mr. Melville right to his door, now."

This parting admonition gave a sinister tension to the foggy carriage-ride home and Herman, his nerves and stomach agitated by a prodigiously strong cup of coffee taken prior to departure, was frequently made to start by shadowy emanations or weird wailings from side alleys.

When he reached his room he tried to write in his Journal but found himself utterly used up. The hotel was silent and Herman became acutely aware of his breathing as he sat with elbows on the table and hands cupped over both ears. The lids of his eyes became heavy so that his dark lashes flickered across his pupils distorting the shadow of his head that fell across the empty page.

He imagined Gansevoort sitting alone in his chamber at this same late hour, in just such profound silence, and the association, together with a sinking into the arms of Morpheus, made him imagine he was leaning over a freshly filled-in grave, with no grass growing on it yet. He heard himself calling to the coffin, "Why don't you speak to me?" and saw himself bending his head close to the earth, putting his ear right against the clod, straining for a reply. "Speak but one word. Speak just one word. It is I." On and on he wailed, until a rustling in his ear made him fancy that an insect was entering his drum, but his eyes opened and in cross-eyed focus saw the handwriting on the opposite page of his Journal, and a closing of his mouth convinced him that the rustling was the sound of his beard scraping against the paper. He

226

had rested there for some considerable time and it was not far off dawn when finally he got into bed.

Between November 27th and December 13th Melville was away in France and Germany on what was the merest apology of a European tour, compared with his original prospectus. In Paris, as well as indulging in more solitary tourism (which he reported in stark schoolboyish style: "to the Louvre and spent threee hours in the museum. Heaps of treasure of art of all sorts. Admirable collection of antique statuary. Beats the British Museum.") he met up once again with Adler and passed further evenings of metaphysical speculation.

The days spent outside Paris were in large part doleful, the only really pleasant stop being in Aix-la-Chapelle, a city full of the historical and artistic associations that suited Melville's ponderous nature. But the cumulative effect of this fortnight amongst foreign speakers was to intensify his homesickness and, returning to London, he felt, both in spirit and direction, that he was homeward bound. Two letters from Lizzie, awaiting him at Craven Street, in which she spoke of Malcolm's crawling abilities, made him sensible of a paternal regret that he was missing important stages in his son's development; so that an invitation from the Duke of Rutland to pay a New Year visit to Belvoir Castle, which was also waiting for him at the hotel, was initially rejected out of hand.

However, the invitation played havoc with his intentions, and two days later he was writing:

I am in a very painful state of uncertainty. I am all eagerness to get home – I ought to be home – my absence occasions uneasiness in a quarter where I most beseech heaven to grant repose. Yet here I have before me an open prospect to get some curious ideas of a style of life which in all probability I shall never have again. I should much like to know what the highest English Aristocracy really and practically is. And the Duke of Rutland's cordial invitation to visit him at the Castle furnishes me with just the thing I want. If I do not go, I am confident that hereafter I shall upbraid myself, for neglecting such an opportunity of procuring "material". And Allan and others will account me a ninny. I would not debate the matter a moment were it not that at least three weeks must elapse ere I depart for

227

Belvoir Castle – three weeks! If I could but get over *them*!
And if the two images (of Malcolm and Lizzie) would only
down for that space of time – I must light a second cigar and
revolve it over again.

This passage, written on a Sunday afternoon after attending
morning service at St. Thomas', Goswell Street, nicely states the
conflict between domesticity and artistic independence but as is
often the case with precisely poised dilemmas the real irreconcil-
ability had little to do with Art.

The second cigar decided in favour of home, and on the next day
he booked a passage on the *Independence* and concluded his agreement with Mr. Bentley. He spent his final week in London
roaming the bookstores and purchasing a large number of
volumes – two of which he read immediately: De Quincey's *Opium
Eater* and Goethe's *Autobiography*.

The final nights on land were spent in that quiet absorption of
good living, good drinking, good feeling and good talk that
Herman increasingly felt to be no longer part of his estate. He was
a married man and there were too many twinges of conscience to
allow unfettered enjoyment of these pleasures.

Part Three

"Oh, my leg is so tired of Julian's complaining."
Una stamped her foot on the station platform to accentuate a favourite form of expressing her displeasure, which always seemed to centre on her lower limb.

Julian stamped his foot too. "It could have come. Could have come. Me carry it." The little boy, not quite four years old, had been utterly disconsolate for two days, ever since having seen, while out walking with his Aunt Elizabeth, a rocking-horse in a shop window. Impulsively he had gone into the shop before his Aunt could waylay him and, taking from his pocket a small pewter cup which was his only and greatly valued treasure, had offered this in exchange for the horse. He had been vastly grieved on being whisked out of the shop without the horse, and had arrived home roaring.

"Home" for Sophia and the children during the spring of 1850 had been in Boston, with the Peabody in-laws, although Nathaniel, who for the sake of space resided at a boarding house nearby, spent the greater portion of these weeks, for the first time since his marriage, on independent forays to Portsmouth (to see Bridge) and to Cambridge (to dine with Longfellow). Even in Boston he had pursued a largely solitary existence, sitting to have his portrait painted by Mr. Thompson, or visiting Parker's smoking and drinking shop on Court Square, where he had admired the bar-tenders' artistry in tossing long parabolas of Tom and Jerry cocktails from one tumbler to another. He had attended this grog-shop ostensibly to observe the manners of its toping community but the amount of time he spent in this kind of amusement is suggestive that he enjoyed the redolent atmosphere of his bachelor days.

His ill temper and lack of stamina during preparations for their departure had also indicated, especially to Sophia, that he was

231

temporarily and temperamentally afflicted. The Red House, at Lenox, to which they were now journeying, had been offered to them some months ago rent free by its original owner Sam Ward. A period of hesitation during which other, hoped-for opportunities had not transpired came to an end with the Hawthornes finally agreeing to rent the red cottage from the new lessees of Highwood for a nominal sum of seventy-five dollars over four years.

The "new lessees of Highwood" were Mr. and Mrs. Tappan. The formality with which Mr. Hawthorne refers to his landlord and landlady in the Journals during the coming months tends to obscure the fact that Mrs. Tappan was none other than Caroline Sturgis, a close friend of Margaret Fuller, a warm acquaintance of Nathaniel's since his Brook Farm days, a close friend of Sophia's before that, an occasional Transcendental poet, and author of a children's book which was a favourite with the Hawthorne children.

"Come along then, Una. Let us think of a game to play while we wait for the train." Sophia looked beseechingly at Nathaniel, implying that the organising of this was his prerogative, but he wandered away from them towards the edge of the platform, where he stood arching a stiff back and exercising his shoulder blades.

The children had said goodbye to their aunt when alighting from the carriage and there was no one to see them off at the station. Sophia was more concerned about this move than she had been before any of the others. Although *The Scarlet Letter* had just been published it was too early for its popular success to have become apparent and she could not but be aware that eight years' marriage and the birth of two children had seen little improvement in their material position.

Mr. Hawthorne had seen the Hillside estate the previous autumn, and he knew that his wife had been deceived by written reports of the cottage, which described it as a four-bedroomed farmhouse. It was in fact a tiny, ramshackle shanty with inadequate means of heating, but all his emphasising of this had been treated as playful teasing. His eyes felt heavy and his back ached. His tongue was dry and his mind was filled by a restless resentment of the fact that he was moving away to a cut-off inland region of the state, just when he seemed to have developed a taste for city observation. He heard Sophia remonstrating with the children and turned to see her trying to pull Una off the only spare place on a wooden bench.

"No, no, no. My leg is tired. It *is*!"

Julian, with his little shoes, was doing his best to give his sister a real pain in her leg, but both children summarily forgot about the bench when the steam engine drawing the cars gave jarring signal of its engagement. Running away from Sophia so that she was left with the embarrassment of appearing to other occupants of the bench devoid of authority over her children, they each took hold of one of Nathaniel's hands and watched as two railroad employees pulled open the carriage doors to invite passengers to take their places.

This was the Worcester Depot on Beach Street, opposite the recently extended United States Hotel, which derived much custom from the visiting businessmen out of Albany, at that date the furthermost stop on this westerly line. It being a Tuesday morning (May 28th 1850), it was mainly families and casual travellers who now made preparation to board the train. The Hawthornes had put back their departure by one day on being advised that Monday's trains would be overcrowded with people travelling to the cattle market in Brighton, at that period the busiest livestock venue in the whole of New England.

Nathaniel made sure his wife and children were comfortably seated, before walking to the rear of the train to make certain that their main baggage had been put on board and was positioned for unloading at Richmond. Heavy rain had been falling during their journey to the depot so that the luggage labels had been converted to pellets of yellow pulp, but he was able to reassure Sophia that each of their trunks was in the baggage car.

When he sat down opposite Una she impishly put her "bad" leg up on his knee.

"What is your leg tired of now?" he asked.

She was slumped back in her seat, her chin on her chest, and her eyelids half-closed.

"She wants to use you as a toadstool," intoned Julian, and immediately giggled at his imagined drollery.

Una sat forward, removing her foot from Papa's knee and, turning to her brother, said, "*Foot*stool, silly. You mean a foot-stool. Doesn't he, father? Julian, you should have said footstool."

Julian was adamant that he had meant toadstool. "My turn now."

But Sophia had had enough of their nonsense and certainly wasn't going to let herself be used either as a footstool or a toadstool. She knocked Julian's shoe off her knee so that his

233

relaxed limb dropped with a bang to the floor of the carriage. He pretended for a little that it was badly hurt and then, catching Onion's eye, began once again to giggle.

Rain was still falling and Nathaniel changed places with Julian so that the two children might both have window seats and trace the scurrying slantwise fall of raindrops. As he took up his new position opposite Sophia he opened his mouth and massaged the back of his neck.

"I don't feel all that well."

Sophia, as if entranced by the noise and motion of the train, sat with hands in her lap, unresponsive; her shoulders rocked gently and her eyelids blinked rather rapidly as she looked back at her husband.

"My mouth is dry and my back aches."

Then Nathaniel, for the first time in his memory, became unsettled by his wife's gaze, and turned to watch Una and Julian following the rainstreaks with their fingertips. Sophia, meanwhile, seemed gradually to break free of her enchantment and at last, when Nathaniel glanced back towards her, said, "Do you think you have a chill?"

"Some such malaise."

"We shall get you wrapped up as soon as we arrive. Didn't you say the Tappans had arranged for help for us?"

Nathaniel nodded.

"There then. I expect the bedrooms are already prepared." She leaned forward and pressed both hands on Nathaniel's knees. "We'll soon get you better. I think this Red House is going to be another Manse for us."

But now it was Nathaniel's turn to be unresponsive. He felt himself a good deal changed since those times and his past self, especially as exhibited in the early stories, was not very much to his taste. His recent solitary existence made him bristle a little at the prospect of being tucked up in bed and cared for as an invalid. The train made its first stop and the torrential rain could be heard on the roof of the car.

"When will we dine?" Una asked. The engine started up again and she and Julian vigorously rubbed away the mist of condensation which was now forming on all the windows.

"At Springfield."

"Where's that?"

Nathaniel looked at his route sheet. "Eighteen more stops."

234

"Eighteen!"

"It's a hundred miles from Boston."

"Where are we going?"

"Richmond."

"I thought the Red House was in Lemacs."

"Lenox."

"Why aren't we going there then?"

"We are."

"You said somewhere else."

"The railway doesn't go to Lenox."

"So we won't see the train from our new home?"

"I shouldn't think so."

Mr. Hawthorne had wanted to stop their journey at Pittsfield, thinking it best to arrive in what was the nearest main town but Sophia, who had completed the final details of the move and transaction, had considered it worth the extra thirty-five cents fare and the extra ten minutes to go on a further two stops to Richmond, where it would be much more convenient for Mr. Tappan to collect them in his own carriage.

Una and Julian had continued their wickedness until Springfield, where they were allowed to run up and down outside the cars and the passengers in general took advantage of a thirty-minute stop to stretch their legs and purchase articles of sustenance and refreshment from a variety of perambulating vendors. For the less encumbered there was the opportunity of eating in an adjoining dining room, and several of the male travellers were seen to leave the area of the train altogether and seek out the nearest grog shop. The Hawthornes contented themselves with cups of soup and bread, followed by a piece of fruit.

After their exertions, and with stomach warmed by the soup, Una and Julian spent the second half of the journey in more quiescent mood. Eventually they grew tired and yawned, Julian actually falling asleep soon after passing the United States Armoury, but Una appearing merely contemplative as if she were conscious that her young life was leaving one set of habits behind, and journeying towards new ones.

Such thoughts were certainly at the fore of Mr. Hawthorne's mind and with all his theoretical love of sloughing off the old he managed to convince himself that he was feeling better and that the morning's distemper had played itself out. He even considered – without consequence, but the thought did cross his mind –

walking along to the smoking car and lighting one of the cigars which he had been given by Bridge on his recent trip to Portsmouth.

Sophia's thoughts were understandably more practical. With proper regard for her domestic and maternal responsibilities she was busy contemplating the several jobs which she would like to have done that evening before retiring.

Nathaniel looked at her and smiled. "I see mops and buckets in your eye." He was not mocking, for he genuinely considered it one of his greatest blessings in life – his wife's industrious capacity for cleanliness and order. It was a quality which might never have been guessed at in his young bride, except insofar as her artistic sensibility might be expected to excite an interest in design. Certainly there was a danger – the more so with a couple such as Nathaniel and Sophia, whose romance had been ethereal – that these concerns might become obsessive and leave no room for any luxury of mind. For just this reason, Mr. Hawthorne, unlike Mr. Melville, never needed any prompting to keep his wife connected with his creative output. For the same reason, his remark about mops and buckets was intended as teasingly instructive; and Sophia knew it as much.

Nevertheless she began, for the first time, to question Nathaniel about the precise layout of the house, and in particular the kitchen. He had at all times stressed the smallness of the building, and did so again now, saying that four Red Houses at least could be put inside the Manse.

"But all those rooms upstairs?"

'They are very small rooms."

"That doesn't matter," Una said. "There are four of them. We can have one each. You and Mama won't have to share."

The parents smiled and, as they were just then pulling in to Pittsfield, leaned over towards the window to see what they could of the town through the rainstreaked glass. When they got off the train two stops later they were pleased to find that it had stopped raining, but the sky was still dark and threatening and the carriage ride to the Hillside estate took them along a route which adequately introduced the dramatic characteristics of the hilly region to Sophia's eyes. And also to the children's. Julian, who had had to be carried from the train, was now awake, and looking around himself speechlessly, as if he had awoken in another kingdom, which, in a sense, he had.

236

Mr. Tappan was most obliging with the luggage (some of which was left with the stationmaster for collection later in the week) but less welcoming in the conversational sense. It was a strange, quiet and awesome ride.

At the house they were surprised to be introduced to Anna Alcott, the temporary helper promised by the Tappans. Caroline was sitting there also and she immediately dissolved the awesomeness of the carriage ride with vivacious chatter. She spoke as much to the children as to Nathaniel and Sophia and they told her that they had her book with them and that it was a nice book and Papa read it most beautifully and they had told him that he too must write a book for children.

"Yes, you must," Caroline said. "In this house."

Anna had beds ready and a little early supper warming on the stove – more soup, but even the children did not comment. She returned to the Tappan house as soon as Sophia seemed to be in control, saying she would be back in the morning.

Sophia was, as Nathaniel predicted, initially disappointed in the size of their new house, but she liked the lowish ceilings and could envisage the homely atmosphere that she would aim to concoct once their belongings were unpacked. She did not think the room with the unmade bed was quite suitable for Mr. Hawthorne's study, so she undid some of Anna's work and made up the bed in this fourth room, although they were undecided whether or not to make Una and Julian sleep in separate rooms.

Nathaniel, having arrived at the house, once again felt unwell and, resigning himself to the fact that he was suffering from a cold or some such malady, sank into a comfortable armchair. After his soup he closed his eyes, and did not open them although still awake when the children kissed him good night.

"What is the matter with Papa?" whispered Julian.

"I think he is dreaming up a story to write for us," Una said. "You heard Aunt Cara tell him to, didn't she, Mother?"

*　　　*　　　*

The next morning, when Anna arrived to offer her services, she was speedily despatched back to Hillside for a dose of belladonna to be administered to Mr. Hawthorne, who had been restless and feverish in the night and was clearly unwell enough to have to spend several days in bed.

Caroline Tappan returned with the medicine in person and, because Sophia was busy giving the children breakfast, went up to the sickbay herself. Returning downstairs after some ten minutes she promised to send Anna straight back and told Sophia to hold on to her until Nathaniel was better.

At the end of a day during which continuing inclement weather had kept the children indoors drawing pictures for father Sophia, who now felt as if she had stamped the house as home, sat and conversed with Anna, the latter seemingly starved of a listening ear at Highwood, for she willingly unburdened her life story on the new mistress. "Which brings me to why I'm here. At first I was happy to get away. For the past week or two mother has been so feeble and weepy. Louisa was going out to teach in a school on Suffolk Street when I left. She was reading your husband's latest book. I had no idea that you were to be here until I arrived. Had Louisa known I'm sure she would have swapped places. She's much more the reader than I, and always making up plays for us to perform. She acts the men and I the women. At times this entertainment and diversion has been all that's kept us going."

"Anna, you *must* tell me what your sister thought of *The Scarlet Letter*."

"Well, she hadn't finished when I left, although she was reading it very quickly. I think she described it as 'lurid' but in such a way that showed she was admiringly fascinated by it."

"Lurid? Oh dear, I'm not sure I shall pass that on to Nathaniel. Although I know what your sister means. It is stranger than anything my husband has written before. And now, you were saying, you're not so happy at being away."

"I know there's a real necessity for my having to take work of this kind. I don't mind that so much, although Mrs. Tappan doesn't think very highly of my housework and I find Ellen, her child, difficult to warm to. If everything were happier at home it wouldn't be so bad, but even with the train link I feel so far away and certainly I shall not be able to afford visits home, at practically five dollars each way. That's as much as I earn in . . . Well, I mustn't tell you that, I suppose."

"From what you say of your mother I'm sure she'll soon start to feel hopeful again. You know, Mr. Hawthorne and I have had our prospects dashed too. We're only here by virtue of the generosity of our friends."

"But don't you think your husband, being a writer, an artist, makes it easier to accept charity?"

238

"I don't think we see it as charity exactly; more as friendly support. I take your point, but your father is no mere teacher, he's a thinker like Mr. Emerson surely."

"Oh, he'd love to hear you say it. It warms my heart to hear it said, too. I only wish mother could always recognise that. Don't you ever, when things go badly and Mr. Hawthorne isn't earning, well, wish say that he were a banker, or has it ever come to your thinking of getting work yourself?"

"No, never to both, although I have sometimes sold a piece or two of art. I'm happiest when Nathaniel is writing, rather than when he was earning money at the Custom House. And although I suppose if we were ever desperate I could once again make a few dollars by painting and embroidering firescreens, Nathaniel would never contemplate letting me leave the house to work."

Mr. Hawthorne heard the murmur of voices from his room upstairs. On the first evening he thought it was Cara's company that filled the house with a continuous stream of sound and, as often when he was feverish, he fantasised amorously about the distant voice. When the chatter continued for a second and third evening, and after he had been told it was Miss Alcott rather than Mrs. Tappan, he felt about it as he had felt about Margaret Fuller's company in the Manse: excluded and resentful. There was something in the sound of distant, indistinct conversation which disconcerted his ear, especially when one of the participants was his wife. So that, on the Friday morning, when his temperature was a good bit lowered, and when Sophia began to tell him something of Anna's story, his sudden insistence that she never set foot in the Red House again had a little more than its ostensible and more justifiable reason behind it.

"What did you say!"

Sophia had let it out that when Anna Alcott had left Boston both her mother and father, as well as being utterly disconsolate, had been suffering from smallpox.

"I think they must have it quite mildly."

"Huh! I suppose we must hope we get it mildly too when it comes to us. Fancy Caroline letting her into her house. I presume she knows about it?"

"I can't be sure. She's got a child too. I'm sure, away from the city, it can't be so contagious."

"She's not coming here again, and that's that. I shall be up and about later today so we can manage quite capably till after the weekend before engaging someone from the village. And Julian and Una are not to play with Ellen so long as that Alcott girl is at Hillside. Do you hear?"

For much of the time so pliant, Mr. Hawthorne did occasionally give displays of autocratic ruling. They were usually more pleasantly decreed and Sophia ascribed his present aggressiveness to the belladonna.

She changed the subject. Neither argument nor discussion would be worthwhile or expected.

"Do you need any more medicine?"

"No. I shall be up by the afternoon."

"By the way, Anna's sister was reading *The Scarlet Letter.*" Sophia busied herself with knocking out Nathaniel's pillows for him. so that he could sit up.

"Oh, yes? What did she make of it?"

"'Lurid.' Although I gather she was using the word admiringly."

"Admirably lurid, eh. Well, that's a new . . ."

Nathaniel sat up in bed reading. Una and Julian visited him and he asked them how they were finding the new house. While they were answering they sprang their knees, vault-fashion, up on to the edge of his bed, which was high.

"There are rooms . . ." Julian began. Una giggled. And he giggled in response.

"How many rooms?"

"Sixty-four." More giggling.

"And where does Una sleep?"

"Over there." Vague pointing.

"And Julian?"

No answer.

"Doesn't Julian go to sleep?

"No. He rides a broomstick and goes to see the Black Witch."

"Do not."

"Do."

"Farver, tell Una to stop teasing."

"Only if *you* tell me how many rooms there are in the house."

Both children began seriously to count their fingers.

After most of the fingers of one hand had been turned out, Una stopped and said, "Upstairs or downstairs?"

"Altogether."

More fingers were turned out, Julian watching his sister closely, and copying her finger-turning, whilst at the same time managing to retain an expression of seriously independent calculation.

The hands were begun again; whether in a second attempt or a continuing count Nathaniel could not be sure. A dramatic quietness was broken by the sound of Sophia banging a rug on the wall of the house. The children were not distracted from the task.

Fists were closed and finger-turning began a third time. There was a reverberation on one side of Nathaniel's bed. He looked to see Julian trying to suppress a series of giggles. Still the Little Man managed to copy Una, finger for finger. But in the fourth set of ten fingers his knees slid off the bed and he let out a strange gasp of relief. Una let her fingers fly in a flurry which was impossible to copy. Finally she stood back from the bed, holding up four fingers of one hand, and Julian was once again able to emulate this static attitude.

"It is as we said," she announced, in a voice deep and serious in the extreme.

"Zas ee zed," Julian tried to copy, giggling all the time.

"There are sixty-four rooms."

Julian immediately fell upon the floor and worked his legs in the air as if this anticipated punchline were causing him much agony. The door opened. And Sophia arrived to take the children away. She had heard Julian's thumping on the ceiling downstairs and did not want her husband tired. He was left alone for the rest of the morning.

* * *

The next morning Cara walked into their parlour while they were eating breakfast. Without apologising for the interruption she handed Sophia a folded note and said, "I warned William the family was unreliable, but I never expected this." And then, looking at Nathaniel, "The Alcott girl – she's run off. Did you know anything of this, Sophia?"

Sophia refolded the note and handed it back. "No. Of course not."

"Only she seems to have spilled her heart out to you."

"What makes you say that?"

"She said it herself. Came home saying she'd done nothing but sit and talk and what a marvellous listener you were."

"That's not true, Cara. She played with the children which was just what I needed while I sorted out."

"I wanted William to catch up with her. She must have been on

241

foot. But he said he wasn't going to behave like a prison warder."

Nathaniel asked where the note was left.

"Oh, on the breakfast table. Together with all the wages we'd paid her so far."

"Oh, no!" Sophia let out. "You'll have to send that on, Cara. The family is quite desperate for money."

"All the more reason why we were expecting her to stick it out."

"She may have been able to, had she known more about her mother's state of health. She has been enormously worried about her mother, as she says in the note."

"Yes, did you know anything about that?" Nathaniel had presumed Sophia was talking about the smallpox and was still keen to establish the facts.

Sophia would have blocked the enquiry, especially in front of the children, who were quietly and wonderingly poking at their eggs. In the event, Cara's child, Ellen, burst in and hung around her mother's skirts.

"So – we shall be competing for local help I suppose. Stop dragging, Ellen!"

The Tappan girl, after her excited entry, had become absurdly shy, hiding from the stares of Una and Julian.

"Eat up your egg, Julian."

"But, Mother, I've got the no-est bit left."

"Then the no-est little bit won't take the no-est little moment to swallow. I expect Ellen finished breakfast an hour ago."

"No, I didn't." She darted out from behind her mother's legs to deliver this aggressive piece of information.

Mrs. Tappan confessed that breakfast had been overlooked, what with the drama of a runaway, and debate about the proper reaction. On hearing this Mr. Hawthorne invited her and the child to sit down. "We must have a little bread, at least, to offer. Does Ellen like it toasted?"

Una and Julian were allowed down from the table, and began playing with a box of dolls' furniture and cutlery. They set up a rival breakfast table with the result that, just as the toast was ready, Ellen decided that an imaginary breakfast was more to her taste than an actual one. The adults were left to devour the toast on their own.

Sophia talked to Caroline about her plans for the house, while Nathaniel watched alternately the playing children and the conversing women. Ellen continued to be treated as a guest, even in the game. She had to sit down and wait to be served. She was told if she picked up the wrong plate and if she ate too quickly. Una and Julian offered only a limited menu, and when Ellen began to request things which were not on it, Una asked her, in a most accomplished sardonic tone, if she were deaf.

It did not strike Nathaniel that Caroline Tappan had any natural enthusiasm for domestic management. But she was a good nurse. The quarter of an hour she had spent in his sick room was to prove the inspiration for the opening pages of *The Blithedale Romance*.

Ellen came and put her head in her mother's lap.

"What is it, dear?"

"They keep giving me worms to eat."

"Only when she asks for cold meats." Una had heard the complaint, and was up at the table to defend her behaviour. "We keep telling her that cold meats are not on the menu."

"You should have accepted the toast that Mr. Hawthorne offered you, Ellen. I think it's time we went back. We left Bruin loose in the garden."

Caroline got up and they all went to the front door of the Red House.

"I do think you should send Anna's wages on as soon as possible," Sophia said. "We shall have to go into town today now that Nathaniel's up. Would you like us to go to the Post Office?"

"Oh, there's no need. William's always back and forth on his horse and cart. Yes, I'll send the money off. Ellen – say goodbye."

"Bye bye, Hawthorn-tree."

Caroline raised her brows and whisked Ellen off, saying "Goodbye" herself as she moved away.

Later in the morning Nathaniel went in to his "study" for the first time. He stood at the window staring at the luscious-leaved chestnut trees. There was no hint as yet, either in his notes or in the room itself, of anything he might produce here, but with his fever gone, and the belladonna nausea having worn off, he felt at last a degree of expectation proper to the occupation of a new dwelling.

Like many restless, creative men, he had a tendency to package his past into periods: the solitary youth, the communal experience, the first Custom House job, the Manse etc. He liked to think that these pockets of time were evidence of an educating Destiny, and so he stood at his window with all the excitement and trepidation of a boy who has just enrolled at a new school. Beside the chestnut

243

trees some slighter, slimmer trees swayed – they were paint-strokes that left no writing in the sky.

*   *   *

The Melvilles had long had a connection, through Herman's uncle, with Pittsfield, and in July Herman brought Elizabeth and Malcolm, who was now an eighteen-month-old toddler, to the Berkshire countryside to escape the claustrophobia of a New York summer.

Now that Malcolm was on his feet the prospect of two growing families (Allan's wife was already pregnant a second time) continuing to share the Fourth Avenue home with Maria and the the sisters was clearly not on, and ever since his return from London Herman had been considering a move.

He had fond memories from childhood of the Pittsfield area and, without saying so to Elizabeth, intended to use this summer vacation as a reconnoitring exercise. Unlike Mr. Hawthorne, he had every wish to leave the city which, apart from the Duyckinck library, held less and less of interest for him. He regularly declined opportunities to go to the theatre or the concert hall on the grounds that, having been cooped up all day, reading and writing, he had no wish to be cooped up again all evening. He preferred to take a walk, but his observant mind, made dormant by recent travel, and supplanted by ruminations that arose from his reading (which at this time was Shakespeare and the Bible, especially the Apocrypha) derived no stimulus from the many facets of metropolitan fashion.

He had written to Dana as early as 1st May, only three months after disembarking from the *Independence*, that he had a new book about a whaling voyage "half-finished", but this was bravado. The spring and early summer of 1850 were contemplative rather than productive periods and Herman was increasingly realising that his reading, scribbling and smoking life was more suited to the country than the town.

On Thursday July 18th he accompanied Robert, his cousin, on a rail and wagon tour of the southern part of the county of Berkshire. For both men, it was a viewing time. Robert was Chairman of the Berkshire Agricultural Society and undertook the journey to investigate the state of the crops. For Herman it was an excellent opportunity to get the lie of the land and take note of any vacant properties.

Before leaving Robert's farm Aunt Mary handed Herman a package, saying he might like his birthday present early, for reading matter on the tour. He thanked her, but in the end left it, unwrapped, with Elizabeth.

The excursion took three days, day one being the most significant since it brought them almost within throwing distance of Mr. Hawthorne and the Hillside estate.

They set out in the morning for the Lenox meeting house, and then on to Richmond, where they took lunch. In the afternoon they climbed a hill outside the town and inspected a crop of rye on the mountainside. Afterwards they returned to Lenox, where they had arranged to put up for the night with a retired naval captain named Caleb Smith.

The old gentleman entertained them grandly, and although he had not read any of the books found much to converse with Herman about. His house stood to one side of the Stockbridge Bowl, adjacent to, but not immediately neighbouring, the pair of homes at Hillside. When he heard that Herman was thinking of moving to the area he exclaimed, with a jocular acidity, "Hmmm! I suppose you writers have ganged together and propose colonising the place. Why, we already have Mr. James, the Englishman, and Mr. Holmes, the doctor, and only six weeks ago another writer fellow moved in across the way, just on this corner of the Bowl."

"Oh? Who was that?"

"Mr. Hawthorne."

A chill spread over Herman's scalp. Mr. Hawthorne was being much talked about back in New York. His reputation as the stylistic inventor of romantic allegories had been enhanced by the publication of *The Scarlet Letter*, and although Herman was not yet a reader, let alone an admirer, Captain Smith's information affected him profoundly. At the most superficial level it firmed his resolve to move into the county; but it also opened up the prospect of making the acquaintance of an older and more practised wielder of the pen.

"I see that's caught your interest. We'll take a walk by the Pond in the morning and give you a viewing of his place. Not that I've set eyes on the man yet."

Herman looked at Robert.

"Yes, we'll have time for that."

The three men sat up late, drinking hard liquor and talking

about crops and storms, the breaking-off of Table Rock at Niagara Falls, the death of President Taylor and Herman's southern impersonator.

An itinerant personality of North Carolina and Georgia had been passing himself off as the author of *Whitejacket*, claiming Herman Melville as his pseudonym. Only two days after their dismissive remarks about the prankster the *Morning Express* printed, in its Personal Column, the information that, "Melville, author of *Typee, Omoo* etc., has gone on a cruise to Europe once more".

Such an impersonator had a much more certain chance of success than he would have today. Overseas, there was no telling what deceptions he might manage, especially with some forged letters of introduction.

"He's probably only a womaniser," said Robert. "You ought to be impressed that he has adopted your mantle and no other."

"Just so long as no woman goes claiming Herman Melville as the father of their babies," Captain Smith wheezed.

In the morning their intended walk by the Pond was thwarted by torrential rain. It was noon before they could depart, by which time Robert needed to press on with his farm-viewing schedule. They travelled beside Monument Mountain to Egremont, where they stayed with a Mr. Joyner. The third and final day of their tour took them through the two villages of Sheffield, and back to Stockbridge, where they at last boarded a train for Pittsfield and arrived home on Saturday night.

Elizabeth, after she had greeted him and enquired about the tour, reminded him that he had left Aunt Mary's package behind. She picked up the parcel, and put it on her husband's lap.

"It didn't matter. Robert kept us moving and our hosts were good talkers." He nonchalantly unwrapped the package and turned the book onto its edge so that he could read the spine: *Mosses From An Old Manse* by Nathaniel Hawthorne.

The initial reaction to Captain Smith's information had worn off, and had it received no other stimulus Herman might have dismissed it as the effect of good whisky and warm conviviality. But this gift from his aunt was hauntingly apposite, and seemed indeed like a Providential prod.

"Oh, dear," said Elizabeth, struck by her Herman's delayed reaction. "Is it something dreadful?"

"Not at all, not at all." He showed her the book and went

246

through to the drawing room to thank Aunt Mary for it, explaining the coincidence.

"But that's why I got it. I thought you'd know that Mr. Hawthorne was living here now."

"No. I didn't."

The very next day, a Sunday, taking the book into one of Robert's barns, he began his relationship with Nathaniel Hawthorne. Perching himself on a high ledge of bales where he could lean back beside an opening in the wooden slats and position the book's pages in a beam of light, the reading engrossed Herman for the final days of July, while the summer burned magnificently and the two Broadhall dogs licked and slobbered over Malcolm. In the evening he talked to Robert about his love of the area and his determination to find a property there.

On August 1st he was thirty-one years old. He had been away to sea, had published five books, had mixed with the best London society, had married and started a family. And yet he was sensible of a lack of substance to his mental life. Most of the thoughtful passages in his books had been culled almost directly from reading, but when he read Goethe or Seneca, say, the plainest thing about their work was that they were men with minds of their own. The writer of the Manse was clearly of like tenacity – the statements about character and occasional authorial comments were expressed with the calm resolution of Scripture. A man capable of such original certainty must possess a personality unlike anything previously encountered in the flesh. He spent his birthday yearning for such an encounter, with an intensity akin to prayer. The prayer was just four days in being answered.

*   *   *

The next day, August 2nd, Evert Duyckinck and Cornelius Matthews (a poet and editorial associate of Evert's) arrived on the 10.30 p.m. cars in Pittsfield and settled for the night into Cooley's hotel. Herman rode out in the morning to fetch them back to Broadhall where they were to stay for one week. The same afternoon Mrs. Morewood arrived, dressed in a linen sack, and carrying a bait box, to take them away on a fishing excursion to the Pontussac Lake.

Elizabeth put on a great flopping straw hat tied under the chin, its brim so wide that only a slight inclination of the head was needed to obliterate her face. Herman played country squire with Duyckinck and Matthews, behaving as if he were already resident in the area and instructing the two city dwellers in the mysteries of bait and casting, of which he knew little beyond a few childhood lessons given him by his uncle.

"I'm after bigger fish than this," he said, when they were all sitting on the bank, rods cocked and waiting. "In the new one."

"Ah, yes, the whaling romance. Ever since you let Dana know about it, the rumour's out. Any of it ready for my eyes yet?"

"No, Evert. I'm not as far on with it as I had supposed."

"Going to be a Leviathan, is it?"

Herman grinned. The truth was that he had never been "as far on with it" as he had claimed, but that the material he had amassed, begun in much the same tone as *Whitejacket* and *Redburn*, appeared lacking in substance beside his reading of Hawthorne's *Mosses*. If he was going to make this one carry the hallmark of his own mind it would need a good deal of re-writing.

There was a high-pitched shriek and Elizabeth jumped up from the grass, her straw hat falling off her head, the string tie almost choking her in the excitement. She put up a hand to insert fingers between the string and her Adam's apple and the rod dropped onto the ground. Herman, racing over, swiftly picked it up and bellowed. "Kee-hee! Kee-hee! Haul in! Haul in!" He was, as when telling his sea stories, utterly transported, and managed to give the impression that he was really high up a mast, standing on the deck of a ship, boarding a rowing boat, aiming the harpoon, or dragging on the line, all of which he managed to mime, while at the same time keeping perfect hold of Elizabeth's rod.

Cornelius Matthews was agog. He had found Mr. Melville, to this moment, a disappointingly retiring and soft-spoken companion, but here he was, bellowing on the bank without restraint. In his later articles for the *Literary World* Matthews referred to Melville as "New Neptune" and it was as a god that he appeared to them now, with none of the usual embarrassment that such theatricality off the stage commonly engenders. But there was much mocking and merrymaking when Herman at length pulled in Elizabeth's line to reveal a little silver whippet of a finned being, no more than an inch and a half from tail to pinhead mouth. While the others lay back on the grass laughing helplessly he disengaged the little mite and let it slide gently off his hand back into the water, saying to Elizabeth, in his normal voice,

248

"It may as well serve its purpose as titbit to the larger fish."

Elizabeth was appreciative of neither the dramatic display nor this final remark, both of which seemed to mock her – the first her own overdramatic response to the bitten bait, the second her sentimental belief in a benign creation. Herman's quiet cameraderie with his two friends further isolated her the following day, their third wedding anniversary. For Matthews, and indeed for the rest, it was "a Sunday of delicious beauty". The sun burned. The air was still. The bees set up a dozy drone. The three literary men lay down under a tree after breakfast, smoking and talking about books. From her room Elizabeth watched them and tried to dampen the annoyance that their laziness aroused in her. There was no real cause for it beyond the general one of woman's resentment of the other sex's capacity for relaxation, and the specific one of Herman's disregard for their anniversary. She stared at them, as one concentrates upon a toothache in an effort to ignore it by a demonstration of mental bravado. When this failed she fetched her Bible to the window and let it fall open at the folded piece of paper which contained the four-leaf clover. She opened the folds very slowly, taking care that the clover stem did not fall onto the floor. There it was, in its creased frame; shrunken and dull green now, but still in existence. A memory, a saving, a lasting grace. But as she looked more closely one of the petals appeared separated from the stem. She tapped the edge of the paper twice with her forefinger. Sure enough, the clover separated, the single petal apparently stuck, the other three sliding free. As her eyes welled with tears she hurriedly folded the paper shut, not bothering to order the folds correctly, so that as she placed it back in her Bible the book would not close properly. The paper, like a map folded in too great a hurry, resisted closure.

"We met Field on the train," Evert told Herman. "It should be quite a day tomorrow."

"I should say!" Matthews' voice was full of boyish enthusiasm. "He has quite a cast cut out for us. Holmes and Fields. Fields J. T., that is, who has his young wife with him."

"Wait till you see her, Herman. The violet of the season, a human flower of sixteen years. She'll become your next Fayaway figure."

"Who's Field?" Herman seemed to ignore the promise.

"Dudley Field. New York attorney and something of an amateur socialite it seems."

"And Mr. Hawthorne who has just moved to Lenox hopes to join us. Yes, it should be quite a day."

Herman stared up at the portion of sky beyond the crinkled outline of the tree. Somewhere within that blue eternity the finger of Providence was patiently making a complicated series of moves, so that these two might meet. It was akin to the puzzle squares that children amuse themselves with, finding always two which refuse to take up their contiguous places. There had been times before when they might have come face to face – in Boston, here in Berkshire, in New York. On hearing Matthews' announcement, Herman felt the same quiet confidence that an infatuated admirer senses when he or she sees the prospect of their meeting the adored one looming ever closer. There was, too, the expected nervousness. Indeed, Herman felt a sudden shock of it create an intestinal spasm and, excusing himself, he went indoors.

Malcolm, now popularly known as Barney, was tottering up and down the wide hall of the house pulling along a little horse on wheels. Herman, remembering that a patch of grass outside had been recently scythed, went back and fetched a handful.

"Give horsey some hay," he said, placing it in a corner.

Barney was delighted and, with a sweep of his tough little arm, pulled a toppled-over horsey up to the hay. Putting his hand on the creature's back he thrust the animal's snout with some force into the food.

"Hay gone," he said, almost immediately.

Herman took horsey and re-offered the grass. "Give horsey more. Horsey, take some more."

Malcolm smacked the ground and levered Herman's hands off horsey's back. "No. Hay gone."

"I see. And is horsey still hungry?"

Barney nodded.

"Then come with me." Herman took Malcolm to the side of the house and showed him the cut grass. "Plenty of hay here. Horsey have all he want."

He left the boy to gorge the horse and went back indoors.

Elizabeth was sitting downstairs, reading her Bible in lieu of going to church. She had been forced to fold the clover leaf with greater care and had then put the little packet at the bottom of her valise, determining to find a new keeping place for it when she was back in New York.

"Lizzie, it is a splendid morning. Why don't you read outside?"

250

"Did you see Malcolm in the hall?"

"Yes. He's playing with horsey."

"I shall go back to him just as soon as I finish the lesson. Are our two guests still lying on the grass?" Herman nodded. "What have you got planned for them?"

"Nothing."

"Herman, they *must* do something!"

"No. They're fine."

"Won't they think us terribly dull?"

"Let them. Anyway . . ."

"Oh I know they don't find you dull but . . ."

"Lizzie, it's all right, and by the way . . ." Herman came behind her chair and kissed her on the top of the head. It was hardly an ardent show of affection but it went some way towards mollifying Elizabeth, for he kissed her not once, but three times.

She closed her Bible and stood up. "Let us find Barney. I think I shall come outside now."

Elizabeth was first out of the room and thus to see the busily gathered mound of grass at the end of the hall. She ran forward. "Malcolm Melville, you naughty child, what have you been *doing*?!" The last word was delivered with such deep reverberation as Herman had never before heard uttered from his wife's lips. It scared him, as well as the boy, for it was so unlike the Elizabeth he had married three years ago, and seemed to threaten that the admonition of childish waywardness might, after practised usage, be turned upon him.

Malcolm had indeed been busy. The mountain of grass was higher than himself and its sloping side extended some considerable way into the centre of the hall.

"I meant you to keep horsey outside, Malcolm."

Elizabeth turned. "Did you tell him to do this, then?"

"No. I showed him the cut grass outside. He wanted to give horsey some hay."

"Papa bring it in."

"Only a little handful, Elizabeth. Then I took him outside."

"But I had told him to play *in*doors and not to leave the hall without telling me."

"I didn't know."

"Come along, Malcolm. We'll leave Papa to take the hay back outside. And do be quick, Herman. If Robert's wife sees it we'll be sent straight back to the city."

Mother and son walked out into the sunlight. Herman gathered an armful of grass and took it to the side of the house. He did this just twice, and then spent a longer, more laborious time picking up individual stems and dusted seed-heads off the floor.

* * *

The next morning the Pittsfield party breakfasted early, ready to take the first cars for Stockbridge. Elizabeth, who was not of the party (the proposed ascent of Monument Mountain being considered too strenuous for ladies), did not appear at the table. Malcolm had had an unsettled night, his sleep broken by successive sneezing bouts, which were conveniently blamed on the grass episode. When Herman rose she commanded him to be as quiet as he could, and allow Malcolm to sleep on, so that the boy might not be too unstable during the day. As Herman crept out of the curtain-dimmed room, and turned the handle of the door so that the catch didn't click closed, he experienced the disturbing sense of disassociation which he was to spend the greater part of his married life trying to smother.

The three men from Pittsfield – Melville, Duyckinck and Matthews – were joined at the station by Dr. O. W. Holmes, who owned a summer place adjoining Robert's land on the ancestral estate left by his grandfather. He arrived carrying an india-rubber bag of occupational instruments and explained that there would be nothing more embarrassing than one of the party suffering injury or some other sudden manifestation of illness up the mountain and he, the doctor, being unable to minister to them for lack of tools. "M' tools" became the subject of an elaborate monologue, which was neither prompted nor interrupted by the other three who, for varying reasons, sat quietly, and only half-listening.

Matthews, a deep sleeper and normally a late riser, was not yet properly waked. Mr. Duyckinck composed, in his head, the opening paragraph of a letter to his brother George, while Mr. Melville, as soon as the car shuddered into motion, surrendered himself to anticipation of his meeting with Mr. Hawthorne.

Meanwhile, the Hawthornes were up and about in the little Red House at Lenox. The whole family was astir. Staying at the cottage were James Fields, the publisher, and his sixteen-year-old-wife, Eliza.

252

Una helped her mother cater to the guests and Eliza sat a wriggling Julian upon her knee. It had been decided that Eliza, by virtue of her youth, could join the ascent of the mountain, so she was kitted out this morning in hiking clothes. Nathaniel thought her almost more beautiful than yesterday, when she had walked by the lake in a blue dress, very much playing the part of violet of the season. Here in the breakfast parlour, clothed in brown and cream, with a child on her knee, she looked maternally magnificent.

"Are you climbing the mountain with Farver?"

"Trying to, Julian."

"Will there be ice at the top?"

"Of course there will." Una had brought extra cutlery to the table. "Haven't you heard Papa talking about the Icy Glen?"

The two men chuckled.

"There won't be any ice at this time of the year. And it isn't a craggy mountain."

"But, Mr. Fields, you will be careful and not let Father fall."

Nathaniel's two children had been admirably concerned about his safety, ever since the proposal of the trip. Eliza turned to Sophia. "Isn't that sweet? I'll look after your father, Una, surely I will. Mr. Fields, I fear, will be too preoccupied talking."

"And panting."

Nathaniel blushed at the thought of being looked after by Eliza and Sophia showed that she was not unaware of the implications. "Just so long as you don't hold his hand."

Julian, finding the notion of his father having to have his hand held funny in the extreme, writhed on Eliza's lap and she exacerbated his amusement by digging her fingertips into his ribs so that in the end his knee came up and hit the underside of the table, knocking a plate of toast onto the floor.

"I am sorry, Sophia. It was my fault." She pushed Julian aside and bent down to pick up the débris.

Sophia insisted she leave it alone. "I really think you ought to be leaving. Mr. Field wanted you early and you can see that Una's in a helpful mood today."

"Isn't Mrs. Peters coming?"

"Yes, she is. But you can help me till she does."

Una made a mock scowl but laughed when Eliza said, "That's pretty."

James and Eliza went upstairs to finish getting ready. Sophia

253

kissed Nathaniel goodbye and told him that she too wanted him to be careful and not to try and keep pace with the younger men.

When the Pittsfield party arrived at the home of Dudley Field, the wealthy attorney who had masterminded the gathering, they were welcomed by his daughter, Jenny, who said that the departure for the mountain would be in about half an hour, after the arrival of Mr. Hawthorne and friends. Meantime, they could wait either in or out.

They decided to wait outside and, wandering Mr. Field's grounds, they came upon a mound so steep-sided that it seemed to have been devised for sacrifice or some other pagan rite. Matthews proposed they scale it in rehearsal for the grander climb, and the doctor, outvoted in his reluctance to expend energy in advance of the main attempt, offered to supervise proceedings.

Bags were put down to mark the start. The first to reach the summit must stand with feet astride and arms raised. Herman bent down and rubbed life into his shins. Evert practised elbow jerks. Matthews crouched in classic starting pose.

It was the type of hillock that can be scaled by a fit adult in one bullish dash, barring the final yards, where deceleration would require the use of hands. In any event the sprint start and early lead could be decisive. The first laurels went to Matthews, his greater determination in the first few yards giving him just this advantage. Coming back to the bottom, with short little juddery steps, the other two proposed a re-run. Matthews declined the attempt on his title, so the second race was a duel between Evert and Herman.

Duyckinck had his elbows working to good effect in the first paces and Herman received a diverting blow in his ribs that effectively put him off course. He took his revenge by giving the vulnerable victor a mock punch in the exposed midriff. Evert doubled over and tumbled down the hill. Herman took over the winner's stance and raised his arms in proud supersession.

Below, Evert intrigued with the others and after a time they all, Holmes included, took up positions on three sides of the hillock, and were just starting to march upwards in a collective attempt to put right a wrong and overthrow a usurper, when a voice from the house called, "Stockbridge to Pittsfield, Stockbridge to Pittsfield".

Herman, from his elevated position, and with his sailor's experience at projecting the voice, took it upon himself to reply, "We hear you and are heaving to."

"That must mean Mr. Hawthorne has arrived," Evert

254

remarked when the four of them were turned to the house and walking on the level. Duyckinck had known Mr. Hawthorne for some time, and had acted as an intermediary between the author and Wiley and Putnam, both on Hawthorne's own behalf, and on that of his friend Bridge, when the latter published his notes of a cruise along the West Coast of Africa.

Herman had said nothing about his eagerness to meet Mr. Hawthorne. He walked behind the other three now, a sense of panic keeping his pulse pounding at the same strenuous rate it had been driven to on the hill. As they neared the house he stayed in the rear, keeping his eyes to the ground.

"Well, here are our fellow mountaineers. And how have our two New Yorkers been since our train-ride together? Not set upon by cannibals, I hope. Mr. Hawthorne, Mr. Fields, do you know these four?

Dudley Field did the introductions; there was much shaking of hands and Herman was required to come forward. First of all Herman was dazzled by the beauty of Mrs. Fields. When he did turn to the two men he knew immediately which of them was Mr. Hawthorne. An older man than he had anticipated, his high-browed head was nevertheless a good correspondence to the unarticulated inner vision of the man he had had as a reader.

The mountain party completed, they set off in procession without further delay, carrying turkeys and loaves for lunch. Field's daughter Jenny joined the expedition to be a companion to Eliza and these two walked behind Mr. Field, who took the lead with Matthews. Evert joined J. T. Fields and Mr. Hawthorne, leaving Herman to bring up the rear with the doctor.

Holmes kept up a steady stream of conversation to which Herman only half-attended, reserving the other half of his concentration for the observing of the three walkers in front, and in particular the personal conduct of Mr. Hawthorne.

He seemed totally self-engrossed, walking alongside Fields and Duyckinck, but allowing them to converse without making any effort to intervene. At one point Evert, who was in the middle, looked towards Hawthorne, obviously expecting some comment, but the other's eyes were turned to some interesting effect of the landscape beyond. A little later Mr. Fields talked directly to Mr. Hawthorne, leaning behind Evert and tapping Nathaniel on the shoulder. The incommunicative man nodded his reply but gave no further elaboration in answer to the question and the two publishers continued their dialogue.

"Are you a churchgoer, Mr. Melville?"

"Yes. Not as regular as my wife. But, yes."

"That surprises me," said Holmes. "I do not think the public gets that impression from your books."

"Well, you can be proud and independent at your desk, but there are times, especially when travelling, when it is humbling and comforting to enter a common building."

"And listen to the sermon?"

"Why yes! I heard some very good sermons while in London."

"Perhaps then the English clergyman is superior to the American. I confess I find the reverend population of our own land horribly hypocritical."

"Hypocrisy is a problem we all have. We are all victims of the conflict between Truth and Reality."

"Oh, I take the point. They are like two plates upon the geological surface, pushing against one another, and we all like to keep a foot on each side of the crack. Tremors send us reeling, and if ever we step fully onto one side or the other, when we replace the moved foot, it takes a devilish lot of footshifting to regain a balanced stance, and make allowance for the still-shifting plates."

"Earthquakes swallow us up completely."

The doctor jiggled his black bag. "Quite so. Quite so. I see I have interested you in the analogy, although it is noticeable in your books that this type of comparison does not appeal to you. You prefer allegory to metaphysical conceit, do you not? You take my point? You make a whole episode, or in *Whitejacket* a whole book, stand for something else."

"I'm not sure what you mean by the mention of *Whitejacket*."

"Come, it's surely not about the navy only!"

"No." Holmes seemed not to notice any hesitancy in Herman's negative.

"There you are then. It signifies. But I have a predilection for the small-scale, European conceit. For example, do you play chess?"

Herman nodded.

"Well, I like to characterise persons, merely as an amusing classification you understand, according to the movements of pieces upon the chess board. You can do it both for outward behaviour and for inner thought, assuming you know anything about the subject's mental processes. For example, one man, in his day-to-day behaviour, may be extremely predictable, and always keep on the straight and narrow like the conservative rook which never strays from its vertical or horizontal course. But the same man's mental life may show all the panache and adaptability of the knight and be capable of tackling a subject from roundabout points of view. Similarly, there are those people who, both in thought and deed, move through life ploddingly, one step at a time, one thought following rationally upon another, until . . ." Holmes raised and then slapped his bag with the palm of his free hand, regaining Herman's full attention, which had been drifting. "Until, provoked by deepset, predatory instincts, he makes a swift sidestepping killing. It is the unpredictability and shortreached action of these men which make them so interesting."

"Of these men?" Herman emphasised the last word, querying the limitation to one sex only. There had been something of his mother in both analogies.

"I confess, I find it more difficult to apply the chess board to the female sex. The rarity with which they play the game ought not to affect the analogy, but so it does. Take the resplendent Mrs. Fields up yonder. Although there is beauty in the game, there is nothing representative of visual beauty. One can of course talk about beautiful styles of play, beautiful formations. But look at her! It is not the same thing, is it? However, this question of moves . . ."

Herman allowed Holmes, in the periphery of his hearing, to develop further ramifications of his conceit. Their group had already fallen into opening formation.

Mr. Hawthorne had, by now, taken his eyes off the landscape. He was hearing something of the conversation behind (a fact of which Herman was self-consciously aware, and which made him more than normally unresponsive to Holmes' intellectual stimulation), but hardly attended to it. Of much more interest to him were the two young women in front. They seemed to find an interminable stream of things to chatter and giggle about but the precise content of their conversation was difficult to pick up, since the voices carried in the wrong direction. It was sufficient for Mr. Hawthorne to gaze upon their vivacious intercourse. However conscious of his years he might be in the company of men, the company of women, particularly of young women, always dispelled regard of his age. He felt once again the identity of the Salem loner, the mysterious and unreachable bachelor eyeing the girls to tantalise both himself and them. Only a slight shift in the

257

balance of his personality might have turned him into an unprincipled womaniser.

Every so often the girls would bend to pick up a flower and the men behind would have to adjust their pace.

"Come along, ladies. Let's not have any collisions."

The remark of Evert's interested Nathaniel, for it was the type of social pleasantry that he was utterly incapable of delivering. He practised it silently on his lips and felt a physical rejection of it. The majority of men and women conduct their day-to-day communication in a tone of artificial bonhomie. Those unable to do likewise are labelled "silent", no matter how much they use their voices in less lightly social contexts.

Matthews dropped back to join Evert, and Mr. Field walked with his daughter. He turned to Mr. Hawthorne and asked him to walk with what was now the front party.

"How have you settled in Lenox? It is very pleasant at this time of year, but the winters can be hard." The conversation proceeded at this level until Eliza Fields, who was still walking with them, inspired by an enquiry about Nathaniel's wife and children, began to wax lyrical over the family atmosphere in the Red House.

It was flattering to have his domesticity so publicly extolled – anything that humanised was welcome and he listened to it all with a shy smile on his lips.

In the rear, Herman was aware that the party was proceeding in three groups instead of four and also that the cerebral conversation of Dr. Holmes was isolating him from the others. It was very easy to trap oneself in such a position and to spend a day in bondage to one instead of another.

"To go back to our theory of personality," Holmes went on, "it is of course simplistic to isolate just one piece from the chess board and hope to sum up one individual. One produces only a kind of caricature. But who can say that an individual is of such or such an humour? We know, and you novelists more than others, I suppose, that we grow, we change, from moment to moment. And those times when individuals behave out of character suggest that we have co-tenants of our personality. Now, who might those co-tenants be? Mr. Hawthorne, I dare say, would claim they are our ancestors, vying for influence in the present age. A parson would claim them to be the angelic voice of God, or the demonic voice of the Devil. Naturally, you don't expect me to share that view. If we have a guardian angel it is probably in human form – our wife or our closest friend. No, but there is something in an old Judaistic notion I have read about – Qumran it is called – of two angels at our side, one of justice, one of wickedness. It is nothing but a metaphor for the ever-present struggle between good and evil, but you have seen how partial to metaphors I am. God forbid that I should be supporting the metaphysicality of evil; look around you, Mr. Melville, is there . . ."

Herman permitted Dr. Holmes to address three or four rhetorical questions on the neutrality of nature, endorsing nothing more than the current anti-Calvinist, transcendental orthodoxy, and which Herman would have gladly taken issue with had not the urge to extricate himself from this rearguard isolation proved the stronger.

"Neutral or no, I think the sudden steepness of the path demands a catching-up exercise."

They had fallen a good distance behind the others, and Herman took Dr. Holmes' bag while they jogged forward to close the gap.

The climb became strenuous enough to preclude all conversation other than odd, grunted comments on individual states of stamina. Turns were taken with the two picnic boxes, the heaviest one containing champagne and a set of silver goblets. It was noticeable that Mr. Hawthorne was never given the second box.

The wind began to flap jacket tails and skirts and to make fulminating sounds out of the immense and invisible materials of the air. Rocks now strewed the path. Herman, still carrying the doctor's bag, scrambled past the other men and began to compete with the two females in a race for the top. He allowed them to win but made several mock advances encouraging them to shriek and giggle. Too exhausted to stand and acclaim their victory, it was Herman who waved triumphantly to the others, while Jenny and Eliza conspired to hide behind one of the larger boulders on the rocky peak.

"Well, Mr. Melville – what have you done with my daughter?"

"We shall find the two ladies, Mr. Field. Leave it to us." Matthews and Duyckinck went off in search, while Dr. Holmes, panting and pale, took his bag from Herman, and crouched down on some scree.

J. T. Fields and Mr. Hawthorne were last up the mountain, the latter however appearing robust and unwearied by his exertion.

"It appears Mr. Typee has spent too long among the cannibals. I am afraid, sir, your young wife has been devoured."

The voice, pitched in a tone of convincing seriousness, came from behind them at ground level, so that a momentary look of horror on Fields' face seemed to suggest he actually believed the accusation. Mr. Hawthorne was the first to chuckle and knocking his friend with an elbow said, "Come on – I'll help you find the bones."

"Come and sit down out of the wind, Mr. Melville. Once more we are on our own."

Reluctantly, Herman put his back against a huge rock beside Holmes' couch of smaller stones. Resting his head against its smooth surface he looked directly up towards the sky, half of which was covered with a dark ragged cloud.

"Did you see the look on Fields' face just then? I'll swear he believed me until Hawthorne chipped in. Ah, what evidence of Love's . . ."

There was just then an excited scream and the two young ladies bobbed up from behind their rock, discovered by Mr. Hawthorne. He held Eliza's hand in an unnecessary but courteous attempt to assist her rising and, turning, he passed it on to Fields who rushed up and embraced his beloved. After they had kissed he heard Fields say, in the childish lingo of lovers' endearments, "I thought you'd been gobbled up."

Gobbets of rain began to issue from the black cloud and the party hurriedly re-assembled to discuss how best to shelter from the storm. Herman saw a large shrub a little way down the slope of the mountain and asked Holmes if he had a knife in his bag. The two of them went and cut three branches from the plant that they brought back to be used as umbrellas. Evert had found two high rocks which sheltered them from the angle of the rain and here they gathered round, under their leafy canopies.

The rain fell for some ten minutes but never with any ferocity. The drops were large but well interspersed. There was one rumble of thunder, which frightened Miss Field. It was not repeated and served to strengthen the atmosphere of protective communion. Herman noticed for the first time Nathaniel's eyes. They were strikingly blue, with long lashes, which flickered across them in the nervous way he had of blinking three times in quick succession.

The picnic box containing the food was opened and the bread and the victuals passed round. The rain, the need to hold the leafy boughs steady, and the chewing of bread and bird, precluded much conversation. Even Dr. Holmes was content to watch the changing light through gaps in the branches. He was the first to notice when the rain had stopped, and put aside his own woody limb, causing a sprinkling of rain from the wet leaves as he did so. Dark spots suddenly appeared on Eliza's coloured skirts and she threw a lump of bread at the back of the doctor, which hit him on the seat and made everyone cheer.

"There you are J. T.," said Matthews. "No stepping out of line with this one about."

"Has she as true an aim with more pointed weapons?" asked Evert.

The arrows of desire, thought Mr. Hawthorne, but did not state it.

Holmes was rubbing his rear as if it had been pelted with lead shot but the others were not responding to the intended humour.

"Come back into the circle, Holmes," said Mr. Field. "It is time to pour the Heidsieck. Can you open these for me?" Field passed a bottle each to Hawthorne and Melville and then delved back into the basket for the set of silver mugs.

Mr. Hawthorne nervously attacked the cork, encouraged by the gleeful excitement of Eliza Fields to consider it a race. Mr. Melville, whose fingers and thumb moved with greater assurance, had the wire restrainer almost released, when he paused to examine the bottle's label. Out of the corner of his eye he had seen Mr. Hawthorne turning the wire in the wrong direction and thus tightening the restraint. He had no wish to embarrass his rival and thus, ostensibly just to tease the thirsty party, had interrupted his own manoeuvres.

"The trouble with literary men is that they are as interested in the label as they are in the liquid inside." Dr. Holmes took breath and then developed his observation into what threatened to be a highly involved metaphorical dissertation on body and mind, based upon bottles and their contents. Herman, satisfied that Mr. Hawthorne had been given time enough to make right his early fumbling, and wishing to interrupt the doctor before he got into full stride, proceeded to push up the cork. Both bottles shot out their stoppers at the same instant, and with a cheer a wheel was made, with arms as spokes and silver mugs at the hub.

"Thank you, gentlemen," said Mr. Field, when the cups were filled. "What harmonious timing. And now, to our descent."

Glasses were raised and the words "our descent" mumblingly repeated.

261

Holmes, thwarted in the midst of one of his observational metaphors, was not to be thwarted overall. Taking a paper from his pocket he stood and announced that this was the time for a recitation. Would the party please lend their ears to a rendering of Bryant's poem?

Herman's and Nathaniel's eyes had met at the instant of cork-popping and Herman spent the moments of the recitation recalling the exchange. There was something bullish about the Hawthorne physique – that same quality which had led Mr. Emerson to extol its masculinity was still evident despite the advance in years. The eyes were as alert and reactive as those of an animal. They watched and dropped away, preserving an isolated security. He was a bull with the eyes of a rabbit and those eyes had reacted to Herman as if he were danger personified – or so it seemed, in the instant dropping of the lashes. No sense of professional fear communicated itself to Herman. The reluctance of one author to parley with another would have been understandable. It seemed that the other man's natural timidity had been intensified in the presence of one who posed more than the average amount of threat. Perhaps Herman had been too obvious in his eagerness to make the acquaintance of the older author. But that was impossible. He had spent so much time with Holmes, no such impression could have arisen. The personal fear and reticence must therefore be instinctive. What was there in his own personality that provoked such a pronounced timidity? How many of his books had Mr. Hawthorne read? Had his companionship with Dr. Holmes for almost the entire ascent of the mountain made him appear intellectual and aloof? He would drop Holmes in the afternoon. He would be more open, make his voice heard . . .

To such an extent had Mr. Hawthorne exerted a fascination that Herman spent the dying lines of the poem, and the short reverential silence thereafter, in a series of such minor resolutions as if he were a young infatuate, planning a campaign of courtship.

The silence was broken by Matthews. He raised his silver mug and said, "Long life to the dear old poet." After this popular toast all were ready to have their cups replenished and then the rain having truly stopped and the sky having become much brighter they all stood up to stretch their legs.

They scattered over the cliffs, Mr. and Mrs. Fields walking hand in hand, Mr. and Miss Field trying to spot their own home in the low distance, Matthews and Duyckinck strolling the rocks with a cigar, Holmes creeping about protesting the altitude affected his life "ipecac" and Herman bestriding a peaked rock which ran out from the side of the mountain like a bowsprit. He pulled and hauled imaginary ropes and shouted out nautical commands for the delectation of the others and in particular Mr. Hawthorne, who was the only one to remain seated in their picnic place, looking mildly about him as if for the Great Carbuncle. He turned away from Mr. Melville, not through any distaste for the maritime posturing but because of the phallic obscenity that Herman's position on the rock suggested.

In the afternoon they were guided, by a newcomer to the party, who joined them at a prearranged point of the descent, through the Ice Glen, a dark crevice in the rock. They experimented with the echo, bouncing shouted jests off the sheer walls of stone and Mr. Hawthorne not the least, bringing up the rear, put on a ghoulish voice of doom and predicted certain destruction for them all. Herman, who at the time attributed this sudden fulsomeness to the effects of the Heidsieck, would later take an over-serious view of the fiendish side to the other man's playfulness. But for now the champagne, and the exercise, made him less concerned with the proposed friendship than he had been in the morning, and he spent much of the return walk talking with the two young ladies and treating them to some of his stock South Sea sagas.

Dr. Holmes tried to latch on to Mr. Hawthorne but Nathaniel, who was never unprepared to be rude in a silent, disregarding way, gave him short shrift.

Eventually they left the ankle-straining slopes of the mountain behind and came out on the peaceful fields of the Housatonic. They crossed the river to their host's house, where they took tea and conversation before dining early enough for the return.

The doctor, who had spent a recuperative hour on the couch, was in his finest table-talk form.

"To all Americans!" he proposed, lifting his glass before the meal commenced. "May they grow in stature, both physical and intellectual."

Having proposed this toast he then demolished it by laying down various arguments for the superiority of Englishmen, to which bait Herman responded with vigour.

"Oh, yes, to be sure," Holmes responded to Melville's attack, "in these United States it will be a common thing to grow sixteen and seventeen feet high."

263

"Well, there is a remarkable bullock at Great Barrington," chipped in Mr. Field, "bigger than . . ."

Mr. Hawthorne looked on, unready as usual to become sociably hearty but also extremely tired from the day's pursuits. He was missing Sophia and the children and especially the children's bedtime routine.

As the day drew to its end and they rose from the table Herman began to panic at the lack of direct communication between himself and the author of the *Mosses* and he drew Duyckinck aside to press him into obtaining an invitation from Fields. He confessed his ulterior motive and Evert, amused by Herman's timidity, obliged. It turned out that they would be welcome at Lenox the day after next, although Mr. Fields and his wife would be returning to Boston at some point during that same day.

*   *   *

With such an invitation in prospect, the day immediately following could not fail to be, in Herman's view, a day to pass by. And yet he did not want it to pass by too quickly. He was conscious of wanting to prepare himself for this second encounter, which would naturally be more intimate, more inescapable than the first.

Lizzie, still upset by Herman's disregarding of their anniversary, insisted on being included in the plans. She therefore accompanied the three men on their excursion to the Shaker village at Lebanon, sitting between Duyckinck and Matthews, while Herman took the reins. It was a silent and rather pleasureless outing, with the presence of a lady inhibiting the men and with Herman, in particular, just wanting to get through the day.

The next morning was different. There were four in the carriage again, but this time all male. Herman had been persuaded to take Malcolm with them. Elizabeth was feeling unwell and she did not want to impose on Robert's wife. She had assumed that Herman would have to postpone his trip to Lenox and made it plain that this was what she expected him to do, but her husband's expectations were not to be dashed.

Her temperature, or cold, had manifested itself during the return ride from Lebanon, and in their own rooms at Broadhall she had declared, "I really don't think I can cope with Malcolm tomorrow."

"Well, I'm seeing Mr. Hawthorne in the morning."

"I know you've arranged to. But what about Barney? I really can't . . ."

"We'll see if Robert's wife . . ."

"Herman! She looked after him for the whole day today, we really can't expect her to offer hospitality *and* a baby-minding service."

"I'll take him with me, then."

"Don't be preposterous."

"Are you too ill to look after him or not?"

"Yes, I am."

"There it is then."

"But I don't think he's old enough to go gallivanting with city gents and gabbling authors who won't pay him much mind."

Herman laughed. "You think Mr. Hawthorne and I are going to gabble, do you? I doubt it."

"Anyway, he can't go with you."

"He's not allowed out with his own father?"

"Not in a horse and carriage. Who would hold him?"

"Duyck would hold him."

"The idea is preposterous."

"Lizzie. I am going to Lenox tomorrow. Either you are well enough to look after Barney or not."

The hour before breakfast was one in which Herman and Elizabeth both refused to communicate further on the matter, each waiting for the other's bluff to be called. Duyckinck and Matthews were a little annoyed by the tension and by the delay, for they knew Mr. and Mrs. Fields would be leaving during the morning and did not want to miss them. The delay was caused when Elizabeth, at last realising that Herman was adamant in his intentions, took Malcolm away to dress him in a double napkin, and to prepare a little parcel of his favourite food. In addition a whole string of admonitions had to be delivered to Herman when all four men were at last seated in the carriage.

She stood and watched the carriage depart, Matthews holding Barney up to wave, then she wept bitterly for half an hour, chastising herself for allowing a marital battle of wills to supersede her maternal instinct.

They met Mr. and Mrs. Fields on the road a little way from the Red House, using the Tappan wagon to take themselves to the

265

station. Duyckinck made a casual arrangement to meet with Fields in the city in a day or two's time while Eliza made faces at Malcolm.

"You look very much at home with him, Mr. Matthews."

Barney was kneeling up at the side of the wagon with Matthews' open palm supporting his back.

"Una will be delighted . . ."

Herman, staring unsociably ahead, inadvertently exerted some pressure on the reins, which caused the carriage to start forward. The jarring made Barney knock his mouth on the hard carriage side and he began crying profusely. Eliza leaped from her wagon and lifted the chubby mite into her arms. There was no bleeding and he quickly responded to her sympathy. Herman, now having turned round, thanked her and asked either Duyckinck or Matthews to take the reins for the rest of the journey. He would sit in the back with his boy. The two city dwellers tussled physically for the privilege of steering the wagon along its country track and the horse gave another start. Herman had not yet taken Malcolm from Eliza and she had to run forward to hand him over. Mr. Fields shouted out his goodbyes.

Una and Julian had been posted as look-outs at the end of the track leading off the road to the small Tappan estate, and Evert, who had successfully achieved the driver's position, reported seeing two little figures scurrying away.

"This must be the turning, up ahead. I believe Mr. Hawthorne will be forewarned of our arrival."

*   *   *

Down at the Bowl Mr. Hawthorne pops two corks off the Heidsieck bottles given to him by Mansfield. Malcolm is taken in hand by Elizabeth Peabody and Julian rocks on the horse that his aunt has brought him from Boston.

Melville tries to recollect the phrases he has used in the critical essay to be published any day in the *Literary World*. He could reach out and touch the man now. Interview him. But they say nothing. Duyckinck and Matthews smoke cigars. Mr. Hawthorne watches the outer leaves burn and retract, burn and retract. Ash falls onto a lap to be roughly scuffed away; the cool breeze and the overcast sky making the city men over-vigorous in their gestures.

To have De Quincey at arms' length, or even Seneca in his toga – would it be like this? The dry champagne winces the tongue with

266

its bitter fizz. When all is said and done what *do* you say or do at a first intimate meeting? How much rent do you pay? Is Julian quite dry at night? How long is Miss Peabody staying? Have you thought at all about Una's schooling? Do you believe in God? What is the secret of happiness? From where do you get your wild witch voice?

What ineptitude. He sees that now, in Hawthorne's white shirt and sturdy, tanned collarbone. The hair, though receding, surprisingly thick and glossy. The eyes beckoning, then downcast. Open, but secretive.

"You do not have much of a library here," says Duyckinck.

"No. Just the volumes you saw in the case by the Hall." Volumes chosen for reading aloud to one another by the betrothed pair eight years since.

"I must get some new things to you. Certain quayside texts, eh?" Duyckinck says this rising, with a hand pushed down on Herman's shoulder. He tosses his cigar butt into the lake. Matthews out-throws him.

Herman sees that Mr. Hawthorne's pulse shows at the temple. The skin between his eye and ear oscillates with a strange display of light and shadow.

*   *   *

"Now it is that blackness in Hawthorne that so fixes and fascinates me." Melville receives his copy of the *Literary World* on publication day, August 17th. He reads it in a tiny garret room at Broadhall, sitting at a desk which once belonged to his uncle, and which has since been rescued from the cornloft over the carriage-house. It had been white with pigeon mess, and eggs had been laid in its drawers. He flicks a small brass handle on one such drawer, letting it swing back and sound out a tut-tut for every printing error he finds. Yesterday he had been at the Red House again but had spoken only with Mrs. Hawthorne, to whom he had handed a large packet addressed to her husband and posted from New York by Evert Duyckinck. It was the addition to the Hawthorne library already promised and so promptly made good. In return she had given him some Salem moss to use as a frontispiece in his copy of *Mosses From An Old Manse*.

Herman journeyed home carefully with the triangular talisman. He dared not show it to Lizzie whom he had so often rebuked for her attachment to the clover stem, and so he brought the volume to this new-found smoking and reading den.

Sophia Hawthorne had taken quite a fancy to the bearded literary colleague, in many ways the perfect counterpoint to her own husband. "When conversing he is full of gesture and force and loses himself in his subject. There is no grace nor polish." But he is "very agreeable and entertaining, with life to his fingertips". Perhaps she sensed an indolence creeping over her husband more middle-aged than temperamental, and thought that he would benefit from the company of an enthusiast. At any rate she was very much in favour of their association, so that, if there was any holding back, it was on her husband's side.

The parcel left by Herman contained, unknown to him, his own entire works and these kept Mr. Hawthorne busy for the next ten days, reading, as Melville had done his own *Tales*, in a haybarn. It was during this period that the anonymous review appeared in the *Literary World* and both the Hawthornes were captivated by it – she by its insights (a vision of her husband that no one hitherto had expressed) and he by its laudatory excesses. The reception of the article at once gives a clue to Sophia's interest in Mr. Melville. As soon as its authorship had become broadcast she knew that Herman was a man who saw her husband as she did.

The Indian summer did not produce any sensual relaxation in Elizabeth. Her face became drawn with a grey pallor and her temper was shortened by the continuing uncertainty surrounding Herman's plans and by the lack of physical union between them. Herman stayed up late each night talking to his cousin Robert and then, for fear of waking the baby Malcolm, he slept downstairs. Elizabeth would have been more tolerant of her empty bed had she been sooner informed of the exact nature of the conversations which kept her husband so assiduously away from her arms. He was campaigning hard to buy a small section of the Broadhall domain which, five years after the death of Uncle Thomas, was being sold off in order to provide an equitable sharing of the estate. In fact he eventually picked upon a small farm on Broadhall's eastern perimeter, after he had been introduced to its owner, a Dr. Brewster, who was wanting to move. Elizabeth heard nothing of this until the day before his first extensive visit to Lenox.

It was Monday September 2nd. He said, "Lizzie, do you think your parents would care to visit us here for a few days before the old place goes?"

"But we go back to New York in the middle of the month. Is there time to arrange . . ."

"Could you?"

"Could I . . ."

"Could you get them to come? At least your father. It's rather important. You see . . ."

"You want us to borrow more money." Lizzie took his hand. Their fingers linked limply.

"I'll tell you all about it when I'm back from the Hawthornes." He bent to kiss her forehead and then walked to the door. Holding the handle he turned, made as if to say something more, but then proceeded to leave the room.

The next day he rode to Lenox. At first the Hawthornes entertained him stiffly. Nathaniel and he sat opposite one another in easy chairs. Sophia brought them tea. Even Una and Julian seemed shy and nervous. They eyed the visitor strangely. Eventually he gave them a squint-eyed frown and bent to put his cup down on the floor. On their knees they scurried to the side of Papa's chair. Herman slapped his own knee.

"I suppose your father's been telling you how I lived amongst the cannibals. Only *lived* amongst them, mind. I'm not a cannibal myself, only . . . that bare little arm . . ."

Herman began to get up, reaching his hand forward as if he intended to strike Una's forearm. She screamed. There was a knock on the door. Sophia told them to behave. Herman made a naughty-boy grimace.

"It's a Mr. Hadly, dear, will you see him? He asked if that sweetest man of mosses were at home."

Herman guffawed. The children looked wide-eyed. Such extravagant reaction was unusual in their household. "Tell him there's more green mould than sugar in your husband's pen." When Sophia left to open the door he added, "I cannot understand how your stories acquired such a reputation."

"No," said Mr. Hawthorne. "Have you seen the piece about me in the *Literary World*?"

"Ay. That hits the mark."

Both gentlemen stood as a third entered the room. He was a thin clerical-looking fellow. Mr. Hawthorne greeted him as Mr. Hadly, and immediately introduced Mr. Melville.

"Mr. Melville! Mr. Melville, too! And Lydia in her carriage still. She wouldn't come to the door, not knowing if Mr. Hawthorne were married. Mr. Hawthorne and Mr. Melville. My, my! Would you mind if I fetched Lydia? We shall keep our call very brief. Oh, there we are."

He drew out his calling card which he left with Mr. Hawthorne while he went to fetch his lady companion.

"It says Hackley here. Rev. Charles Hackley, New York. I thought you said Hadly."

"I thought *he* said Hadly."

"Know the man, Mr. Melville? In your parish?"

Herman shook his head. The two New Yorkers returned, the female dressed in black also.

"Lydia insists we stay not a moment longer than we need. As you have company. But would you be so kind as to inscribe these two volumes for her?" Turning to Mr. Melville he added, "I'm afraid we had no notion that you, sir, would be here. Otherwise we might have brought our *Typee* with us."

"Yes," piped in Lydia. "Are you still writing? Or have you gone back to sea."

"To sea. I'm a whaling man now, ma'am."

"What fun! A book will come out of it no doubt."

"I hope that it might."

Mr. Hawthorne dashed off the second inscription and Sophia took them to the door.

Una and Julian immediately paraded the room impersonating the lady named Lydia, calling out "What fun!" and turning their heads this way and that.

"Sshh! They are still on the path," said their father.

Herman rose to see if this were true. "And there, my sweet sir, are the recipients of our labours in the fabulists' honeycomb. Do they not make your sting quiver?"

Una and Julian looked at Herman and then at Papa. Nathaniel smiled and then said, "I must ask Sophia if Mr. Tappan will drive us to Pittsfield tomorrow."

Herman had insisted that they both return to Broadhall the following day to dine. He passed the afternoon taking a walk beside the Stockbridge Bowl. Nathaniel excused himself and went to his study to write. Sophia busied herself in the house. The children played outdoors.

Walking beside the lake, Herman looked forward to settling in Pittsfield. He would live here in the Berkshires, a neighbour to the most acclaimed tale-teller in the eastern states.

At nine o'clock that night, alone with Mr. Hawthorne, and smoking cigars at the back doorway, it was difficult to be so positive about the hoped-for friendship.

270

"I had little idea that Providence would despatch us to this extraordinary region," stated Mr. Hawthorne.

"You prefer your home town? Salem, is it?"

"Not Salem! Never! But the coast somewhere, yes. I have a yen for political office although I know it runs counter to my temperament. It is strange the way these incongruous yearnings afflict us."

"Elizabeth and I have to move out of New York. The house we share with my brother's family is too cramped. I have half an eye on a property in Pittsfield."

Mr. Hawthorne's eyes darted across to scrutinise Herman's. His cigar moved sideways, with a twist of his lips. He removed it and said, "Is that so?" The words were spoken with a cold neutrality which mocked much of the puppyish expectation that had so diverted Herman during the afternoon.

A defensive caution instantly pervaded the manners of the older man. He put out his cigar, said "Well," and retired into the house. Herman remained for as long as it took to finish his own smoke, feeling just as if he had had a first kiss rebuffed by an uninterested maiden.

The next morning, at ten, Mr. Tappan agreed to take the two authors back to Pittsfield to dine. According to Sophia it had required some considerable persuasion to secure his services, not through any un-neighbourliness, but an acute shyness that had made him wary of being introduced to Mr. Melville. While such negotiations as were necessary took their course, Herman played wild chasing games with Una and Julian. They ran round the house, through back and front, until they were beside themselves with exhausted glee.

"Do you have to go back?"

"I'm going to make Papa trap you."

They each grabbed one of his forearms.

"There – you can't go."

"Oh, can't I?"

"No!"

"Well, we'll see." Herman lifted them bodily, one arm for each, and made one more rampaging circuit of the house, tossing the two children onto the parlour sofa at the end.

"Mama, Mr. Omoo wants to stay. He said. He said."

Sophia blushed. She explained to Herman that Nathaniel had spoken of him to the children as "Mr Omoo".

"Actually, would you mind returning with Nathaniel tonight

271

because William Tappan says that he will be perfectly able to drive you *in* to Pittsfield but that he will be taking the cars to Albany this afternoon and will then be staying there for at least three days. Have you anything to drive the two of you back in?''

The children cheered. They were told to leave the room. Nathaniel arrived with William Tappan at his side.

If there is nothing disingenuous in Sophia's explanation of William Tappan's original reluctance to help out with this journey it nevertheless raises more questions than it answers. She states that he ''particularly did not wish, for some reason, to be introduced to Mr. Melville''. So that even though Tappan may have suffered from a general shyness that made all fresh encounters irksome, it appears he had some special cause to be wary of *this* one. If Melville had been a complete stranger to him, if he had been acquainted with no more than the literary reputation, there would surely have been nothing ''in particular'' to fear. It is reasonable therefore to deduce that Tappan's protestations and prospective embarrassment arose out of some reported knowledge of Mr. Melville. This is supported by the subsequent sentence in Sophia's letter: ''I have no doubt he will be repaid by finding Mr. Mèlville a very different man from what he imagines.'' Who, we must ask, had been telling him stories; and for what reason?

The carriage ride to Broadhall was sufficiently charged to support these contentions. Tappan dropped them off en route to the station, not having passed a word of conversation with Herman, and not going one yard out of his way to lessen the walking distance to cousin Robert's.

''A sour man that,'' said Herman.

''Just painfully quiet.''

''Ah, but we are sweet silent men.''

Mr. Hawthorne's demeanour at Broadhall, when introduced to Mrs. Melville and the rest of the residents, was strictly cordial and need not detain us. But let us linger with Herman and Lizzie as he took her aside to communicate the new arrangements.

''. . . and so I must go back with him this evening and as he's been pressing me to stay for some time I think I shall do so and not return till the end of the week.''

''But you have only just been for the night!''

''A mere ice-breaker, Lizzie. We hardly passed a word of any consequence.'' He placed his hands on her shoulders. ''This is important to me, Lizzie.''

She lifted her eyes to his.

"At last I feel there's someone who might listen."

Those raised eyes gleamed.

"There are weird things rolling out of me in this *Whale* book. I need a Solon or a Nestor."

The lids dropped. Herman kissed each one, apparently not noticing their dampness, for the gentle patting of her shoulders assumed assent had been given.

"You mustn't whisper a word about the Virginian in Vermont. They know nothing yet."

Before leaving for Lenox, Herman had a quiet word with Robert, firstly to negotiate for some bottles of liquor which, aside from the Heidsieck champagne, the Hawthorne household seemed sadly lacking in, and secondly to check that his overtures to Dr. Brewster were proceeding as planned. He had further upset Elizabeth by pestering her to confirm that she had written the letter to her father as promised.

"Of course there is no reply. I only posted mine yesterday. And if you're so keen on hearing their answer why go charging off to Lenox?"

"Dear Lizzie. Please be patient."

They arrived at the Red House at 8 p.m., Herman holding the reins and Nathaniel the bottles – two Amontillado sherries, one gin and one brandy. There was a note downstairs from Sophia saying that she had a headache threatening and had gone to bed at the same time as the children. Nathaniel fetched glasses and the two men settled themselves down with one of the bottles of sherry.

"You've made yourself very comfortable here."

"Ah, that is one of my Sophia's gifts. But yes; a little cramped indoors, we yet have space enough outside."

Herman drank his first sherry and immediately refilled the glass. Raising it, and squinting through the amber liquid as if to check for sediment, he said, "I'll let you into a secret. I'm making a bid for the Brewster place. That is, if I can raise the capital. Know it?"

Mr. Hawthorne shook his head. "You'd already mentioned you were looking around."

"Yes. Elizabeth hasn't really made a home yet. Not like this. It's time we separated from Allan. Time to plant ourselves now, to tread the roots in."

"You don't think planting a family is at the bottom of most of the wrong and mischief men do?"

Herman moved his shoulders back. Noticing his guest's hesitancy Nathaniel added, "I do not mean to criticise. You understand? Of course, if Sophia and I could afford it we would do the same."

"You like this spot, then?"

"Not a great deal, no. I meant buy a place."

"With your latest success that possibility cannot be so remote."

"Well, you know as well as any I'm sure how unclear these things are until a publisher draws up its account."

"I was thinking more of home as haven, an island about which flows the river of life. I don't think possession of the deeds is important in itself."

"You'd describe yourself as a family man, then?"

Herman again filled his glass. "I think we should have started on the brandy."

"We could smoke a cigar but would need to move out to the kitchen."

Herman nodded understanding. "That is a question of deep significance for me." He stared at his replenished glass. They were drinking from narrow-bowled copitas and he found the tipping of the glass made his nose feel extra-large.

Mr. Hawthorne detected from the statement and the thoughtful expression on his companion's face that he had sauntered upon ground not quite applicable to so early an acquaintanceship. He quickly added, "Very amusing the other evening. That supper debate. Between you and the Doctor."

"Family names, you mean. How did that come up now? Oh, we were talking about the English peerage, yes. There's mischief in that all right. Although I think both of our own families are guilty of a little tinkering with the hereditary nomenclature."

"You mean the added letters."

"Yes. All vanity really."

"But in itself an example of our Republican fluidity in matters of station?"

The two of them talked on like this at some length and the evening ended with Herman giving a long account of his recent London visit. When Nathaniel got to bed Sophia was awake.

"I'm sorry, dear. Have we been making a babble?"

"I heard your voices, but no, I've been asleep and woken again."

"The children are all right?"

"They haven't stirred, but are worried that Mr. Omoo will mistake their room for his own."

"Don't worry. He's already a-bed. I stayed downstairs clearing up."

"Gallant Monsieur l'Aubépine."

Bridge had visited them a week or two earlier and there had been much merry reminiscing of the Frenchman and the month spent in Maine.

The next morning Mr. and Mrs. Hawthorne were woken early by screaming coming from the children's bedroom.

Herman had bathed his head, slicked back his hair, and gone bare-chested into the children's room. They were wild with terror and when Sophia appeared at the door, still wrapping herself in her gown, they fled to her side. At the breakfast table Herman helped explain his behaviour by telling them that the book he was now working on began with a scene in which the narrator has to share a hotel room with a savage.

"His name is Queequeg."

The children exploded in giggles.

"Kwee-Kwee!"

"Mr. Ki-Wi."

Nathaniel gave them a stern eye and Sophia tapped the back of Una's hand.

"Let them laugh at me. I fear it won't be the reader's reaction. But look; I must leave you, sir, to your morning's work. I am determined that my stay here should not impede your own labours. I shall go and put on my boots and lead my horse a trot round the barns."

When he had gone Sophia beamed at her husband. "No excuses today, then. Up you go."

He walked over and embraced her. "Oh, Sophiechen. Adorablest." And kissing her brow he mounted the stair to the study.

Herman while cantering the horse, met Mrs. Tappan.

"At last! A bearded stranger to carry me away on his steed." Caroline did not get the response which her dramatic witticism might have been expected to elicit. Neither Herman's general temperament, nor the particular mood he was in this morning, cut him out for flirtatious banter.

"I am just a guest. Of Mr. Hawthorne's."

Caroline's feet were bare. They were wet with dew up to the

ankles. The Melville horse bent its head and nuzzled her toes. She did not withdraw them and step out of range, but fell forward across the horse's neck and mane, letting out a delighted groan. There was, in this exaggerated and sensual response, and in the woman's open, rather impish features, something that worried away at Herman during the day, and made him refer to Mrs. Tappan in conversation that night.

Mr. Hawthorne worked all through the morning. He had been more flattered than he was willing to admit by the *Literary World* piece and both the success and notoriety which his *Scarlet Letter* was bringing him made him feel as if at last his star had turned.

He was forty-six years old. There had been a time, only a year or two ago, when it seemed as if he had put down the pen for ever. Literature had become a mere tool for preserving his observations of family life. His Sophia, their two children, and the job that kept them adequately provided for marked a hermetic perimeter around his life.

Now requests for his autograph began to reach him through the post. Magazines and annuals pestered him for stories that he might have written since the *Mosses From An Old Manse* had been collected in 1846. But, looking back on much of this work as a pitiful waste of effort, he sent apologetic replies. The sudden success of the longer form, the Romance, as he would term all his major novels, seemed to taunt him for having so weakly abandoned the form in his twenties, after the failure of *Fanshawe*. Already he was contemplating the shape of a sequel to the *Letter*; and he embarked on these early notes – it was just so that he filled his time this particular morning – with the conscious intention of making this next book a sunnier creation.

He remained somewhat appalled at the identification with sin, in the shape of fallen woman, that lay at the heart of his last Romance's power and persuasion. And now he was profiting dollar by grubby but grandiose dollar from that adulterous coupling and its repercussions.

Referring to old Journal entries he crafted various tentative paragraphs, sketching both setting and character. It was his manner as diarist and notemaker to work at fairly expansive first drafts, yet it is rare to find him lifting verbatim such passages into the final work. Rather he seemed to make several long-running assaults on an idea and the best performance stuck. He was not a pernickety re-writer. The prevailing quality of his style, not to every modern reader's taste, is a rhythmic clarity and exactitude of expression which has more to do with the shape and loading of sentences and paragraphs than with the painstaking choice of *le mot juste*.

He scribbled down a sentence which had sprung to mind in response to Mr. Melville's remarks the other evening. "There is no unwholesome atmosphere as that of an old home, rendered poisonous by one's defunct forefathers and relatives." And having full-stopped and bracketed it he leaned back, linked the fingers of both hands behind his neck, and tipped his chair onto two legs by pressing down with his foot.

His guest was outside exercising his horse. His wife was brushing Una's and Julian's hair. The black woman from the village was clearing away the breakfast things. He, an author, was upstairs earning his daily bread. It was difficult to resist a grin, not of self-satisfaction perhaps, but certainly of well-being.

What a saviour the ex-Cardinal was! Horace Connolly, the arch-fiend responsible for his dismissal from the Custom House had blessed where he meant to curse. Nathaniel's grin broadened as he remembered once again their chance encounter in Boston, before moving to the Red House. Despite the vituperative blasting he had rehearsed for such an event, a miracle had taken place. They had got corned together and laughed the whole affair off as a foolish vanity. He had written Connolly a comical letter, praising up his own Christian forgiveness and promising not to satirise his enemy in the next book. He felt less certain of that assurance now. Perhaps it might be possible to develop, without unkindness, his good and his evil, as combined so queerly together.

Horace Lorenzo Connolly, born illegitimate, had been adopted by a cousin of the Hawthornes. The cousin lived in an old house on Turner Street, Salem, which is supposedly the model for *The House Of Seven Gables*. The guardian, and the boy, had at one time played cards with the Hawthornes and it was this pastime that furnished their nicknames: Cardinal and Duchess. Connolly worked first as a preacher then as a lawyer and wheeler-dealer local politician, making enemies of everyone until Hawthorne began to dedicate all complimentary copies of his book to his "pet serpent". And yet he took an interest in literary matters; it was he, reputedly, who gave Longfellow the idea for *Evangeline*.

Nathaniel's mind wandered to these card games and the old, old days of his life with sisters and mother. And then his reclining position recalled the lethargic evenings he had spent in his little bedroom on Beacon Hill, while staying with the Hillards in Boston, and courting Sophia in Salem. Arriving back exhausted from a day in the open, checking cargoes of salt and coal, he would begin a letter to his adorablest, working himself up to an unbearable pitch of sensual longing till he had to throw himself onto the bed and resume the letter at the end of half-sleeping dreams of union.

In the past he might have whiled away an entire hour or more in such idle recollections or vague meanders of the mind, while purporting to "work". But writing *The Scarlet Letter* had finally adapted him to a more productive manner of composition; the fiendish angel which had inspired that book may have deserted him, but there were reverberations of creative intensity which stirred him, for example, now to rock back suddenly onto all four legs of his chair, pick up pen in his right hand, bend left arm across the top of the page and dip his head to the task of adding another sentence to his set of notes for the new book.

*   *   *

"I met your neighbour this morning. Tappan's wife. The two don't seem to go together."

Sophia had once again left the men to talk alone in the little front parlour. They sat either side of the fireplace, which was covered up by one of Sophia's hand-painted screens. She, who had long since given up the brush in favour of the needle, sat darning in the back room, with the door open to the garden.

"No. We've been acquainted for some time. Do you know her children's book?"

Melville shook his head. "Isn't she part of the Morewood set?"

"Not as far as I can tell. I suppose her husband is too shy. They are a bit of a mismatch in many ways. She and her sister have had poems published."

"Then it must have been the response of a poetess this morning. My horse licked her toes and instead of starting away she groaned with pleasure and bent over its mane, inviting it to repeat the stimulation."

Mr. Hawthorne's eyes seemed to fill with an imagined conception of the scene. His mouth lengthened into something approaching a smirk. It was not one of the enigmatic smiles which, in later conversations, were so to frustrate Herman, but a self-gratifying savouring of the reported incident.

"She stayed with us for a month once. When we were at the Manse. Near the end of our time there."

The mouth closed suddenly. He was about to say more but stopped. There is a barely resistible temptation to open that mouth again; to let Mr. Hawthorne himself confess to a secret in his past. I remain curious about Mrs. Tappan. Some of the nudgings and veiled hints that come from the biographies, the letters, the journals and the fiction itself are beginning to adhere. It is time you had some facts.

CAROLINE STURGIS TAPPAN: born August 1819, same month and year as Herman Melville. Grows up in Boston. Father is wealthy shipping magnate, whose firm Bryant and Sturgis dominated American–Far East trade for a generation. Caroline, her four sisters and one brother receive a cultivated education at home. In her teens she becomes an ardent admirer of Margaret Fuller, who takes her with her on vacations to the Emersons in Concord. Already writing poetry, Caroline's society is cherished mostly for her charming and gently probing conversation and she, in turn, enjoys the company of the Transcendentalist set, appearing for a while to harbour a romantic attachment for Ellery Channing, until ousted by Margaret Fuller's sister. In the summer of 1845 she boards with the Hawthornes, Nathaniel having previously refused two other requests to accept lodgers; his change of heart being officially attributed to financial exigencies. Caroline marries in 1847. Her husband, William Tappan, an acutely shy man, with no natural aptitude for business, works in the family merchant bank. Besides once having been a walking companion to Thoreau he seems not to have made much of a mark on the literary or cultural scene. He has once contributed a poem to the *Dial* but is probably satisfied enough, after his marriage, to leave literary efforts to his wife. They live mainly in Boston but spend summers on the Highwood estate in Lenox. (It was this estate which was eventually bequeathed by Caroline's daughters to the Boston Symphony Orchestra and renamed Tanglewood.) Mrs. Sturgis died in 1888, aged sixty-nine.

I blush to admit once again that this picture of a younger woman, member of the Transcendental literary establishment,

279

exact contemporary of Melville's and wryly effervescent conversationalist is a recent revelation. There is no excuse. The facts were always to hand. It was that business with the apples (of which, more in a moment) and all those strait-laced nineteenth-century references to "Mrs. Tappan" which led me, like little Julian in the opening scene of our saga, to concoct a prejudiced view of the lady.

The altered and corrected vision immediately suggests that Caroline Sturgis, a frequent if impermanent resident of Brook Farm, is much more likely than Margaret Fuller to have been the inspiration behind the female characters in *The Blithedale Romance*. Take the following as a possibility: Nathaniel fell in love with Caroline at the farm and the delayed announcement to his family of his engagement to Sophia was attributable to this bewitchment. Eventually, seeing no future in the affair, he proceeded with the marriage. For nearly three years he protected their privacy in the Manse but when Miss Fuller suggested Caroline board with them in the summer of 1845 he accepted. She stayed for a four to six week period and whether or not there was any direct romantic involvement between them then, the horrific discovery of the drowned girl on the night of his and Sophia's third wedding anniversary, and their ensuing eviction from the Manse, were perceived by Nathaniel as tangible recompense for an infidelity of the heart if not of the body.

Nathaniel produced the quart bottle of medicinal brandy he had bought at the apothecary's in the village. They had already emptied another Heidsieck during an afternoon mostly spent lying about the garden, reading and paying attention to the children.

"You can take yours back with you. This won't be of the highest calibre, I'm afraid. I've written to my friend Zack Burchmore who runs an off licence in Boston, for some gin and some cigars. I'd rather have gin than champagne, though it seems ungracious to say it."

Herman lifted his first glass of the rather muddy looking brandy. "May there be gin in these glasses then, the next time we meet."

"You're staying another night?"

"Oh, yes. When I entertain you in my new property then."

Mr. Hawthorne raised his glass too. "A successful transaction."

Mr. Melville, sipping his drink, and then snapping his tongue away from the roof of his mouth, said, "I feel a bit of an upstart, thinking of buying a farm, and you with such a list of titles, and longer family . . ."

"I know – while I rent this poky old shanty, you were going to say. And only pay a farthing for it at that. We could have had the place for nothing but the Brook Farm experience taught me to value the formality of money. The right of purchase is the only safe one. This is a world of bargain and sale and no absurdity is more certain to be exposed than the attempt to make it anything else."

It was an attitude which Herman had not quite anticipated. Just as he felt himself abandoning the requisites of the market place in his book about the whale so did Mr. Hawthorne seem to be in a mood keen to capitalise upon the success of *The Scarlet Letter*.

"I thought you did not approve of wealth and property."

"I approve the rites of exchange, not of possession."

The image of Caroline Tappan embracing his horse's mane obtruded itself once again. Mr. Hawthorne's head was bowed. Herman could look at him without having to meet his eye. They were easier in one another's company now and talking more freely. Nathaniel, bent forward in a low-seated couch, in these domestic surroundings seemed to have taken on the sort of sphericity associated with European burghers. But then his face lifted. There was that maddening twinkle in his eye. "In patience possess ye your souls," he added.

Was it said in all seriousness, or did Herman detect a mild mockery there? No ordinary sphericity that – a man who would mock the very words of Christ. Again the guest's discomfiture returned. No, he wouldn't play dainty intellectual games and bury his own response in veiled ambivalency. Pour another brandy, sailor! Let loose the line!

By the time Sophia had gone to bed, and the level of the brandy had sunk well below the narrowing of the bottle's neck, the conversation struck deep ore.

"Fellow I shipped with to London last winter would have liked to join us now. Adler was his name. Though he'd have no stomach for this corrosive cordial. A nautical nip this is, by the Devil!"

Herman splashed more of the liquor into his glass.

"What he lacked in stomach for the liquid ether he made up for in a prodigious appetite for metaphysical moonshine. He was full of continental lore, the German philosophers I mean, and we tramped the deck at the chilly midnight hour talking about Futurity and Chance."

281

Herman raised his glass.

"Here's to the future. And some day, though it be far in that metaphysical and hypothetical distance, may we find ourselves once again on some grassy bank in Paradise, our glasses filled with aromatic London gin, and a smoking Havana in our hands."

Nathaniel shifted in his seat. Though he was several tots behind Herman he did lean forward now to fill his glass, making at the same time a rather limp excuse for their not being able to smoke indoors. He was embarrassed by this response to his companion's lucid overture, and reddened.

"Hang the cigars! Your Zachariah will provide for you in time. Behold, the hour of the cigar cometh! Not at day nor at night shall it come to pass but at evening, and men shall put down their burdens . . . ah, but I do not mean to mock. I fear I have offended the Great Society Lady Mrs. Morewood already with my Biblical parodies. Still our Fate holds in that book, though no new canons have been added to it for nearly nineteen centuries. Our vastly prolific age of print and text – will it produce anything at all to challenge the authority of tablet and scroll? I was going to say I have finally acquired a wonderful edition of the Holy Book, with text at last propórtioned to my weak and overwrought sight. I cannot read for more than ten minutes by lamp or candle flame, you know. But it isn't the Bible at all. No, the Bard of Stratford it is who has come into my life in letters tall enough to be perceived by these useless orbs. A typically blasphemous thought association. I feel I am rather renowned for having the audacity to speak of the divine, the immortal, and the temporal in the same breath."

"You have, have you?" Nathaniel sat up straight, speaking the words lowly, accusingly.

"I must own up to a tendency of that nature, yes, sir."

"And is there anything else you think it would be in order to own up to? A recent trip to a plantation perhaps, tobacco lover that you are."

Herman raised his glass again. "To Virginia," he said. "And Abolition."

"Sophia'll be tickled. Her response to your over-generous praise was, Amen Nathaniel, at last someone sees you as I do."

"Well, face to face you know it gets a little delicate. I'd rather we return to ontologicals, as Duyck calls them, before we get to criticising my own Yays and Nays."

"I have been reading them – the ones Mr. Duyckinck sent me and . . ."

Melville lifted the flat of his palm toward Mr. Hawthorne's face. "Hold to! We can ponder my *White Whale* if you wish, but the little squibs and porpoises which have preceded it I'd rather we let dance out their days in an unmolested ocean of oblivion. Look, this brandy is for the high atmosphere, which makes me think of that story of yours about a steeple. You do those vignette pieces, life in its various busy aspects, so well."

"Ah, but I fly high only to pry. It is not my impulse to help or hinder, but to look on, to analyse, to explain matters to myself."

"Schuck! You are speaking in the voice of some adopted character."

"Yes; but isn't that all we can do? I mean when we write."

Mr. Hawthorne sipped his brandy and continued. "I sometimes imagine I have been enrolled as the great Recorder and I was quite serious when I referred, in that story to which you have just made mention, to the idea of being an invisible witness, able to hover undetected from subject to subject."

"But as an angel wouldn't you be moved to help and comfort people in distress?"

Mr. Hawthorne sat back on the couch, quite lucid and alert but certainly by now well-primed with alcohol. "There are those who charge me with having too blatant a moral purpose. And I cannot dispute that my style of composition lends a certain amount of credence to this view, but the only consistent moral I draw is that none but the pure of heart should point a finger. And the pure of heart? Where are they?"

"Yes, but in addition you do manage to put into your narratives the impression of secret arcane knowledge regarding the human heart."

Nathaniel leaned forward again. "I met a Frenchman once. He was appalled when I suggested that his character might not be as unblemished and lacking in dark secrets as he proudly boasted."

Melville felt uneasy, as if his own mind were to be probed by the aspiring Paul Pry. The light in the room had dimmed and the atmosphere seemed set for mesmerism. Mr. Hawthorne's face contained a greater proportion of shadow than was usual.

Herman took up the bottle and poured a little more – the merest splash.

"You are not a mesmerist?"

Mr. Hawthorne, with lips to his glass, coughed, and took out his handkerchief.

"That, my dear Melville, is a subject I will not even talk about."

283

Such an embargo on conversation shocked Herman and though he knew it was an effect of the adulterated brandy he was unable to dispel a distorted and devilish image of his companion. There seemed to be a long silence, in which Mr. Hawthorne primped and preened his eyebrows. It made the quiet, subdued, smoke-free intimacy of the little shanty parlour room unbearably oppressive. Herman got up, and throwing open a window leaned far out into the night. His head immediately cleared and reeling round he saw Mr. Hawthorne picking up the empty glasses and bottle, apparently turning in for the night, and once again the picture of phlegmatic provincialism.

"Shall we drink a measure outside? I feel the need to quaff the air myself."

A stormy breeze blew from off the Bowl and even using the house as shelter they soon felt more refreshed than intended. The ground was wet with September dew and they walked into the small orchard to lean against a tree. Nathaniel picked up two early windfalls and tossed one to Herman. The two men bit their fruit and sipped their spirit glasses, for a moment lost in independent revery.

Herman chewed the apple then spat out the pulp. He found it too tart to swallow. He hoped Lizzie's parents had agreed to visit Berkshire and that letters and travelling could be arranged in time for a speedy transaction. If affairs moved quickly enough they might not need to return to New York *en famille* but transfer themselves from Broadhall, returning to Fourth Avenue individually to pack up. Such would be the. . . . A chunk of apple crept to the back of his throat and made him cough. When he had cleared his throat he looked at the stars through watering eyes.

Nathaniel was beginning to enjoy the brandy, and to seriously regret the lack of cigars. He looked at the rear of the cottage. He had been a resident in Lenox for three months and there was little remnant of the dysphoria he had been prey to on moving in. Their own bedroom window faced the orchard. He thought of Sophia alone in their bed, and wanted her.

"What is it the philosophers say?" Herman pondered after his coughing fit. "Man does not know the place he should occupy."

Nathaniel smiled. There had he been thinking of his own domestic station and a bricks and mortar type of occupancy while Mr. Melville so much more worthily of an author had been thinking of the stars, of Heaven.

"You smile as if it is an old conundrum no longer bothering to you."

Nathaniel's face was quickly drained of expression. "No, no. Whether to curb the passions and become as God. Or down all scruples and live as beasts. Is that it?"

Herman laughed. "You state it with a cool accuracy. There is a Jewish teaching I have read of which says that man's soul originates on a higher plane than angels."

"I rather pity the angels if this is so."

"It leaves them little room for manoeuvre, surely. Ours is the more perilous condition, as you convey in your stories."

Nathaniel turned his head to Herman, with the chin thrust foremost, as if asking for chapter and verse.

"I mean those examples of the chain of human sympathies being broke loose from. Dash, my words are addled. Well, you're familiar enough with the sin of spiritual pride."

"I fear so. From time to time."

Herman, deeply embarrassed, spluttered, "I am just talking clumsily. Not you, Heaven forbid. You have such a clear vision of error."

"If only we avoided all the pitfalls that we see in our way."

Momentarily Herman's head cleared of awkwardness and befuddlement and he was made alert to the possibility that he was being played with; that his companion had been dealing in mischievous condescension. The feeling passed as quickly as it had come, but it was indicative of the mutual watchfulness that impeded a quick sealing of their friendship.

"So, you've known Mrs. Tappan some time?" Herman took advantage of the lull, by throwing in a piece of his own mischief.

"Mm, at the Farm, and . . ."

It was Herman's turn to throw his chin out in query.

"Brook Farm. Ripley's community experiment. I was one of its founding members."

"Before your marriage?"

"Oh, yes. I quickly saw that the Community was no environment in which to start a marriage. Though in the beginning that was what Sophia and I intended."

"You were engaged then?"

Nathaniel didn't answer. His eyes, focused on a horizon which was in fact masked by hedgerow, seemed filled with private reminiscence.

285

"I have a mind to write its history one day," he said.

"Of your love affair?"

"My love affair! What do you mean?"

"With Mrs. Hawthorne."

"No!" Nathaniel's emphasis of the word was both relieved and categorical.

The wind had turned slightly and their position in the orchard was not as sheltered as when they had first leaned against their respective trees. By an act of uncanny dexterity, Nathaniel caught a piece of falling fruit and tossing it to Herman said, "Take it indoors with us. I'll carry the bottle."

The brandy bottle which had been standing in tall grass was soaked in dew. Nathaniel wiped it on the wings of his coat and then led the way back to the house.

Creeping into bed behind Sophia, Nathaniel meditated upon Caroline's delight in the equine lick. He put his own feet on Sophia's feet, felt their familiar shape and naked warmth, and was quickly asleep.

Herman, on the other hand, when he got to his room, sat on the edge of the bed and without making any effort to undress drifted off into head-throbbing ruminations regarding the night's talk. He had not drawn Mr. Hawthorne out. He had had one line of conversation totally rebuffed and another dealt with in a schoolmasterly repetition of the classical dilemma which he, Herman, had proposed. There was the added embarrassment of having seemingly accused his host of spiritual pride. The gaffe had been caused by a slip, or rather a boozy entanglement of the tongue, but he found himself making much the same mental accusation now. Not pride perhaps; but a superior dismissiveness. His pulse, perceptively rocking his spinal column, set his whole torso swinging to and fro, a motion which he gradually accentuated. He breathed deeply through his nose, rocking thus, on the edge of the bed. And then he sat straight up, stock still. He had reminded himself of a picture carried over from a nightmare of his dead brother Gansevoort, rocking himself dementedly in just such a way, in his lonely London room.

*   *   *

In the morning he woke late, to find the family already up, and the noise of children at their breakfast. He recollected little of the comatose musing on the edge of the bed but, discovering that he had gone to sleep in his dirty underclothes, he was reminded how severely affected he had been by the apothecary's brandy, so that he was delighted when he swung his legs on to the floor to find that they were steady and that the throbbing in his head had stopped.

Downstairs Nathaniel's mental mood did not tally with Herman's. He had snapped once at the children for not answering their mother quickly enough, and had been otherwise silent.

"Are you all right, dearest?"

"Is Papa sick again? Will Mr. Kwee-Kwee have to go home?"

"I am quite all right and I believe Mr. Melville is staying one more night."

Sophia stopped to study her husband. He was eating his breakfast and staring away from the table, berating himself for various excesses. He had drunk too liberally of the brandy. He had been too free with information about Mrs. Tappan. He even remembered speaking about the moralistic purposes in his *Tales*. He had been betrayed into a false position, and could not recognise the drinking partner he had been last night.

The two men passed one another on the stair.

"Good day. Did you sleep well?"

"I was a little enlivened by our talk. But don't let me keep you from your room."

Mr. Hawthorne raised and turned a hand, as if to say such a delay was of no consequence and might be extended without detriment to anyone, but passed on to his study door all the same. Before closing it, noticing that Herman was still on the stair and turned his way, he made as if to say something; but instead he raised and turned the same hand, this time in the condescending kind of wave he might have used for Una or Julian. It was just that sort of inappropriate gesture which we all make from time to time and cringe over cruelly once behind closed doors. Mr. Hawthorne closed his own door and, still holding the handle, leaned back against it, his eyes tight shut.

Downstairs Herman was rather pampered, being waited on by both Sophia and the children, but once he had all that he needed in front of him the children were instructed to find something to play with.

"It's rude to stare at people eating."

"Why is it rude?"

Sophia, ignoring Julian's predictable question, suggested Una find her blackboard and do some drawing.

"Mama, why isn't breakfast supper?"

Sophia, clearing the main breakfast serving, answered, "Why isn't a cup a plate?"

"Because it's a teapot." Julian grinned proudly at Herman and then, giggling, crashed down onto his knees to see what Una was drawing.

"Is it a cow?"

"No, it's a horse. I'll just kick this leg out a little more."

Julian keeled over, pretending to be floored by a hoof. "And this one," he said, sitting up again.

"Julian! Mama, he's smudged my picture!"

"It kicked me."

"Don't be so silly."

Sophia seemed out of hearing and Herman intervened.

"What are you both going to be when you grow up?"

The children took up the enquiry with enthusiasm.

Julian first. "I'm going to grow and grow, and grow and grow, and grow and grow, into *two* men!"

"Ah, but which one will be Julian?" Herman thought it an interesting notion. One worthy of the brandy bottle.

"Both. One would be my servant and do as I said."

Herman smiled. "Does that other one sound like Julian, Una?"

But she was ready with her own reply. "I shall be like Mama but marry someone rich and I shall make children's books like Cara."

"Like Mrs. Tappan."

"Yes."

"Yuk!"

"You like the book, Julian."

"Yuk!"

"He used to like the book. He's just being silly. Let me show it to you."

While his sister was away Julian confided, "They're horrid." What, or whom, he meant by "they" Herman could not enquire, for Una promptly returned with the book. He finished a piece of toast and wiped his hands on his handkerchief, then turned sideways on the chair to take the volume from her.

There was a dedication in the front and Herman fended off Una's impatient fingers.

"It doesn't start there. That's just scribble. Look. Over here."

Herman had to let go of the title page lest Una tear it in her determination to move on to the proper starting of the text. But he had not read much past the first three words when Sophia walked into the room and told Una to take the book away from the table.

"It might get marked, and I'm sure Mr. Melville would prefer to look at it *after* breakfast. Papa would be upset if it was to get marked."

"He wouldn't. I know Papa very well and I'm sure he wouldn't mind in the slightest." Una said this in her most haughty tones, hugging the book to her chest and apparently refusing to put it away.

"More coffee?"

Herman said that he wouldn't, and that what he would do was go to his room to prepare for a walk into town.

"Then you won't be able to look at the book."

"Una, put the book away now, there's a good girl."

Breakfast, little though it had been, settled uneasily on Herman's stomach, and he was in no mood to help Mrs. Hawthorne humour Una out of her stubbornness. He made for the stair with the determined madame still insisting that Papa wouldn't have minded marmalade marks on every single page. Treading past Nathaniel's closed study door, and then sitting on the edge of the bed to put on his boots, Herman couldn't help thinking how strange it was that, at just that moment, the older author might be writing a sentence which he, Herman, would read in the leaves of the next successful Romance, when it was published in due course. It was a thought that made him angry with his own stalled start on the whaling book. He had arrived back from London in February, had been diverted by the publication of *Whitejacket* in March, but had then spent three good months reading and writing preliminary chapters for the next sea epic. But the summer had drydocked the effects of that first sweat – the exodus to Pittsfield, the reading of Hawthorne's stories, their first encounter, negotiations for the Brewster place, and now these indulgent days at Lenox failing to make any real and satisfying contact with the composed and penetrating moral eye of the man, had dislocated him almost entirely from the initial inspiration. "Almost". for he was not the man to waste labour; and a use would surely be found for those early, unemblematic chapters.

He tied the laces of his boots with a businesslike rapidity, gathered his things, and left the house with no effort to quieten his step on the landing or the stair. In his study, Nathaniel heard the flamboyant departure of his guest and bit down hard on the top of his pen.

* * *

The introductory preamble to *The Scarlet Letter*, that unimpeachable piece of prose "The Custom House", had severely undermined the main tenet of Mr. Hawthorne's fictive craft. The story itself had certainly followed the dictates of the Romance, as Mr. Hawthorne understood them, rather than what passed in those days for the realistic Novel; but, preceded as it was, by such an authoritative and worldly-wise frontispiece, the atmospherical medium of the story had been somehow authenticated. (Therein of course lies its power. To read *The Scarlet Letter* without first reading "The Custom House" must be a wholly different and diminished experience.)

Nathaniel wrote down the phrase, "Keep undeviatingly within my immunities". It was a phrase he was to use again in the New Year, when composing the short Preface for the completed *House Of Seven Gables*, a Preface just two pages in length, and totally devoid of circumstantial reference. The words, as he wrote them now, formed a prospective commandment to keep a surer control over the balance of shadow and light in this book. The *Letter* had been too dark a tale. It had made his wife weep. The new book should have the power to move, but with a mellower influence.

The memory of an aunt's seven-gabled house, brought back to him by the recent exchange of letters with Connolly the Cardinal, and the vague picture of an elderly female character much reduced in circumstance combined with that conversational reference of two or three evenings ago to produce the following paragraph:

> In this republican country, amid the fluctuating waves of our social life, somebody is always at the drowning point. The tragedy is enacted with as continual a repetition as that of a popular drama on a holiday; and, nevertheless, is felt as deeply, perhaps, as when an hereditary noble sinks below his order. More deeply; since, with us, rank is the grosser substance of wealth and a splendid establishment, and has no spiritual existence after the death of these, but dies hopelessly along with them.

Nathaniel put down his pen and read the lines back to himself.

He went to the window and saw Mr. Melville riding off towards the village. He had made a start, though the paragraph was not quite the stuff of which opening chapters were made. As he had done so many times in the past he returned to his desk and sat quite still, letting his compositional eye relocate the house. Before the reconstruction was complete he picked up his pen and wrote: "Halfway down a bystreet of one of our New England towns there stands a rusty wooden house . . ." The Romance had begun and, uncharacteristically, he continued working into the afternoon, stopping for a brief lunch with Sophia. Mr. Melville had not returned and Nathaniel, going back to his room, hugged Sophia and said, simply, "I have started something new. I think I'll do a little more."

He managed that day to compose the greater part of the opening chapter, tracing the history of the old Pyncheon family and the curse that had pursued them generation by generation, since the first Colonel Pyncheon had executed one Matthew Maule for witchcraft and thereby taken possession of the martyred man's wooden dwelling, on which site the grand seven-gabled mansion had been built. He already knew that one of the main characters would be an old woman named Hepzibah, latest descendant of the Colonel to occupy the dwelling. She would be living there in very reduced circumstances and would be observed in the first scene of the narrative proper having to resort to the opening up of a petty shop in the front gable, under the impending brow of the second storey.

In just this way did the narrative speed ahead of the writing so that in four or five days time, when Mr. Hawthorne had done little more than perfect the opening chapter, and write the much shorter second one, introducing Miss Hepzibah and her Little Shop-window, he had the entire course of the story charted out in his mind, right up to, and most certainly, the happy ending, but not, of course, the full and convoluted explanation of Clifford's innocence, which could only be determined by the less predictable exigencies of created plot.

Herman turned up in the middle of the afternoon. The day was very warm and the doors of the cottage were open. Una was in the garden helping the Hawthornes' servant take down some washing that was already dry. Julian could be seen running hither and thither in the orchard, pouncing at imaginary targets. Sophia was indoors sewing some gold beading round the perimeter of a cushion. She put down her needle when Mr. Melville came in and asked him if he had eaten lunch. Herman said that he had ridden on to Stockbridge and had taken a little refreshment there.

"Did you see Julian outside?"

"Yes, he's dashing about in the orchard."

Sophia took a disapproving inhalation of breath. "I've warned him about the wasps. I think I shall get out the ointment in readiness."

She moved a dining chair over to a tall dresser and made to step onto the seat, but Herman intervened.

"Is it on the top shelf? Let me."

Sophia directed him to the box of medicaments and thanked him for his help.

"My husband is still at work. Most unusually, I might add. It must be the influence of a fellow-author in the house. Perhaps you can prolong your stay," she added with a smile.

"No, not this time, though I hope my visits may become fairly regular. You see, on my return to Pittsfield I shall be making a bid for a small farm on the edge of the Broadhall estate. It is time Elizabeth and I moved out of New York."

"That is good. Nathaniel is not a great mixer, but I think he does like to feel a part of a community. That is why we were so happy in Concord, and why at first he was rather frightened of moving out here, though these summer weeks ought to have cured him of those fears. You have just the one child, I think you said."

"Yes; though my mother and sister will be moving out with us."

Again Mrs. Hawthorne used an inhalation of breath to indicate a reaction, but this time with an open, rounded mouth, betokening astonishment. When Herman looked at her perplexed, she laughed and explained, "It is only that such a plan would be inconceivable for Nathaniel and me."

"Well, you do have more children."

"Oh, it isn't that. Not a bit of it. Mrs. Hawthorne lived with us while she was dying but it couldn't possibly have worked while she was fit. And, as for Nathaniel's sisters, well I fear their early relationship with him, for the first thirty years or more of his life, was such that they could never live in close proximity with him as a married man. And as for my own kith and kin, well, Elizabeth – you met her briefly the other week – has the type of personality which Nathaniel can only stomach for twenty minutes at a time, and my parents, though dear enough as they are, could never board with us without wholly altering the family state. Such is Mr. Hawthorne's firm and unflinching view."

"As in all things pertaining to human behaviour your husband is correct. But what am I to do, with my father and older brother dead and gone?"

The despairing tone of this plea took Sophia by surprise. She had not envisaged this bearded adventurer as a victim of domestic circumstance.

"No, you have no alternative," she quickly reassured him, and then, with the organising instincts of a hostess, she changed the subject and asked if there was anything he would like to do while waiting for her husband to finish.

"Oh, I'll continue talking to you, if you'll permit, but do get back to your cushion."

Sophia blushed. She was into her fourth decade of life and could no longer be described as a beauty. Indeed, one later visitor to Lenox complained that her appearance was unashamedly dowdy. But the perpetrator of this rebuke was Ellery Channing, a character who had little sympathy for the domestic situation. Nevertheless it cannot be doubted that the artifices of glamour with which so many forty-year-old women successfully prolong their good looks in our own age were not available to the ordinary American woman of the 1850s. Yes, time and the cares of motherhood had certainly brought Sophia unequivocally to the plainness of her middle years, but Herman, who, unlike Nathaniel, had never had a great eye for visual charms, responded to the freshness of her personality, which seemed to have held on to a certain core of the younger Sophia Peabody much more successfully than Elizabeth, ten years her junior, had retained the vestiges of Miss Elizabeth Shaw.

Mrs. Peters came through the house, her laundry basket heaped with washing.

"Una is playing with the young gentleman now, ma'am."

"Young gentleman indeed!"

Sophia quickly closed up her sewing case and excused herself to Herman, explaining that she must help Mrs. Peters sort through the washing. He went outside, to stalk Una and Julian.

*   *   *

The little orchard appeared deserted. He stood for a moment

293

between the two trees which, as best he could remember, he and Mr. Hawthorne had occupied the previous night, but the chance for reflection was cut short by the sound of voices from beyond the hedgerow. Crouching down, he darted in and out of the apple trees to the corner of the orchard. The hedge was thickest here and gave him the cover to ascertain the exact position of the voices. They were quiet now. Perhaps the children had been stalking *him*; but no, there was Una's voice urging Julian to follow her, and the scampering of feet away from the hedge.

Herman moved forward to a spot where the roots of the hedge were spaced widely enough to see through. He lay flat and put his face to the opening. The two children had run across a stretch of grass and were now bent together, whispering and giggling in turn. It was clear that Herman was no part of their adventure for they were using a shrub as cover from some other party.

Looking along the hedge, Herman realised that the children must have wriggled through one such hole as this, for the orchard seemed enclosed on three complete sides. He strode up and down on his haunches, picking at last on the largest opening, and then waited for the children to make their next move. It was soon enough coming. They dashed round one side of the shrub and were out of sight. Herman lost no time in following them but made a clumsy job of getting through the hedge and had to waste precious seconds disengaging a pocket on his jacket that had become snagged. He sped to the shrub and began to edge round it, ready to halt as soon as he had again sighted the children.

They had already gone some distance, flitting from one choice of cover to the next, across land which was obviously part of the Highwood domain. They were heading for what appeared to be a summer house, except that it was somewhat far off from the main house, only the roof of which was visible, above a dense copse of pines. Herman began to follow. It was not a difficult operation, for they never looked behind them, since they had no reason for believing that they were being followed; nevertheless there was sufficient excitement in the pursuit for Herman to thoroughly lose himself in the game, and just as the children were guilty of an over-confident sense of security, the same was true of Herman, for, unknown to him, this piece of land was clearly visible from the Hawthornes' bedroom, and Sophia, busy putting clean clothes away, often kept an eye on her children's wanderings from this elevated watchtower.

The children's progress slowed down as they approached the summer house. Behind the last opportunity for shelter Una appeared to be reciting an eeny-meeny-miny-mo rhyme, pointing her finger back and forth at Julian and herself. Her brother was dissatisfied with the outcome. He pushed her in the chest and she fell backwards. Scared that he had given their position away he grabbed her arm and pulled her upright again. She repeated the rhyme. The result must have been the same for she shook her head and made an "Oh" shape with her mouth, as if to say, she didn't mind, Julian could do it.

He began to venture forth, towards the square wooden construction, but displayed a nervous hesitancy now that he was on his own. He kept stalling and looking back towards Una, who agitatedly waved him on with sweeping outward movements of her palms. Still he dithered, and seemed about to turn back. Una jumped up and down. The urging gestures with her hands became frantic. Her feet began to stamp. At last she made a break for it herself and pushed her brother to the side of the hut. They stood with their backs to the wooden beams, for the first time looking in Herman's direction, but he had foreseen such a turn and had taken cover. Now Una took charge and led the surreptitious creeping round to the side of the summerhouse.

The children were soon out of sight and Herman had little alternative but to be bold and head for the house himself, trusting that he would make the rear wall before they had completed their reconnoitre and appeared round the other side. He sprinted as hard as he could, twisting one foot slightly on a fallen pine cone. Arriving at the hut he took care to lighten his step and avoid breaking his approach by colliding directly with the wall. He heard the children talking. It was clear that the summerhouse was unoccupied.

"Shall we go to the house and find her?"

"No! Mr. Tappan might be there."

"I thought he'd gone away."

"He might be back."

"Doh, all that trouble!"

"We can frighten her another day. Come on."

With a sense of panic Herman realised that he could not predict from which side of the summerhouse the children would appear. Having concealed his watchfulness for so long it would be deeply embarrassing to have it discovered now. He reacted instinctively and flattened himself on the ground. Fortunately it was a stilted construction and he was able to roll completely out of sight underneath the floorboards. He watched the children walk disconsolately away. He heard Julian complaining that his arm hurt where Una had gripped it to yank him towards the hut. It was evident that the boy would become tearful before they reached the Red House and Herman felt that he should, after all, declare himself and create a new diversion for the return journey. But something bright caught his eye on the other side of the hut. Mrs. Tappan – or so he supposed, from the mere fact of it being a woman's dress – was approaching. The children had just missed her. Herman felt an uncomfortable swelling in his throat. Bands of light penetrated the floor of the hut, through quite substantial gaps between the boards. He put his hand up to one such gap. It was just wide enough for his middle finger to pass through. His face became suffused in sweat. If Mrs. Tappan were to enter the summerhouse, as she plainly intended doing, it would be quite improper for him to remain in hiding. But too sudden a movement under the boards might be noticed. He should go just as she stepped up to the door, and then make his flight behind the safety of the un-windowed rear wall.

She came nearer. There were two steps up to the door of the hut. She stepped on the first. He should go. But her entrance was too swift, his hesitation too paralytic.

Herman turned his head to one side. Caroline's wide skirts occluded several bars of light. The summerhouse must have been newly built for there was still a good covering of grass beneath it. Herman stared at the darkened stems, conscious of the surrounding brilliance. Caroline settled in one position but her little fidgetings were amplified by the hollow floor. A clothes-scent, used in place of regular cleaning, seemed so strong that Herman fancied its very powder was falling through the boards and getting into his nostrils. He crooked his forefinger and pressed it hard against his nose until he was aware of pain.

He had made up his mind to make a run for it, and was slowly shifting his knees to initiate the wriggling motion, when Caroline began humming. It was a mere accompaniment to thought (she was starting to compose a letter) and held no particular melody, but it beguiled Herman into postponing his escape. He let the full weight of his head rest upon the ground, the cool roughness against his cheek a counterpoint to the warm mesmeric tones from

296

above. Whether he had lost consciousness or not he could not be certain, but he suddenly became aware that the humming had stopped. In a fit of panic he felt convinced that his presence had been discovered and that Caroline was peering beneath the boards, or had actually left the summerhouse and was on her knees outside looking beneath the floor. He screwed his eyes closed, in a childish attempt not to be seen, but his ears gradually picked out a rhythmic scratching sound which suggested that Caroline was not in fact staring accusingly at him, but preoccupied with her own affairs. As soon as he realised this he scrambled out from beneath the hut, in a much greater rush and with more noise than originally intended, and ran for cover.

It was just as well that he did not turn an ankle on a fallen pine cone this time for no sooner was he concealed behind the nearest bush than Mrs. Tappan appeared on the right-hand side of the hut, calling, "Una, Ju-li-an". She used a wad of writing paper to shield her eyes while they scanned the vicinity.

Herman made shambling and stumbling progress back to the Red House, feeling for all his life like an army deserter fleeing from a skirmish, his mind as discomposed as his appearance and gait. Nor was it a subjective impression, for Sophia said as soon as she saw him, "Why, Mr. Melville! Have you been in an affray? Your pocket hangs loose!"

Nathaniel was standing with his wife, just outside the back doorway, enjoying the late afternoon sun, and this fact was sufficient to ensure that Herman made a clear-minded reply.

"I saw Una and Julian beyond the orchard and went after them. The little mites led me a merry scrape."

Mr. Hawthorne chuckled. "Ah, they've been giggling over some such secret while eating their tea." And then, calling to the children, he added, "Papa will want to see those plates clean in a moment."

"I thought they'd been annoying Caroline again. Not playing hares and hounds." Sophia examined Herman's torn pocket. "I'll be able to mend that for you tonight; if we send you back to Mrs. Melville in that state my husband's gentle reputation will suffer radical amendment!"

"My mother isn't in Berkshire with me."

This unconsidered response set the seal on the final evening of Herman's stay in Lenox. The two men reverted to a cautious handling of one another, and no advance was made on the

297

ontological discussion begun in the orchard the previous night.

*   *   *

Herman left the Red House immediately after breakfast the next day, with his pocket mended and with Una and Julian taking a short ride on his buggy. He let them down about two hundred yards from the cottage, telling them to watch out for the monster who lived in the wooden hut. Giggling, they shouted out that it wasn't a monster, it was a princess, a genie, a white witch, a fairy godmother, a . . . Their words became inaudible against the wind and the trotting of his horse's hooves.

He arrived back at Broadhall to discover that Malcolm had developed a mysterious lameness and that Elizabeth was beside herself with worry. The boy seemed quite unperturbed by the incapacity and this blasé state only increased his mother's concern.

"Did he do anything before you left? Fall, or something? There couldn't have been any poisonous plants amongst the cut grass you let him play with?"

Herman had to control his fury at being blamed in this way. He knew that his real crime had not been any negligence with the boy, but going away to stay with the Hawthornes against Elizabeth's wishes. Yet he also knew it would be pointless to argue this out with her, especially since he had just seven days to win her over in favour of the Brewster place.

He put Malcolm on his shoulders, and piggy-backed him around for the rest of the morning. After lunch, while the boy was asleep, he began to explain the proposals to Lizzie.

"Have you heard from your father?"

"Yes; they're arriving in the middle of the week. I don't know what they think is the matter. They probably imagine I've had a miscarriage or something."

"No!" Elizabeth's suggestion shocked Herman. "You did hint to your father that it was something to do with money, didn't you? Anyway, listen, you know the whole of this estate is up for sale, to the Morewoods, well there's a little farm on the eastern edge, with a house big enough for us all, though eventually we can build . . ."

"Big enough for your mother and your sisters."

"Well, I have to provide a home for them too, Lizzie. You know that."

298

"Can't they stay in New York?"

"Not really. Allan's baby is due any day, and that won't be the last, will it? Then he'll be needing more office space as his practice expands."

"It would seem that this is sewn up. All you need, I suppose, is for my father to come along and buy it for you."

"I have so many books out now, we ought to be able to pay it back." He reached out and held her upper arms. "I like it here. This is where we're meant to settle. We'll ride out together tomorrow afternoon. And Dr. Holmes is only just down the road. If Malcolm is still limping we can consult with him."

"On a Sunday?"

"The doctor is a rationalist."

"Poor man."

Herman roared aloud, still squeezing his wife's arms. "And you, my dear, are a humorist."

Elizabeth looked at him with a coquettishness which came into her eyes too infrequently. She tried to keep her face straight and stern, but finally a smile beamed through and she put her arms, almost resignedly, round Herman's neck.

"I do love you, Herman. Please forgive me. It is the summer heat makes me sour."

*　　*　　*

Malcolm's leg seemed much better the next day and they left him at Broadhall. The buggy ride alone out to the Brewster place reminded Elizabeth of that earlier ride when she had been on the threshold of her present life. The memory was poignant but it did not make her despondent, and when she saw the Brewster farm it was as if the four intervening years had been a dream rather than reality and here she was once again the betrothed maiden being shown round the bridegroom's estate. True, the place was a bit run down; especially the outbuildings. But the sheer expanse of the grounds excited her, a town girl, more than anything. This was fine. It would surely be possible to keep a certain distance from Mrs. Melville Senior here.

"Would it all be ours?"

"Yes. We'll walk right round the boundary lines if you like. I thought eventually we could build on the side of that hill up there. But the house is big enough at present, don't you think? Brewster

299

is away till next weekend. That's when the deal must go through. Fifteen hundred dollars is the price, though we'll need a fair bit more to spend on the place. Do you think the Judge'll approve?''

Elizabeth stood looking wonderingly at the farm, without replying. Eventually she said, "If I say so, yes.''

The Shaws arrived in Berkshire on Tuesday, but stayed with acquaintances of Lemuel in Lenox. Elizabeth was given the job of broaching the subject of the purpose for their visit and Herman dealt with the details.

The Judge was happy with the proposal in principle and offered to advance them three thousand dollars. His wife was noticeably less comfortable about it all and spent some considerable time discussing with Elizabeth the disadvantages of living in the country. Had she considered Malcolm's education? Did she realise he might have to move away from home to attend a good school? What about entertainment? There were no theatres in the country and, except in the summer, no parties. Did she realise how much snow fell in this region? And in the summer might not the trees exacerbate her hayfever? To be fair, Elizabeth *had* given insufficient thought to these matters and Mrs. Shaw was perhaps right to bring them to her attention. But again one wonders whether she may also have been jealous of her husband's bountiful support of Elizabeth, as compared with the less liberal degree of favours bestowed upon her own two sons.

Elizabeth's enthusiasm for the Pittsfield farm couldn't be deflected. Most of the advantages of living in the city were negated by aspects of Herman's temperament, and she was now beginning to accept that she would have to live with these. Anyway, she hoped that it would always be possible to visit Boston, either with Herman or without.

The sale was finalised on September 14th, Herman having given the Judge a promissory note for the three thousand dollars, just as he had done for the two thousand advanced for the purchase of the New York house. Lemuel Shaw was to make judicious use of these two notes in ten years time, before Herman embarked on his Eastern tour.

"Arrowhead'' is designated a Registered National Historic Landmark. Between June 1st and October 31st it is open to the public from 10 a.m. until 4.30 p.m., except on Sundays when it closes at 3.30 p.m. It is open in the winter by private appointment. The local historical society maintains it as a "national literary shrine – the author's study, his piazza, the original fireplace from Melville's short story *I And My Chimney*, and the newly restored barn in which Melville and Hawthorne spent hours discussing their writings, are all open to visitors." Adults 2.00 dollars – Senior Citizens 1.50 dollars – Students 1.00 dollar. The admission charges include access to a Gift Shop, a Nature Trail and a Wild Flower garden. If there is indeed gin in Heaven it must be sorely tempting to chuck measure after measure of it into the faces of a public who spurned him when he was actually living, and the majority of whom, even now, have only a passing knowledge of his books.

Helen came out from New York the following week, sent ahead by Maria to ensure that Herman was not expecting them to move into a haybarn. By September 20th all the Melvilles were back in town, preparing for the disestablishment of the Fourth Avenue home. Allan and Sophia's second child had been born on the fifteenth so that due regard had to be paid to the young infant and the convalescent mother.

Herman's announcement of his removal surprised the small circle of his literary friends, particularly the Duyckincks, who had long supposed that his reliance upon libraries would hold him in the city. Little reference is made to Allan's reaction, but one supposes that he did rather well out of it, and was therefore disposed to take the suddenness of it in good heart.

The Brewster farmhouse being ready to move into, Herman and the family spent only a week in New York packing up and otherwise preparing for their retirement to the country. By the time they arrived back in Pittsfield, September had turned to October and the leaves of the maples had turned red. Herman worked single-handed throughout the autumnal month at minor rehabilitations of the farm's outer fabric and grounds, his intention being to make it more of an ornamental place than a working farm. He helped indoors only when his mother, sisters and wife required assistance with the lifting of a bedstead or a bureau. It was one of those intensive, moving-in onslaughts when each person discovers a degree of energy and perseverance which buoys them up. The mood was good. The weather was dry. The scenery changed imperceptibly from russet to brown.

* * *

On October 1st Mr. Hawthorne wrote to his friend Bridge that he was already deeply into the book which he had begun halfway through Melville's visit in the first week of September. Yet on the same day he wrote to James T. Fields, his publisher, warning him that the new book would not be ready until some time beyond November. "I am never good for anything in the literary way till after the first autumnal frost."

The truth is that Mr. Melville's presence had prompted him to start the book a little before the time of natural readiness. He was still managing to work diligently, but not so rapidly as he had hoped. He was finding that the book required more care and thought than *The Scarlet Letter* and that he had to wait oftener for the mood. In the *Letter* he had had only to get the right pitch and then go on interminably. He was trying in this one to achieve the minute finish of a Dutch painting and was conscious that the writing often careered on the utmost verge of a precipitous absurdity. "You won't get it out before January," he told Fields in his next letter.

"So wholesome is effort! So miraculous the strength that we do not know of!" Mr. Hawthorne wrote in his manuscript, just as Mr. Melville was hammering away at his outbuildings, turning his thumb black and blue. "As a general rule," Nathaniel put in, in relation to Hepzibah's first cent-shop transaction, "Providence seldom vouchsafes to mortals any more than just that degree of encouragement which suffices to keep them at a reasonably full exertion of their powers." There are sentences enough like this in the book – wonderful extrapolations of perennial law, in which even the earliest stories had abounded. (This is what must have so amazed Herman as he calculated at what age each of the *Twice Told Tales* had been written – it was not the wisdom of fifty-year-old experience but an innate gift of clairvoyance.) And yet alongside these general strokes one can see the difficulty which Mr. Hawthorne was having with his new material, as he tried to make his treatment of Hepzibah both particular and emblematic: The Sallow Spinster's Scowl, Chiselled in Marble, Moulded in Mud.

The onset of harsh weather also impeded his progress, preventing, as it did for the first time since their arrival in the early summer, the children from playing out of doors in any continuous way; they were still able to snatch the odd hour between squalls, and they went on organised walks with their mother, but they had to be got up in winter coats and their boots had to be changed when coming back indoors; and the necessity of suddenly imposing an indoor-discipline on the two of them, who for months had run around in the open air shrieking at the tops of their voices and who, even when indoors, had forgotten about Keeping Quiet for Father, since he had not been working in any serious way at that time, the difficulty of this sudden imposition was very taxing on Sophia and she did at last begin to berate the cramped dimensions of her new home.

Her first objective was to prevent sudden incursions into the realm of Mr. Hawthorne's study. One morning, after the children had been forced indoors by rain, they dashed away from her while she was scraping mud from their boots and made for the stairs.

The door burst open and Nathaniel turned round. Julian hurtled forward, his hands clutching a jagged bundle of dripping red maple leaves.

"Farver! Farver!" was all his gleeful little mouth could find to say.

Una, standing back in the doorway, through a consciousness that she was perhaps old enough to know better than to burst in on "Farver" like this, added, gigglingly, "He wanted to bring you a handful of fire." (The word "fire" pronounced with eyes wide and mouth exaggeratedly open, as if it were a word forbidden to young lips).

"Mmm. Fi-yah," Julian added more matter-of-factly, and tipped the incendiary bundle onto the corner of his father's desk, one or two of the leaves falling onto the floor in the course of a manoeuvre made clumsy by the sudden arrival of Sophia, the muddy boot-knife still in her hand.

"And will you give me at least three reasons for being here" she said, with much earnestness.

Nathaniel wagged a finger at her. "Not too prospective, divinest. Two reasons will suffice for this pair."

Sophia had missed a period in September, and they were awaiting confirmation of conception. She blushed and scurried the children out of the room.

More of the leaves fell from the corner of his desk in the draught created by the closing of his door. There was a glen between their house and the lake, through which wound a little brook, with pools, and tiny waterfalls over the great roots of trees. The glen was deep and narrow, and filled with trees; so that, in summer, it was all a dense shadow of obscurity. Now, the foliage of the trees being almost entirely a golden yellow, instead of being full of shadow, the glen was absolutely full of sunshine, and its depths were more brilliant than the open plain or the mountaintops.

Distracted from his struggle with Hepzibah, Nathaniel took his notebook and wrote a paragraph about the glen. It was Wednesday October 16th 1850. By the end of the month, the trees were bare and sleet had fallen on the Red House roof.

But, as if in compliance with the analysis sent to Fields, the first winter frosts induced a more settled momentum in the composition of the book. For one thing, Una and Julian had grown more resigned to staying indoors, playing in front of the "breath of the stove", as Julian called the vapour that vibrated about it when hot. For another, in chapter five of the *Seven Gables* Nathaniel introduced the redemptive character of Phoebe, conceived, in large part, as a tribute to Sophia. Phoebe had been a name of endearment he had used for his wife in many of their engagement letters and he made a point of stressing at the outset a characteristic which Sophia herself had in high degree – the homely witchcraft which enabled both the real and the fictional characters to transform the rudest of dwellings into comfortable habitableness by the gift of practical management.

Phoebe's entry into the house and her taking over some of the practical affairs of the shop lead easily into the contrasting of new Plebeianism and old Gentility which is part of Hawthorne's republican theme. His ridiculing of the gentrified life of a lady is scrupulously pitched:

> To find the born and educated lady, we need look no farther than Hepzibah, our forlorn old maid, in her rustling and rusty silks, with her deeply cherished and ridiculous consciousness of long descent, her shadowy claims to princely territory, and, in the way of accomplishment, her recollections, it may be, of having formerly thrummed on a harpsichord, and walked a minuet, and worked on an antique tapestry stitch on her sampler.

*   *   *

In November Mr. Melville also began to settle into a routine that allowed him to get back to his *Whale*. Let us join up with him one

304

morning in the latter half of the month. Lizzie has left Pittsfield a day or two since, taking Malcolm to Boston for Thanksgiving. Since they did not return to Arrowhead until the New Year it would not be unfair to suppose that Elizabeth had been disappointed in her earlier hopes of a freer, more independent family life with Herman and her son. Even here, Maria and the sisters are Queen and Princesses of the establishment. The sisters display consideration for Elizabeth's position it is true, especially Helen, but there is more than a touch of stooping sufferance in their graciousness. It would be easy to say that Elizabeth's retreat to Boston, no more than six weeks after moving to Berkshire, betrayed a weakness of character, a rather cowardly unwillingness to stay and brazen it out with the other women; but such a judgement does not take into account either the things we *do* know about Elizabeth, or the things that we do *not* know about the particular circumstances of this time.

We *do* know that Elizabeth was a Christian who took a serious view of her faith. Resigning herself to the more wilful influence of Herman's mother was, therefore, a mark of non-resistance which she felt incumbent upon her. We *do* know that she had probably not been to Boston since the previous winter, the whole of the summer vacation having been spent at Robert's farm. We *do* know that Arrowhead had been purchased largely with her father's money and she would therefore be desirous for him to get as much grandfatherly pleasure out of Malcolm as possible.

Of the petty maladies, bodily or spiritual, which prompted her departure and delayed her return, we shall not conjecture.

We were about to join Mr. Melville as he pulled on his daytime clothes, one typical morning at this time.

It is eight, or thereabouts. He walks, in thin socks, to the back door of the house, and there pulls on his outdoor boots. Putting a heavy woollen cape round his shoulders, for the chill of winter, even at this relatively unSpartan hour, blows determinedly from the slopes of Graylock, he lifts the latch and walks out to the barn. His horse whinnies and knocks against the side boards of its pen.

"Agh, it goes to my heart to give you a cold breakfast in this weather, but it can't be helped. And you seem well enough on it." He pats the beast between the ears as it stoops to its replenished trough, and then pays a visit to his cow and cuts up a pumpkin or two for her. He stays and watches her eat, thinking how mildly and with what sanctity she moves her jaws.

He takes two empty buckets back to the house and sits down to his own breakfast, prepared by Augusta.

"It seems cruel that we expect the animals to eat cold raw food this weather," he observes.

"Just imagine! Recipe books for the farmyard."

Herman's sisters enjoy themselves with the train of thought set off by his remark and he leaves them concocting the ingredients for Friesian Fricassee, Pigsty Pie and other girlishly inspired recipes.

He goes to his workroom and lights his fire made, in Lizzie's absence, by one or other of his sisters. Then he moves to his table, spreads out his manuscripts, takes one business squint at them, and falls to with a will, or so he puts it in a letter to Evert Duyckinck.

It is fairly easy to ascertain, from the books themselves, his manner of working up to this time. Each chapter (they can be as short as one page in length) represents a burst of effort. He sits in front of his source books: his naval histories, his travel stories, his mythological dictionary, his Bayles, and beckons a discursive propulsion to the narrative. The book thrusts forward in staccato jumps. There is no grand design.

In *Redburn* he had begun to depart from this method. Working in a freer style, with more familiar material, and keeping to a tight deadline, he had achieved, in the opinion of the Penguin English Library jacket, "a new spare and compelling idiom, a new mastery of his material". The chapters are a little longer; they follow smoothly one from the other. The story, of an American sailor-boy's first voyage across the Atlantic, has its own momentum.

Moby Dick begins in similar vein. The arrival of Ishmael in New Bedford, his encounter with Queequeg at the Spouter Inn, the sermon of Father Mapple, the passage out to Nantucket and the signing aboard the *Pequod* are as vivid a hundred pages of fiction as you can find in any nineteenth-century writer, American or English, Dickens included.

But we have it on Mr. Melville's own authority that he was profoundly unhappy with *Redburn*. It was not the book he wanted to write. It had been a commercial enterprise, and he had vowed this summer, since making the vivid start on *Moby Dick*, that dollars could be damned, he would write as he wanted. And so when he turned again, in this autumn of 1850, to the *Whale* material, it was with a determination to make it more than just another yarn of the seas.

What he wanted to achieve was the sort of moral authority he had found in Hawthorne's work, and a manner of displaying the deep thinking he had come across in the classical and modern writers of his recent reading.

And so once more the source materials are spread before him. Scholars and academics have their own theories I suppose, stemming from much enjoyable detective work. Look at the fun Merton Sealts and Charles Olson had tracking down books that had belonged to Melville's library. But the evidence of the novel itself is difficult to gainsay. Chapter twenty-two ends with the sentence, "We gave three heavy-hearted cheers, and blindly plunged like fate into the lone Atlantic."

Herman leafs through those twenty-two launching-out chapters. He is little enough satisfied with them, but at least they set the thing in motion. If he had gone beyond this in his first New York effort, writing actual sea-going chapters, I believe he scrapped them. He touches the calluses on his hands, rubbing the ball of one thumb across the hardened areas. He had found the physical labour on the farm easeful to the mind; a glimpse of an ordinary thoughtless existence. Thinking thus, he catches up the papers of chapter three and re-reads a paragraph describing a mariner just landed at New Bedford. It was the brawny, barrel-chested Bulkington, introduced into the narrative as the result of one of those witless whims familiar to all writers. But Melville sees a part for this Bulkington, in the relaunching of the epic.

Thinking of his own brief respite from the cares of authorship and the likely attempts of his family to persuade him to take up a more congenial occupation, perhaps to make a go of the farm, he identifies with this exile from the mountainsides of Virginia, who, just landed from a four years' voyage, so promptly re-enlists. "The port would fain give succour; the port is pitiful; in the port is safety, comfort, hearthstone, supper, warm blankets, friends, all that's kind to our mortalities." Along with the *Pequod*, along with Bulkington, Herman perceives that he must quit the cosseted life of husbandry. Perverse imperatives impel him towards an intolerable truth: "that all deep, earnest thinking is but the intrepid effort of the soul to keep the open independence of her sea; while the wildest winds of heaven and earth conspire to cast her on the treacherous, slavish shore".

At half-past two in the afternoon he is called out of his landlessness by a prearranged knock at his door, which continues until he

307

answers it, so great is his tendency to write on for half an hour or more at a passage which has seized his fancy. Today the Bulkington piece has reached a swift crescendo and the first knock weans him effectively from the desk.

He pays a second visit to his horse and cow, and gives them their dinner, once more talking to the horse, watching the cow, and smoking a pipe the while. He has his own dinner in the middle of the afternoon and then, with his mother and sisters, rigs up the sledge, for the first snow has settled, and starts off for the village, to buy various supplies, and to see if any mail has arrived from New York or Boston. He spends the evenings in a mesmeric state in his room, now and then skimming over some large-printed book and planning any number of future works, and drinking glasses of sweet Montilla wine.

*   *   *

In the lee of Monument Mountain our other writer plies his more craven craft. It is not unkind to Mr. Melville to suggest that, after his visit to Lenox, this was partly how he saw it. Every artist, whatever the doubts which make them hesitate or rethink, must essentially believe that theirs is the truest manner of looking honestly at the world. Mr. Hawthorne had seemed afraid to encounter the spray of deep earnest thinking.

The only creatures at the Red House, beside the rabbit, were two broods of chickens. The Hawthornes had recently acquired a wooden roosting coop and positioned it at the side of the cottage, in front of the washing area. Una and Julian delighted in feeding the birds crumbs of bread and cold potatoes (especially the latter, for it gave the children ready excuse to leave the disliked vegetables on their plates) and Una had developed a peculiar call which the chickens seemed to recognise, responding to it by creeping through the pales of the coop and running to her feet.

Phoebe had been made to feed such chickens before encountering the daguerreotypist, Holgrave. Mr. Hawthorne had sped past this meeting, but dwelt longer on her first sighting of the elderly Clifford. That was in the seventh chapter entitled "The Guest", and the miniaturist pen was again at work in the succeeding chapter, in which Phoebe comes face to face with the new Judge Pyncheon, across the shop counter.

The modern reader will be inclined to think Mr. Hawthorne's

308

exacting attention to the shifts and contours, and the symbolic atmosphere of a character's countenance, a waste of effort – a vain attempt to achieve the plasticity of Fine Art. Certainly, as compared with the effortless asides on the eternal truths of human character, his descriptive writing can reach for similes as ridiculous as any overblown Virgilian. Witness:

> It [the Judge's face] was quite as striking, allowing for the difference of scale, as that betwixt a landscape under a broad sunshine and just before a thunderstorm; not that it had the passionate intensity of the latter aspect, but was cold, hard, immitigable, like a day-long cloud.

There is a sluggish centre to the book – during which this interplay of countenance and temperament is related to the main characters – which robs the novel of the pace that makes *The Scarlet Letter* so difficult to put down.

Mr. Hawthorne and Mr. Melville met again towards the end of December. Elizabeth and Malcolm were still away in Boston and already more weeks had passed since the ending of summer than Herman had intended letting go by before consolidating his acquaintanceship with the author of the *Mosses*. He set out on his sledge one day when the snow was not falling too thickly, having sent no note ahead of him, and was perfectly prepared to be turned away at the door by a protective Mrs. Hawthorne.

The hens clucked and several of them ran about on the snow, their legs sinking into it fully up to their bellies, so that the art of extricating them and making the next step was wondrous to behold. Melville stood at the fence and watched the comical commotion he had stirred up, and chuckled to think of the kind of anthropomorphic parallelism a mind such as Dr. Holmes' would make of the spectacle. The doctor was no longer in the county; nor were the Tappans. Mr. Hawthorne's little shanty, surrounded by the bare orderly trees of the orchard on one side, the bare wilderness of the glen on the other, and the Bowl not yet frozen beyond, seemed touchingly isolated.

Sophia was on her own in the house, Mr. Hawthorne having gone out for an afternoon stroll at the end of his writing session, with Una and Julian.

"Did you see them down by the Bowl? They've been gone an hour already. They're sure to be back in a minute. You will wait?"

Herman said he would and stamped the snow from his boots before properly entering the house.

He and Sophia sat down in the warm back parlour. She did not occupy herself with sewing.

"Lizzie is away in Boston for Thanksgiving. At least, she was. I mean still is. But that's why she went."

"And Malcolm?"

"Him too."

"Nathaniel and I thought of retreating to Boston as well. But then the winter set in and there's not much we can do about it now, and so much to be done here by way of sawing logs and digging paths clear."

"In the New Year you must all come over to Arrowhead. We have space enough."

"Oh, if the snows are not too deep. A few days ago, when the first really heavy ones came, Mr. Tappan offered to drive me into the village. He had come over from Boston especially to shut Highwood up for the winter. While I was in the store his horse bolted, I don't know what for, and broke up the sleigh. I felt far from civilisation. We had to hire the carriage home."

Herman was prevented from responding to this episode by childish knocking at the door.

"There they are." Sophia got up to help unclothe her two little ones. Herman followed her.

"I'm glad to find I do not interrupt you at your desk. Unless you were returning to it, that is."

Nathaniel unbuttoned his outer garments. "I think I like the winter here better than the summer. It certainly keeps the world at bay."

"Me, you mean. Forgive me for bursting . . ."

"Ah, yours is a world I don't mind letting over the lintel," Mr. Hawthorne said with more politeness than honesty.

"I feel more like a forlorn traveller flung across a tempestuous sea into a quiet harbour."

"Not so quiet, with these two home again, I promise you."

"I like the snow because, for a season, the land becomes an ocean. Wild and fathomless. An eternity of wild warbling holiday weather would ruin a man's mind."

Nathaniel answered with one of his quizzical smiles and Sophia hurried the children through to the warmth of the fire.

"I shall not stay long. I only wanted to pay you another visit before the year was out."

"Well – let's sit and take a little tea together."

Nathaniel spoke quietly to Sophia and then the two men sat in the front parlour.

"It is colder here, but the children will not giggle at us. Your move went well?"

"Oh, yes. I spent six weeks acting the landlubber, mending fences, clearing scrub, and hardly looking at a printed page. I'm back in the swim now."

"With the Leviathan I suppose."

"Yes, I'm back with my spermacetti. It is the story of a madman. Never have you contrived such a monomaniac as my Captain Ahab."

"Drawn from the life, perhaps?"

"Now who are you to ask me that?"

"Let me surprise you. The Minister with the Black Veil; an unlikely enough character you might think; but he existed; in moderated form to be sure; but the veil was there; there *was* a minister who wore a veil."

Sophia entered with a tray of tea and fruit cake.

"Your husband is pulling my leg."

"Just telling him about the Minister's veil."

"No one ever believes that story, Nathaniel."

Mr. Hawthorne shrugged, with a humorous look of resignation on his face. "Why trouble to tell the truth, if it's not to be believed."

Mrs. Hawthorne went back to the children, and Herman helped himself to a slice of cake.

"Your own book goes well?"

"Yes; better now the snow has come. I always do my best work in the winter."

They talked on in much the same way, while finishing their tea, never getting close to the intimacy-manqué of their orchard ontologicals. But they had renewed their acquaintance, which was sufficient, at least on Herman's part, to heighten their self-awareness as creative men. Mr. Melville, was, by nature, inclined to indulge in unauthorised surmisings about the thoughts going on with regard to him in the people he met; especially if he had reason to think they disliked him. His days at sea had heightened this mild paranoia, and as his sledge scudded homeward, although he had no reason to feel unliked by the Hawthornes (indeed, they were still deeply grateful for his fulsome review) he did wonder in what true regard they held his own literary talent. There is little

311

doubt that part of his motivation in buckling down to the remainder of his madman's story was an urge to prove himself to his senior neighbour.

*   *   *

The two men got on with the business of writing their books, and both made good progress, although, as with Mr. Hawthorne's rather heavy-handed attempts to emulate a Dutch master's visual touch, Mr. Melville succumbed to a convoluted and labyrinthine style to convey the craziness of Ahab:

> But as the mind does not exist unless leagued with the soul, therefore it must have been that, in Ahab's case, yielding up all his thoughts and fancies to his own supreme purpose; that purpose, by its own sheer inveteracy of will, forced itself against gods and devils, into a kind of self-assumed independent being of its own. Nay, could grimly live and burn, while the common vitality to which it was conjoined fled horror-stricken from the unbidden and unfathered birth. Therefore, the tormented spirit that glared out of bodily eyes, when what seemed Ahab rushed from his room, was for the time but a vacated thing, a formless, somnambulistic being, a ray of living light, to be sure, but without an object to colour, and therefore blankness in itself.

Such leaden complexities would be all but indigestible were they not invariably deflated by a winsome appendage, as in this case: "God help thee old man!"

His recent reading of Shakespeare had helped him learn to vary his tone, and not to write at the same pitch all the way through a book. His emulation of Shakespeare is less successful when he attempts it in the form of dramatic colloquies, such as are found in chapters thirty-nine and forty, and the continual labouring and leavening of tone quickly dissipates the distinctiveness of Ishmael's first-person narrative voice, so authoritatively established in the first hundred pages. Those one hundred sides are stamped with a storyteller's wizardry. The remaining three-quarters of the book bears the heavier seal of creative artistry.

If Melville did begin again on *Moby Dick* at chapter twenty-three, it appears that he must have written 150 pages in the space of something like six weeks, for on December 16th he was, if we make the by no means certain conclusion that he was writing honestly (within an exact twelvemonth), already two-thirds of the way through the book, and writing chapter eighty-five, in which he declares the time is, as he writes, fifteen and a quarter minutes past one o'clock on the sixteenth day of December 1851 (1850). The brackets are Jay Leyda's, whose Log entry for this day 1850 has required me to explain the apparently prodigious progress. Firstly, on analysis, it isn't that astounding. Six weeks is forty-two days and 150 divided by 42 equals 3.57 (by my son's calculator), and three and a half pages a day is *not* fantastic progress for a writer of Herman Melville's free-blowing facility, working regularly from breakfast till 2.30 p.m., especially considering that several of the intervening chapters are made up of loosely précised source material concerning "Huzza, Algerine and Mealy Mouthed Porpoises" etc. Secondly, I don't accept Mr. Leyda's simplistic conveyance of dates. It seems much more likely to me that Melville wrote this chapter in January, or even February 1851, but altered the *month* in manuscript to make it more commensurate with an anticipated publication date. He was seeking to give his contemporary readers a buzz of immediacy.

Nevertheless, he must, by the turn of the year, have been somewhere around the halfway stage. The chapter strangely and hauntingly entitled "The Hyena" comes just before this point, and I place its composition at the end of 1850.

Lizzie is still away in Boston. It is the season of the Nativity. Mr. Melville is made conscious of a certain absurdity in his position and, feeding his horse and cow one afternoon, he delays returning to the house for his own dinner to smoke more than one bowlful of his pipe. He meditates upon his mood, which is unlike any that has come over him before. Holding the pipe in his hand and allowing the bowl to warm the fleshy part beneath his thumb, he pushes his top lip up and inhales the aroma of tobacco left in the hairs of his moustache. In the midst of his earnestness concerning the *Whale* he feels another kind of earnestness has been shrugged off. The juvenile keenness to escape his condition by going to sea, by publishing, by marrying, and in philosophy and reading, has, in some incalculable moment of development, been outgrown. All his adventures, all his reading, seem but the script for a vast practical joke, the wit whereof he but dimly discerns. There is nothing dispiriting in the awareness. He feels perfectly happy, sitting on this bale of hay, watching his two animals at either end of the barn. He even has to admit that, in this odd sort of wayward mood he is in, it hardly seems to matter whether Lizzie returns from Boston or not; he could contentedly live on alone with his mother and sisters. Something of Mr. Hawthorne's phlegmatic being must have rubbed off on him, and this new nonchalance is to be savoured. Nothing needs disputing. Perhaps all his recent dissertations on whiteness, on madness, on the mark between the visible and the invisible, on the liquid and the solid, are all futile. But there is always the memory of Gansevoort's morbidly mortal apathy to shake him out of a comparable indifference.

Suddenly he knocked out a hard grey hunk of tobacco from his pipe and then blew through the stem. He stood up and cocked his head at the cow. As Kant said, in some preface he had read recently, and marked: "Human Nature cannot decline the questions which its own nature calls it to consider".

Leaving the barn, he ran back to the house and, bursting through the lower rooms, ignored several plaintive enquiries regarding his meal, which had been spoiling. He returned to his desk and seized a pen, to write, in Ishmael's voice:

Now then, thought I, unconsciously rolling up the sleeves of my frock, here goes for a cool, collected dive at death and destruction, and the devil fetch the hindmost.

Back in July the *Virginian* had fallen for the magnetism of Mr. Hawthorne's "wild-witch voice", and whilst the central theme of his laudatory article is the espousal of the republican need to elevate American writers to the ranks of Old World worthies this is really an argumentative excuse for extolling the particular enticements of a new-found author. Most of us fall in love with a writer's voice in adolescence but the submission can work its alchemy at any time. Crucial to it is a sense of being *in*vaded and *per*vaded by the power of an irrepressible personality. Although it is possible for a reader to be charmed by a writer of the opposite sex there is, usually, a strong degree of sexual identification involved in the reader's submission. Of course it is always possible to equate analogous writing with subconscious confessional, so that ofttimes the following passage has been quoted as evidence of Melville's latent homosexuality:

Already I feel that this Hawthorne has dropped germinous seeds into my soul. He expands and deepens down, the

314

more I contemplate him; and further and further shoots his strong new England roots into the hot soil in my Southern soul.

But in order to do that one really has to make a very questionable leap from the ethereal to the physical, from metaphor to literal fact. Melville is pursuing the theme with which he had introduced his article, namely that excellent books have only the "ever-eluding spirit of all beauty, which ubiquitously possesses men of genius".

> No man can read a fine author, and relish him to his very bones while he reads, without subsequently fancying to himself some ideal image of the man and his mind.

Melville, in this midsummer article, fancies aloud that the key temper of Mr. Hawthorne's mind is that of a "seeker, not a finder yet". A seeker after Truth. A *fellow* seeker? Might Herman himself not be a fellow genius?

> May it not be that this commanding mind has not been, is not, and never will be, individually developed in any one man? And would it indeed appear so unreasonable to suppose, that this great fulness and overflowing may be, or may be destined to be, shared by a plurality of men of genius?

No one man can "be regarded as in himself the concentration of all the genius of his time".

This article – on the surface the effusive outpouring of a naïve and uncritical spirit – is really a skilful exercise in self-advertisement. For, moreover,

> Whatever Nathaniel Hawthorne may hereafter write, *Mosses From An Old Manse* will be ultimately accounted his masterpiece. For there is a sure, though secret sign in some works which proves the culmination of the power that produced them.

Here, in this book, with his sleeves rolled, he was going to seize the initiative. He would call forth the same occult powers as had driven Mr. Hawthorne to write his blackest of stories, *Young Goodman Brown*.

*   *   *

315

Lizzie came back from Boston in the first week of January, but it was Herman's sister Augusta who wrote to the Shaws commenting on the health and vitality which the stay had induced in both of them. The husband himself was hurtfully oblivious to their reappearance, commenting upon it merely to draw attention to his new routine.

"Oh, of course, I forgot, I wasn't working when you went away. No, I can't eat before three o'clock. But you and Malcolm can. I expect you've been having four table-laid repasts at home."

"Helen tells me she has been knocking for you at half-past two."

"Yes, she does. But I can't eat straightaway. I feed the horse and cow."

"Perhaps Malcolm can help do that."

"No. He can't."

"Herman! Haven't you mised your Barney? He'll have to get to know you all over again you know. My stepbrothers were so good with him, they . . ."

"I'm not taking him to the barn. Look – Lizzie . . ." (They were standing upstairs in a cold bedroom. Herman made clouds of vapour as he began to pontificate.) "I've started that Whaling book all over again. It has a grip on me. I'll have it done by the spring and we can make plans for the farm and really get to know the Hawthornes; I'm hoping to get the whole family over soon and maybe increase the size of our own." In a display of rather studied affection he clasped his hands over his wife's stomach and, standing behind her, bent his cheek to the tightly drawn hair on top of her skull. The words he said at times like these rang false in his own ears and jangled harshly against the language of his pen. Nor did Lizzie find his forced optimism convincing.

"You'd best first show interest in Malcolm," she said, and unclasped his fingers. She went straight to bed, though it was not yet half-past eight, and while Herman sat smoking by the fire, with mother and sisters busy in the lamplight, she wept. It was a homesick weeping, but its desperation and lack of control shamed her. She reached out for her Bible, took it beneath the bedcovers, and prayed to God for strength to suffer her afflictions.

In Lenox Mr. Hawthorne had been making admirable progress in the convivial atmosphere of his homely dwelling. In the centre of his book there is a description of Clifford that seems to borrow some of Herman's conversational terminology.

Perhaps Clifford required to take a deep, deep plunge

316

into the ocean of human life, and to sink down and be covered by its profoundness, and then to emerge sobered, invigorated, restored to the world and himself.

If this addition to a continuing gallery of folk who had broken the links of brotherhood with their kind was inapplicable to Mr. Melville at the present time, it did prove remarkably prophetic, since from this moment on Herman was to turn himself into a Hawthornesque recluse par excellence.

The House Of The Seven Gables was finally erected by early January 1851 and Nathaniel read it aloud (as was his custom with completed work) to Sophia on the three evenings of January 13th–15th. There was a good deal of Mr. Hawthorne himself in the character of Holgrave, and Sophia smiled, on the middle evening, at some of the exchanges between the daguerreotypist and Phoebe contained in chapter fourteen. It was intended that she should recognise familiar goadings, but direct comment upon them was prohibited before the reading of the book was complete. Since in his correspondence to his publisher Mr. Hawthorne did not announce that his book was officially complete until January 26th we can assume that such comments, when they were permitted, elicited some slight final revisions. The nights came early. They were dark and crisp. In between chapters Sophia put her notepaper down to prod the fire. Nathaniel took a sip of water and even-ended the pages of his manuscript. Sophia sat back down. She picked up notepaper and pencil and, having made several jottings on the topside, turned the paper over. Four months' pregnant, the early swelling of her tummy made a comfortable little desktop. She jockeyed her wrists into position and then gave her husband an upturned glance which, on one level, was a simple sign for him to begin, but also communicated, in the meeting of her eyes with his, a mutual sense of unutterable happiness. It is difficult not to envy Mr. Hawthorne this moment of quiet conspiratorial ecstasy. The silence of the household itself is something we might readily enough savour for its own sake. No humming of refrigerator or freezer; no whoosh of distant motor traffic; no manic, over-regular panic of a quartz clock mechanism; no dishwasher or automatic washing machine in mid-cycle; no recorded music playing. It was a silence which has all but disappeared from the civilised world for ever and if, perhaps, there was nothing inherently wonderful in such silence itself, it was a critical medium for the exchange of unspoken sympathies.

317

Nathaniel had written a book which he knew his wife was enjoying and which held no grievous dénouement in store. He knew the public would like it too. Sophia had passed the risk of miscarriage, to which she was prone, and they would, God willing, in early summer, have a baby in the house. Una and Julian were fit and sleeping sweetly in their beds. They possessed no great wealth but they were comfortable and occasionally received generous gifts from Nathaniel's devoted friends.

As he began to read one more paragraph describing the dismal, gabled mansion of his fiction, a smirk of irony tightened over his cheeks and, for a line or two, tightened his diction. Sophia looked up again, with the same, upturned, meaningful glance. He had to pause before continuing, overcome with elation.

It is impossible to imagine Mr. Melville, at this point in his life, succumbing to a similar sense of domestic delirium.

Sophia delighted in the adroitly engineered happy ending.

"You don't think the unveiling of Holgrave too marvellous?" Nathaniel asked her.

"No, no. But do you have to have those lines about our mortal sphere never really being set right. Surely it is, isn't it?"

"Set right? Yes, but only after the old Judge has been disposed of. He had to be removed . . ."

They talked in general for a little while about the ending and its relation to the ending of *The Scarlet Letter*, and then Sophia handed her husband the piece of folded paper, upon which she had been making occasional notes. These consisted, in the main, of single words, followed by question marks. No chapter number or other references were given. She was accustomed to her husband being able to relocate a phrase or a particular word in his manuscripts with alacrity. The brief submission required no further comment. Nathaniel would consider each of Sophia's queries in turn and then change or not change the given vocabulary, as the case may be. The understood meaning of each question mark was: Do you intend so strong a word here?

There were not many such decisions to make so that when, on January 22nd, Mr. Melville finally made his first New Year trip to Lenox, Mr. Hawthorne was at his ease, with the manuscript just about ready to send off to Fields. Prior to its inaugural reception by his wife, while he had still been hammering away a little on its roof, he had composed a preface for a re-issued edition of the *Twice Told Tales*. It is a shorter, more restrained Introduction than any of his previous and, in its self-assessment, typically deprecating. It is interesting that just a few months after his newest admirer had lauded these early stories, equating their literary worth to American literature with that of Shakespeare's plays to English literature, and predicting that their author would never better them, Mr. Hawthorne himself should be minimising their qualities and, whilst retaining personal affection for them, in the literary sense well-nigh dismissing them.

(To new readers of Hawthorne's early work, let me make a recommendation. Do not begin with a famous, most-often anthologised story, but with one of the so-called lesser works, where the authorial voice is more obvious. To be specific, why not try *The Seven Vagabonds* and then ask yourself whether it does not remind you of that modern allegorist or emblematic writer, Samuel Beckett.)

At any rate Mr. Melville arrived at a time when Mr. Hawthorne was at his most buoyant. He had finished a good, life-enhancing novel to which Sophia had given tear-free approval. He had reassessed his early work and concluded that those lonely bachelor stories had represented an attempt to open up an intercourse with the world, which attempt Sophia and the children now made redundant, freeing his energies for a more substantial form of literary pursuit. He was, at last, a writer in the accepted nineteenth-century sense, and there was now no reason at all why he should not continue to concoct popular Romances with the same vigorous fecundity of a Walter Scott.

Herman was not the only guest that day. A young girl from the Hawthornes' Boston circle was visiting and, her visit having been expected whereas Mr. Melville's had not, Nathaniel and Sophia divided their attention equally between the two guests. They had cold chicken to eat and nothing stronger than cinnamon tea to drink. Outside the snow was deeper than ever and Herman could really have done with some grained red meat and a nip or two of firewater. A cigar wouldn't have gone amiss, either. But there was no opportunity for any of that on this occasion and instead of an intimate soirée with his fellow Truth-seeker, Herman concentrated on issuing an invitation to the whole Hawthorne household to spend a day in Pittsfield.

"I have some excellent Amontillado sherry. We can crack jokes and bottles from morning till night. Or you can spend the period of your visit in bed, if you like. Every hour of your visit."

"But your work – it would be an unforgivable disruption to have the whole lot of us descend upon you."

"Not a bit. I shall carry on regardless."

Nathaniel looked at his wife. She read in his expression an entreaty for help in extricating himself from this invitation, but she was inclined to receive it as an instinctive defence of his privacy, which she reckoned at that time could perhaps benefit from an incursion by this other man, for whom she felt a vicarious attraction. Unable to want him for herself she had, from the beginning, wanted him for her husband.

"And with the *Seven Gables* done you could leave your desk for a day or two quite honourably."

"Gables?" Melville quizzed.

"Another sombre Romance. And not *quite* yet finished, I should add."

"It isn't sombre at all."

Sophia, having said this, became aware that the other visitor had awkwardly turned to the children and was pretending to engage their attention, whereas in fact both Una and Julian were agog at the subtle ploys of overheard adult conversation. She asked Una to help the guest collect up the plates and left Nathaniel to extricate himself from the dilemma single-handed.

"Can I see some of the book?" Herman asked, as soon as they were alone.

"No." And then blunting his definitive refusal: "I am still putting a tile or two in place. But I do have something for you here. Same old things."

Nathaniel handed him a copy of *Twice Told Tales*, Second Series.

Herman flipped through its pages. "Five days. Make it six. I can read these in six. Get your masonry work finished in six and come over to me then. That makes it next week then, weather and sleighing permitting. I had better be returning before the freeze sets in. We'll have your rooms prepared. I shall ride out for you at eleven."

At some point during these intervening days Nathaniel prevailed upon Sophia to perform the act of extrication which she had originally resisted, for, at the last minute, a note arrived in Pittsfield to the effect that Mr. Melville should not call for them on the appointed morning, since Mr. Hawthorne had still not despatched his book into the express man's hands. They would make their own way to Arrowhead some time at the end of the new month, and would look forward to spending a day there, perhaps when the snow had begun to thaw.

Since it is my contention that the majority of *Moby Dick's* chapters were written consecutively, and that chapter eighty-five was completed at some point well-advanced in the New Year, I am of the view that Mr. Melville was busy with one of the Whale's Head/Spermtapping chapters when he received this note. These physiological chapters were difficult and unpleasant to work on. His temper was always fragile when he had to rely heavily on reference material and, in this stretch of the book, he was conscious that the overall effect was not oily, but dry, and efforts to make the descriptions analogous, such as "This Right Whale I take to have been a Stoic; the Sperm Whale, a Platonian, who might have taken up Spinoza in later years" were so manifestly unlike anything that Mr. Hawthorne might come out with that he almost despaired of ever lifting the material onto the plateau of its new conception.

When he was given the note he refused to leave the room for lunch but, in the first surviving letter to Mr. Hawthorne, wrote out his reply, not caring to conceal his annoyance that the other man had chosen to hide behind the protectiveness of a wife:

> That side-blow thro Mrs. Hawthorne will not do. I am not to be charmed out of my promised pleasure by any of that lady's syrenisms. You, Sir, I hold accountable, and the visit (in all its original integrity) must be made. What! *spend the day* only with us? A Greenlander might as well talk of spending the day with a friend, when the day is only half an inch long. As I said before, my best travelling chariot on runners will be at your door and provision made not only for the accommodation of all your family, but also for any quantity of baggage.

Mr. Hawthorne, obviously aggravated by this insistent letter, the annoyance of which is inadequately veiled by the exaggeration of its vocabulary, marched straight off to the Post office with a note which basically reiterated the points made in Sophia's earlier one, except that he did not mention the novel, not wishing it known that it had already gone to the publishers.

This second refusal from Lenox had the effect of improving Mr. Melville's self-confidence. He wrote a characteristically bravado chapter on the Honour and Glory of Whaling in which Perseus

321

figured as the first whale-slayer and St. George was revealed as the conqueror, not of an evil Dragon, but of a perverse Leviathan. Skilfully, but apparently effortlessly, threaded through this brief chapter was the information that the City of Joppa had long contained the vast skeleton of a whale reputed to be the bones of the monster which had terrorised Andromeda. And it was from Joppa that Jonah had set sail.

If Mr. Hawthorne's hallmark was his succinct revelations of experienced truth, Mr. Melville's was just this ability to assimilate referential information and sift it for appropriate but original associations.

His reading of *The Twice Told Tales* had the effect of reducing the awe in which the older writer had initially been held. He could not forget the cold white slivers of dry chicken flesh he had been served with latterly. In these stories the human insights seemed served up in the same way. The meat should have been red, and connected with the rest of the meal by slipways of gravy.

"I think Mrs. Hawthorne should change her butcher."

"I dare say there isn't much choice in Lenox."

"Then I must deliver to them from Pittsfield."

Lizzie benefited from Herman's newfound confidence to the extent that, during the first half of February, a second child was conceived.

He fancied that he might have found a new equilibrium, perhaps somewhat similar to the unflinching poise of Mr. Hawthorne. Neither despairing indifference, nor the theoretical wisdom of a middle way characterised his new mood, but a mixed brew of doubt and intuition. Just as, from time to time, a whale's spout would be crowned by a rainbow so, through all the thick mists of the dim

doubts in my mind divine intuitions now and then shoot, enkindling my fog with a heavenly ray . . . Doubts of all things earthly, and intuitions of some things heavenly; this combination makes neither believer nor infidel but makes a man who regards them both with an equal eye.

At the end of the month he wrote briefly, and in a manner not to be gainsaid, to the Red House, announcing that he would ride out on March 12th, stay the night, and then transport the Hawthornes *en famille* to Pittsfield the next morning.

*　　*　　*

He arrived in a household visibly affected by the winter's siege.
Both Mr. Hawthorne's and Julian's boots were worn out and Mrs.
Hawthorne's attire was badly in need of some expert cleaning.
Nevertheless the occupants bore their somewhat dilapidated
existence with good cheer and Herman was entertained to some
champagne foam.

"This is the last of the Manfield bequest."

"You kept it all this while?"

"Had it been a more spirited brew we might have used it by
now, but in these past winter days a sparkling acidity hasn't quite
fitted . . ."

Mr. Hawthorne's explanation of his restraint tapered off while
the two men watched in fascination as Sophia served up the
champagne with beaten eggs and loaf sugar. The element of
protein in the cocktail evidently transformed the frothy mixture
into a substantial foodstuff for the only other victuals on offer were
bread and cheese. Herman waited until he had spooned up all the
foam – he did not feel comfortable consuming such airy stuff –
before, turning a piece of hard and cracked cheese between his
fingers, he said, "And you will come back with me tomorrow."

The other man, mysteriously sucking on his foam, as if it were a
hard-boiled sweet, eyed his wife before saying, "We have decided
that we can't possibly burden you with the whole crowd of us.
Onion and I will accompany you, yes."

It was enough for Herman, and he didn't really listen to Sophia
elaborating the "decision".

"Julian has been really impish lately. To tell the truth we
thought we might be quite ashamed of his behaviour, especially in
front of your wife and mother. And it will do Una good to be away
from him for a while. I hope you haven't made up beds in
advance?"

Sophia received no pacification on this point, for Herman,
turned fixedly in her husband's direction, could not contain a
whoop of delight. "I have saved that Spanish sherry for you, and
Allan has sent me cigars from New York." Then, turning to
Sophia, but still not to answer her concern: "Fail to accompany
him at your peril, madame."

A curtain moved at the bottom of the stairs and Una appeared.
Sophia led her quickly away to the kitchen for a drink of water.

"It is some while since my friend Burchmore sent me any. But, as you can see . . ." here Mr. Hawthorne turned the backs of his hands over onto his trouser knees, "the winter has taken heavy toll on our resources."

The rest of the night passed tamely enough. Nathaniel got out copies of the new daguerreotype portrait of himself to be used in all future publications.

"Sophia thinks my expression far too melancholy. I suppose it *is* a cheerless phizz, but not unfitting for the author of *The Scarlet Letter*, don't you think? Although I'm not at all sure about this trend for appending an author's likeness to all his creations."

"I'm all for it; if it can put a stop to my impostor. The latest is, the fellow's in England, meeting all kinds of lord and lady at my expense."

"At your expense?" Sophia didn't quite follow.

"At the expense of Mr. Melville's reputation. Some rogue has been passing himself off as the writer of *Typee*."

"Which is more or less what they accused me of at the time."

They did not talk late. Mrs. Hawthorne, before going up, apologised for the bed in the guest room. "I'm afraid the children were bouncing on it – well, Julian was to be exact – pretending to stamp dead a snake – something quite fiendish anyway – I think you had just read them a story about the baby Heracles – and a leg went – we've propped it up with some old books – none of yours I assure you – but it's still a bit askew."

Mr. Hawthorne followed his wife, first assuring that Herman knew how to find his way up after extinguishing the lamps.

"I'll try and get a long night tonight. I'm sure your place is most comfortable; but I'm just as sure I shan't be able to get a settled sleep there."

"I shan't let you, old Melancholy-face. With beef and cigars, and nutbrown sherry we shall . . ." Mr. Melville didn't say this aloud. Instead he stood and said simply, "Good night."

The following morning began with such a snowstorm that, for a while, it looked as though the trip to Pittsfield might have to be postponed, but by eleven the snowfall had lightened sufficiently to allow them to proceed. Julian must have been previously apprised of the arrangements, for he took Una's preparations in good heart and vexed her only in a good-natured way by hiding things she wanted to pack.

One side of Mr. Melville's neck was stiff from having slept at an awkward angle due to the uneven bed-legs, and he spent much of the time waiting for the storm to abate massaging the nape with the back of his hand. His hair was cut according to the orthodox fashion of the time – that is, shorter than the earlier generation, but not as short as the more militarised later generation. It is always difficult to tell from black and white photographs how grey a person's head of hair was; in the one taken by Rodney Dewey in 1861 there are certainly hints of grey in the beard but not sufficient to suggest that it was already greying ten years earlier. The reader should remember that Mr. Melville was not yet thirty-two years old and the sciatica which laid him low during the writing of *Pierre* and many times thereafter had not yet gripped him; but he had been working sufficiently hard and, beneath the still youthful energy, was tired enough to be more than usually bothered by petty aches and pains.

"Can I touch your beard?"

"Come away, Una."

Una did as she was told and went to her mother, who bent down and whispered, audibly, "I don't think Mr. Melville slept very well. Try not to disturb him." But even as she said it little Julian popped up beside Herman's chair, put one hand up to Mr. Melville's chin, and gave a sharp stroke, before retracting his fingers and yelling, "It's sharp and prickly, sharp and prickly." Una raced back to her original station.

"Did he really?"

"Oh, yes, really."

"And is it really?"

"Why don't you find out?" Herman projected his beard at her.

"Mama says you didn't sleep well. I know why you didn't sleep well. Julian broke the bed."

"Did not."

"Did."

"Did not."

"He did, Mr. Omoo, he . . ."

At the same moment Julian ran bawling to Sophia and Una screamed as Herman grabbed her hand and forced it into his beard.

Nathaniel stood aside from the instant of bedlam. He had been up early and was now restlessly waiting with, at last, some excitement for his venture abroad, after so long cooped up in the close little cottage. His imperviousness to the brief outbreak of

325

uproar was not, as Mr. Melville perceived, bred of staunch disapproval, but more the result of his transported expectation. At any rate, when Una fled into his arms, he seemed to blink awake and wonder whence she had come, in such a state of panic.

"Why? What is it?"

She stared up into his face with that primaeval, bewitching scrutiny which had been the inspiration for so many attitudes struck by Pearl in *The Scarlet Letter*.

"Papa, if you grew a beard, would it be like Mr. Melville's?"

"If your mother hasn't packed my toilet case, we might find out. Sophia, is everything ready?"

It was, and Mrs. Hawthorne began to dress Una for the drive to Pittsfield.

*   *   *

The drawing room at Arrowhead had, by now, become stylishly comfortable in the middle-class manner of the time. Its spaciousness and grandness beat anything that Mr. Hawthorne had ever dwelt in, including the Old Manse, the rooms of which, though large, had never attained to the atmospheric gentility of this room, achieved in large part by the array of oil paintings, all of which seemed to speak of family solidity, so that, although there were many maritime pictures in the collection, an uninformed visitor might justifiably have concluded that this had been the family residence for several generations.

As he was shown into it, Mr. Hawthorne was not without feelings of envy. Although, philosophically, he affected to despise this kind of gentrified theatre of permanence, he had nevertheless grown up with the notion that a revenging Fate had dispossessed his own family of just such cultured comforts. The death of his mother, the dispersal of his two sisters, and the present poverty of himself and Sophia seemed the nadir to which this malevolent requital had been leading.

"This of course is not the genial heart of the house. Come, let me show you my smoking corner."

"Herman, perhaps Mr. Hawthorne would like to leave Una with us."

It was his mother who spoke and, without waiting for a reply from her son, turned to the guest and repeated her suggestion.

"Herman's wife is upstairs with Malcolm. She'll be down soon.

Augusta, Helen – take little Una's hand and let her come and talk with me for a bit."

Maria Melville was sitting regally in the centre of a long settee, vast folds of her dress spreading out on either side. As Herman led his guest out of the room, between the bowed back of this settee and a large sash window, Nathaniel wondered how his primitive offspring would fare in such stiff company.

They went out again into the small entrance gallery and, having closed the drawing-room door, Herman began, in hushed voice, to educate Mr. Hawthorne on the architectural peculiarities of his hall of residence.

"It begins in the cellar and goes up through the house like an elongated pyramid, foiling my mother's plans for a modern home split in two halves by a continuous hallway from front to back. But look in here" – he opened a door into another room – "here is the chimney's true face. Its others are all showy or pragmatic, but here it can be its own smoky self. This is where I sit, smoking a pipe and watching the logs burn. Three old cronies they call us. Me, my pipe and my chimney."

Herman had sat himself down on a wooden bench that was fixed to a low partition wall separating the door from the chimney. The hearth was enormous with open brickwork at its back, charred both black and white.

"And so, at the back of this, is the hearth in the room we have just left?"

"Yes, everyone in the house faces towards this one column of stone, as if it were some Druidical talisman."

"I rather like that notion."

"Then please say so to my mother. Her dreams of reconstruction are quite impractical of course – we would have to redesign the entire dwelling – but that doesn't prevent her from continually taking out her measure and calculating the amount of living space taken up by this totem pole as she calls it. And she has great influence over my sisters and Lizzie, so a word to them would be of value too. But we can sit here later, four old cronies smoking and philosophising together. In the meantime I'll take you up the stairs and show you another advantage of this smouldering taproot."

They went back out into the entry bay and Herman led the way upstairs, stopping before they had reached another floor. "Here, you see, the stair must turn about the chimney piece and the

327

landing up there follows the side of the house. Rather theatrical, that gallery, don't you think? But let me show you into my sultry stowaway vault." So saying, he opened a cupboard door in the wall and, crouching down, led the way inside. It was not an understairs cupboard with a sloping ceiling but a storage area built against the side of the tapering chimney.

"Put your hand against the wall there."

Nathaniel did so. It was exceedingly warm.

"This is where I keep all my old wines. The sherry I told you about is in here, and some port. I should have brought a lamp."

Herman turned, ready to push open the door, which had drawn closed until just a crack of light illuminated the cupboard; but before providing further brilliance he turned and put his finger to his lips. Someone was descending the stairs. Nathaniel could make out the rustling of skirts and a child's voice. From what Melville's mother had said earlier it was plain that this must be Lizzie bringing Malcolm downstairs, and Nathaniel found her husband's childlike subterfuge disconcerting. As Herman took his finger away from his lips there was, left on his face, an expression of intent concentration. Finally he heard the drawing-room door open, and close, interspersed by a chorus of female introduction. Looking up, he saw Mr. Hawthorne standing in the middle of the cupboard, all but his boldest features obliterated in the poor light, his eyes opened wide with perplexed timidity.

"Oh, that'll have been Lizzie with Malcolm. I'll introduce you later. First of all I'll take you to your rooms. It's a bit of a maze upstairs, with one room leading off another." Herman spoke as he bent his way out of the cupboard. Nathaniel followed him up the stairs, the experience of closeted proximity with his new friend having made him withdraw into a reflective silence. Not simply the strange, secretive behaviour of the other man had unsettled him, but the mere fact of having been cooped up together in a dark and tepid space had seemed to assume a confederacy more intimate than the friendship was ready to sustain.

In due course the tour of the house was over; Nathaniel had been properly welcomed by the younger Mrs. Melville; polite conversation had been had regarding Mrs. Hawthorne and Julian; regarding children in general; regarding Pittsfield and Lenox; the rail link with Boston; the latest edition of Appleton's *Travelling Compendium*; and the troublesome architecture of the house – at which point, Herman, his eyes smiling at Nathaniel, suggested he take Una to see the cow in the barn. Nathaniel stayed in, to talk further with the Melville women, and to order his and Una's things upstairs. Malcolm went with his Papa, and Lizzie, by now more or less certain that she was pregnant again, took an afternoon nap.

At the evening meal Nathaniel began to appreciate how different Herman's domestic life was from his own. The dining room had no less than nine doors leading off it, and the table was of course large enough to seat all of the Melville women plus guests. Herman himself was not only outnumbered by the female side of his family, he was overshadowed by Mrs. Melville Senior, and seemed not quite at home amid the rather austere décor in this part of the house. He and his mother sat at either end of the table, but it was Mrs. Melville Senior who acted as its head, giving directions to the servant and prompting the conversation in a way which clearly defined her position regarding her son and his occupation.

"Of course, Herman's older brother, Gansevoort, was much more the . . .

"Now you, Mr. Hawthorne, write for the magazines, I think that's much more sensible.

"Una seems very fond of you; you must spend a lot of time with your children.

"Did you hear that, Herman? Mr. Hawthorne often takes his boy and girl for a walk.

"What do you think of our place, then? We shall be doing something about the monstrous old chimney, of course.

"I expect you were very sad to lose your job at the Custom House; a man needs a regular occupation, don't you think?"

If Herman seemed willing to submit himself to this barrage it was not any kind of masochistic humility which kept him quiet but an habitual and resentful sense of his place in things. Nathaniel, for all his insight into the ways and wiles of individuals, possessed no key to the sometimes darker dynamics of family relationships, and he can be forgiven for finding this dinner-time spectacle psychologically disturbing. More unsettling than Herman's sullen silence was the supernumerary presence of Elizabeth. The Melville sisters did at least make some attempt to engage Mr. Hawthorne in general chitchat, enquiring about his favourite authors, his next book and so forth, but Elizabeth sat at Herman's elbow, not unresponsive, but simply ignored by the rest of the table, with the result that her polite smiling made her appear feeble-minded. When he had seen her the previous summer she had been in an ill humour, but there had been more colour in her complexion and Mr. Melville had paid her more attention.

At the end of the meal Nathaniel went upstairs to see if Una had settled in her bed. She was still awake and said her prayers aloud, for Mama, for Julian, and for the brother or sister to be. She said what a nice big house this was and how beautifully warm it had been in the barn, with such a cosy smell.

"Mr. Melville says that Malcolm was born in the cowshed, because it's so warm and cosy there."

Nathaniel, sitting on the side of the bed, gave a spluttering shake of the head.

"Don't you believe that, Papa? I do. It really is warm. And Jesus was . . ."

"Little Onion, I don't think the Melvilles lived here when Malcolm was born."

"Well, you'll see anyway."

"I'll see what?"

"The barn. Mr. Melville said that you and he would be smoking cigars in there tonight. Papa, you will come into the house to sleep, won't you?"

He reached out and squeezed her shoulder beneath the coverlet. "Of course. I dare say the night will be too cold for us to stay out of the house for more than a minute."

"It really is warm in there, Papa."

Nathaniel kissed her smooth forehead and then went next door to his own room and made sure that his things were properly arranged for the night. He put his face-cloth next to the wash basin and jug, and then practised stepping blindly from the door to the bed. He did this twice, the first time tripping on a tasselled rug, and causing a chair to scrape on the floor with the hand stretched out to steady himself.

"Papa, is that you?"

Nathaniel rushed to Una's door. She was sitting up in her bed.

"Yes, my pet. I'm sorry. I tripped on a mat."

She giggled. "Did you break anything? I shall tell Mama you broke something really precious, something Mr. Melville had been given by the cannibals."

"Has he been talking to you about cannibals again?"

"Yes. In the barn."

"Well, try not to dream of them."

"Don't frighten me with any more noises then."

They said good night for a second time, and for a second time Nathaniel stepped with his eyes closed from the door of his own room to the side of the bed. Opening his eyes he stood still for several seconds in the centre of the room, making certain that he had got his bearings. In the silence he fancied that he could sense Sophia thinking of him, and he sent his love to her and he wondered if Julian was being a good child.

On the stairs he met Elizabeth, who seemed to be making tracks for an early night. She smiled a little grimly at him, and then passed by, but suddenly turned, as if remembering her function as hostess, and asked if Una were asleep.

"Not yet; but she is quite comfortable."

"And you?"

"Not asleep yet either, but yes, quite comfortable."

"You must excuse me, but I am a little tired tonight."

"That's quite all right."

"You'll find the others by the large fireside."

"Thank you."

Nathaniel regretted that he could not make this staircase exchange less formal. Elizabeth's upper jaw was larger than the lower, and the chin weak. She had inherited a large nose from her father. But her eyes were kindly and seemed to betoken an inner life richer than her outward behaviour signified. Of all the female occupants of the house she interested him the most.

Herman had already lit a pipe and was sitting apart from the others on the bench that he had earlier pointed out to Mr. Hawthorne. Mrs. Melville Senior and two of her daughters were playing cards at a table positioned too closely to the fire for a fourth player to join them. Augusta sat in a high-backed chair directly opposite Herman. A book was in her lap and Nathaniel had the impression that she had been reading aloud before he had entered the room.

"Mr. Hawthorne, are you a card player? We can never get Herman to join us these days. Says it makes his eyes ache. You wouldn't think he was in the prime of life, would you? How old do you think I am, Mr. Hawthorne?"

Nathaniel smiled and turned his head to one side, but he was spared the effort of concocting a diplomatic reply.

"Sixty. Sixty years old this year. Born in seventeen ninety-one

331

and not an ache in my eyes nor any other part of my body to speak of. Sixty, clean-living years." She played a card nonchalantly. Herman stood up and thrust the poker at a charred log, with a vehemence which captured all their attention. He was thinking of the psychological warfare his mother had waged in the past, with her supposedly fragile health as a weapon. This robustness of body and spirit which she had discovered in old age was enough to make him strike a second log with even greater force. It was less charred than the first, and the blow jarred his wrist. He dropped the poker onto the tiles in front of the fire.

"No, Mother. I want to take Mr. Hawthorne to the barn."

When the two men had left the room, Augusta stood up and placed the poker back in its rack.

*   *   *

The barn was indeed warm, and the aroma of cigar smoke mixed sweetly with that of the dung. Herman had lighted two oil lamps at either end of the building with a third lamp brought from the house. Nathaniel had carried the bottle and glasses. He put them down on the straw and watched the snow turning grey then clear at the rims of his cracked boots. They were very worn and let in the wet. His toes were cold. He hoped that Una would not wake and find him out of the house.

"This is a good cigar," he said, when Herman had seated himself on a bale nearby.

"We'll hope the drink is too." Herman stood up again and filled both the glasses. Handing one to Nathaniel he said, "To American writing."

Nathaniel steadied his glass in a muted response to the toast and then drank. It was one of the old, incubated sherries from the stairway cupboard.

"There's good fortification to that, is there not?" asked Herman. "I have grown fond of these older blended wines ever since my trip to England. Have you tasted stout?"

Mr. Hawthorne shook his head.

"A thick black bitter number that is. A drink to dye the arterial system and make the very brain black. If you were an Englishman they'd be saying you wrote with a nib dipped in stout." Herman scuffed up a pile of straw with his heel. "They'll say I used the devil's pitchfork for mine."

332

"They said as much about *The Scarlet Letter*."

"Well, let the popular novelists give the public cider froth and let them be popular for it. We must stay popular only with our good guardian angels and damn what anyone else might want us to write."

"I do most of my work in the winter but this summer I'm thinking of beginning a children's book." There was something impishly deflating in Mr. Hawthorne's announcement. It was honest, and to the point, but coming as it did straight after Herman's "damn what anyone else might want" its effect was calculated to surprise. Herman looked suspiciously at his companion through narrowed eyes. "It's something Sophia has wanted me to do for a long time." This additional remark compounded the rebuff. "I've been telling the children some of the Classical myths. Just modernising them a little as bedtime stories. I think I might write one or two down and see how it goes."

Herman was uninterested in this possibility. He decided to change the subject. "You know, apart from the horse and cow here I've hardly talked to a soul since the snows came down. When we first moved in I started befriending some of the local farmers and landowners, but after a bit they were bored by my sailing yarns just as I was by their landed concerns. And as for philosophising, well, anything that didn't bear upon yields and livestock, market prices and machinery, bovine sickness and barn-building, bored them silly. To tell you the truth I find obsessive practicality a bit unmasculine. Like my mother's dauntless tape-measuring. My sisters, with all the time they have on their hands, do little more than sew and bake, and hold the tape – apart from Helen, who does a bit of scribing for me. It takes the horse and cow here to share a pipe with me. We do some musing together, don't we?"

Standing up, Herman had continued speaking while moving over towards the horse, who had put its head across the gate of its stall and seemed to be paying its master intelligent attention. It got its snout patted while Herman continued, "The irony is that while my family at least consider that I have isolated myself through too-heady reading it's the two beasts here which offer me greatest companionship. But anyone who's been to sea and has shared a bunk-deck with the general rabble of skullduggerers in the merchant navy can tell you it isn't reading that sparks off questions about Fate and Providence, though I sometimes wonder what a boatful of women would find to talk about if thrown

333

together in similar circumstances."

You haven't met the likes of my sister-in-law or Miss Fuller, Nathaniel thought to himself, but he made only a general comment. "Perhaps the decisive quality in the matter of which you speak is youth and not sex."

"What! And don't old men lead more reflective lives than the young?"

Mr. Hawthorne would not immediately grant the ridiculousness of his statement. "There is an independent quality to the cogitations of the senile. They are different from and bear no necessary relation to youthful speculation."

Herman came back to his original bale. He picked up the bottle and refilled their glasses. The horse turned round in its stall. After the noise of its manoeuvring a late-night silence established itself in the barn. Nathaniel felt as if they were once again shut up in the stairway cupboard. When he continued, Herman's voice had a different timbre, affected by the background silence and by the unexpected antagonism of Mr. Hawthorne.

"That sounds remarkably like my mother, trying to persuade me that in middle life I should put away philosophising and become the pragmatic provider for a family."

Mr. Hawthorne frowned through the cigar smoke he had just exhaled, and Herman, sensing that his analogy had been mistaken for personal criticism by the older man, quickly added, "Though your own dedication to the pen denies it."

Lifting his head to one side and smiling, his cigar held down between his knees, Mr. Hawthorne said, "I was quick enough to put down the pen when it came to working for the Custom House."

"But now, after the success of *The Scarlet Letter*, I imagine . . ."

"Oh, it hasn't made me rich yet. Look at the hovel we inhabit. When a man has a wife, and two sturdy children, with a third on the way, it is a little difficult to live in glorious isolation from the world. And, anyway, I've lived out my hermit years. At your age I was still at home, in my mother's house, confined to a single chamber. And yet when I re-read the *Tales* I wrote there, as I did this Christmas past, before adding the new introduction, what strikes me is that they have the style of a man of society, that they are not the talk of a secluded person holding private conversations with his own mind and heart but that they are attempts to open up an intercourse with the world. I think inevitably that which

334

actuates an author's work shifts ground as soon as such an intercourse is begun."

Mr. Hawthorne looked around for a safe place to extinguish his cigar butt. Mr. Melville took it and dropped it into a nearby water-bucket. "That'll be changed in the morning. We won't give the cow marinaded Havana for breakfast." The little speech just past had pleased him twofold. It was the first time his guest had put more than two or three sentences together at a time since arriving and suggested that the two of them were feeling more relaxed in one another's company; secondly, the analysis corresponded with his own view, recorded earlier, that Mr. Hawthorne was never likely to repeat the quality of those first tales. Herman did not pursue that point now, for he did not want the question of his own intercourse with the world examined. "Coming back to the subject of reading, what I said before notwithstanding, I date the whole of my mental development from my discovery of Duyckinck's library. And I don't mean fiction, or even contemporary things. Cooper was good to read as a boy but I have really been more affected by authors like Thomas Browne and Robert Burton. I read De Quincey's *Opium Eater* in London. I must lend it to you if you haven't read it. Quite wonderful, and our own people, Emerson and Thoreau I suppose, seem pretty watery when put alongside."

"I knew them both in Concord, and used to go skating and boating with them. Have you ever met Mr. Thoreau?"

Herman shook his head.

"Ugly as sin. Long-nosed, queer-mouthed; the most unmalleable fellow alive."

This outspokenness was again pleasing, and so surprised Herman that he roared his approval. Later he would worry about the kind of fearless and pithy epithets Mr. Hawthorne might use to his own detriment.

"But an expert rower." Mr. Hawthorne sat up straight and beamed. Then he drained his glass. He was a bigger man than he appeared. Five foot, ten and three-quarter inches was his recorded height and his weight was usually in the region of twelve stone. But he was long-backed and his shorter legs, together with the impression of sphericity which Herman had earlier noted, reduced his observed height.

"Although" – Mr. Hawthorne held out his glass, watching the lamplight shine through the russet liquid – "my kind wife says I outdid them both on skates. There doesn't seem to be so much skating here as there was in Concord. Although the Bowl would make a fine venue. We don't have any skates with us, but I've walked across it with Una and Julian.''

"Ah, yes, those walks." Mr. Hawthorne did not fill out Herman's pause. "How do you get on with your mother?"

"My mother died over a year ago. No, it's Sophia's sister, Elizabeth, who plays the maternal figure in our family now. Don't ever come out to Lenox when she's visiting. We don't often see the older Mrs. Peabody now. At least I don't."

Herman turned his head as if he had heard a noise. The new domestic angle of the conversation had made him fidgety.

"Rats?"

Herman turned round again. "Oh, no. Well, there probably are. But not then. This is good." The last three words were spoken as a toast, with glass raised. Herman eyed the sherry but clearly included in his tribute more that was unseen. Sensing this, and that Herman's gaze was just about to meet his own, Nathaniel put in, "You have a fine prospect of Graylock from the house."

"Oh, and from your room." Herman chuckled, then added, "The mountain is another source of disagreement between me and my mother. I want to build a piazza onto the house facing the peak, but it lies to the north. The ladies, you see, want a sundeck, but I . . ."

Nathaniel could see that this domestic wrangling about the architecture of the house could become very tedious to an outsider, and in due course he began to yawn so uncontrollably that Herman showed the way back to the house.

*   *   *

In the morning, Mr. Hawthorne, keeping to his room, wrote to Evert Duyckinck in New York.

> I write to you from the house of our friend Herman Melville, and have only to glance my eye aside to obtain a fine snow-covered prospect of Graylock.
>
> May we not hope for the pleasure of seeing you again in Berkshire next summer? If you were to see how snug and comfortable Melville makes himself and friends I think you would not fail.

The letter was in part occasioned by one Mr. Hawthorne had received inviting a magazine contribution, but the different kind of invitation he sent back on his host's behalf was perhaps prompted by those things which Herman had said regarding his relationship with the locals.

Herman spent the morning dutifully working, partly in compliance with a condition laid down in advance by the guest, but also in an effort to appear just as professional as the older author. He did not get much done that morning but, thinking of Mr. Hawthorne's inner calm, he wrote, apropos of a chapter in which the *Pequod* becomes encalmed within a vast circle of whales, "But even so, amid the tornadoed Atlantic of my being, do I myself still forever centrally disport in mute calm; and while ponderous planets of unwaning woe revolve around me, deep down and deep inland there I still bathe me in eternal mildness of joy." Such deep inland mildness was, at this stage in Mr. Melville's life, a craving, and not a reality.

Downstairs, the seven-year-old Una played with the two-year-old Malcolm, to the gallery of grandmother and aunts.

"Did you hear that, Helen, he called her Onion. You're a cheeky thing young Malcolm Scollay. Don't mind what he says, Una."

"But it's my name. It's all right for him to use my name."

Maria continued, fawningly, to Helen, "She thinks he was trying to say her name." And then back to Una, "No, dear. Malcolm can speak quite well now. He was slow starting but he can now tackle most words. He made it up."

"He didn't."

Maria turned back to Helen. There was no mistaking that she was aggravated by the Miss Hawthorne's categorical refutation but she continued to smile wincingly. "The dear's put out. You're a naughty boy, Malcolm. A naughty cheeky boy."

Malcolm, sensing that the word was at the root of these exchanges, began to scurry round Helen's chair, burbling, "Onion, Onion, *un, yun, un, yun, un, yun, un, yun, un, jun, un, jun, jun, jun, jun, jun!*"

"All right. That's enough." Helen held out her arm and barred any further circumambulations.

"Anyway," Una piped up, "I told him it. Mama and Papa often call me Onion. Don't they, Malcolm?" With this last question she turned down to the little boy and put her arm across his shoulder with all the cutting grace of Maria herself.

"Is Mr. Hawthorne the kind of man who would call one of his children an onion?" Maria addressed the question, which she hoped was rhetorical, to all her daughters, but they were able to evade it for, at that moment, Elizabeth came in and asked Una if she would like to help change Malcolm's napkin.

"I'll do that, Lizzie. You sit down for a bit."

But Elizabeth had woken up in no mood to accept Augusta's kindnesses. She had prayed hard in the night, while Herman and Nathaniel had been in the barn, and her conversation with the Mighty One had determined her to fight against the mood of resignation which had hung over her at last night's meal table. The Christian is forever caught in this ambivalence of the faith. Be selfless, be pliant, be submissive; but also be optimistic, be joyous, be, above all things in the nineteenth century, energetic. There were Scriptures to support both sets of exhortation, so one swung as one's mood pushed one, or as one's prayers instructed.

"No, I'll take them out to the barn afterwards. I expect Una used to help Mrs. Hawthorne with Julian's napkins."

Una giggled. "He still disgraces himself sometimes."

"Oh dear. Only when excited I expect."

The Melville women were surprised by this calm and confident exchange as Elizabeth left the room with her two charges, since it contrasted markedly with her normal manner when left to cope with Malcolm. She was never harassed or incapable but, by the same token, she was hardly ever composed, and when Malcolm behaved naughtily she pleaded with him, rather than told him, to be good. This particular morning had started woefully enough. Though she woke up mentally invigorated by her prayers, physically she was racked by a bad bout of morning sickness, yet once the nausea had cleared she felt possessed by just that "eternal mildness of joy" which her husband was describing in an upstairs room. It was a religious calm which irradiated the everyday world with an indeterminable celestial lustre, and it was in this sense that the feeling was eternal. She knew what perhaps Herman did not know – better than to expect the mood to be perpetual.

*   *   *

The two authors took cigars into the barn on the second night.

"Just such a birth-place did the God-child have." Herman

338

spoke as if in soliloquy. His chosen speech had been long deliberated; this was not spur of the moment stuff. "In straw or weed they always rest. Christ the earthborn, counterbalance to the empyreal Jehovah. Jesus is the indulgent God; homely, four-walled and canopied. The other is wild and elemental, a Moby Dick psychopathically indisposed to being hauled in and weighed up ounce by ounce by ounce. There is some such Gnostic nonsense creeping into my book. But such a mighty faith the Judaic faith. And now? In Protestant repose it snores toward a mortal close." This last had not been so perfectly prepared and Herman chuckled at the chance couplet. "Shakespeare. I mean the influence, not a quote."

Mr. Hawthorne seemed ill to brook the weary length of arguing which this preamble clearly augured. He picked up a length of straw and began tickling the shadow his glass made on the barn floor. Moving the glass to one side with one hand he pursued its shadow with the other, and once catching up with it he tickled away again, so that it seemed to Herman, who perhaps made too much of this concrete doodling, that Nathaniel was emblematically scratching away at the surface of an enigma. It seemed, in short, that his guest, though silent, was attentive and making coded responses. Was he teasing or upbraiding? Herman eyed the doodling for a second or two, then continued. "Doubt has cast its shadow over our whole epoch, undeifying the day." And then, because Mr. Hawthorne remained silent, choosing to elucidate what he thought was meant by the other man's talismanic response, Herman said, "Is it good to fight such gnats? And leave the poor world in the lurch?"

"You have a line in one of your books."

"Yes?" At last Mr. Hawthorne put down his straw and spoke.

" 'Our lives are our Amens.' "

"*Mardi* that is. Yes?"

"A good line. It reminded me of my sister-in-law."

"Ah yes, but it was spoken in character, I didn't mean to . . ."

Mr. Hawthorne waved his glass at Herman, the clear liquid slopping up the sides but not spilling, so that the younger man reddened at his unnecessary defensiveness. "They say that belief is like a maze. Those that are just at the gateway can be nearer the heart of the faith than those who are busy exploring the labyrinths within."

The analogy typified the different mental geographies of the two

339

men. Herman spoke in altitudes and depths; soaring and diving. Nathaniel spoke of chambers and edifices; entering and turning; slipping, or keeping balance.

Herman frowned. "There is not much solace in that metaphor. And there is even something more frightful about the hidden truth than the hedgerowed centre of a maze." But, mixing another pair of drinks, it was Herman who found that he had lost the desire to pursue such matters.

Both men sipped their drinks and concentrated on the taste. Then Herman lifted his and said, "My mother favours the Dutch church. Though I've tried to tell her that the gin she drinks is the London concoction."

Nathaniel seemed not to attend to this observation. There was another silence and then he said, "I hope Sophia is all right. Before I came away she dreamt that the Duke of Buckingham was stabbing her in the bosom."

Herman kept some spirit in his mouth, letting it burn around his gums and under his tongue. He looked at Mr. Hawthorne but the other man seemed genuinely to be thinking about his wife, his eyes staring vacantly through the far wall of the barn, and apparently unaware that Herman might find Sophia's dream in any way remarkable.

His friend's engrossment gave Herman the panicky feeling that this second night was going the same way as the second night he had spent at the Red House at the end of the previous summer. Now, even more than then, he was anxious to draw Mr. Hawthorne out. He had returned from London in the early part of 1850 convinced that his days as a travelling adventurer were over. He had come home determined to become a truly professional author and good head of the family. It had been in just such a spirit that *Moby Dick* was begun and the Pittsfield farm had been bought. But the intervening twelve months had resulted in radical alterations to this vision. Elizabeth, he had learnt, could not satisfy him as a soul-companion. Her spiritual life was too fettered by convention and Holy Scripture to be much interested in Herman's own brand of searching faith; and she lacked the domestic poise to make a wholly satisfactory manager of the home – family circumstances hardly allowed for that anyway. His own attempts to enter the world of rural practicalities had met with either ridicule or plain incompatibility, and he was happy enough to steer clear of a serious view of life's trivialities. He had read, and met, Mr.

Hawthorne. The unworldly dedication of the early stories had inspired him and he was ready now, albeit at a different period in his own life, to take a less obsequious view of public acclaim, so that the *Redburn*like opening of *Moby Dick* was giving way to a style which put more emphasis on allegory and symbolism, and less on narrative. The availability of this admired and senior author as neighbour had opened up the prospect of artistic and spiritual communion which his marriage had not proved capable of delivering. It was this last that had produced the sense of panic. In their several meetings thus far, Mr. Hawthorne had opened up just so far and then drawn back. Herman swallowed the spirit, now neutralised by saliva, and with a smack of his tongue against the roof of his mouth, to stir Nathaniel out of his reverie, he said, "It is the pregnancy, I presume."

"That makes me think of Sophia?" There was a tone of astonishment in Mr. Hawthorne's response.

"No – that makes her have such nightmares."

"Oh, I see. The Duke of Buckingham, you mean. No, no, my wife has always suffered from periodic tensions of the head, severe headaches and so on, together with nightmares. They were particularly acute before we married."

Herman nodded. He was struck by the way in which the information had been expressed – as if to a neighbour, hitherto unknown, at a dinner table. There was nothing in the least intimate about it and Herman feared that his friend was consciously adopting a formal tone to signify that this night's conversation would be different from the last. He decided to press for a greater sharing of confidences.

"Elizabeth suffers badly from hayfever. We expect she will have to spend part of the summer in Boston. Do you like being left on your own?"

Perhaps Mr. Hawthorne was puzzled by this non-sequitur of a question; perhaps he purposefully failed to grasp the connection of Herman's sentences. Leastways he did not reply; nor did he remain silent, but surprised Herman with a reference to his time at Brook Farm.

"Sophia never joined me on Ripley's plantation, though we had intended to begin our married life there. Whatever else I may repent of, never let it be reckoned among my sins or follies that I had faith or force enough to form generous hopes of the world's destiny!"

Herman was struck by the still-vacant look in Mr. Hawthorne's eye. Fancying that his guest, rather than becoming cold and formal, was alcoholically transfixed, he quickly took the other man's glass and replenished it.

"I rejoice," Mr. Hawthorne continued, raising the newly filled glass as if in toast, "that I could once think better of the world's improvability than it deserved. It is a mistake into which men seldom fall twice."

"You believe then that Destiny conspires to spoil men's hopes?"

The conversation, having surprisingly taken a turn which allowed Herman to make one of his ontological queries, he foolishly made it straight away. Mr. Hawthorne answered, almost in annoyance, "Destiny had best answer that herself."

"And does?"

"Yes, yes – of course."

It seemed to Herman that gin did not agree with his friend, making his temper uncharacteristically ruffled.

"It must be strange, your having Mr. and Mrs. Tappan as neighbours."

"Why do you say so?"

"I think you said once that Mrs. Tappan had been at Brook Farm with you."

"I did? Well, yes, she was. But really only as a friend of Miss Fuller."

"A hanger-on?"

"No, Caroline is more than that." Mr. Hawthorne's eyes, having lost their vacancy for a moment, again became unfocused. "You know, I fancy more than ever writing a Romance about those times." Then, the eyes blinked back to alertness, and a rather embarrassed flush appearing on his cheeks, Nathaniel added, "With a capital 'R', of course. Not a love story."

Herman seized the opportunity for sharing artistic plans. "Yes, do! I have often fancied that these communities are much like ships. On land, but divided off from earthly society by their Utopian dreams, as well as the walls and fences around their plot. And then each sect has its leader, its captain, whom you could make into one of your monomaniacs. I think when you see my Ahab you'll recognise pieces of your own creations."

"Ahab?"

"Captain of the Pequod. Hunter of the White Whale." Nathaniel nodded and sipped a little more gin. "Who was it again?"

"Who was who?"

"Leader at Brook Farm."

"Ripley."

"Yes, well there you are, you could make him some kind of overblown philanthropist, or mesmerist even."

Mr. Hawthorne chuckled. "Perhaps I should scribble down a few recollections and allow you to write the Romance for me."

"Well, I could do with getting away from the sea. But no, do what you can with the idea first."

Mr. Hawthorne arched his brow a little. He had never expected his offer to be taken seriously. "The children's books first."

"Oh, yes. Is Mrs. Tappan helping with those?"

"No! Why on earth should she?" Nathaniel was beginning to be vexed by Herman's continually bringing Caroline into the conversation.

"Only that Una and Julian showed me her book once. I suppose she must have some idea what the publishers want."

"The Tappans are still away."

"Does she still write?"

"I believe another children's book is on its way."

"Perhaps you should collaborate."

"I think it time I went in. Una may not settle so well a second night."

Mr. Hawthorne stood up and Herman began gathering up bottle and glasses in silent compliance with his friend's sudden desire to retire. It was obvious that Caroline Tappan touched a raw nerve somewhere in Mr. Hawthorne's emotional past or present and Herman was unsure whether to be pleased with this certain discovery or disappointed that it had brought about an early culmination of their discussion.

Going through the house Mr. Hawthorne stopped to admire the kitchen clock, and asked if it had been acquired locally.

"Yes, in Pittsfield. Though they are manufactured in Connecticut. Only a dollar fifty. Excellent timekeepers. I have a comical notion about Christ and timepieces."

Mr. Hawthorne smiled wryly. "I really must get up to Una."

"You'll stay another night?"

*   *   *

Mr. Hawthorne did not stay another night. Herman drove him back, taking Malcolm and one of his sisters along for the ride. It

343

was the fifteenth day of March and one of those early tastes of spring that hold out false promise of a prompt end to winter. Not much was said on the journey by the adults, who were content to listen to a one-sided conversation between Una and Malcolm.

The next day, while writing to his friend Zachariah Burchmore for a new pair of trousers, Sophia came up to his room and, apologising for disturbing him, explained that there was a cabinet maker at the door.

"A cabinet maker?"

"Yes; all he says is Mr. Melville sent him to measure up."

Nathaniel went quickly down the steep flight of stairs and pulled the two children away from the doorway to reveal a short bald man in an overall with a folding-rule in his hand.

"Good day to you, sir. I've come to measure up."

"So my wife tells me. I'm afraid we know nothing of this."

"All I know myself is they says you had a broken bedstead at Brewsters and to come over here and fix it for you."

They let him look at the broken bed and he said they'd best let him make up a new frame. "Especially as there's a rich author paying. And what I'll do is nail a sacking bottom all around it so your Missis can use the space underneath for storage. That's all the rage now, that is. And judging by the size of your rooms here you need every bit of space. I've never been out here before. You know your window frames need some attention? The place your own?"

The carpenter had walked to the window and was running a finger along the perimeter of a pane of glass.

"No, we rent it."

"Well, you tell the owners that these windows at the very least need re-puttying. Very well, I'll get this ready in a little over a week."

While he was in the process of leaving – the children detained him for some minutes at his carriage and he being a slow, sociable country sort did not hurry away – Nathaniel helped Sophia replace the pile of books beneath the broken bedstead.

"That's nice of Mr. Melville."

Her husband's "Yes" was pensive. On leaving Arrowhead he had been presented with a four-volume work entitled *The Mariner's Chronicle*, originally a present from Herman's Berkshire uncle, and evidently a work which had been a prized reference source. As has been shown by Mr. Hawthorne's insistence on paying a nominal rent for the Red House, he was not a man to feel easy with over-generous favours and he was already beginning to find Mr. Melville's friendship a little too zealous.

"Now you'd better get that letter finished. You will remember to enclose the tape. I did give it you?"

"Yes. You gave me the tape."

Nathaniel had begun his letter by explaining the piece of tape:

> Dear Zack / You will wonder what this piece of tape means. The fact is I want you to get me a pair of pantaloons, either at Oak Hall or Smith's, or any other cheap clothing· establishment that you think proper. The piece of tape is the precise length of the last pair that John Earl made me, from waistband downwards. I have likewise marked the measurement around the waist and around the thigh; so that I think you will be able to suit me. Be sure and have them large enough, and any other defect is of less consequence. As for the material let it be of some stout dark cloth, suited to the gravity of my character; it need not be black though that would be no objection. I would rather not have them blue.

Sophia had bullied him into making this request on his return from Arrowhead, having been appalled by the contrast between Mr. Melville's appearance and that of her husband. He also wrote off for a waistcoat and a pair of size ten country boots.

Herman put in another month of hard work on the *Whale*, which he combined with a gradually increasing load of tinkering and patching-up jobs around the farm. Writing, "I have perceived that in all cases man must eventually lower, or at least shift, his conceit of attainable felicity; not placing it anywhere in the intellect or the fancy; but in the wife, the heart, the bed, the table, the saddle, the fireside, the country," he was no doubt recalling the mood in which he had returned from England. A few pages on, and considering his spellbound absorption in the character of Nathaniel Hawthorne, he writes, "Hardly have we mortals by long toilings extracted from the world's vast bulk its small but valuable sperm; and then, with weary patience, cleansed ourselves from its defilements, and learned to live here in clean tabernacles of the soul; hardly is this done, when – *there she blows!* – the ghost is spouted up, and away we sail to fight some other world, and go through young life's old routine again."

Ten days after writing off to Boston, the box from Zack

Burchmore had still not been delivered to the Red House and feeling certain that it had become holed up at the Pittsfield depot both the Hawthornes wrote a note to Melville requesting him to see if it were there, and if it were, to pick it up for them. Sophia's postscript contains a strange, last-minute panic about the bedstead:

> If the cabinet maker intends to make a bedstead which cannot be taken down and put up with ease, on account of the sacking bottom which he is going to nail on, I think it will not be worth having – and I wish he would not do anything about it. Will you tell him so?

Behind these words in Sophia's hand there lurks her husband's discomfort in the face of material favours. Both of them must have realised it was too late to avert the good deed. Mr. Melville was perhaps sufficiently dismayed by this reaction not to deliver the box in person but simply to direct it to the Post Office in Lenox. However, on April 11th he did get over to Lenox, to deliver both the bedstead and a kitchen clock, of the same model as the one in his Arrowhead kitchen. There were others at the Hawthorne home that day – John O'Sullivan, editor of the *Democratic Review*, and Mr. Farley – so that Herman's visit resulted in little furthering of the friendship. But when it transpired that Mr. Hawthorne was contemplating going to New York, to meet with O'Sullivan there, Herman was quick to point out that he would be going there too, eventually, to get his *Whale* through the press. The prospect of a jaunt together was one to be throughly explored, even if, predictably, Mr. Hawthorne was lukewarm in his reaction to the proposal.

"Oh, I have to go to Boston and Salem first. And Sophia must get away too."

Herman addressed his response to Mrs. Hawthorne. "I'll be down your way again shortly to talk him round. I hope the clock keeps good time now."

"Oh, you shouldn't have."

"And the bed is easy enough to put up. I did have a word with the cabinet maker, but let me know if it's bothersome. And now, is there anything else I can fetch for you hermits?" Herman turned to O'Sullivan and added, "Fair set of recluses these, you know." He then looked back at Mrs. Hawthorne for a reply to his query.

"Well . . ." (There was a hesitation while she looked timidly

346

towards her husband, who staunchly avoided her gaze, and in fact walked some paces away, to separate himself from the conversation.) "Well, Julian *has* quite outgrown his shoes."

"Speak no further – I am sure the capital of Berkshire will be able to furnish you what you want. I suggest you jot down some details of the type of thing required and I shall get one of my sisters to procure them for you."

"Oh, of course, your wife must be far too busy with that big household, I shouldn't have asked it."

Herman put his hands on Sophia's shoulders and turned her in the direction of the house. She scurried off with both hands lifting up her skirts. The men exchanged an uneasy sally of chuckles although Mr. Hawthorne in reality was most unamused by the episode, and would tell Sophia about it later. He had intended giving Melville a copy of the *Seven Gables*, fresh from the press, and had already inscribed one for him, but now decided that this could await a more pleasing occasion. However, when Sophia came out with her note concerning Julian's shoes she brought the book out also, saying first to her husband, "You'd have forgotten this, wouldn't you? Look, I've dated it in my own hand. Is that all right?" There was no response from Nathaniel. "Is that all right, Mr. Melville? This is Nathaniel's new novel. The signing is by him. The date is by me."

Nathaniel made a point of passing an inconsequential remark with O'Sullivan, partly through straightforward embarrassment, but also because he was by now genuinely angry with his wife, with an annoyance which rarely manifested itself between them, for they generally read one another's minds well.

"Excellent. I shall get straight back and dive into this. Mr. Hawthorne, you will have robbed me of a day. Come to New York with me and let my *Whale* rob you of a week."

Melville's response to the *Gables*, recorded in a letter to Nathaniel five days later is, by Melvillian standards, muted:

> . . . the Author who declares himself a sovereign nature amid the powers of heaven, hell, and earth. He may perish; but so long as he exists he insists upon treating with all powers upon an equal basis. If any of those other powers choose to withhold certain secrets, let them; that does not impair my sovereignty in myself; that does not make me tributary. And perhaps, after all, there is *no* secret. We

incline to think that the Problem of the Universe is like the Freemason's secret, so terrible to all children. It turns out at last, to consist in a triangle, a mallet and an apron – nothing more!

What this seems to say is that Mr. Hawthorne was beginning to lose some of his mystique; that Melville was losing the sense of inferiority which had affected the opening stages of their friendship; that now he considered himself a Power equal to Mr. Hawthorne; and if Hawthorne chose to withhold certain secrets, let him; perhaps there was no secret anyway. It is Melville's use of pronouns in this letter which suggests that this reading is defensible. Beginning systematically, but uncharacteristically, with the royal "we", Melville administers some stagey and unexceptional criticism of the novel, all favourable in a fairly pandering but honest way. Then, identifying with the authorial figure he shifts to "he" (i.e. Hawthorne), and finally, in the middle of the quoted paragraph, the identification intensifies, the pronouns used become "my" and "me" and Melville ends up talking about himself.

The whole letter ends with a different kind of exhortation. "Walk down one of these mornings, and see me. No nonsense; come. Remember me to Mrs. Hawthorne and the children." This sounds less intense, less bothered, than his previous insistencies. The other end of the letter informed the Hawthorne household that shoes of the desired size and pattern could not be had in all Pittsfield.

*   *   *

The next three months or so – the rest of April, May, June, July – were very different for each of the two authors. For Mr. Hawthorne they were dominated by the favourable reception of *The House Of Seven Gables* and by the birth of his third child, Rose. His father-in-law, Dr. Peabody, stayed at the Red House for a few days either side of the birth (it was he who actually took charge at the instant of delivery, in the absence of the nurse), but Mrs. Peabody had become ill soon after moving to West Newton, so that she was unable to come, and Dr. Peabody had to return to her as soon as Sophia had recovered a little of her strength. Nathaniel had hoped to take advantage of a longer stay by making his own planned trip to Boston and Salem. This was not possible and he spent much of May writing letters and planning his proposed collection of children's stories. His only vexation, other than the scuppering of his Boston trip, was the necessity of responding to various persons who considered that the family name of "Pyncheon" had been impugned in his novel. He had to counter suggestions that reparation was due or, at the very least, the plates of the book should be altered so that future printings of the text contained a different family name. His replies to these complaints were courteous, but he staunchly defended an author's right to the use of any surname he chose. The recipients were apparently pacified although in an introductory section to The Gorgon's Head, the first of the *Wonder Book* stories, he wrote, of the children:

> I am afraid to tell you their names, or even to give them any names which other children have ever been called by; because, to my certain knowledge, authors sometimes get themselves into great trouble by accidentally giving names of real persons to the characters in their books.

So that names such as Sweet Fern, Squash-Blossom and Buttercup, so twee and whimsical on first reading, in fact had a background ironical bite to them.

His preparation had been good. The children were once again able to play out of doors. Although Sophia was some time regaining her strength, the baby did not unduly disturb their nights. Nathaniel wrote his stories in a mood of effulgent pleasure, so that within a period of six summer weeks he had produced nearly three hundred manuscript pages.

Nothing more need be said in detail about the way this time passed at Lenox, but sections from a letter which Mr. Hawthorne wrote to his sister-in-law Elizabeth Peabody will testify to the contrasting ways in which his and Melville's mental weathers were then operating:

> Dear Elizabeth / This subject of Life Insurance is not new to me. I have thought, read and conversed about it long ago . . . I know that it is an excellent thing in some circumstances – that is, for persons with a regular income . . . We must take our chance, or our dispensation of Providence.
>
> Sophia and the baby are getting on bravely. She gazes at it all day long, and continually discovers new beauties. As for me, who look at it perhaps half a dozen times a day, I

must confess that I have not yet discovered the first beauty. But I think I never have had any natural partiality for my children. I love them according to their deserts.

Your father, as I see him here, presents as comfortable an aspect of old age as I can possibly imagine. He does not appear to suffer any disquietude from your mother's precarious condition . . . The children hang about him continually, and find him an excellent playmate; merely a playmate however, for he is the most heedless and venturesome of the three, and when left to his guidance, they do things and undertake adventures which they would never dream of by themselves . . . Happily he finds my surroundings so rough and rugged that he has continually some little job or other to do.

For Melville these three months were full of hot, sticky unproductive effort. On May 1st, to cover the cost of improvements to the farm's outbuildings, he had had to take out a commercial loan of two hundred and fifty dollars for five years at nine per cent. This was after Harper and Bros. had finally refused his repeated requests for an advance on the *Whale*. If the publishing firm had known what problems Herman was having with the final section of the book they wouldn't have bothered excusing their inability to help. As it was they drew up an account which made it evident that Herman owed *them* seven hundred dollars. Such financial distractions inhibited his progress and in particular made him, once again, uncertain as to what kind of work he was trying to produce – one that would be pleasing to the public or one that would please himself.

In the middle of the month he visited New York for twenty-four hours to arrange the occupancy of a room in June when he was hoping to see the main bulk of the book through the press and to finish writing the end chapters. While there he seemed not to be able to escape the presence of Nathaniel Hawthorne. He saw a portrait of the author; heard and read many favourable allusions to the *Seven Gables*; saw bookshop displays of the republished *Tales*; and noticed advertisements heralding a "New Volume by N. H.". All of which provoked, in his next letter to Lenox, a rather sour aside on the subject of fame:

All Fame is patronage. Let me be infamous: there is no patronage in *that*. What "reputation" H. M. has is horrible.

Think of it! To go down to posterity is bad enough anyway; but to go down as a man "who lived among the cannibals"!

He had not taken the reading of *The House Of The Seven Gables* as placidly as at first appears. The book had impressed upon him the futility of trying to write against the grain of his own ability. His own style was better – beefier, anyway. In addition, the other man's character exasperated him. Holed away in his cramped little shanty he had no interest in exchanging philosophical truths with another writer but preferred to spend his summer writing children's stories. The story "Ethan Brand" had recently been republished in the *Dollar* magazine. Melville had read into it a prospective denunciation of his own self-education. A key passage read:

> Then ensued that vast intellectual development, which, in its progress, disturbed the counterpoise between his mind and heart. The idea that possessed his life had operated as a means of education; it had gone on cultivating his powers to the highest point of which they were susceptible; it had raised him from the level of an unlettered labourer to stand on a star-lit eminence, whither the philosophers of the earth, laden with the lore of universities, might vainly strive to clamber after him. So much for the intellect! But where was the heart?

This struck home to the sailor-turned-philosopher as one more example of Mr. Hawthorne's eerie and almost spiteful clairvoyance. But the man's indolence was the most maddening attribute. He would never think of walking the six miles to Pittsfield; no great trek by that century's standards. The friendship, which had promised so much, had progressed to the marvellous point where the Hawthornes could unashamedly use him as an errand boy, to do the shopping and collecting which they were too lazy to do themselves. But he wouldn't cease to hammer at their emotional self-sufficiency.

> I mean to continue visiting you until you tell me that my visits are supererogatory and superfluous. With no son of man do I stand upon any etiquette or ceremony, except the Christian ones of charity and honesty.

The work on the out-buildings, which he was doing in large part

351

himself, kept him away from the Hawthornes' door up until his departure from New York.

> I have not been to Lenox because in the evening I feel completely done up, as the phrase is, and incapable of the long jolting to get to your house and back. In a week or so, I go to New York, to bury myself in a third-storey room, and work and slave on my 'Whale' while it is driving through the press. *That* is the only way I can finish it now. I am so pulled hither and thither by circumstances. The calm, the coolness, the silent grass-growing mood in which a man *ought* always to compose – that, I fear, can seldom be mine.

Let Nathaniel know there was no way he, Herman, could share his well-guarded domestic repose. He had been pestered into the out-of-doors work by his family, but it was at least some kind of physical therapy for the difficulties posed by *Moby Dick*'s "fin." He could see the book turning into a final hash, another botch like the ones before it. Physical toil in the open air made him slightly contemptuous of the incessant shut-away application of the winter.

> What's the use of elaborating what, in its very essence, is so short-lived as a modern book? Though I wrote the Gospels in this century I should die in the gutter.

He went to New York in a mood to have done with it.

*   *   *

The journey was more circuitous than the one from Pittsfield to Boston. First one had to take the stage to West Stockbridge and then travel the length of the Housatonic Railroad to Bridgeport on Long Island Sound. From there one picked up the newly opened New York and New Haven line and finally, to get into the centre of town, changed again at William's Bridge for a fifteen-mile shuttle on the Harlem Railroad.

He arrived in his meagre third-storey room at six in the evening, having brought with him, apart from normal travelling baggage, a securely tied carton of manuscript, to which he had persuaded Elizabeth to attach an umbilical cord in strong triple-plaited thread which travelled, from the parcel, through the waist of his trousers and down an inside leg, to be tied about his ankle, so that all day he had boarded and unboarded the rail cars with a veritable ball and chain about his person.

It was a mean room, unadorned and uncarpeted. The bed was low, and pushed into one corner, so that it looked like a prisoner's pallet. The only furniture, beside a chest of drawers covered in cheap blue chintz, was an oversized mahogany chair, weak about the joints, and a six-inch-long board of oak set upon two empty flour barrels. The lowness of the bed, combined with the shortness of the umbilical cord, forced Herman to kneel down on the floor whilst he opened his suitcase to find his penknife with which to separate himself from his paper and ink foetus.

Having made the cut, and thus able to sit down in the chair and survey more closely his surroundings, he felt no less a prisoner. The view from the window was mainly of brick; he had to strain his neck in order to see one small parallelogram of sky. He had taken a few dry biscuits from a packet in his case, and he broke one of them in half, brushing the crumbs onto the floor with the side of his hand. He continued the sweeping motion after the wooden surface was clear, enjoying the numb sense of friction created by a large callus beneath his little finger. Remembering the sunsoaked muscular effort which had gone into that accumulation of hardened skin he could not help but wonder at the different sort of occupation he had committed himself to for the next three weeks. The thought that the commitment was rather more lasting, that he had dedicated his life to the pen, the ink, the desk, was suddenly ghastly to consider. Thinking of the books which had first enchanted him, the works of Fenimore Cooper, his imagination became filled with vignettes of pioneering life, and in particular with images of Red Indians crashing like wild deer through the green underbush. Civilisation and Philosophy, behold your victim – he grinned ruefully at this idea, but nevertheless turned back to the packet, broke its restraining strings, again with the penknife, and began to set out on the oaken tablet the completed chapters in numerical order.

Over the next few days, as he finished ordering his manuscript and sent the early corrected chapters off to the printers for setting, and as these came back to him in the form of proofs for final correction, he was aware that his book was becoming already limited, bound over and committed to imperfection, so that he became inhibited in the execution of what was to have been the main purpose of his summer hibernation – the writing of the final chapters.

It was nearly seven years since Melville had returned home from the sea to begin his writing life; just over five years since his first book was published. The educating process that had begun during those first eighteen months ashore seemed now to have hit still water. Although, in this leprously white-walled room he was unable to push the narrative along, he did compose a few reflective paragraphs that found their way into the later chapters, one such being:

> There is no steady unretracing progress in this life; we do not advance through fixed gradations, and at the last one pause: – through infancy's unconscious spell, boyhood's thoughtless faith, adolescence's doubt (the common doom), then scepticism, then disbelief, resting at last in manhood's pondering repose of If. But once gone through, we trace the round again; and are infants, boys, and men, and Ifs eternally.

He kept his presence in the city as quiet as possible – in particular he did not want to meet the Duyckincks. He dined with Allan and Sophia just twice and on each occasion drank over-much, so that his conversation became disjointed and rather morbid, a fact which was duly conveyed to Pittsfield by letter, this representing the beginning of the family's concern for Herman's health and state of mind. He spent much of each daytime at the printers, unnecessarily standing over the typesetters, and getting to know an old man by the name of Preston, who had been with the firm all his working life, and whose hands were now too arthritic to handle the pieces of type, so that he generally stood around idle, keeping an experienced eye on things. He impressed Herman with the sense of repose that exuded from his stance and gaze. He was a simple man and a Christian; appending his conversation with phrases like "All in God's time" or "He sees it, if we don't". He was well-liked by his colleagues and the younger apprentices treated his smallest piece of advice with the utmost respect. Such unpretentious, small-scale renown suddenly seemed very enviable to Herman, so that he was rather taken aback towards the end of his three-week stay when Preston began speaking ruefully of a certain failed ambition. It seemed that as a youth he had harboured thoughts of becoming a scientist and all through his manhood had developed an amateur's interest in machinery. He had attempted to develop and patent a form of hydraulic pump for

354

the drying up of swamps. "Ten years I gave to that infernal machine before I admitted of defeat. Ten years when the work here meant nothing to me. I was fretting to get back to the workshop. Ten years when my own bairns saw nothing of me, unless it was to hold a screw in place or help create a false quagmire for a test run. In the dead of winter, when it was too cold to work in the evenings, I bent over blueprints of the next spring's model. In the end the patent office wrote to tell me someone else had registered a similar pumping machine, but by then I was glad enough to admit my failure. My good wife tried to comfort me. Said surely there was something else to invent. But I know now there's not much left in an old world to invent."

The whole of the printing floor was listening to old Preston's story. Herman and the rest of them said nothing.

"Boys, take my advice, and never try to invent anything but happiness. Praise be to God for that failure!"

This last, deep fervent cry echoed in Herman's mind up until his departure. He left New York with less than half the finished chapters in proof form and, disgusted with the brick-kiln heat of the city, returned to the country determined, as he had been when he had left London, to attend himself more fulsomely to the domestic felicities of hearth and home.

He took about his person both the handwritten manuscript and the printed proofs, but since this time he had had no second person to tie the parcels to his ankle he spent the entire journey clutching them to himself, so that he arrived in a state of nervous exhaustion. Unfortunately Elizabeth was suffering badly with hayfever and, with her face buried in a wet towel, was in no fit state to give her husband anything like a loving welcome. The other members of the household were strangely inquisitive of his health – had he been having proper meals, had he been sitting up late at night, straining his eyes perhaps. Unaware of the Fourth Avenue letter these enquiries at first mystified Herman and then, when they continued beyond the bounds of natural curiosity or even normal family concern, infuriated him. He left the house and took a pipe into the cowshed.

Before going away he had broached his idea of a piazza on the north side of the house. Unbeknown to the rest of his family much of his work on the outbuildings and outer walls of the farmhouse had been to clear the way for this proposed edifice. On the first morning after getting back from New York, ignoring the storm that it would provoke, he rode into town and arranged with a local timber firm for a man to come and measure up. The man rode straight back with him, made his calculations, and the work began the following day. The piazza was completed in less than two weeks – a simple wooden platform, supported on short brick pedestals, with square wooden posts holding up the sloping roof. The autocratic way in which Herman had chosen both the design and the aspect, and his imperious disregard of attempted criticism (he simply walked away, normally to the barn, whenever anyone raised a voice in opposition) seemed to confirm the Fourth Avenue reports; something had destabilised the man of the house.

On one of the last days of June he had been sitting at his desk in his small upstairs room, with the window open, and the sound of the carpenters' planing and hammering beneath him, knowing that he ought to attack his manuscript again, but strangely unbothered. He looked a little differently on the attack of doldrums which had overcome him in the city and found himself writing in free and easy manner to Mr. Hawthorne:

> This most persuasive season has now for weeks recalled me from certain crotchety and over doleful chimaeras, the like of which men like you and me and some others, forming a chain of God's posts round the world, must be content to encounter now and then, and fight them the best way we can . . .
>
> Come and spend a day here if you can and want to; if not, stay in Lenox, and God give you long life.

Having sent off the letter and with the family treating him with an odd but welcome degree of reserve, he was able to devote himself to a pleasant mix of haymaking and writing. Elizabeth, now six months pregnant, was becoming large and uncomfortable. He became very courteous towards her and let Malcolm ride out with the nag to the hayfields.

Hawthorne remained domiciled at Lenox and, in a reply which he sent to Herman (an "easy-flowing long letter"), did not take up the offer of seeing "a fin of the Whale by way of a specimen Mouthful". He and Sophia, becoming conscious of a growing prosperity, began to talk openly about their manner of living.

"I think our Mr. Omoo finds me an exasperating acquaintance."

"None but us can count the cost to you of having a stranger in our courts."

"Am I really such a hermit?"

"You know you are. Why, I could see the way even Father, much though you like him, destroyed your artistic and domestic life. I never intend to have a guest for so long again."

Nathaniel, hanging his head, said, "No – that is too harsh on yourself. I have just had Mr. Emerson here."

"Only for a night. And anyway he spent more time with Caroline than you."

"Well, I shall have solitude enough next month."

Sophia had arranged to visit her parents in West Newton, taking Una with her. A week ago they had finally declined an offer to rent the Mann house in West Newton for nine months, while Horace and Mary were in Washington. Sophia had told Mary that they would be unable to pay a fair rent and would have nothing in Lenox to return to when the lease was over. But the prime reason was Nathaniel's disinclination to be close to his parents-in-law. However, they were considering a move out of the Red House. Fanny Kemble, the English actress, owned a summer cottage and a few acres of land in Lenox, which she had offered to the Hawthornes, ready-furnished and rent-free.

"When you get back we must decide on our move."

"I shall miss it here."

"Oh, but it is the most inconvenient and wretched little hovel I've ever put my head in. Besides – you know we can't stay here."

"No. I suppose we can't."

This last agreement was a reference to the deterioration in relations with the Tappan family, which had resulted in a ban on the use of the orchard.

"If things continue to prosper, next year we shall be in a position to buy a place."

"Nathaniel, that's wonderful. Be busy while I'm away, then."

"With Julian? No; I am going to read foolish novels, and smoke cigars and think of nothing at all – which is equivalent to thinking of all manner of things."

"Just as long as the cigars stay out of doors."

"I have just sent off to Zack for one thousand of the beauties."

"We shouldn't find a place here for that price."

"I want to take you back to the coast – somewhere on the Manchester shore. Pike has written to me about a place on

Marblehead-neck. But there are not enough trees there and the society in summer would be made up entirely of Boston aristocrats and capitalists. We must have plenty of trees and little fashionable life."

"But, dearest, as soon as my distinguished husband moves there, society will flock to his door."

Nathaniel picked up a copy of the *Literary World* and swatted her in the lap.

The bare outlines of the disputed rights to the fruit in the cottage grounds are as follows. At the outset Mr. Hawthorne had insisted on the payment of a nominal rent to establish certain "rights". Among these he considered the right to the fruit of the orchard, a right which seemed to have been tacitly conceded the previous year, when no complaint had been made about their picking of currants, plums, pears and apples. It seems that around this time of high summer 1851 one Mary Beckman, a friend of Mrs. Peters the Hawthorne servant, was approached by Mrs. Tappan while carrying a basket of fruit. Caroline had enquired, with some acidity, whether the fruit had been sold or given away. Mary returned to Mrs. Peters to complain that she had been accused of conspiring to denude the fruit bushes. The incident was immediately followed by a note of remonstrance to Sophia, taking her to task for presuming the property of the orchard, and for distributing its produce to friends and servants. Sophia had replied with a gentle assertion of the right which Nathaniel insisted had been conferred with the payment of the annual rent. Another note came swiftly back from the Highwood estate (itself, at that time, rented and not owned, a fact that Mr. Hawthorne made much of in a long letter to Caroline Tappan at the height of the dispute), this second note repeating in much clearer terms than the first that the Hawthornes had no right whatever to a single pip or berry, and would it not be more appropriate for them to receive a kindness rather than assume rights.

There is much in this episode that must remain mysterious, but one thing is crystally clear – Mr. Tappan played no part in the controversy. It was he, and not Caroline, who eventually replied to Nathaniel's letter, in terms that the Hawthornes described as "noble and beautiful" and as making "one ashamed of any narrower or ignobler sentiment than those of universal beneficence and goodwill".

Something other than the fruit must have aggravated Caroline into acting spitefully. It was she, and not her husband, who had been on close friendly terms with the Hawthornes; she, and not her husband, who should have been loath to take the contractual view.

Elizabeth travelled out to accompany Sophia and the two girls to West Newton. They said goodbye to Julian and Nathaniel at 7 a.m. Monday July 28th 1851. When they had gone Julian ran around shouting and squealing as loud as he could for half an hour.

Part Four

U na and Julian had taken themselves to the back of the end
car so that they could watch the track, and the small towns
and villages of the Berkshires, receding. They had lived in the Red
House for eighteen months and were now moving to their Aunt
Mary's and Uncle Horace's place in West Newton. It was a wet
morning in the latter half of November 1851. Una, who was seven
years old, enquired of her brother, who was four, whether he
recalled the tantrum that had spoiled the beginning of that earlier
journey.

"Yes," he said. "You were so cross you stamped your foot till it
got a pain."

Una giggled and flung her head back against the seat, greatly
amused by the recollection of a childish eccentricity. She sat
forward, her face red and her eyes watery.

"Not me! You were the one who was miserable. Pining for
horsey!"

Julian, refusing to be reminded of his own infantile vagaries, put
his heels up on the seat opposite, which was unoccupied, and said,
"I'm going to play toadstools."

His sister gave a loud hiccupping laugh and collapsed into his
lap.

Nathaniel, sitting at the other end of the car, leaned into the
aisle to make sure the children were not making too great a
disturbance. He and Sophia sat with the six-month-old Baby Rose
perched between them. Although it was cold, and the cars were
unheated, the child's legs were bare, and an ugly big blister
halfway down her right shin was given to the air. Nathaniel looked
down at the mark, and then frowned at his wife.

"It's healing well enough," she said.

"Are you sure?"

"If we can keep it dry . . ."

363

The accident had been his own doing. Sophia had been standing in the kitchen, holding Rosebud in her arms, on one of the last warm days of autumn, when Nathaniel had turned with a hot pan of chocolate. The lip of the pan had touched the child's leg, instantly etching a two-inch weal into her soft fleshy skin.

Their departures seemed often to coincide with such disasters, as if a disintegration of the quiet pattern of their lives echoed the decision to move on. Leaving Lenox had been arranged so suddenly it almost seemed they were in a state of flight. There had been vague talk of their staying in the district having become impossible, the impossibility being bound up both with Caroline Tappan and Herman Melville. Both embroilments were entirely separate, but as Mr. Hawthorne had become bothered by them, they had been confused in his mind.

He had suffered a recurrent dream during that autumn in which Melville and Caroline stood on either side of his bed, leaning across it to exchange a kiss. The dream revealed to him that in some irrational way he held Mr. Melville responsible for the transformation in Caroline's attitude to his family – a transformation that was represented by the contrast in her affectionate sickbed tête-à-tête with him on their arrival, and the later frosty notes concerning the orchard.

*   *   *

Melville had finally finished *Moby Dick* in a six-day flurry, after the Duyckinck brothers had departed on August 14th 1851. *Pierre*, which had been brewing in his mind all summer, was begun straightaway. "Silly thoughts and wayward meditations", in the words of a letter to Mrs. Morewood in early September of that year, had sparked off the opening chapters; the implied discovery of a moral waywardness in his father; suspicions of an emotional entanglement involving Mr. Hawthorne and Caroline Tappan; the strange relational disorientation affecting his wife and mother; the frustration and demystification of his failed intimacy with Mr. Hawthorne; perverse suppositions regarding his father-in-law; the obsession with incest – all had compelled him onwards in his Tale of Ambiguity.

He was well into it when Stanwix had been born on October 22nd and, given the disorientation that was the motivating force behind his novel, the mistake he made in the filling-out of the birth certificate is explicable enough; but interesting.

Next to the name of the child's father he put his own.

Next to the name of the child's mother he wrote, "Maria G. Melville".

Lizzie had been generous on discovering the error, dismissing it as the result of a miscomprehension. Herman, she argued, had taken the questions as applying to himself. Maria, after all, *was* his mother. Credible enough, for the unsuspicious.

His immersion in the new book was such that the London publication of *Moby Dick*, and the imminent American unveiling, showed little sign of distracting him, his main diversion being the axing down of wood for the ravenous multi-mouthed chimney, already in full blast. But early in November he had received a letter from Evert Duyckinck sending him news of the sinking of the ship *Ann Alexander* by a large sperm whale.

Melville's reply:

> It is really and truly a surprising coincidence – to say the least. I make no doubt it is Moby Dick himself, for there is no account of his capture after the sad fate of the Pequod about fourteen years ago. Ye Gods! What a commentator is the Ann Alexander whale. What he has to say is short and pithy and very much to the point. I wonder if my evil act has raised this monster.

By the same post he received, from Mr. Hawthorne, a copy of the *Wonder Book* for Malcolm. He flipped through its pages. "Once upon a time", "Long, long ago". He had begun *Pierre* with the intention (at least, its inception was based upon such an intention) of emulating the other man's style. But the element of disdain which had been creeping into his view of Mr. Hawthorne, born of his frustration with Nathaniel's placid withholding of himself, and evidenced now by the contrast between his own monster-raising art and the juvenile renderings of mythical texts in this children's book, had sharpened the tone to one of pastiche.

A week later he had been made to feel differently. *Moby Dick* was out and Mr. Hawthorne read it quickly. His reaction, handed to Herman in the form of a letter while he was walking one evening to Mrs. Morewood's, put him in an ecstasy. The old feelings of fraternity came flooding back. Oh, how right he had been to dedicate the book to Nathaniel Hawthorne. He had understood it and the knowledge inspired ineffable socialities in Herman. He felt pantheistic. He skipped on the road. If he had had his horse and cart he might have galloped off to dine with the Hawthornes. Later that night, the elation had calmed itself to a feeling of contentment, in which there was neither hopefulness nor despair. He felt himself blessedly irresponsible. An ear had been granted his weird and coded explanations.

But atmospheric scepticisms stole over him in sleep. He woke to find that his own angel, sympathising with the new day, had turned over another page. Perhaps Mr. Hawthorne had cared for the book only in essence. His letter had been short on detail. He had despised its imperfect body but embraced its soul.

His own reply, when it turned to confessing these doubts, became unhinged:

> . . . truth is ever incoherent, and when the big hearts strike together the concussion is a little stunning. Farewell. Don't write a word about the book. That would be robbing me of my miserly delight. I am heartily sorry I ever wrote anything about you – it was paltry. Lord, when shall we be done growing? As long as we have anything more to do, we have done nothing . . . Lord, when shall we be done changing? Ah, it's a long stage, and no inn in sight; and night coming and the body cold. But with you for a passenger, I am content and can be happy. . . . Knowing you persuades me more than the Bible of our immortality.

He signed himself, for the first and only time to anyone other than a close member of his family, plain

Herman

But the mood of fraternity hadn't done with him. He added a P. S.

> I can't stop yet . . . The divine magnet is on you, and my magnet responds. Which is the biggest? A foolish question. They are *one*.

The reply to this letter was devastating. It came from Sophia and consisted in the announcement that they would be leaving Berkshire for good on November 21st, and moving to West Newton. She enclosed an engraving made from Thompson's portrait of her husband.

The engraving captured the ambiguous smile, so that Mr. Hawthorne's demeanour in the picture appeared flirtatious, and

366

Herman, in long midnight gloatings over the print, read licentious mysteries into the gaze, fancying that the artist had captured the evidence of a secret involvement.

During the final weeks of the year the new book possessed him with the kind of continuous pull that had not been the case with *Moby Dick*. The family had Christmas lunch with the Morewoods. Elizabeth, fully recovered from the birth of Stanwix, and possessed of a new sense of confidence, stemming partly from the satisfaction of being a better, more experienced mother to her second baby, and partly from a closer personal relationship with the Melville sisters, as well as with Mrs. Morewood, delighted in boasting of her husband's stupendous industry.

"He often doesn't leave his room until quite dark in the evening, does he, Augusta?"

"And then to his first solid food of the day," added the mother.

Mrs. Morewood laughed. "This reclusive life will soon enough make your city friends think you slightly insane."

There was a momentary silence around the table, during which Herman quickly scanned his family. "I long ago came to the same conclusion myself," he said. And, turning to Mrs. Morewood, added, "A damned devilish and perverted tale, the *Whale*, was it not?"

But on the whole Herman was quiet and less irreverent than the Morewoods had experienced before.

In the New Year he and Elizabeth went to New York. Sophia Hawthorne had read the *Whale* book by then and on December 29th had written to Herman full of praise. He replied, on finest embossed, gilt-edged Bath paper, that she was the only woman to say as much. He thanked her for that, and attributed it to her "spiritualising nature". The wittiest paragraph of the letter was a dig in the ribs of her husband:

And now, how are you in West Newton? Are all domestic affairs regulated? Is Miss Una content? and Master Julian satisfied with the landscape in general? And does Mr. Hawthorne continue his series of calls upon all his neighbours within a radius of ten miles? Shall I send him ten packs of visiting cards? And a box of kid gloves? and the latest style of Parisian handkerchief? He goes into society too much altogether – seven evenings out, a week, should content any reasonable man.

367

The book *Pierre* further elaborated the themes of *Moby Dick*. One paragraph fairly states the conundrum which, in their energy to extricate particular allegories and subsidiary meanings, the critics have sometimes obscured.

> There is a dark, mad mystery in some human hearts which sometimes during the tyranny of a usurper mood leads them to be all eagerness to cast off the most intense beloved bond, as a hindrance to the attainment of whatever transcendental object that usurper mood so tyrannically suggests. Then the beloved bond seems to hold us to no essential good; lifted to exalted mounts, we can dispense with all the vale; endearments we spurn; kisses are blisters to us; and forsaking the palpitating forms of mortal love we emptily embrace the boundless and unbodied air. We think we are not human; we become as immortal bachelors and gods; but again, like the Greek gods themselves, prone we descend to earth; glad to be uxorious once more; glad to hide these godlike heads within the bosoms made of too-seducing clay.

It was finished in the spring, after which Herman must have felt reasonably fit, for he spent three months moving to and fro between New York and Arrowhead, and visiting Nantucket and the Elizabeth Islands with his father-in-law Judge Shaw. On his return from this jaunt he had found waiting for him a copy of Mr. Hawthorne's new book *The Blithedale Romance*, together with an invitation to visit Concord.

*   *   *

Mr. Hawthorne's third novel, in which the dream involving Melville and Caroline had become a centrepiece, was written quickly during the winter spent in West Newton. There are many ways of interpreting the characters in the Romance, none of them watertight of course, but for those who go to it for the first time, or go back to it in the light of the friendship between the two authors, the following key may prove suggestive:

> Hollingsworth=MELVILLE
> Priscilla=SOPHIA
> Zenobia=CAROLINE
> Coverdale=HAWTHORNE

The book also reveals Mr. Melville's influence in its surface features. It is lighter in touch than the two previous novels. It is written in the first person and, in the opening chapter, when Coverdale finishes off his last bottle of sherry with a friend before setting out for Blithedale, there is a hint of Ishmael casting off from the Spouter Inn.

Nathaniel had been genuine in his response to *Moby Dick* and had been more touched and affected by the personality of the younger man than Herman would ever know. Indeed, a good part of the writing of *Blithedale* was a form of exorcising the other man's influence. As he makes Coverdale say:

> Our souls, after all, are not our own. We convey a property in them to those with whom we associate, but to what extent can never be known, until we feel the tug, the agony, of our abortive effort to resume an exclusive sway over ourselves.

Herman's gushing reply of November 1851, which he had signed, significantly, with his bare Christian name, may well have hurried the Hawthornes in their planned departure, Nathaniel being unwilling to chance another close encounter. Writing later in his life, phrasing it just a little differently, but demonstrating a continuing obsession with the effort to retain the individuality of his personal soul, he said:

> Nothing is surer, however, than that, if we suffer ourselves to be drawn into too close proximity with people, if we overestimate the degree of our proper tendency towards them, or theirs towards us, a reaction is sure to follow.

In the summer of 1852 Mr. Hawthorne's earnings, principally from *The Scarlet Letter*, enabled him to purchase the Alcott home in Concord. Soon after moving in, his sister Louisa had been drowned in a riverboat accident. He had received the news at the same time as posting off an invitation to Mr. Melville to visit them at Concord. It had been sent with the basest of motives – to show off the family's current prosperity in contrast to their days as tenants in the Red Shanty – and Nathaniel felt so chastened by the sad tidings that he felt only immense relief when Herman declined to come. He was even more relieved when he read *Pierre* soon after it was published, for he found it difficult to take the book's exaggerated style seriously. And when, at the end of the summer,

369

Herman began sending the "Agatha" material (all of which related to a lengthy case of bigamy reported to him while at Nantucket) together with detailed instructions as to how it should be handled, he became positively cross.

The matter was to be worked up into a book by Nathaniel. There should be a liberal interpretation of the husband, whose sin had stolen upon him insensibly. The book should begin with a wreck. The young heroine comes wandering along the cliff. She gazes seaward. A sheep joins her at the very edge of the cliffs, to emphasise the innocence of the land placidly eying the malignity of the sea. Agatha's sea-lover is coming to her in the storm. It was the stuff of which another *Scarlet Letter* might be made, should Mr. Hawthorne choose to give fullness and veins to this skeleton of actual reality.

Herman finally visited Concord in November of 1852, taking with him further documents appertaining to "Agatha". The reviews of *Pierre* had been very bad. Few commentators cared for the style or conception, and Herman himself suspected that there had been insufficient of actuality in the book. The Agatha story was something he could spin out himself perhaps. A talk with Mr. Hawthorne, to see what he had made of it, might help him to decide.

He had travelled with Lizzie and the children to Boston for Thanksgiving. A day or two afterwards he took the cars for Concord and spent a night with his old friend from the Berkshires – it was to be their last night together in America.

*   *   *

The house, although near the road, was almost entirely concealed by shrubbery. A motto, in white letters on dark wood, attracted Herman's eye as he prepared to knock on the door: "There is no joy but calm". He smiled, in what was an instinctive replication of Mr. Hawthorne's ambiguous countenance.

Sophia opened the door. She carried Rose in her arms. Una and Julian, older and more shy than before, shrank back behind her skirts. Herman growled, and, with his fingers shaped into claws, went after them. They fled up the hall of the house and into an adjoining room. Sophia, with her free arm, dragged Mr. Melville's carry-all over the portal, with Rosebud's face buried in her neck. Then she went through to find Herman hunting behind every piece of furniture in the parlour.

"They'll be away through to the kitchen and out to the garden, I shouldn't wonder," she told him.

"I think our not-so-little Stanny has stolen a march on this frail little mite." Herman tickled the nape of Rosebud's neck. The child giggled, but refused to turn round. Her nose was rubbed back and forth on her mother's shoulder.

"I'll look in the garden, then."

The land rose steeply at the back of the house. Upon the summit of the ridge was a rough seat, the back of which was a simple board nailed to two trees. In the half-light of a late autumn evening the well-trodden path leading up to the ridge seemed a pale, meandering cord by which Mr. Hawthorne kept precarious contact with this world.

Una and Julian suddenly scampered up the hill to their Papa. They had been hiding behind a wheelbarrow near the back door, and had Herman been quick enough he would have been able to grab one of them as they scurried past.

Mr. Hawthorne sat with his back to the house, looking off into some invisible vista. Evidently the children had grown accustomed to treating this perch of their father's with gingerly respect for they slowed to a halt behind his seat and, without tapping his shoulder or making any audible sound, waited for him to become aware of their presence. When at last he turned, they pointed down the hill to where Herman was standing, outside the back door. With an awkward wave of the arm Nathaniel lurched to his feet. The children took one hand each, which they kept hold of when the two men were face to face, so that there could be no shaking of hands, nor arm about shoulders. After a moment's mutual scrutiny Nathaniel said, "Well, let's go in," and, by moving his arms in front of him, propelled the children ahead, adding, "Go and ask your mother if we are ready to eat."

They were, and when Herman was comfortably seated he was asked about his journey, and about Elizabeth, about Malcolm, and Stanwix, about Pittsfield and Lenox.

"Is there anyone in the Red Cottage this winter?"

Herman didn't know. He hadn't occasion to go out there now that they were gone.

"I don't even know if the Tappans are about."

"Mr. Melville should have gone and stripped the orchard, shouldn't he, Mother?"

"Yes, Omoo, you should have made the trees all naked and

bare." Julian giggled at this joke in a manner which betokened his advanced age. He was now five and a quarter, and Una eight and a half.

"Julian shouldn't make such rude remarks. Go on, Papa. Tell him he shouldn't."

"And Omoo shouldn't take trees' clothes off."

"I didn't."

"The wind does."

"Tell him, Papa. Julian, you're being as silly as can be." Then she looked at Herman straight in the eye and beamed. "I have to reprimand him, you see."

Both Sophia and Nathaniel had been sitting aside from this, but now they laughed, as if at the conclusion of a party sketch. Herman felt how swiftly the contrast in family atmospheres, between this household and his own, had once again made itself felt.

"Wayside", as this house was called, was significantly more spacious than the Red Shanty, and Herman and Nathaniel were able to get themselves well out of the way while Sophia, with the house servant's help, put the children to bed.

After they had seated themselves a familiar preparatory silence established itself. Neither of them was a man for whom such a silence was intimidating but the quietness recalled to Herman the many meetings with Mr. Hawthorne that had failed to deepen their bond.

"I saw your clue to the Talismanic Secret on the door," he said, hoping to charge their conversation with a soulful purpose from the start.

"I like that phrase. The Talismanic Secret."

"That reconciles this world with our own souls."

"It never has been found," said Mr. Hawthorne. "And in the nature of things it never can be."

"Yes; I begin to believe it. There was a time I put great trust in the vile brogue of foreign philosophers. But their discoveries have been absurd. How can a man conjure a voice out of silence? Perhaps companionship and an understanding heart is all we can expect of . . ." Herman found himself struggling for words, and Nathaniel dropped his eyes, as if aware that the loss of faith was not founded in any German or Scottish metaphysician, but in himself.

"Anyway, tell me if you have made anything of my 'Agatha' material."

372

"I'm afraid not. The Pierce biography has kept me busy."

"Do you think you'll use it?"

"Your ideas seem very good. Why not use them yourself?"

"No, it is much more your material. Besides, the public didn't care for my turning to a rural bowl of milk."

"But you were suggesting shipwrecks I remember . . ."

"Only for the beginning. You hold on to it. With the election over you may decide to turn to it after all."

There was a knock on the door. Una and Julian came in, dressed for bed, each with a tortoise in their arms.

"Not tortoises! Turtles. They're our pets."

Herman took Una's from her and turned it over. "Look what bright bellies they have, compared with their dark top-shells."

Julian turned his creature over, almost dropping it in the process, curious to see if it also exhibited the pale bright underbelly.

"And look what mastery you have over your little subjects." Herman placed Una's turtle on the floor, white side up, its four feet flailing uselessly above the rug. "Put yours down too, Julian. Bright side up. There – do you note the golden tinge of their sunny faces? But we mustn't deny the dark side, must we, Nathaniel? So, I turn them over, and there you have them in their blackness again. And which do you think they like the best? The bright or the dark?"

"They like it up the proper way." Una had reached the age where she answered all questions of this kind as if there could be no doubt about the sensible answer.

"And very appropriate pets for this household, I declare."

After the children had said good night and taken the turtles away, Herman asked Mr. Hawthorne if he approved of them. He answered that he did.

"You're not driven to dispose of them, then?"

"Dispose of them?"

"I recollect you had once to suppress a violent instinct towards a rabbit at Lenox."

Mr. Hawthorne seemed to have forgotten about the remark to which Herman was referring. He changed the subject.

"Seeing the children reminds me of a frighteningly close encounter we experienced last week. A friend called Colonel Miller had been to visit. We had driven him in a chaise to the Lincoln depot – Una and Julian were with me. We were returning across the railroad after dark, when the horse pricked up its ears, conscious of danger. We were scarcely off the track before the express train whizzed by. The children took it quite calmly, and Julian, a moment later seeing a shooting star, observed that it must be an express train in the sky."

Herman did not respond immediately. He suspected that Mr. Hawthorne was about to make something of the experience, but when nothing was added he did say, "There, you have . . ."

*　　*　　*

Another express train seemed to whizz by and drown out the rest of his sentence with its passing. Herman opened his eyes and realised he had been recollecting all of this in a deep swoon on the cabin bed. It was October 1856. He was fourteen days into the Atlantic aboard a new-style "propeller" bound for Glasgow. He felt sick in his stomach. There was a pain in his kidneys and a sense of pressure in his bowels. He cursed the unmoving motion of the vessel which, having encountered a gale, had been forced to lay-to for sixteen hours just north of Ireland. Even the dull light coming through the bullet window pained his eyes.

Una would be turned twelve now. And Julian ten. He tried to work out how old Rose would be, but something began to roll around the floor, interrupting his calculations. He rubbed his brow against the back of his hand, as if trying to ignore the noise, but the momentum suddenly picked up as the object ran loose of its obstruction and travelled the entire width of the cabin. When his feet hit the floor he winced as the contact sent shock-waves through his sore shins. He shuffled over to where the object was still rolling back and forth, caught in a new trap. It was a metal ring; far too large for a finger – not large enough for either a wrist or a napkin. Deciding that it must be, in its rightful place, a decorative feature of an item of cabin furniture, he placed it inside his case, intending to hand it to one of the crew when next he ventured forth. Pushing his case back beneath the bed, and straightening up, an amount of bile was deposited in the back of his throat. This lurching about at anchor, so close to the journey's end, exasperated him. As the metal disc had made its bolt across the cabin, he willed the ship to burst its chains and surge across the last stretch of the Atlantic.

He had wasted much time after that visit to Concord, trying to work up the Agatha material himself. In meeting once again the man fifteen years his senior the brevity of a human lifespan had dawned upon him. Those fifteen years would soon pass, and there *he* would be, fifty years old, no more likely to reconcile the world with his own soul than he had been at thirty-two or thirty-seven. He had reached, and was now passing, the fulcrum of life beyond which the inevitability of death makes circumspect the romantic and expansive aspirations of youth. The book, which he had nearly ready in the spring of 1853, was a failure. He did not submit it to a publisher.

It was then that every effort had been made by his family to procure for Herman and Elizabeth a foreign consulate. The constant working of his brain and the excitement of his imagination had brought him to such a turn that a change of occupation was the only remedy. Such was Maria's view, and she voiced it in letters – particularly to her brother Peter.

It must have seemed to Herman, having Uncle Peter of Albany called to the rescue like this, as if the hateful period following his father's death were repeating itself. Elizabeth was close to delivering their third child and can only have been a tacit party to the machinations, all of which had been encouraged by the recently announced selection of Mr. Hawthorne for the consulate in Liverpool.

At any rate, all the manoeuvring failed. Mr. Hawthorne, in his quiet way, had kept contact with several notable men of the world, whilst Herman had few friends outside his family, besides literary associates. In the end, he lacked connections.

The third child was his first daughter; named Elizabeth. The baby's arrival had given the older Elizabeth three children under five to look after – Malcolm was four and a half and Stanwix not quite one and three-quarters. This summer of 1853 had been one of the happiest times, domestically, at Arrowhead. Malcolm made his debut as a scholar, the grand feature of his day being the emptying of his dinner pail beneath the school-house tree; Stannie had a hacking cough which threatened to be the whoop; little Elizabeth was restive and not very fat. But Herman himself had seemed suddenly fit again. There had been no grandly organised picnicking this season because Mrs. Morewood had been unwell, and one of her own children had been seriously sick. All the socialising excitement of the summer had therefore centred upon the marriage of Herman's sister Catherine. As far as his work was concerned he had put aside the failed novel and turned, for the first time, to short stories. These stories, eventually collected together as *The Piazza Tales*, but originally published in Putnam's and Harper's *New Monthly* magazines, portray fairly accurately the new mood of the writer, who had come to see a failed anonymity as more harmonious with the divine order than acclaimed success. The conflagration that occurred on December 10th, reducing Harper's six houses on Cliff Street to one mass of rubbish, and destroying all the unsold stock of Herman's books, seemed a fit enough statement for an angel of Fate to be making at that time.

The *Glasgow* had eventually pulled anchor and braved the scarcely subdued elements for the last leg of the journey, arriving in the mouth of the Clyde on October 26th. Herman had disembarked a visibly wounded man. Preparing to move off from Greenock, their Irish refuge, a sailor had been lowering a boat by one of the tackles. The rope got foul. Herman jumped to clear it for him, when suddenly the tackle started and a coil of the rope flew up in his face with great violence, and for a moment he thought his nose ruined for life.

For the week succeeding the accident Herman had presented the aspect of one who had been in a bar-room fight. After three or four days in Glasgow he took the "Parliamentary" train to Edinburgh. This was the cheapest form of rail travel, but entailed catching the cars before daylight in the morning.

Waiting for the cars to Edinburgh, fingering the large rutted scab on the bridge of his nose, and skewering some spilled unburned pipe tobacco into the ground with his boot, Herman found himself thinking of his mother. She and he were walking across the rails of the Housatonic Depot, the gleam from a lantern every now and then lighting the surface of a puddle of water. She had just returned from Uncle Peter's and he, having received her into his arms as she stepped down from the train, directed her through teeming rain, to the horse and cart.

Their outward relationship had mellowed somewhat, largely as a result of Herman's sense of resignation, and this interlude, in which he acted the very part of a doting son, was not untypical; nor had it ever been, but, whereas before such a show of filial affection might have angered him subsequently, he now looked back upon it quite tranquilly, and let the recollection slide into another, also concerning the local railway station. Only a day or two after greeting his mother, he, Lizzie and the children had set off to town, intending to travel to Boston. A regular departure had been organised, including an early breakfast and the allowance of more than an hour to drive to town. But they had arrived at the depot just in time to see the cars steam off, a discrepancy of an hour in Boston and Pittsfield time having resulted in a mistaken reading of the timetable. They had returned to the farm in good humour; Bessie had been put to bed; the boys played outside; Lizzie read a book before the fire; and Herman took himself to his study. It had been a very different and more acrimonious false start that had prefaced his earlier trip to England. And now he was apart from them again. And this time on a much longer tour, the itinerary having been planned in advance, as a restorative to his belea-guered health. He had been suffering from rheumatic pains in both his back and head for several years but in the previous summer (1855) he had been gripped by a first attack of sciatica, and had not felt properly well since.

The Parliamentary train was late. Other passengers paced up and down. A cart piled with packed sacking was pushed to a certain point on the platform. Herman pressed the scab on his nose a little too firmly. A small piece of dried blood fell at his feet, and he gently felt the altered surface with the tip of a middle finger. Arrowhead was a long way off. He felt neither family man, nor lone adventurer. His children were young, but he felt a grand-fatherly detachment from them. Not yet forty, he nevertheless felt fatally gripped by the infirmities of old age.

A young woman joined him on the station seat. He immediately stood up and attached himself to the group of impatient pacers. Trying to hold himself erect he attempted to block out the twinges of sciatica and to convince himself that such morbidity was ridiculous in a man of thirty-seven. He would meet Mr. Haw-thorne, and, by the brilliance of his conversation, wring from him the secret of inner calm.

Eventually settled in the carriage his ruminations shifted into a third gear. The inner calm was already his; he was no longer hungry for success; he did not hanker after acclaim; he did not really need this adventure, except as a recreational cure; he no longer believed in the sorcery of metaphysics. He would be happy almost to go home and please his mother – go home, put down the pen, and take up a salaried appointment; live out the rest of his days as husband, father, provider. Happy, that is, if he could reach some understanding with Mr. Hawthorne. There was a man with whom he felt total empathy on the printed page – reading the old stories had been as if meeting, for the first time, a man who looked upon the world with the same kind of vision as his own – and yet, so often when they met face to face, there was little to connect Mr. Hawthorne's taciturn matter-of-factness and his resistance to speculative discourse with the deep dark matter of his stories.

He had remained five days in Edinburgh, sightseeing in the company of a rather uninteresting theological student from Troy; and then, by way of Berwick and Newcastle to York, before arriving in Liverpool on November 8th, where he put up at the White Bear hotel. After dining in a convivial atmosphere in which he was invited to take some ale as a guest, though charged for it, he walked a little way round the city in the rain, marking where to take the steamboat in the morning for Rock Ferry. He returned to the hotel and spent the evening drinking ale with an agreeable young Scot.

"I sail for the East on the *Damascus* this Monday. Come with me."

Herman told the youngster that he was sorry, but circumstances prevented him.

"I have to meet an old acquaintance over in Rock Ferry. Do you know Mr. Hawthorne, the author?"

The Scot shook his head, and the two began to talk of sailing vessels and sea crossings. They consumed a good amount of ale and when Herman at last stretched out upon the bed his back and hip felt much better, and also his head.

He woke early, quite refreshed, so that there was no great rush to get up. On the bedside table, where he had emptied his pockets the night before, lay a pile of English coinage. The short stories for the magazines had earnt him nothing, and he had been forced earlier in the year to sell off eighty acres on the western half of his estate, including that land on which it had originally been proposed to build a separate dwelling for his immediate family. The book he had completed before coming away, entitled *The Confidence Man* (there had been another novel since *Pierre*, a re-rendering of an historical narrative called *Israel Potter*) was by no means certain to earn him much lucre, becoming, as it had, the repository of all his obsessions.

Mystery is in the morning, and mystery in the night, and

the beauty of mystery is everywhere; but still the plain truth remains, that mouth and purse must be filled.

Nodding assent at his own words he jumped up, pulled on his trousers, swept the pile of coins into the palm of one hand, and tumbled them into his pocket. He had been ashore two weeks, and, by stint of the strictest economy, in rail carriage, lodging and eating, had spent just thirty-five dollars.

He took a good breakfast, paid his dues, said farewell to his Scottish friend, and set off for the steamboat. But at Rock Ferry he discovered, at the only residential address the Hawthornes had given him, that they had removed themselves eighteen months previously, and word had it that they had recently established themselves at Southport, a small resort some twenty miles out of town.

He returned to the White Bear, much to the Scotchman's amusement, and his own embarrassment, resolving to see Mr. Hawthorne at the Consulate in the morning.

*   *   *

Mr. Hawthorne's office consisted of two rooms in an edifice called Washington Buildings. It was situated near the docks, on the corner of Brunswick Street, and from his window he had a view of a tall, dismal, smoke-blackened, ugly brick warehouse, from the windows of which, on several levels, bags of salt were often being raised or lowered. It was a noisy place to do business, the continuous rumble of heavy wheels making conversation rather difficult. The room in which Mr. Hawthorne's own desk was situated was hung with a map of the United States, another of Europe, a hideously-coloured life-sized lithograph of General Taylor, one or two smaller engraved portraits, and three paintings of naval victories. The mantelpiece was adorned with the American Eagle, painted into the wood frame, and on the shelves there were several leatherbound volumes of United States law.

A side of Mr. Hawthorne had always hankered after this – the holding of government office in a European commercial centre – and the appointment had come as no surprise. He had been angling for some such posting when writing the campaign biography for his friend Pierce in the summer of '52. It was inevitable, on Pierce's accession to the Presidency, that such assistance should be rewarded.

The American consul's duties in the day consisted largely in waiting at his desk inside the office, ready to receive American visitors who required his services, either as persons who found themselves in some kind of difficulty, or as persons who simply required his signature upon a document. The work was made interesting by the number of destitutes who laid themselves at his mercy, many of whom were not American at all, but mere paupers after a crafty half-crown.

In such a job there were naturally days when hours would pass by between calls, hours in which, watching the salt sacks go up and down, he could indulge his indolence in reflection. Despite these opportunities for reverie, Mr. Hawthorne had composed nothing new by way of a Romance during the three years that had passed since their arrival in England.

He had one early visitor on the morning of November 10th – a woman pretending to be an American abandoned in England by her husband. She wished to return to America. Although believing her to be a fraud he had given her half a crown and promised to persuade some shipmaster to take her on as a stewardess. After she had left, and the few documents of the day that needed signing had been signed, he settled down to as long a period of solitude as Fate would permit.

Some salt sacks were hoisted up to the fourth level of the warehouse opposite, but the persons retrieving them were youngsters with insufficient strength or expertise and one of the sacks fell back to the ground, bursting its rock crystal on the stones. Mr. Hawthorne laughed at the cursing and the mêlée.

He knew that Mr. Melville was thinking of a European jaunt, but did not know how hard his failure to assist him in '53 had been taken. If he did stop off in Liverpool much embarrassing explanation might be required to ward off renewed requests for him to exercise his influence. The last time they had met had been in Concord. That must be four years ago now. He remembered only that the visit had been dominated by the wretched Agatha papers which he, Nathaniel, had discussed at such length only to avoid the more sensitive subject of *Pierre*. Nor, too, had he much relished discussing the Berkshire guidebook *Taghonic* which Melville had sent him just before the visit. The chapter about himself was full of abusive phrases like "unsympathising morbid spirit". He was accused of "abjuring all communion with this our gross humanity". The six-page chapter was ostensibly by a Mr. Buckham of

Lenox, but the whole thing having been got together by J. E. A. Smith, editor of the *Berkshire Eagle*, and just about Melville's only Pittsfield friend, the unpleasant notion presented itself that perhaps the Virginian was once again vacationing in Vermont.

Mr. Hawthorne puckered his face and shook his head from side to side. Whence came such absurd suspicions? A shovel scraped rhythmically on the paving as the salt pieces and salt dust were transferred to a new sack.

The Consulate had no official residence in Liverpool. Casual entertainment seems to have been centred on Mrs. Blodgett's boarding-house. The Hawthornes' personal dwelling had first been at Rock Park. Now they had moved out to Southport, to another lodging house. As September turned to October, and the holiday season came to its close, they had started to question the wisdom of spending the winter so far out of the city. But Nathaniel liked the poolly, plashy breadth of yellow sands and the wild wind that blew off the Irish Sea. It was near enough a twenty-mile rail-ride into the centre of Liverpool, but barring dinner engagements he could be home by five in the afternoon.

Sophia had become awkward about clearing the Rock Park house, prior to their removal, for fear that an unfortunate experience on their departure from "Wayside" might be repeated. Ellen, their maid, had been clearing the garret when she found an immense snake, fat and outrageously fierce, thrusting out its tongue. She had killed it mercilessly enough, with the hard shoulder of her broom, but Sophia had declared it a fiend, haunting the house. Earlier, in that same garret, Nathaniel had burnt great heaps of old letters, and other papers, to save taking them to England. Among them had been many of Sophia's maiden letters. Fire was the trustful guardian of secret matters; but there was a morbid fear in Sophia's mind that the snake had risen from the ashes.

Nathaniel looked at his watch. It was ten minutes to ten. He stood up at the window, peering down into the street between the Consulate and the warehouse. The last of the salt had been shovelled up, leaving just a smattering of glassy-white crystal on the stones. The watch had cost twenty-eight pounds two years before and was made by Bennett of Cheapside, London. He should have been content with a much inferior one had he not thought of Julian wearing it after him. He remembered, last year, having introduced himself, while in London, at number sixty-five

Cheapside. Mr Bennett's establishment had a large figure of a watch over the door, a good but not gorgeous display of watches in the window and just two chairs in the little room behind the shop front. The man himself, whom Mr. Hawthorne already knew by letter, and by a good many of his poems which he had sent him, was small and slender, with coal-black curly hair and a very animated expression. He wore a dusty black suit, stooped a little, and looked like a clerk off his desk.

The two of them had walked to the Bank of England together, Mr. Bennett for the purpose of identifying Mr. Hawthorne so that he could cash a post-bill. But the bill was not yet due, having two days to run, and the kind Cockney, seeing that Mr. Hawthorne was almost shillingless, offered to exchange it for him; which they did back at the shop.

"There hain't enough trust in this world, Mr. Hawthorne, there hain't. You must take my new poem with you now, and come to see us at Greenwich."

The poem had been in the manner of Lowell's satire, but wretchedly inferior. Nathaniel gave a hiccupping laugh, wondering if Mr. Bennett were still composing. He sat back at his desk, and looked again at the watch. It said six minutes to ten.

Whenever in Liverpool on his own, either returning to the city on business in the midst of a holiday tour, or when Sophia was away somewhere with the children, Mr. Hawthorne would stay at Mrs. Blodgett's boarding house, an establishment which catered mainly for American visitors. It was always a great fillip to spend an evening there and hear American conversation, see American women, who, slight as they might look after the beefy rotundity and coarse complexions of English dames, always proved themselves sufficient for the purpose of life.

He had acquired the habit, after attending municipal functions, of describing for Sophia the various types of women on display.

"Just when I thought I had seen the most hideous animal that ever pretended to human shape another figure, so puffed out, so huge, so without limit, and dressed in a way to show all manner of fleshly abomination to worst advantage, this new atrocity stepped into view, walking about with entire self-satisfaction. The trim, respectable gentleman who escorted her on his arm should take a sharp knife and cut away at the mountainous flesh until he has brought her back into reasonable shape, shredding off all the alien, encrusted layers that have grown over the slender creature whom he married."

382

Sophia held in her own stomach, placing both palms over her waistband, as if protecting it from her husband's scalpel.

"You are a nymph beside these hellish Gorgons, my Dove!"

There was an exchange of voices in the outer room of the Consulate. His assistant clerk must be taking the particulars of another visitor, and Mr. Hawthorne, tugging the creases out of his jacket and shifting one or two items on his desk, prepared to receive the stranger.

*　　*　　*

It being Monday morning, and thinking that Mr. Hawthorne might be busy early in the day, Herman had taken a leisurely breakfast and then lounged for twenty minutes or so against a wall with the entrance to the Consulate in view, waiting to see how many visitors came and went. He had witnessed the clearing of the salt but had missed the departure of the female hoodwinker, so that it seemed as if either the Consul was engaged in a very lengthy interview or had nobody there. Deciding then that it was pointless to wait any longer, Herman was nevertheless prevented from moving off up the street by a powerful sense of hesitancy. Mr. Hawthorne was not expecting him. His arrival might provoke a curt and unfriendly dismissal, so that the rest of his Tour would continue under the dejected gloom of a repulsion. But such must be risked; he wanted once again to present Mr. Hawthorne with the same speculation about fate and futurity as had failed to enliven him five years before, when he, Herman, had dashed his tumultuous waves of thought up against Mr. Hawthorne's great, genial, comprehending silences.

He took his hands from the pockets of his rough outside coat and walked towards the entrance to the Washington buildings.

"My name is Melville. I am an old friend of the Consul's."

"I see. And you are expected?"

"No. I don't think so."

"But you are an American?" Herman flickered assent. "If I could just have some particulars of your visit to England, then."

Herman acquiesced in the officious matters of dates and places of sojourn, until, an adequate amount of information having been collected, the clerk went away to see if Mr. Hawthorne would "grant an interview", passing through the door without opening it further than the width of his own shoe.

"There is another visitor, sir. He claims to know you. A Herman Melville."

Nathaniel stood up behind his desk. The clerk held out the visitor's particulars, but Mr. Hawthorne walked straight to the door of his office and opened it wide.

"Melville! Come in. Come in." At last taking the listed information from his clerk, he added, "I'm sorry you were inflicted with this."

The clerk apologised also. Both to his master and to the visitor.

"No. No. It is a matter of form. I understand."

The door of the office was closed and the two men were alone. Mr. Hawthorne, out of habit, sat behind his desk, and Herman took the visitor's chair, so that there was a reserved formality about their initial exchanges.

"So . . . You are on your way to Constantinople?"

Herman explained that he had been unwell lately, affected by neuralgic complaints in his head and limbs, so he had been sent away, to take an airing through the world. He had crossed from New York to Glasgow in a screw steamer, and had spent a fortnight since, seeing Edinburgh and other interesting places.

Mr. Hawthorne felt rather awkward at first, not knowing how much of an apology to make for his ineffectual attempt to get Herman a consular appointment from General Pierce.

"We are living out at Southport now."

"I know. I went to your old address . . ."

"Will you have time to stay with us? Then I suggest you come out with me tomorrow, leaving your main baggage here at the Consulate."

Herman did not relax his gravity and reserve of manner in this interview. He agreed to the arrangement and as he left the office turned to say he was looking forward to seeing Mrs. Hawthorne and the children again.

Mr. Hawthorne smiled – not his teasingly suggestive smile – but a professional smile which he had obviously acquired as a fixed adjunct to his duties.

And so Herman had to spend, against expectations, yet another night at the White Bear hotel, and the following day, at noon, as arranged, hired a carriage to take himself and his trunk to the Consular buildings. This time Julian was spending the day with his father. The boy was no longer the infant Herman remembered, but a serious, watchful ten year old.

Mr. Hawthorne was busy, dealing with papers, so that he could leave the office early. He made conversation in a semi-distracted manner.

"And what have you done with yourself since yesterday?"

"Oh, I went among the docks to see the Mediterranean steamers." Julian's steady eye disconcerted Herman, and he didn't elaborate. The conversation continued in a manner which was unintelligible to the boy who, by contrast, remembered the improvisational style of the Red Cottage days, and rather hoped that Mr. Melville would break out of his stilted politeness. But he was no longer capable himself of making the kind of impertinent contribution to a conversation by which the four or five year old can vivify adult company.

They took the afternoon train for Southport and found Mrs. Hawthorne and the two girls waiting with tea ready in their small, square parlour. The dwelling shocked Herman by its shabbiness. The Hawthornes' rooms, the bargain for which had been struck only three weeks previously, were in a tall stone house styled "Brunswick Terrace". The parlour they were now gathered in was about fifteen feet square, covered with an old carpet, with an extra layer of rugging in the middle to conceal areas of utmost wear. There were four dining and two easy chairs; a shabby sofa; a bureau; and a cupboard. On the mantelpiece, at either side of a pock-marked looking-glass stood a tinted glass vase. On the walls there was nothing besides two cheap coloured prints, one of Prince Albert and one of Queen Victoria.

Conscious that Mr. Melville's gravity denoted surprise at their quarters, Mrs. Hawthorne began to explain their circumstances.

"So you'll be able to say to your wife that you haven't exactly missed out on the grand life by failing to get a consular posting. Southport is just a little watering town. Full of these lodging houses, which are now beginning to empty of their summer visitors. We have to pay so much for each bed and then again for the parlour. We were promised a better than this, but it hasn't yet become available."

Una helped her mother serve tea without giving any indication that she had met Mr. Melville before. And since neither of her parents was the kind of person to embarrass her with reference to how tall she had grown in the interim there was no requirement to include either of the children in the conversation. They were silent witnesses to a most awkward and restrained reunion. The girl was taller than the mother, and helpful in a degree which suggested that Mrs. Hawthorne had not recently been in the best of health.

The nature of the lodging-house rooms meant that Herman was given the sofa in the parlour. Mr Hawthorne did open a door at the bottom of the cupboard and produce a bottle of sherry; but it was only a third full and anyway, after one glass, he declared that he would leave Herman with his toothbrush and nightshirt (the only luggage which the traveller had brought to Southport) and retire early with his wife who, he confirmed, had not been at all well lately.

The next day Mr. Hawthorne stayed in Southport and the two men took a long walk on the promenade and sands. It was wild and desolate with too strong a wind for the majority to be taking anything but the most necessary of walks. Away from the ribbed sand of the shore there were sand-hillocks covered in coarse grass and one of these provided sufficient shelter for the two men to sit and light a cigar.

Mr. Hawthorne, for once, was the first to raise the conversation above the mundane. "It is a strange thing. Living in a foreign land. One longs to return home, but is afraid nevertheless, that the native air will have lost its invigorating quality, and that life will be found to have shifted its reality to the spot where we deemed ourselves only temporary residents."

Herman pressed the top of his tongue into the butt-end of his cigar, dampening down a protruding tobacco stem. "You don't intend to stay in England?"

"Oh, no."

"What you say reminds me of my old conundrum regarding Providence and Futurity. I have pretty much made up my mind to be annihilated; that is, surrender to the unseen pull of events. Look at those gathering gulls. It wouldn't help one of those gulls to develop an individual viewpoint."

"These don't sound the thoughts of a solitary traveller."

"No? Well, my rheumatism feels better than it did in America but, to tell you the truth, I don't anticipate much pleasure in my rambles."

"The spirit of adventure has gone out of you?"

"Yes."

"We have done a fair bit of travelling around England. But I find that a man with children in charge cannot enjoy travelling; he must content himself to be happy with them, for they allow him no separate and selfish possibility of being happy. I should enjoy your independence."

The last sentence was spoken as advice, but Herman mistook it for a statement of envy.

"I don't think so. We are all temperamentally bound to the life which suits us best." Herman dragged on his cigar, reconsidering this view. "No. Only the wisest. I finished another book before I came away, and I feel utterly emptied. My family don't want me to write another. They want me to return from this tour and take up an office position."

The wind shifted momentarily and swept round the side of their sand-hill. They each protected their eyes from the flying sand.

"Is it the 'Agatha' material?"

"The book? No, it is a masquerade. I have stolen ideas from you again."

"Just as well. I doubt the world will see another full length Romance before my duties are over."

"Are they very taxing?"

"No. But I never have been able to do two jobs at a time."

Mr. Hawthorne then gave Herman some idea of how he spent his days at the Consulate.

The exchange of this information, and the manner of it, characterised the alteration that had taken place in both men. Mr. Hawthorne, although once again refusing to be drawn on the subject of Fate and Futurity, was nevertheless more talkative than in previous years and more willing to initiate conversation. His work as Consul had at long last brought him to that mature station of life where he was placed in the position of talking to others in an advisory capacity; just that sort of rôle in which his friend Bridge had impressed him when dealing with the Irish labourers. But Mr. Hawthorne would not have been so conversationally relaxed had Mr. Melville not become correspondingly more silent. In the past, Nathaniel had been constantly on guard against the other's boyish onslaughts and at the end of their time in the Berkshires had begun to feel his privacy – his own soul's independence – to be under threat. Herman, all too clearly, had become too enthralled with his own self to pose this same threat over again.

Herman listened to Mr. Hawthorne's description of his duties and then said, "Life is something of a fancy dress picnic. I think it's time I too took up a new costume."

On the walk back they searched for colourful shells to take to the five-year-old Rose. She was a quieter, less rumbustious youngster than either Una or Julian had been, and in later life would complain mildly that her father had paid her less attention and had kept her too long the baby of the family.

The tide was so low as hardly to cover the shallow basin of the bay. The wind, which had not quietened, was beginning to howl, and a donkey cart carrying a brave band of autumn pleasure seekers to the sea shore was struggling against it. The donkeys were three abreast and their donkey ears were flattened by the blast. Mr. Hawthorne commented that donkey riding was the only public amusement beside sea-dipping yet available at the small resort.

In the evening, Mrs. Hawthorne feeling unwell again, Nathaniel took Herman to a local inn, the Fox and Geese, where they had one or two bottles of stout, and listened to the local tradesmen's forecasts for the winter, both fiscal and meteorological. They didn't talk much themselves, beside making plans for the rest of the week. The two of them would travel back to Liverpool together the next day, a Thursday, at noon; they would meet again at the Consulate on Friday; and on Saturday Mr. Hawthorne would take Melville to Chester, the only place within easy reach of Liverpool that possessed any old English interest.

Walking back to Brunswick Terrace, Mr. Hawthorne asked Herman where he would stay in Liverpool.

"Oh, I'll go back to the same hotel."

"You wouldn't prefer Mrs. Blodgett's? I could get a room at her lodging house. Americans only."

"No, no. I may not anticipate much pleasure in my rambles but I can at least stay at an English hotel."

In the parlour Sophia had set out a supper table, and Una helped her mother serve up soup and dry crusts. Mrs. Hawthorne sank into an easy chair while the two men ate and Una retired to her bed, making a most ladylike exit, and promising that she would look in on Rose and read her a story if the child were still awake.

"By Mrs. Tappan, I wonder?" Una had closed the door, but Sophia asked Nathaniel to check it. There was a beast of a draught at her ankles. Mr. Hawthorne rested his spoon at the side of his soup-bowl, got up from his chair, walked to the door, opened it and reclosed it, pulled at the doorknob to make sure it was caught in the catch, and returned to his seat.

"We have already agreed to take these rooms until December, but we are a little trepidatious about the winter."

Thus was Mr. Melville's little query averted.

Mrs. Hawthorne sat up with them a short while. Herman fancied that she did not really enjoy life abroad; certainly the climate did not seem to suit her health.

"You will be in the sun in a week's time, Mr. Melville, and we will be on these desolate sands. I hope that when my husband's term of office is over he will take all of us to Italy before returning to America."

"That is our plan, yes."

Suddenly – for no direct connection – Herman found himself likening Mr. Hawthorne to Tyson, the self-sufficient smallholder he had stayed with as a young teacher. The taking of an important government position seemed to have altered, awfully, the old harmony of the Hawthorne household, throwing a conventional weight upon Mr. Hawthorne as Victorian head of the family, and diminishing Sophia in proportion.

"I look forward to that more than anything," Herman said. "The sun. Life seems so full of shadows these days."

The three glanced at one another, and communicated a sympathetic sense of unspeakable disappointment. It was a sad moment and each of them quickly turned away towards the warm glow of the coals. Sophia had put some wet clothes to dry in front of the fire and a fine mist was forming on the pock-marked mirror, and on the glass fronts to the prints of Queen Victoria and Prince Albert.

*   *   *

When Herman arrived at the Consulate on Friday, it was to be told that Mr. Hawthorne, through having been away in the middle of the week, would be too busy to spend much time with his friend, and had therefore arranged for a Mr. Henry Bright, a Liverpudlian industrialist of twenty-six years, to show him whatever was worth seeing in the town.

Bright, a young member of a family firm, found time to contribute to leading English periodicals and while in America in 1852 had been introduced to Mr. Hawthorne, an acquaintanceship both were glad to pick up when the latter arrived in England in 1853.

In the event, since the weather was bad, instead of sightseeing Bright took Melville to dine at his club, and Herman asked him how well he knew Mr. Hawthorne.

389

"I go to his rooms pretty often."

"At the Consulate?"

"Yes. And stand at the fire letting forth about literature in my amateur way."

"And Mr. Hawthorne responds? He rises to the discussions?"

"Oh, yes. His friendship was not easy to win, I grant you. He is reserved and shy, proudly independent, as I'm sure you know yourself. But once the ice is broken then that noble and gentle heart shows itself as it truly is. I stand there rattling on in my opinonated way about books and national character and he, though delicately sensitive, is so little apt to take offence, and the 'amari aliquid', that something bitter or pungent which mingles in his writings never taints our conversations."

Herman cut a piece of gristle out of a slice of roast beef; he pierced the crisp crust of a potato and, with the flat side of his knife, tipped some gravy down into the opening.

Bright added on an afterthought. "Except perhaps when he fancies his dear country is being looked down upon or despised. Then he assails me with exuberant republicanisms."

"How do you respond?"

"With frank and amiable assertion of all sorts of English prejudices."

In the afternoon Bright took Melville to view his Unitarian church and cemetery but the American was quiet and pensive and they parted well before evening. The young Englishman did not make apposite company for Herman at this time. His vivaciousness jarred; and the glowing impression of his friendship with Mr. Hawthorne, its openness, its warmth, its reciprocity, could not fail to make Melville jealous, and invite him to question his own failure to melt the Hawthorne ice. He lingered in the churchyard after saying goodbye to Bright. Perhaps it was the young man's earnest superficiality which permitted Nathaniel to let down his defences in safety; but this was a supercilious view, and there might have been more to Bright than first impressions suggested.

On the following day, a Saturday, Herman met Mr. Hawthorne at the landing stage, ready for crossing the Mersey on their way to Chester. It was a fitful day, and began to shower just as they boarded the ferry; but the weather was brighter in Chester and they had glimpses of sunshine as they walked around the wall with hardly a spatter of rain.

Mr. Hawthorne did his best to be an informative guide and

390

sprinkled his commentary on the town with colourful associations – the buttresses on the old Cathedral appeared to him like hard sugar sweets that had been sucked in a child's mouth. But Melville had never been the kind of traveller who either required or wanted interpretative annotations – these were best left to books – and the two-mile circuit of the city wall thoroughly exhausted him, mentally and physically. He had woken up tired (for Friday night had been an uproarious night at the White Bear hotel) and the effort of keeping a minimum of polite concentration on Mr. Hawthorne's historical references to the Romans had given him a dizzy headache, compounded by the fact that as they walked along the wall two abreast he took the innermost circuit, the steep drop beneath being guarded by nothing more than a single railing. Although his rheumatism had improved since leaving America, he had found that he could not keep walking for long before resting and regaining his breath.

He asked Mr. Hawthorne the time. Nathaniel told him it was one o'clock and then began explaining about his visit to Bennett's of Cheapside, and to talk about the dreadful poems that the charming watchmaker was continually sending him, but Herman, reacting to this as if it were another piece of historical exegesis on the town, simply nodded, and mm-mm-ed, before suggesting that they walk down into the Rows, in quest of a place to take lunch.

They settled upon a confectioner's shop which, like modern bakeries with their contiguous cafés, had become popular places, especially with Englishwomen, for hasty refection. They were shown upstairs, into an antique room fronting the street, with cross-beams, panelled walls, tables and a good fire. The waitress brought them two trays, one with little veal pies, the other with damson tarts. She returned, on request, with a bottle each of Bass's ale.

And so did these two great figures of nineteenth-century American literature begin their last serious conversation together in a small chop-house in a northern English town, with perhaps a doctor and his family, a couple of holidaying spinsters, and a solitary gentleman of indeterminate occupation at adjoining tables, all of whom were absolutely unaware of the Americans' identities.

Herman cut his cold veal pie in half, spread some mustard across its mottled contents, and bit into it. The pastry was crisp and crunchy. He declared the pie delicious and put another on his plate. The waitress returned, to take the trays to another table, and both men quickly helped themselves to damson tarts.

"You see a lot of Mr. Bright, then?"

"Yes, he illuminates my dusky little office fairly regularly. He has some eloquent, if conventional, ideas about literature, and he enjoys teasing my rough republicanisms. How did you find him?"

Mr. Hawthorne picked some jelly out of his pie and put it to the side of his plate.

Herman swallowed a mouthful of ale. "A vivacious youngster, to be sure."

The pleasant refreshment of the beer, the relaxing warmth of the log fire and the relief of having descended from the city wall combined to embolden his next line of talk.

"I have concluded that the souls of men can never commingle. The negatives of flesh prove analogous to a noncordialness of spirit."

Mr. Hawthorne dabbed the last portion of his veal pie across his plate, picking up dropped crumbs of pastry. Concentrating on this manoeuvre he made his response without lifting his eyes.

"The one you speak about is love. The other friendship."

"But such division confines the latter to so feeble a sphere!"

Mr. Hawthorne laughed at this expostulation. The two ladies who sat nearest to the American table looked round briefly, but were involved in a discussion of their own. Nathaniel had been amused by Melville's instant railing against his own proposal. It was so typical of the man that he could not rest easy with his own conclusions.

"Enjoy your tour; home to your wife; and let Fate drive!"

Mr. Hawthorne raised his glass, emptied it and, attracting the waiting girl, asked her to bring two more bottles of the Bass. He turned as she went away, admiring her ankle and the click of her shoes on the stained boards.

It was Herman's turn to smile. "And now *you* regale *me* with Fate. Fate is too skittish it seems when it turns us about so."

"There is regularity enough in mortal life, don't you find?"

"To argue a superintending Providence?"

Mr. Hawthorne took the two half-pint bottles from the girl. A little dome of white froth rose above the brim of one of them. He looked at the bottles with that strange enigmatic smirk on his face, and with a shrug decided to let Melville make the choice; but Herman, misunderstanding the gesture, held out his glass to be refilled.

Nathaniel put down the frothing bottle next to his own glass and poured the flatter ale for Herman.

The damson tarts, in comparison with the veal pies, were dry and disappointing, and they were glad of the extra bottle of ale to wash them down. The doctor's family rose to go, and one of their three children was heard to comment that "those men" were eating pudding with their fingers.

Herman turned himself round and, looking at the child whom he thought responsible for the remark, said, "We only use a knife and spoon when we are eating little girls."

The doctor laughed nervously; the wife hurried her children towards the stairs; the accused child blamed her brother for being the actual provocateur. Herman turned back to Nathaniel and said, "You missed a chance to propound your rough republicanisms there."

Having paid for their lunch (a shilling and twopence each) they went to the Cathedral, where they were given a guided tour which lasted much of the afternoon. Afterwards they settled in a small snuggery in the Yacht Inn for a glass of stout and a cigar, but the landlord kept questioning them and they were unable to indulge in private conversation.

When, noticing the time, they had quickly to put out their cigars and hurry to the station, Herman was suddenly overpowered by the conviction that they would never smoke or drink together again. In the train he said nothing; they might have been a couple returning from a day out so disastrous that neither was speaking to the other. Mr. Hawthorne accepted the atmosphere as evidence of the nervous indisposition which had clearly prompted his friend's trip. In the Journal he described Melville as "much overshadowed". Herman, on the other hand, made no reference whatever to this day in Chester.

Mr. Hawthorne changed trains to take the half-past-six cars to Southport. They said goodbye to one another at a street corner in Liverpool, in the rainy evening.

Herman attended two church services the next day, conscious perhaps that Elizabeth would also be at church in Boston. Sophia, apparently exhausted by Herman's visit in the week, had taken to her bed. Nathaniel walked the children across the ribbed sands.

Melville appeared briefly at his office the next day, to empty a minimum of travelling gear from his trunk into a carpet bag. He sailed for Gibraltar on the *Egyptian* and did not pass back through Liverpool until May 1857, when he picked up his trunk and saw

Mr. Hawthorne for just a few minutes.

After the Hawthornes' return to America in 1860, and up to Nathaniel's death in 1864, neither man made any attempt to meet the other.

The friendship, casually described by one commentator as "one of the major events in literary history", had come to its end in November 1856, over a bottle of Bass.